THE VACATION by... : ... on earth embarks on the longest summer vacation in history when a casual remark turns into a wish come true. . . .

THE SAME TO YOU DOUBLED by Robert Sheckley: A visit from the devil's advocate poses a unique problem—what to wish for if your own worst enemy gets your wish doubled. . . .

BEHIND THE NEWS by Jack Finney: Extra! Extra! Read all about it—before it happens—when a magical meteor turns a local nespaper into a chronicle of future events. . . .

THE FLIGHT OF THE UMBRELLA by Marvin Kaye: An English professor studies his subjects a little *too* closely when a magical umbrella takes him wherever his mind wanders, and shows him that some people— like Professor Moriarty and Dracula—are better met between the covers of books. . . .

So think twice before you ask for your heart's desire . . . for wishing will make it so in—

Isaac Asimov's
Magical Worlds of Fantasy #7
MAGICAL WISHES

MAGICAL
WISHES

ISAAC ASIMOV'S
MAGICAL WORLDS
OF FANTASY #7

Edited by

Isaac Asimov,
Martin H. Greenberg,
and Charles G. Waugh

A SIGNET BOOK

NEW AMERICAN LIBRARY

SIGNET TRADEMARK REG. U.S. PAT. OFF. AND FOREIGN COUNTRIES

REGISTERED TRADEMARK—MARCA REGISTRADA

HECHO EN CHICAGO, U.S.A.

SIGNET, SIGNET CLASSIC, MENTOR, ONYX, PLUME, MERIDIAN AND NAL BOOKS are published by New American Library, 1633 Broadway, New York, New York 10019

First Printing, November, 1986

1   2   3   4   5   6   7   8   9

PRINTED IN THE UNITED STATES OF AMERICA

CONTENTS

INTRODUCTION: "WISHING WILL MAKE IT SO"
by Isaac Asimov   9

THE MONKEY'S PAW
by W. W. Jacobs   12

BEHIND THE NEWS
by Jack Finney   24

THE FLIGHT OF THE UMBRELLA
by Marvin Kaye   38

TWEEN
by J. F. Bone   97

THE BOY WHO BROUGHT LOVE
by Edward D. Hoch   121

THE VACATION
by Ray Bradbury   125

THE ANYTHING BOX
by Zenna Henderson   133

A BORN CHARMER
by Edward P. Hughes   148

WHAT IF—
by Isaac Asimov   166

MILLENNIUM
by Fredric Brown   180

DREAMS ARE SACRED
by Peter Phillips   182

THE SAME TO YOU DOUBLED
by Robert Sheckley   206

GIFTS . . .
by Gordon R. Dickson   216

I WISH I MAY, I WISH I MIGHT
by Bill Pronzini   230

THREE DAY MAGIC
by Charlotte Armstrong   234

THE BOTTLE IMP
by Robert Louis Stevenson   321

INTRODUCTION:
WISHING WILL MAKE IT SO

by Isaac Asimov

When I was much younger than I am now, I heard the philosophical comment: "It takes a million dollars to make a millionaire, but a pauper can be poor without a penny."

When I was a little older I listened to Sid Caesar playing the role of a Teutonic mountaineer. Carl Reiner said to him, "Tell me, Professor, how long does it take a person to negotiate the distance between the top and bottom of a mountain?"

Said Sid, "Two minutes."

Carl said, with considerable astonishment, "It takes only two minutes to climb a mountain?"

To which Sid said, with disgust, "Not climb. To negotiate the distance from the top down to the bottom—two minutes. *Climbing* is a different thing altogether."

I've thought about such things, and it became clear to me that both the examples I have given are representative of a general state of affairs that can best be expressed as follows: "Lousy things are no trouble."

For instance, it's no trouble to go hungry. You don't need money, and you don't have to make an effort. You just sit there. Getting yourself outside a square meal can be very troublesome, however.

Again, suppose that someone brings you all the food you can eat. In that case, it's getting fat that requires no effort (if you don't count the tiny effort it takes to lift the food to your mouth, chew, and swallow). To avoid getting fat, however, means eating less than you probably want to and engaging in vigorous exercise besides.

This is not something that has escaped the notice of humanity generally. I'm absolutely certain that even the meanest intelligence has noticed how readily one can be poor, hungry, thirsty, cold in the winter, hot in the summer, while finding oneself with nothing to wear, nothing to read, and nothing pleasant to do.

Not only does one have to take trouble and make an effort in order to avoid all these lousy things for which there is no charge, but there is no limit on the quantity of trouble and effort you may have to make. Most people can work hard all their lives and stint no effort doing so, and yet find themselves far short of the millionaire mark when they're through.

You may want to marry a rich man's gorgeous daughter (or, if you are a woman, his handsome son), and for that purpose you may bring into play every bit of charm you have—and get nowhere. This may start you brooding over the fact that you can probably, without any effort at all, succeed in marrying any number of very poor, very ugly women (or men).

Well, then, what are you going to do? You crave pleasant things which take more of an effort than you can possibly pump up in a lifetime of pumping, and you want to avoid unpleasant things that are being forced upon you against your will and that then stick to you despite your shouts of dismay.

It is easy to decide that there is something wrong with this. In a properly run Universe, surely you deserve to get something simply because you want it. Even though this doesn't *seem* to happen, there must surely be some trick to bring it about. Perhaps there is some formula or spell that will give you anything you want; you need only wish for it. Or else perhaps there is some supernatural being willing to gratify you under certain conditions. Perhaps there is some wishing object that already exists, manufactured who knows how, that you need only find in order to gratify your every wish.

Folklore of every kind includes tales of magic wishes, and the most successful of all such stories is to be found in *The Thousand and One Nights* (more commonly known as *The Arabian Nights*). What child isn't fascinated by the tale of Aladdin and his lamp and doesn't fantisize having such a lamp for himself? I experienced both the fascination and the fantasy in copious quantities when I was young.

(Incidentally, we moderns still believe in the power of wishing. We call it "praying," of course, and, all too frequently, praying is simply a way of substituting God for the Slave of the Lamp and making him run our errands for us.)

Of course, some such tales caution against overweening greed. Midas, having wished that everything he touched would turn to gold, found he had gone too far and had left himself no way of eating or drinking, so he had to beg to get the wish canceled.

In other stories, the wishes are limited in number, most often to three, and then, invariably, there is a problem in deciding what the wishes ought to be. Almost as invariably, the choices prove unfortunate.

This instinctive suspicion that the notion that wishing will make it so is nonsense was given its final support by the laws of thermodynamics. The first law says that the amount of energy is limited and the second says (in scientific terms) exactly what I said earlier—that lousy things are no trouble, but that to accomplish anything desirable takes an effort. What's more, the laws of thermodynamics hold for everything in the Universe, including Slaves of the Lamp.

And yet . . . and yet . . .

Even if we are grown-up, hardheaded, and scientific, and have put childish things behind us, there is still this hankering. Even though we know that wishing will not make it so, we can't help but *wish* that wishing will make it so.

Here, then, are sixteen stories in which wishes, in one way or another, are involved. And just to make sure that you will be hooked by them, the first story, "The Monkey's Paw," is, to my way of thinking, the best such story ever written, and the grisliest. How I envy you, if you've never come across it and will now read it for the first time.

So suspend your disbelief for a while and enjoy.

THE MONKEY'S PAW

by W. W. Jacobs

1

Without, the night was cold and wet, but in the small parlour of Laburnum Villa the blinds were drawn and the fire burned brightly. Father and son were at chess; the former, who possessed ideas about the game involving radical changes, putting his king into such sharp and unnecessary perils that it even provoked comment from the white-haired old lady knitting placidly by the fire.

"Hark at the wind," said Mr. White, who, having seen a fatal mistake after it was too late, was amiably desirous of preventing his son from seeing it.

"I'm listening," said the latter, grimly surveying the board as he stretched out his hand. "Check."

"I should hardly think that he'd come to-night," said his father, with his hand poised over the board.

"Mate," replied the son.

"That's the worst of living so far out," bawled Mr. White, with sudden and unlooked-for violence; "of all the beastly, slushy, out-of-the-way places to live in, this is the worst. Path's a bog, and the road's a torrent. I don't know what people are thinking about. I suppose because only two houses in the road are let, they think it doesn't matter."

"Never mind, dear," said his wife soothingly; "perhaps you'll win the next one."

Mr. White looked up sharply, just in time to intercept a knowing glance between mother and son. The words died away on his lips, and he hid a guilty grin in his thin gray beard.

"There he is," said Herbert White, as the gate banged to loudly and heavy footsteps came toward the door.

The old man rose with hospitable haste, and opening the door, was heard condoling with the new arrival. The new arrival also condoled with himself, so that Mrs. White said, "Tut tut!" and coughed gently as her husband entered the room, followed by a tall, burly man, beady of eye and rubicund of visage.

"Sergeant-Major Morris," he said, introducing him.

The sergeant-major shook hands, and taking the proffered seat by the fire, watched contentedly while his host got out whisky and tumblers and stood a small copper kettle on the fire.

At the third glass his eyes got brighter, and he began to talk, the little family circle regarding with eager interest this visitor from distant parts, as he squared his broad shoulders in the chair, and spoke of wild scenes and doughty deeds; of wars and plagues, and strange peoples.

"Twenty-one years of it," said Mr. White, nodding at his wife and son. "When he went away he was a slip of a youth in the warehouse. Now look at him."

"He don't look to have taken much harm," said Mrs. White politely.

"I'd like to go to India myself," said the old man, "just to look around a bit, you know."

"Better where you are," said the sergeant-major, shaking his head. He put down the empty glass, and sighing softly, shook it again.

"I should like to see those old temples and fakirs and jugglers," said the old man. "What was that you started telling me the other day about a monkey's paw or something, Morris?"

"Nothing," said the soldier hastily. "Leastways nothing worth hearing."

"Monkey's paw?" said Mrs. White curiously.

"Well, it's just a bit of what you might call magic, perhaps," said the sergeant-major off-handedly.

His three listeners leaned forward eagerly. The visitor absent-

mindedly put his empty glass to his lips and then set it down
again. His host filled it for him.

"To look at," said the sergeant-major, fumbling in his
pocket, "it's just an ordinary little paw, dried to a mummy."

He took something out of his pocket and proffered it. Mrs.
White drew back with a grimace, but her son, taking it,
examined it curiously.

"And what is there special about it?" inquired Mr. White
as he took it from his son, and having examined it, placed it
upon the table.

"It had a spell put on it by an old fakir," said the sergeant-
major, "a very holy man. He wanted to show that fate ruled
people's lives, and that those who interfered with it did so to
their sorrow. He put a spell on it so that three separate men
could each have three wishes from it."

His manner was so impressive that his hearers were conscious that their light laughter jarred somewhat.

"Well, why don't you have three, sir?" said Herbert White
cleverly.

The soldier regarded him in the way that middle age is
wont to regard presumptuous youth. "I have," he said quietly, and his blotchy face whitened.

"And did you really have the three wishes granted?" asked
Mrs. White.

"I did," said the sergeant-major, and his glass tapped
against his strong teeth.

"And has anybody else wished?" persisted the old lady.

"The first man had his three wishes. Yes," was the reply;
"I don't know what the first two were, but the third was for
death. That's how I got the paw."

His tones were so grave that a hush fell upon the group.

"If you've had your three wishes, it's no good to you now
then, Morris," said the old man at last. "What do you keep it
for?"

The soldier shook his head. "Fancy, I suppose," he said
slowly. "I did have some idea of selling it, but I don't think I
will. It has caused enough mischief already. Besides, people
won't buy. They think it's a fairy tale, some of them; and
those who do think anything of it want to try it first and pay
me afterward."

"If you could have another three wishes," said the old man, eyeing him keenly, "would you have them?"

"I don't know," said the other. "I don't know."

He took the paw, and dangling it between his forefinger and thumb, suddenly threw it upon the fire. White, with a slight cry, stooped down and snatched it off.

"Better let it burn," said the soldier solemnly.

"If you don't want it, Morris," said the other, "give it to me."

"I won't," said his friend doggedly. "I threw it on the fire. If you keep it, don't blame me for what happens. Pitch it on the fire again like a sensible man."

The other shook his head and examined his new possession closely. "How do you do it?" he inquired.

"Hold it up in your right hand and wish aloud," said the sergeant-major, "but I warn you of the consequences."

"Sounds like the *Arabian Nights*," said Mrs. White, as she rose and began to set the supper. "Don't you think you might wish for four pairs of hands for me?"

Her husband drew the talisman from his pocket, and then all three burst into laughter as the sergeant-major, with a look of alarm on his face, caught him by the arm.

"If you must wish," he said gruffly, "wish for something sensible."

Mr. White dropped it back in his pocket, and placing chairs, motioned his friend to the table. In the business of supper the talisman was partly forgotten, and afterward the three sat listening in an enthralled fashion to a second install-ment of the soldier's adventures in India.

"If the tale about the monkey's paw is not more truthful than those he has been telling us," said Herbert, as the door closed behind their guest, just in time to catch the last train, "we shan't make much out of it."

"Did you give him anything for it, father?" inquired Mrs. White, regarding her husband closely.

"A trifle," said he, colouring slightly. "He didn't want it, but I made him take it. And he pressed me again to throw it away."

"Likely," said Herbert, with pretended horror. "Why, we're going to be rich, and famous, and happy. Wish to be an emperor, father, to begin with; then you can't be hen-pecked.''

He darted round the table, pursued by the maligned Mrs. White armed with an antimacassar.

Mr. White took the paw from his pocket and eyed it dubiously. ''I don't know what to wish for, and that's a fact,'' he said slowly. ''It seems to me I've got all I want.''

''If you only cleared the house, you'd be quite happy, wouldn't you!'' said Herbert, with his hand on his shoulder. ''Well, wish for two hundred pounds, then; that'll just do it.''

His father, smiling shamefacedly at his own credulity, held up the talisman, as his son, with a solemn face, somewhat marred by a wink at his mother, sat down at the piano and struck a few impressive chords.

''I wish for two hundred pounds,'' said the old man distinctly.

A fine crash from the piano greeted the words, interrupted by a shuddering cry from the old man. His wife and son ran toward him.

''It moved,'' he cried, with a glance of disgust at the object as it lay on the floor. ''As I wished, it twisted in my hand like a snake.''

''Well, I don't see the money,'' said his son, as he picked it up and placed it on the table, ''and I bet I never shall.''

''It must have been your fancy, father,'' said his wife, regarding him anxiously.

He shook his head. ''Never mind, though; there's no harm done, but it gave me a shock all the same.''

They sat down by the fire again while the two men finished their pipes. Outside, the wind was higher than ever, and the old man started nervously at the sound of a door banging upstairs. A silence unusual and depressing settled upon all three, which lasted until the old couple rose to retire for the night.

''I expect you'll find the cash tied up in a big bag in the middle of your bed,'' said Herbert, as he bade them good night, ''and something horrible squatting up on top of the wardrobe watching you pocket your ill-gotten gains.''

He sat alone in the darkness, gazing at the dying fire, and seeing faces in it. The last face was so horrible and so simian that he gazed at it with amazement. It got so vivid that, with a little uneasy laugh, he felt on the table for a glass containing a little water to throw over it. His hand grasped the monkey's paw, and with a little shiver he wiped his hand on his coat and went up to bed.

II

In the brightness of the wintery sun next morning as it streamed over the breakfast table he laughed at his fears. There was an air of prosaic wholesomeness about the room which it had lacked on the previous night, and the dirty, shrivelled little paw was pitched on the side-board with a carelessness which betokened no great belief in its virtues.

"I suppose all old soldiers are the same," said Mrs. White. "The idea of our listening to such nonsense! How could wishes be granted in these days? And if they could, how could two hundred pounds hurt you, father?"

"Might drop on his head from the sky," said the frivolous Herbert.

"Morris said the things happened so naturally," said his father, "that you might if you so wished attribute it to coincidence."

"Well, don't break into the money before I come back," said Herbert as he rose from the table. "I'm afraid it'll turn you into a mean, avaricious man, and we will have to disown you."

His mother laughed, and following him to the door, watched him down the road; and returning to the breakfast table, was very happy at the expense of her husband's credulity. All of which did not prevent her from scurrying to the door at the postman's knock, nor prevent her from referring somewhat shortly to retired sergeant-majors of bibulous habits when she found that the post brought a tailor's bill.

"Herbert will have some more of his funny remarks, I expect, when he comes home," she said, as they sat at dinner.

"I dare say," said Mr. White, pouring himself out some beer; "but for all that, the thing moved in my hand; that I'll swear to."

"You thought it did," said the old lady soothingly.

"I say it did," replied the other. "There was no thought about it; I had just— What's the matter?"

His wife made no reply. She was watching the mysterious movements of a man outside, who, peering in an undecided fashion at the house, appeared to be trying to make up his mind to enter. In mental connection with the two hundred pounds, she noticed that the stranger was well dressed, and wore a silk hat of glossy newness. Three times he paused at the gate, and then walked on again. The fourth time he stood with his hand upon it, and then with a sudden resolution flung it open and walked up the path. Mrs. White at the same moment placed her hands behind her, and hurriedly unfastening the strings on her apron, put that useful article of apparel beneath the cushion of her chair.

She brought the stranger, who seemed ill at ease, into the room. He gazed at her furtively, and listened in a preoccupied fashion as the old lady apologized for the appearance of the room, and her husband's coat, a garment he usually reserved for the garden. She then waited as patiently as her sex would permit, for him to broach his business, but he was at first strangely silent.

"I—was asked to call," he said at last, and stooped and picked a piece of cotton from his trousers. "I come from 'Maw and Meggins.'"

The old lady started. "Is anything the matter?" she asked breathlessly. "Has anything happened to Herbert? What is it? What is it?"

Her husband interposed. "There, there, mother," he said hastily. "Sit down, and don't jump to conclusions. You've not brought bad news, I'm sure, sir;" and he eyed the other wistfully.

"I'm sorry—" began the visitor.

"Is he hurt?" demanded the mother wildly.

The visitor bowed in assent. "Badly hurt," he said quietly, "but he is not in any pain."

"Oh, thank God!" said the old woman, clasping her hands. "Thank God for that! Thank—"

She broke off suddenly as the sinister meaning of the assurance dawned upon her, and she saw the awful confirmation of her fears in the other's averted face. She caught her breath, and turning to her slower-witted husband, laid her trembling old hand upon his. There was a long silence.

"He was caught in the machinery," said the visitor at length in a low voice.

"Caught in the machinery," repeated Mr. White, in a dazed fashion, "yes."

He sat staring blankly out at the window, and taking his wife's hand between his own, pressed it as he had been wont to do in their old courting days nearly forty years before.

"He was the only one left to us," he said, turning gently to the visitor. "It is hard."

The other coughed, and rising, walked slowly to the window.

"The firm wished me to convey their sincere sympathy with you in your great loss," he said, without looking round. "I beg that you will understand I am only their servant and merely obeying orders."

There was no reply; the old woman's face was white, her eyes staring, and her breath inaudible; on the husband's face was a look such as his friend the sergeant might have carried into his first action.

"I was to say that Maw and Meggins disclaim all responsibility," continued the other. "They admit no liability at all, but in consideration of your son's services, they wish to present you with a certain sum as compensation."

Mr. White dropped his wife's hand, and rising to his feet, gazed with a look of horror at his visitor. His dry lips shaped the words, "How much?"

"Two hundred pounds," was the answer.

Unconscious of his wife's shriek, the old man smiled faintly, put out his hands like a sightless man, and dropped, a senseless heap to the floor.

III

In the huge new cemetery, some two miles distant, the old people buried their dead, and came back to the house steeped in shadow and silence. It was all over so quickly that at first they could hardly realise it, and remained in a state of expectation as though of something else to happen—something else which was to lighten this load, too heavy for old hearts to bear.

But the days passed, and expectation gave place to resignation—the hopeless resignation of the old, sometimes miscalled apathy. Sometimes they hardly exchanged a word, for now they had nothing to talk about, and their days were long to weariness.

It was about a week after, that the old man, waking suddenly in the night, stretched out his hand and found himself alone. The room was in darkness, and the sound of subdued weeping came from the window. He raised himself in bed and listened.

"Come back," he said tenderly. "You will be cold."

"It is colder for my son," said the old woman, and wept afresh.

The sound of her sobs died away on his ears. The bed was warm, and his eyes heavy with sleep. He dozed fitfully, and then slept until a sudden wild cry from his wife awoke him with a start.

"The paw!" she cried wildly. "The monkey's paw!"

He started up in alarm. "Where? Where is it? What's the matter?"

She came stumbling across the room toward him. "I want it," she said quietly. "You've not destroyed it?"

"It's in the parlour, on the bracket," he replied, marvelling. "Why?"

She cried and laughed together, and bending over, kissed his cheek.

"I only just thought of it," she said hysterically. "Why didn't I think of it before? Why didn't *you* think of it?"

"Think of what?" he questioned.

"The other two wishes," she replied rapidly. "We've only had one."

"Was not that enough?" he demanded fiercely.

"No," she cried triumphantly; "we'll have one more. Go down and get it quickly, and wish our boy alive again."

The man sat up in bed and flung the bedclothes from his quaking limbs. "Good God, you are mad!" he cried, aghast.

"Get it," she panted; "get it quickly, and wish—Oh, my boy, my boy!"

Her husband struck a match and lit the candle. "Get back to bed," he said unsteadily. "You don't know what you are saying."

"We had the first wish granted," said the old woman feverishly; "why not the second?"

"A coincidence," stammered the old man.

"Go and get it and wish," cried his wife, quivering with excitement.

The old man turned and regarded her, and his voice shook. "He has been dead ten days, and besides he—I would not tell you else, but—I could only recognize him by his clothing. If he was too terrible for you to see then, how now?"

"Bring him back," cried the old woman, and dragged him toward the door. "Do you think I fear the child I have nursed?"

He went down in the darkness, and felt his way to the parlour, and then to the mantelpiece. The talisman was in its place, and a horrible fear that the unspoken wish might bring his mutilated son before him ere he could escape from the room seized upon him, and he caught his breath as he found that he had lost the direction of the door. His brow cold with sweat, he felt his way round the table, and groped along the wall until he found himself in the small passage with the unwholesome thing in his hand.

Even his wife's face seemed changed as he entered the room. It was white and expectant, and to his fears seemed to have an unnatural look upon it. He was afraid of her.

"*Wish!*" she cried, in a strong voice.

"It is foolish and wicked," he faltered.

"*Wish!*" repeated his wife.

He raised his hand. "I wish my son alive again."

The talisman fell to the floor, and he regarded it fearfully. Then he sank trembling into a chair as the old woman, with burning eyes, walked to the window and raised the blind.

He sat until he was chilled with the cold, glancing occasionally at the figure of the old woman peering through the window. The candle-end, which had burned below the rim of the china candlestick, was throwing pulsating shadows on the ceiling and walls, until, with a flicker larger than the rest, it expired. The old man, with an unspeakable sense of relief at the failure of the talisman, crept back to his bed, and a minute or two afterward the old woman came silently and apathetically beside him.

Neither spoke, but lay silently listening to the ticking of the clock. A stair creaked, and a squeaky mouse scurried noisily through the wall. The darkness was oppressive, and after lying for some time screwing up his courage, he took the box of matches, and striking one, went downstairs for a candle.

At the foot of the stairs the match went out, and he paused to strike another; and at the same moment a knock, so quiet and stealthy as to be scarcely audible, sounded on the front door.

The matches fell from his hand and spilled in the passage. He stood motionless, his breath suspended until the knock was repeated. Then he turned and fled swiftly back to his room, and closed the door behind him. A third knock sounded through the house.

"What's that?" cried the old woman, starting up.

"A rat," said the old man in shaking tones—"a rat. It passed me on the stairs."

His wife sat up in bed listening. A loud knock resounded through the house.

"It's Herbert!" she screamed. "It's Herbert!"

She ran to the door, but her husband was before her, and catching her by the arm, held her tightly.

"What are you going to do?" he whispered hoarsely.

"It's my boy; it's Herbert!" she cried, struggling mechanically. "I forgot it was two miles away. What are you holding me for? Let go. I must open the door."

"For God's sake don't let it in," cried the old man, trembling.

"You're afraid of your own son," she cried, struggling. "Let me go. I'm coming, Herbert; I'm coming."

There was another knock, and another. The old woman with a sudden wrench broke free and ran from the room. Her husband followed to the landing, and called after her appealingly as she hurried downstairs. He heard the chain rattle back and the bottom bolt drawn slowly and stiffly from the socket. Then the old woman's voice strained and panting.

"The bolt," she cried loudly. "Come down. I can't reach it."

But her husband was on his hands and knees groping wildly on the floor in search of the paw. If he could only find it before the thing outside got in. A perfect fusillade of knocks reverberated through the house, and he heard the scraping of a chair as his wife put it down in the passage against the door. He heard the creaking of the bolt as it came slowly back, and at the same moment he found the monkey's paw, and frantically breathed his third and last wish.

The knocking ceased suddenly, although the echoes of it were still in the house. He heard the chair drawn back, and the door opened. A cold wind rushed up the staircase, and a long loud wail of disappointment and misery from his wife gave him courage to run down to her side, and then to the gate beyond. The street lamp flickering opposite shone on a quiet and deserted road.

BEHIND THE NEWS

by Jack Finney

No one knew how the false and slanderous item on Police Chief Quayle got into the *Clarion*. The editor accepted all blame. It was Friday, press day, in the final lull before the old flatbed press began clanking out the weekly twelve hundred copies, and everything in the one-room frame building seemed normal. Grinning insanely, young Johnny Deutsch, owner and editor, sat before a typewriter at a rolltop desk near his secretary—all three of which had been his father's before him. He sat as he did each week, his long, loose-jointed body hunched over the old machine, his big hands flying over the keys; then he flung himself back in his chair and read aloud what he had just written. " 'Police Chief Slain by Wolf Pack!' " he cried.

"An immature form of wish fulfillment," his secretary, Miss Gerraghty, murmured acidly—as she did each week.

Ignoring this, Johnny pounded at his typewriter again, the carriage jouncing. Then he threw himself back once more, a lock of jet-black hair dropping onto his forehead, his lean, rough-hewn face happy, his brown eyes dancing. " 'This morning,' " he read, " 'Police Chief Wendall E. Quayle was set upon and slain by a mysterious pack of wolves that suddenly appeared on Culver Street. Before the eyes of horrified shoppers, the maddened animals tore Quayle to tattered shreds within seconds.' "

The *Clarion's* printer, Nate Rubin, an ink-smudged youth in blue denim apron, stood at his worktable, setting the back-page supermarket ad and, as he did each week, mournfully shaking his head at the prices. "Johnny"—he glanced up—"Quayle's a slob, but harmless. What you got against him?"

"Nothing personal." Johnny grinned. "But I'm a cop hater," he shouted, "as all true Americans instinctively are. A foe from birth of officialdom, bureaucracy and the heel of tyranny!" Nate considered this, then nodded in agreement and understanding. Johnny's typewriter clattered again for a time, then stopped. " 'Eyewitnesses,' " he read, " 'state that the surrounding area was a shambles, while dismembered limbs were found as far south as Yancy Creek. The body was identifiable only from indecent tattoos and the reek of cheap whisky, which characterized our undistinguished late sleuth.' "

This, finally, as also happened each week, was too much for Miss Gerraghty, and peering over her glasses like a benevolent grandmother, she said witheringly, "A mature mind could never, week after week, compose these childlike fantasies to the uproarious amusement of no one but himself. 'Mayor Schimmerhorn Assassinated!' " she quoted contemptuously from a previous effort of Johnny's. " 'City Council Wiped Out by Falling Meteor' " An old memory awakened, she frowned, then shook her head disdainfully. "Meteors." She sniffed. "You're worse than your father."

"What'd he do?" Johnny looked up.

"Lots of things, all foolish. Found an old lump of lead in a field, for one thing, and claimed it was a meteor. Threw it in the lead box on the Linotype machine to melt. Then he ran a story saying it was the first time in history a paper had been printed with type cast from a meteor." In a tone suggesting that both stories were equally absurd, she added, "Same issue that carried your birth announcement," and nodded at the paperweight on Johnny's desk.

Johnny glanced at the paperweight, then picked it up, hefting it absently. It was a rectangle of lead type, the letters worn almost smooth; he hadn't read it for years. But now his eyes scanned the blurred lines that had once announced to four hundred uncaring subscribers that he had been born. When he reached the last sentence, "It is predicted he will make his mark on the world," Johnny's eyes flicked to the dateline, "October 28, 1933." All elation and well-being drained out of him then. He was twenty-three years old, the worn type reminded him, and there wasn't the least indication that he would ever make a mark or even a scratch on the world—and for the first time he was impressed with Miss Gerraghty's weekly tirade.

Recalling his idea, at University Journalism School a few years before, of what life as a newspaperman would be, he smiled bitterly, contrasting that picture with the life he now led. Owner by inheritance of a small-town weekly, its columns filled with stale and newsless news as boring to himself as to his subscribers, he reflected that Miss Gerraghty's contempt was deserved. For he simply went on, week after week, doing nothing to relieve his frustration but compose childish parodies of nonexistent news. He thought of a classmate, now a copywriter for a large advertising agency, earning an enormous salary. Then, with even greater longing, he thought of two other classmates, both of whom were actually married, he reflected bitterly. Glancing at the half-full sheet of copy paper in his typewriter, he felt with sudden force that he was just what Miss Gerraghty said he was, immature and childlike; and he looked down at the worn type in his hand with distaste. The very fact that he had kept it, he suddenly realized, could undoubtedly be explained by Miss Gerraghty in unpleasantly Freudian terms.

On impulse, a new will toward maturity flaming within him, Johnny stood up, walked to the Linotype machine, lifted the cover of the lead box, and dropped his paperweight into the molten metal. "Miss Gerraghty," he said firmly, his voice several tones deeper, "what would a mature mind compose?"

She glanced up, surprised. "If anything," she said, "something at least distantly linked to the remotely possible." Then she turned back to her proof sheets.

Back at his desk after several minutes of frowning thought, his face set, he believed, in new lines of maturity, Johnny typed "Police Chief Loses Pants." Then he went on, typing slowly, to compose a brief fictitious account of an attack on Police Chief Quayle by a large Dalmatian who, Johnny wrote, had torn out the seat of Quayle's pants. But he felt no urge to read this aloud. As he recalled later, Johnny yanked the sheet of paper from his typewriter, tossed it onto his desk, and then left, feeling depressed, for City Hall, informing his staff, who knew better, that he was going to hunt up some last-minute news.

The item appeared on page one, headline and all, just as Johnny had typed it. How it had gotten in with the remaining unset front-page items no one knew. But it had, and Nate—with his astounding ability to set words and sentences, editing their spelling and punctuation, yet allowing no glimmer of their meaning to touch his mind—had turned it into type along with the others.

In any case, it was Johnny's responsibility to check the issue before the final press run, and he had not done so. Deprived by Miss Gerraghty of even the pretense that the *Clarion* might sometime carry a piece of news worth reading, he had lingered too long talking to the town clerk. This was Miss Miriam Zeebley, a blonde, lithe young woman who resembled Grace Kelly from the shoulders up, though better-looking; Anita Ekberg from waist to shoulders, though less flat-chested; and for the rest of her five feet six inches, as Marilyn Monroe as Miss Monroe undoubtedly wished she looked.

Seated at her desk, in a thin summer dress—polite, cordial enough, but coolly official—Miss Zeebley obviously didn't actually know or care that Johnny Deutsch was alive, and he didn't blame her. There were times when Johnny, staring into his mirror, could convince himself for as long as two or three seconds that he had a sort of offbeat, Lincolnesque good looks. But now, he felt his face flush as the certainty swept over him that he was actually an awkward, crag-faced lout. Then, grateful for even the crumbs of her attention, but knowing that for her anything less than a young Ronald Colman was absurd, he left.

Back at his desk, the *Clarion* already delivered into the official hands of the post office, Johnny reached the lowest ebb of his life. Staring numbly at the page-one libel on Police Chief Quayle, knowing that any jury would regard it as tending to "embarrass, humiliate and defame," he knew too that he was a failure and a misfit, inept in life, libel and love; and he considered simply walking to the edge of town, jumping a freight, and beginning life anew in the West.

The front door opened, and a small boy, wearing cowboy boots, the dress jacket of a full colonel in the Space Patrol, and a fluorescent green stocking cap, stepped into the office. He said, "Hey Johnny, you got some old type I can have for my newspaper?"

"Ask Nate." Johnny gestured wearily at the shabby sink at which Nate was scrubbing his forearms.

"Okay." The boy suddenly grinned. "Gee, it was funny. I sure laughed," he said.

"What was funny?"

"Chief Quayle. Gettin' the seat of his pants tore off. Gee, it was funny; I sure laughed."

"Oh." Johnny nodded. "You've read the story?"

The boy shook his head. "No. I saw it."

"Saw *what?*" Johnny said irritably.

"Saw the dog," the boy explained patiently, "bite off his pants. Gee, it was funny." He laughed. "I sure laughed."

Johnny pushed himself upright in his chair. "You *saw* this happen?"

"Yeah."

"Where?"

"On Culver Street."

"You actually *saw* the dog tear the seat out of Quayle's pants?"

"Yep." the boy grinned. "Gee, it was—"

"*When?*"

"I dunno." He shrugged. "Few minutes ago. He ran all the way back to the station house. It was sure funny. Everybody laughed like anyth—"

Grabbing the boy by both shoulders, his voice grown low and tense, Johnny said slowly, "*What kind of dog was it?*"

"I dunno," the boy answered without interest. "One of them big white dogs with black spots all over." He turned toward the sink at the back of the room. "Hey, Nate!" he called. "Johnny says for you to gimme some type."

For a full quarter minute Miss Gerraghty just stared at Johnny. Then she blinked her eyes and announced firmly, "Coincidence. An astonishing, yet mathematically predictable coinci—"

Johnny slowly shook his head. "No," he said numbly, his

eyes astonished. "It was no coincidence, as any but the scientific mind would know." He turned slowly toward Miss Gerraghty, and in his eyes a glow of triumph was kindling. "Miss Gerraghty," he said slowly, "I don't know how it happened, but what I wrote and printed in the *Clarion* came true. Immediately, and in every detail." Suddenly he grinned, snatching up a fresh sheet of paper, rolled it into his typewriter, and said, "And nothing in the world is going to stop me from trying it again!"

His eyes glittering, staring through the paper at a suddenly glorious and incredible future, Johnny typed "Engagement Announced!" The keys beat out a furious splatter of sound. "Miss Miriam Zeebley to Wed Editor Deutsch!" The type bars jammed, and Johnny frantically pried them apart, then continued. "Town Clerk Zeebley, unexpectedly resigning her position, announced today—"

One week later, the *Clarion* printed, addressed, carried to the post office, and even then, Johnny knew, being delivered, he sat at his desk waiting. Then, as he had hoped, the phone rang; and as he had also hoped, it was Miss Zeebley, her voice lovely as a temple bell. For a full minute Johnny sat listening. Once he said, "But Miss Zeebley, it was an acci—" A few moments later he began, "Typographical err—" During the one time she paused for breath, Johnny managed to say feebly, "It must have been some kind of—joke. A disgruntled employee." Presently, voice dulled and hopeless, he said, "Yes, I'll publish a retraction," and hung up.

For a while, lost in despair, Johnny sat with his head in his hands, staring down at the floor. Then, as some men turn to drink, others to drugs, women, or gambling, Johnny turned to his typewriter. "Quayle Slain by Thug," he typed despondently. "Early this morning," he continued, "the decapitated body of Police Chief Wendall E. Quayle was discovered in an abandoned trunk. Minutes later, his head, shrunken to a fraction of its normal six-and-one-eighth-inch size—"

Presently he tossed the finished story onto Miss Gerraghty's desk. "It came true once," he said sadly, "about Quayle's pants. If I'd only printed this instead."

"It wouldn't have come true then," Miss Gerraghty said, glancing at the headline. "Any more than Miriam Zeebley marrying you. There are some things that are just too ridiculous."

Johnny stared at her for several seconds, his eyes narrowing. "Yeah," he said then, interest and excitement beginning to well up in his voice, "maybe that's it." He nodded thoughtfully. "It's got to be possible, at least; maybe that's the key. You can't go *too* far, you can't go overboard." Suddenly he was elated. "You've hit it, Miss Gerraghty!" He reached for a fresh sheet of copy paper.

As Miss Gerraghty stared at him in icy, unbelieving contempt, Johnny, choosing his words slowly and carefully, began to type. "Among those attending the Old Nakomis Country Club Soirée tonight," he wrote, "will be Miss Miriam Zeebley. It will surprise none who know our ever-popular town clerk to learn that, bearing no malice for an unfortunate error that appeared in these columns recently, she will attend escorted by Ye Ed, Johnny Deutsch."

He pulled the sheet of paper from his machine, dated it in pencil for the following week's issue, scribbled "Social Notes" at the top, then read it through again. "Possible," he murmured approvingly. "Or at least barely within the borders of conceivability." His eyes happy again, Johnny glanced at Miss Gerraghty and grinned. "Shoot the works," he said, and rolled another sheet into his typewriter.

"Psychotic," Miss Gerraghty murmured, nodding soberly. "Like father, like son."

"How do you spell 'bubonic plague'?" Johnny asked, then hastily added, "Never mind; I'd better make it mumps."

The following Saturday Johnny picked up the phone. Miss Gerraghty laid down her proof sheets to listen.

"Miriam," Johnny said presently into the phone, his voice brisk and confident, "I want you to attend the Old Nakomis Country Club Soirée tonight; with me." He leaned back in his chair, feet up on his typewriter, listening. "You have a date? Well, break it," he said firmly. A moment later he smiled and said, "Fine. I'll call for you at eight." There was a pause; then Johnny said, "Quayle, eh? What's the trouble?" Then he nodded. "Thanks; the story'll be in this issue." He replaced the phone, turned to Miss Gerraghty, and waited, humming softly.

For a moment there was no sound in the room; Miss Gerraghty simply stared. Then in a small, frightened voice, she asked, "Is Quayle sick?" Johnny nodded. "Mumps?" Miss Gerraghty whispered.

'Yeah," Johnny said, and turned happily to his typewriter

The quality and interest of the *Clarion's* news picked up sharply in the weeks that followed. With invariable accuracy, the *Clarion* reported that Miss Miriam Zeebley was attending the Flower and Garden Show, the movies, the Women's Club annual bazaar, a traveling carnival, and the Spelling-Bee State Semifinals, all with Johnny Deutsch. In addition, the *Clarion* uncannily announced almost simultaneously with the events themselves that Mayor Schimmerhorn was stung by a swarm of bees, and that the City Council, refreshing themselves with cheese sandwiches after a meeting, was stricken to a man with food poisoning. It was predicted by the *Clarion* that the Girl Scouts would sell 42 per cent more cookies than last year in their annual drive, and this came precisely true. The *Clarion* reported that the Old Nakomis Country Club had elected a new vice-president, Johnny Deutsch, and that Police Chief Wendall E. Quayle, having recovered from the mumps, had promptly come down with hives. Circulation increased by leaps and bounds.

For however it happened and whatever the cause, it was undeniably true that what the *Clarion* printed as fact or prediction always came true—so long as Johnny kept his inventions to the reasonably possible. Once, in his zeal, he violated this principle, and had to rush an extra edition into print on the following day carrying a retraction of the *Clarion's* lead story that Mayor Schimmerhorn, a notorious teetotaler, had been arrested while drunk for peddling indecent post cards in the alley back of City Hall. But, the retraction added; His Honor, understanding how such an error could easily occur, had no intention of suing the *Clarion;* and the mayor explained to friends later that day, his voice faintly puzzled, that this was quite true.

A few days later, Thursday, a hot afternoon in August, Johnny leaned back in his chair, folded his hands complacently in back of his head, lifted his long lean legs up onto his typewriter, and looked across the little office at Miss

Gerraghty. She was sitting, chin in hand, listening to a portable radio on her desk from which a voice was saying, ". . . sacred trust to the American people!" A burst of applause followed this statement, and Johnny nodded at the radio and said, "You know, we have seldom carried national news. We've been more of a local paper."

Miss Gerraghty glanced up, nodded absently, then returned her attention to the radio, as the voice resumed solemnly, "In the immortal words of Thomas Jefferson . . ."

"There is no reason," Johnny continued quietly, "why we shouldn't, though. Once in a while." Miss Gerraghty didn't bother to answer. "It might be fun," Johnny added, nodding at the radio, "with the Democratic convention going on, to score a news beat on the rest of the world."

Miss Gerraghty looked at him, faintly puzzled; then her jaw dropped, and she hastily switched off the radio. "No!" She stared at him wide-eyed. Then, voice frightened and ominous, she said, "No, Johnny, you're going too far. Stick to local—"

He was shaking his head. "There are several possible candidates for the Democratic nomination," he said, nodding at the radio, "and it's time to do something about it." Dropping his feet to the floor, Johnny sat up and rolled a fresh sheet of paper into his typewriter. "Think it's all right if we issue the paper a day early?"

"Nobody will notice the difference," Miss Gerraghty replied faintly, as Johnny poised his fingers over the typewriter.

"We'll get the paper to the post office tonight then," he said, "to be delivered in the morning mail. "Kefauver, Stevenson, or Harriman," he murmured, "I just can't make up my mind." Then he suddenly typed, "Stevenson Nominated!" and said, "Think I'll make it on the first ballot."

The next day, the radio blaring with the voice of the excited announcer above the background pandemonium of cheering delegates, Miss Gerraghty looked up at Johnny. "Anybody could have predicted that."

But Johnny wasn't listening. Hands clasped behind his head, staring dreamily at the ceiling, he was murmuring, "It's Ike for President, of course, but whom shall I give the second spot to?"

Seven days later, the radio on Miss Gerraghty's desk blared that Richard Nixon had been given the Republican nomination for vice-president, in precisely the way Johnny's lead story in the *Clarion* had described. Miss Gerraghty wrung her hands, and moaned. "Johnny," she said pitifully, "why?" She snatched a copy of the *Clarion* from her desk, and shook it violently in his face. "Nixon to Run with Ike!" the headline cried. "*Why* does it work?" Miss Gerraghty begged.

"Why, I thought you knew." Johnny looked at her, genuinely surprised. "I thought you'd guessed; don't you ever read science fiction? It's the meteor, Miss Gerraghty."

"The meteor?"

"The one my father found," Johnny said patiently. "It seems to be lead, but actually it was an unknown metal from another world. And somehow, when you turn it into type, the news it prints comes true. Within reason."

"But where did you get—"

"My birth announcement," he said impatiently. "It was cast from the meteor, as you yourself told me. It was saved all these years, till I melted it with the Linotype lead." Johnny shrugged, smiling happily. "And since we remelt our type after each issue, it's always still there, hard at work, issue after issue of the *Clarion*."

Her voice dulled, finally accepting this, Miss Gerraghty said, "But how? Johnny, *how* does it wor—"

"Miss Gerraghty," Johnny said sternly, "if you had ever read science fiction, you'd know that the dullest part is always the explanation. It bores the reader and clutters up the story. Especially when the author flunked high-school physics and simply doesn't know how it works. We'll just skip that," he said firmly, "and get on to more important things. We've got lots to do now."

But in the weeks following the conventions, to Miss Gerraghty's great relief, Johnny's mind turned from the national scene. For while it was delightfully true that Miss Miriam Zeebley and Editor Deutsch continued to do everything mentioned in the *Clarions's* Social Notes, there was a limit to what could be mentioned. Johnny Deutsch was healthy, normal and reasonably full of animal vigor; and while he enjoyed escorting Miriam to the town's social functions, there

were times—twenty-four hours a day, in fact—when he longed
for more than he could describe in type. He would have
liked, for example, to kiss Miss Zeebley, long and linger-
ingly, full on the lips.

He considered printing this as a news item and burying it
among the legal notices at the back of the *Clarion*, but he
couldn't quite work up the nerve to do it. He also considered
simply kissing Miriam on his own some night; but he couldn't
work up the nerve to try this, either. There were times now
when, shaving before a date with Miriam, he managed to
convince himself for a full minute or more that he was
actually a rather rugged, good-looking man. There were even
times when he felt that Miriam agreed. But these times never
coincided with opportunities to kiss her. At those moments he
alway knew, with depressing certainty, that he was a gibber-
ing clod. Once again he was a frustrated man, and it seemed
to Johnny as the summer went on that his activities with
Miriam were forever doomed to those that could be described
in a family newspaper.

And so it was, one fine fall morning, that when Miss
Gerraghty said, "Did you vote today?" Johnny only looked
at her blankly.

"Vote?" he said.

"Today," Miss Gerraghty said patiently, "is Election Day;
your first opportunity to help elect a President."

He glanced at the wall calendar. Miss Gerraghty was right.
"Thanks," he said, and his face cleared. "Thanks for re-
minding me"—once again his voice was brisk and assured—
"or I might have been too late."

"Too late for what?"

"To make sure," Johnny said, reaching for a sheet of copy
paper, "that the right man is elected."

Slowly Miss Gerraghty rose from her desk, walked around
it, and stood facing Johnny. "No," she said quietly.

"What do you mean?" He looked up.

"I won't let you, Johnny. That's one thing neither you nor
anyone else is going to interfere with."

He sat back in his chair, smiling up at her. "Don't you
want to see the right man elected?"

"Certainly," she said, "but who is he? That's something

no less than seventy million Americans are competent to decide." Her voice rose shrilly. "You hear me, Johnny? You let this alone!"

For a moment he sat staring up at her, and Miss Gerraghty realized how much he still resembled the boy he had been only a few years ago. "Don't be silly, Miss Gerraghty," he said, and turned to his typewriter. "Not many people would pass up this chance."

"And that," Miss Gerraghty said—and now she was speaking more to herself than to Johnny—"may be what is wrong with the world today." She walked back to her desk and for the rest of the morning sat thinking. She considered, first, burning down the office, but she knew she would be stopped. Then she considered rushing out to buttonhole people on the street and tell them the secret only the staff shared about the *Clarion;* but she knew she would not be believed. For a wild moment she considered murder, but knew immediately that she could never harm a hair of Johnny Deutsch's head.

At noon, when Johnny and Nate left for lunch, Miss Gerraghty stayed behind. The moment the door closed she stood up and walked to the files. For the next hour and a half, her fingers working frantically, her face soon perspiring and dust-streaked, she hunted desperately through the files.

"What are you doing?" Johnny asked, as he opened the office door on his return from lunch. Miss Gerraghty turned, her old body moving with a terrible weariness, her face like granite. From the top of the old wood filing cabinets, she picked up a stack of newspapers, and nodded at them somberly.

"I have been going through the back files," she answered. For a moment, her eyes like embers, she stared across the room at Johnny. "Has it occurred to you," she burst out bitterly, "that you weren't the first to use that meteor for type?" She dropped the stack of papers on Johnny's desk; their edges, he saw, were yellowed and crumbling with age. "Your father used it first, remember!" Her bony forefinger, trembling violently, touched a faded column of type. "Read it! Like you, he wasn't afraid to deal with subjects he knew nothing about!"

Johnny leaned forward to study the old story; after a moment he glanced at her, puzzled. "It's nothing," he said.

"Just a column of speculation on financial affairs. Harmless stuff."

"Harmless! 'Stocks will go down,' the old idiot wrote, just as though he knew what he was talking about! And of course it came true. Oh, it came true, all right! Look at that date!" Her shaking finger touched the date line. " 'October 28, 1929,' and the next day the stock market crashed and the worst depression in mankind's history began."

She snatched the old paper from the stack, revealing the next. "Presently," she said with acid quietness, "our genius turned to politics, just as his son wants to do. But he jumped into *world* politics, with an asinine editorial on Pacific developments." Her bony forefinger pointed out the date line. " 'September 17, 1931,' and of course his story came true, in a way he never realized. Japan invaded Manchuria the very next day! Two years later"—she revealed the next paper—"he wrote an empty-headed article on German politics, and Hitler became Chancellor of the Third Reich! In the very same year"—she pointed to another yellowing page—"he very nearly got Roosevelt assassinated, and"—her finger stabbed at still another story signed by Johnny's father—"read this and you'll see that he was directly responsible for the Dionne quintuplets!"

For a full fifteen seconds there was no sound in the little office but the chattering of Johnny's teeth. Then, barely able to speak, he whispered pitifully, "What about—World War Two?"

In a tone almost of kindness, Miss Gerraghty said, "No. I've checked the files carefully, and he wasn't responsible. But he did plenty! Any number of floods, fires, earthquakes and minor holocausts I haven't even bothered to mention! And he never realized it, never saw the connection, and I didn't either, till now. In time, I guess, the meteor metal thinned out. New lead was added to the Linotype from time to time, of course, and by the late 'thirties, as far as I can tell from the files, there wasn't enough meteor metal left to do any harm. Until you melted some of that original type again— your birth announcement, cast in full-strength meteor metal! Johnny"—her voice deepened with implacable authority— "you've got to clean out the lead box on the Linotype machine and throw out every scrap of old lead in the place. Right *now!*''

His voice a humble whisper, Johnny said, "Yes. Of course. Right away. Just as soon as I run one last story—''

"No!"

"—about my elopement!" he said frantically. "I finally figured out what to do about Miriam and the story is all ready to set up!"

For a full minute Miss Gerraghty considered. Then finally, reluctantly, she said, "All right; though I'm very fond of Miriam. And I think it's criminal to risk another generation of Deutschs. This one last story—and that's all!"

"Okay," Johnny said humbly. Then, physically and emotionally exhausted, Miss Gerraghty went home for the day, while Johnny allowed the presidential election of 1956 to proceed normally.

But he did write still one more story, which he personally set up in meteor type. Then he dropped every other scrap of type metal in the office into the deepest part of Yancy Creek. This final story, a little square of type locked in the office safe, has not yet been printed. It announces the birth of Johnny's daughter, giving precise details of her weight and length and stating that she resembles her mother exactly. Since obviously the prediction had come true in his own case, Johnny added, "It is predicted that she will make her mark on the world." Then he dated the story exactly nine months later than the elopment announcement.

Whether this final story will come true or not—whether the meteor metal from an unknown world will continue to have its mysterious effect—it is impossible to say. But it still *seems* to be working okay so far; at least, Miriam Deutsch is expecting.

THE FLIGHT OF THE UMBRELLA

by Marvin Kaye

Exegesis

". . . a long, heavy pole that ended in a large flounce of some silky material emblazoned with orange-and-yellow stripes on which various cabalistic symbols seemed to dance in pastel figurations. It was clearly an umbrella, but its size was rather impractical: too large for everyday use, too small for beach-basking . . ."

When J. Adrian Fillmore (Gad, how he detests that name!) bought the odd-looking bumbershoot, he had no idea it would whisk him away from his prosaic daily routine as a professor of English literature, American drama and Shakespeare at Parker College in mid-Pennsylvania and plant him smack-dab in the middle of a Gilbert and Sullivan cosmos.

The incredible umbrella was obviously some kind of dimensional-transfer engine, and it operated by universal laws he could but dimly discern. But after undergoing several harrowing adventures as a fugitive from the pirates of Penzance, the crew of the H. M. S. *Pinafore*, the ex-daughter-in-law-elect of the Mikado, and finally the entire British legal establishment, J. Adrian Fillmore found himself safely ensconced in the home of the umbrella's manufacturer, John Wellington Wells, the very sorcerer named in the title of the third Gilbert and Sullivan operetta.

The first thing the scholar demanded was why the umbrella took him to G&S-land and then refused to function again.

Said Wells: "I didn't plan it that way. But apparently there are physical laws governing it. You've got to finish a sequence. You have to follow some basic block of activity . . .''

J. Adrian Fillmore nodded. "My adventures followed the developing logic of an operetta. I had to solve the chief plot dilemma before the finale could be obtained, and the umbrella would work again.''

During his struggles to get free of his various predicaments, Fillmore began to take part in the logic of the G&S cosmos: he sang, just as the natives did . . . and there lay his chief danger.

"Subsumption," said the sorcerer. "There is a fine line between participation and total involvement. You were beginning to accept the axioms and tenets upon which my world is formulated. A little more singing and you could have found yourself permanently stuck here.''

"But why did you engineer such a danger into your umbrella?''

"I didn't. The instrument operates on principles and universal dictums that I've never been able to completely pin down. One time I wafted myself into an alien universe by magic and spied a master mathematician explaining the principles of this very device to an associate. It was beyond my comprehension. But when I heard what purpose the inventor had in mind, I stole the umbrella, brought it back to my own clime, and analyzed the working parts sufficiently to manufacture it for discreet, serious people who wish to go to other, better lands . . .''

Fillmore realized that he had been thinking about his thesis on Gilbert and Sullivan at the moment he first pushed the button of the umbrella. Normally, Wells pointed out, the machine would take its possessor to the cosmos desired in his thoughts.

"But participation in other climes will be vastly different from this world. It won't always be so obvious as to what may ensnare you permanently.''

The scholar picked up his umbrella, determined to go someplace where he would not be constantly put upon, a victim, but the sorcerer warned him that man tends to remain stable in whatever dimension he inhabits.

"D'you know where you wish to go now?" asked Wells.

"Yes. I want to seek out the one man who could unriddle the mystery of this umbrella."

"Which mystery are you talking about?"

"Why it takes the user to literary, rather than actual dimensions," Fillmore stated.

"Well, as to that, this world is real enough to me," the sorcerer protested, "and I have no idea what you mean when you refer to it as a gilbert and sullivan place . . . but, pray explain: What enlightened genius could possibly unravel the enigma of my marvelous umbrella?"

The sorcerer's curiosity remained unsatisfied. At the very moment he posed the question, there came a fierce rap at his front door. Fillmore looked to see who it was—and blanched.

During his misadventures, he had won the affections of Ruth, the rather bloodthirsty piratical-maid-of-all-work who spent her best, and second-best, and least-worst years marauding with the Penzance buccaneers. Ruth mistook Fillmore's intentions and thought he wanted to marry her.

As soon as he saw her at the sorcerer's door, the professor pressed the button of the dimensional-transfer machine and disappeared.

There were two people at the front door: Ruth, and a small, bald-headed civil servant, dry in manner and parched of spirit.

"Subpoena for one J. Adrian Fillmore," said the wizened functionary.

"On what charge?"

"What else?" Ruth snapped. "Breach of promise of marriage!"

"Oh, dear," the sorcerer mumbled to himself, "another sequence! I *do* hope he got away in time . . ." *But Fillmore's thoughts were confused when he pressed the umbrella catch. Vivid memories of Ruth throwing herself upon him at the conclusion of his trial in Old Bailey crowded his brain, and muddled the process of selection.*

And what was worse, he knew nothing then of the principle of universal economy. . . .

Chapter One

All afternoon, the equinoctial gales whipped London with elemental violence. The wan October sun, obscured by hueless clouds, shed pallid light but little warmth. Winds screamed down avenues and alleys, while at the windowpanes, a driving rain beat a merciless tattoo. It was as if all the destructive forces of Nature had foregathered, penned beasts, to howl at and threaten mankind through the protecting bars of *his* cage, civilization.

As evening drew in, the storm waned, though the wind still moaned and sobbed in the eaves like a child-ghost whimpering in a spectral schoolroom. From the Thames, great curlings of fog billowed forth, obscuring the green aits and meadows, creeping up alleys and mews, blanketing the city in an impenetrable maisma. Amber streetlamps glowed feebly in the mist-shroud like the eyes of corpses. Few foot travelers ventured out in the mud, and the only sound heard on some streets was the occasional rhythmic clip-clop and simultaneous metallic squeal of a passing hansom.

Newman Street was deserted and smothered by the river vapor. The mud was so thick and the appurtenances of inhabitation so difficult to discern that one might well believe a stegosaurus could wander along its morass-like reaches. But at precisely ten past nine, a less impressive figure suddenly appeared on the empty thoroughfare: a smallish, somewhat stocky man.

His footsteps echoed down the street and he stalked along for a time before assaying a cross-street. He was inadequately dressed in a gray woolen suit with ascot tucked in at the throat. He was hatless and wore no topcoat. Though he carried an umbrella in one hand, he made no effort to use it as a shield from the steady drizzle.

Up one alley, down another, past shadowy blocks of homes, tenements, commercial estabishments, the solitary pedestrian walked, his collar turned up and his head bowed. He hunched his shoulders, but the rain soaked into the material he wore on his back, ran down and squelched soddenly in his shoes, making the toes of his socks into sopping sponges. Once he stepped into a puddle deep enough to drown a cat. Shivering, he extricated his foot and forlornly tried to wring the excess moisture from his trouser leg.

Turning into Lombard Street, he spied the lights of a distant tavern. He huddled into a covered entranceway and fished in his pocket for his wallet. Finding it, he counted over the meager currency therein: roughly $34 in U.S. dollars that had been generously converted to pounds sterling by his benefactor, John Wellington Wells. But would it be usable in this cosmos? And did he, in fact, reach the very place he'd been meaning to visit?

Fillmore meditated briefly, made a decision, then stepped off in the direction of the far-off inn.

After a few moments more of slogging though mud and the rain, he drew near to the place. A sign suspended from an iron scrolled arm set at right angles to the bricks above the tavern door proclaimed the name of the establishment:

THE GEORGE AND VULTURE

That disturbed him. But he wiped off his shoes on the small bracket for that purpose set next to the steps and went inside, grateful to get out of the wetness.

The taproom was sparsely populated that evening. A trio of gamesters took turns at the dartboard, and an elderly, kindly-looking gentleman with a bit of a paunch sat at a corner table taking supper with a young, dandyish companion. The only other individual in the room when the drenched itinerant entered was the bartender.

Fillmore's bedraggled condition drew quizzical glances from the dart throwers, but they said nothing. Approaching the bar, he held out a pound note and ascertained from the bewildered tapster that it was, indeed, acceptable tender. The newcomer then ordered a pint of ale.

"Bit of a foul night for a stroll," observed the bartender as he set the libation on the polished countertop before his customer.

The stranger nodded, downing a quarter of the brew at one

gulp. Wiping his mouth, he eyed the bartender quizzically, then motioned to him.

"I say, would you mind very much if I asked you a question?"

"Of course not."

"Even if it seems a trifle peculiar?"

The tapster grinned, placed his hands flat on the countertop and leaned over to his customer. "If," he said in a low voice, "you think aught can surprise me after twenty-year of tavern-tending, ye've much to learn. Ask away."

"Well . . . this *is* London, isn't it?"

"George Yard, right enough."

"Well and good, but—" Fillmore shrugged. "Well, what I want to know is this: what year is this?"

"Why, 'ninety-five," the other replied, a bit nonplussed in spite of his assurances.

"Yes, yes," Fillmore nodded impatiently, "but—do you mean *eighteen* ninety-five?"

The bartender swallowed, wet his lips and took a breath before trusting himself to affirm the century. Then he found a reason to busy himself at the opposite end of the tavern.

Fillmore slowly sipped his ale, oblivious to the muted buzz that rose when the tapster began to talk to the dart players. He ignored their collective gaze, and busied himself moistening his interior and wondering how to dry off his exterior.

A tap on his shoulder. The dandyish gentleman stood by his side.

"Allow me to introduce myself. My name is Snodgrass—"

(Fillmore's ill-defined fears began to take shape.)

"I beg to be forgiven for invading your privacy, but my companion and I, you see, could not help but notice your somewhat uncomfortable condition. My friend is the most compassionate of men and wishes to make your acquaintance and perhaps assist you in your putative predicament."

The stranger thanked Snodgrass and followed him back to the table at the rear of the room, where the elderly, portly gentleman in cutaway, gaiters and ruffled shirt rose to take his hand in greeting. With his other hand, he adjusted the rimless pince-nez upon the broad bridge of his nose and smiled.

"Pleased to meet a fellow scholar," he said, upon perusing

Fillmore's Parker College business card. "Eh? What? Bless me, yes, quite right, you heard correctly, that *is* my name. I daresay what little reputation I may have established is not the least bit tainted with the calumnies of false report. But sit you down, sir, sit you down and dry off as you may. Won't you share some of this excellent cold beef? And allow me to refill your tankard?"

Fillmore thanked him mightily, and set to with a will, not to mention a hearty appetite. His last meal had been in prison, awaiting trial at Old Bailey. The meat and ale were so excellent that he did not permit the trifle of a possible mislocation of cosmoses to upset him.

After he'd made a clean sweep of a quarter of the beef and had his glass refilled twice, Fillmore apologized for interrupting the dinner colloquy of his host.

"Bless my soul," said the old gentleman, "this is in no way an interruption, my good sir. Mr. Snodgrass here, who is, by the way—"

"A poet," observed Fillmore.

The old man's eyebrows raised. "Goodness, does his reputation, too, precede him? How *did* you know his occupation? I had thought he'd yet to be published!"

The scholar shrugged. "Oh, it's a bit of a fey quality that I have, I fancy."

"Well, well," the other chuckled, "I am suitably impressed. But, as I say, Mr. Snodgrass here is a capital poet—"

"My blushes," the other simpered.

"Now, Augustus, modesty ill becomes a man of true genius. You are a servant of the Muse and there is glory there! At any rate," said the host, turning to his guest, "my friend here is somewhat concerned with an affair of the heart, and I had thought to give him proper advice . . . which, indeed, I did. As I completed my statement, my attention was drawn to note your extremely dampish plight. And how, if I may be so bold, do you manage to be out on such a night as this without adequate protection? I presume your umbrella must be damaged; else it should have shielded you more efficiently from the elemental deluge."

"Well," Fillmore said, somewhat reluctantly, "I do not

know whether I should repay your generosity with a rehearsal of my predicament. It is so wild a tale you would doubtless judge me madder than King Lear."

The consequence of this remark was for Fillmore's host and the poet to positively entreat his adventures. So the stranger at length embarked upon his lengthy personal history, ending with his arrival on Newman Street and his subsequent trek to the George and Vulture.

When he had done at last, the others sat back, their mouths agape.

"Bless my soul," said the elderly gentleman. "That is certainly the strangest romance I have ever had the privilege to audit! No mind if it be true or no—it is an history worthy of the *Arabian Nights*. What do you say of it, Snodgrass?"

The poet had a dreamy look in his eyes. "I see," he sighed, "a major epic, a heroic narrative. I shall apply myself this very night while the fit is still upon me!" Suddenly leaping up, he excused himself and rushed from the room.

His companion laughed heartily, then apologized for the poet's precipitate departure. "When Inspiration descends unto his noble rhymer's brow, it ill beseemeth him to let her wait admittance until he pay the check." Still chuckling, the rotund little gentleman rose. "No matter, though, I am better conditioned than he, I can well afford it and had, indeed, meant to persuade him so." He graciously waved Fillmore to follow him.

In the lobby of the inn, he retrieved his room key, then, turning to his guest, said, "I keep rooms in this establishment. Pray let me loan you some fitting—ho, ho!—apparel, for you cannot hope to go about unnoticed in your present state. No, no! I will hear of no polite declinings. I am very handsomely off, my good fellow, and it will vastly please me to make a present of some necessaries with which you may better shield yourself from the raging elements . . ."

An hour later, the two descended the stairs to the lobby. Fillmore, dry and warm in slightly loose-fitting apparel, carried an oilskin bag beneath his arm. In it was his sopping clothing. Over his arm, the inoperable umbrella dangled.

As they neared the front door, the scholar whispered to his host, but that person vigorously shook his head.

"I repeat, positively not, sir! Your entertaining tale is ample payment now for these scraps of cloth you've accepted. I urge you to keep your monies for a more pressing use. Why, if your story be true, you have but a few odd pound notes on your person!" His eyes twinkled as he "humored" his guest.

At the door, Fillmore asked directions to his ultimate destination, and feared it did not exist. But the old man's answer allayed his doubts.

"Why, indeed, that street is no great ride away, but see here, you cannot walk there on this foul night! I insist you let me fee a hansom for your transport."

The scholar protested vigorously, but to no avail. His host, apologizing for a temporary absence of his manservant on a family matter, himself stepped into the drizzle and smoke to hail a cab. It was no simple matter on such a night to find one, let alone flag one down in the limited visibility the fog afforded. But after much assiduous labor and much raising of the voice, the portly benefactor finally arranged for his friend's transportation.

As he entered the cab, Fillmore thanked his host repeatedly, and the other as often belittled the charity as privilege and necessary duty. Closing the cab door, the elderly gentleman stepped around to the front of the vehicle and told the driver the proper destination. He paid him in advance.

"The address wanted," said Mr. Pickwick, "is 221 Baker Street. Just out of Marylebone Road . . ."

Chapter Two

Inside the cab, J. Adrian Fillmore tried to collect his thoughts. It was not easy because of the unaccustomed joggling and jostling his bones were receiving, but he did what he could to resolve the nagging doubts, as to his whereabouts.

London it was, and the year was correct, but was it the time and situation—in short, was it the *universe*—of Sherlock Holmes?

His thoughts, confused and harried by the sight of Ruth through the front door pane of Wells' shop, had rushed past in a chaotic jumble as he pressed the button to open the umbrella's hood. After that, all was a disordered kaleidoscope of colors and voids as he flew through uncomputed curvings of space. His hurried departure allowed no time to consider personal comfort. When he found himself in the middle of a dark, rainy street, Fillmore had cursed the enforced celerity of his flight. "And, damn it," he muttered in the dark interior of the lurching cab, "what stupidity made me abandon my raincoat and galoshes back on the Cornwall seacoast?"

At least Pickwick saw to it that he would be able to survive the weather until such time as he might expand his wardrobe. But the thought of the old gentleman brought fresh dismay. He was in London all right—but it appeared to be that of Charles Dickens! The benign heroes of the *Pickwick Papers* were pleasant enough, but they hardly qualified to assist Fillmore in his cerebral quest. Besides, memories of the grimmer aspects of some of the "Boz" narratives haunted him and made him most uneasy. His umbrella, ruled by cosmic quirk, would not permit him egress from this milieu until he completed a sequence of action—and Dickens' plots sometimes covered entire lifetimes. And in the meantime, what might he do inadvertently to mire himself permanently in the world of Dickens?

Was there a possibility that by some principle of universal economy, the London of Dickens was also the same world as that of Watson and Holmes? To learn the answer, the scholar was headed towards Baker Street.

"Sherlock Holmes," he mused, with a thrill of anticipation. "If anyone in the multiplicity of worlds that seem to coexist with the earth I know can analyze the umbrella, then—"

The sentiment was interrupted by the abrupt stoppage of the cab and the simultaneous hurling-forward of the passenger. He bruised his head against the edge of the opposite seat.

The driver shouted, "221 Baker." Fillmore dismounted, offering, as he did, an epithet to the cabbie in lieu of a tip.

Picking up the oilskin container of clothing, Fillmore crossed

the road just as the disgruntled hansom driver pulled away. A
bit of mud spattered up from the wheels of the cab, but the
scholar ignored the inconvenience in his excitement as he
spied the large brass plate on the house opposite. His hopes
were high as he scanned the inscription:

221
S. HOLMES, CONSULTANT
Apply at Suite B

Dashing up the steps to the front door, he pushed it open
and mounted one flight. The interior was cheery, just as he'd
always imagined it. Green wallpaper paralleled the staircase
and the flickering of gaslamps set in staggered sconces brightened the interior considerably.

He stopped in front of the B apartment and knocked.
Almost immediately, a powerfully built, mustached man in
dressing gown opened the door and invited him to enter.

Stepping inside, Fillmore asked, "You are the good doctor, I presume?"

"Why, yes," the other chuckled, "at least I hope to merit
the appellation. But I imagine you have come to see Holmes,
have you not?"

"I have, indeed," the scholar replied, his heart beating
rapidly like that of a schoolboy who sees his first love
approaching.

"Sit down, my good man," the doctor invited, meanwhile
pulling on a bell rope in the corner of the cozy sitting room
where he'd ushered his caller. "The fact is, I'm afraid Holmes
is off tending to that dreadful business in Cloisterham. Chap
missing, you may have read about it in the papers: Drood.
But it's a close undercover game Sherrinford is playing and
my presence there would only have confused things, so—"

The doctor stopped, peering at his visitor with concern.
"Pray tell me, sir, are you troubled by some indisposition?"

Fillmore, pale, could barely speak. "What," he whispered, "*what* did you call Mr. Holmes?"

"Why, Sherrinford, of course! All the world knows
Sherrinford Holmes, do they not? Not the least (I fancy I may

compliment myself) because of the narratives which I have penned concerning his exploits.''

"And what," the scholar asked, still hoarse, "and what is *your* name?"

The doctor chuckled. "The fickleness of fortune and all that, eh? I'd thought my little publications might have added some touch of notoriety to the name of Ormond Sacker, but apparently—''

Fillmore rose in agitation and paced the room, thinking feverishly. Why were the names the doctor used so nightmarishly different from the ones he'd expected to hear? Sherrinford, not Sherlock. Ormond Sacker instead of John H. Watson, M.D.

On the other hand, why did they also sound so familiar?

"Here, here, my good fellow," said Sacker worriedly. "I can see you are in considerable agitation. Pray be seated. Perhaps, in the absence of Holmes, I can shed some light on your problem. Meantime, I notice that the storm has not left you untainted. Be seated, be seated, man. I have rung for Mrs. Bardell and she will be up directly with tea and perhaps—''

Fillmore interrupted, even paler than before. "Mrs.— *whom*?"

"Why—Bardell, Mrs. Bardell, our landlady!" the doctor said, greatly amazed.

"Not Mrs. Hudson?"

"Hudson? I should think not. There used to be a Mrs. Warren taking care of this building, but she sold to a Mrs. Martha Bardell, and that is who . . . but see, the knob is turning now. This is the very woman."

The door opened and a plump woman entered, bearing an ornate silver tea service in her arms. But when she saw Fillmore, the woman screamed and dropped the tray. The hot liquid splashed upon the rug.

"What the devil!" Sacker exclaimed. "Mrs. Bardell! Have you taken leave of your senses?"

"It's him," the woman wailed, *"it's him!"*

"What *are* you speaking about, madam?"

"Him!" she howled, pointing an accusatory finger at J. Adrian Fillmore.

He, in turn, stared in flabbergasted dismay at the landlady. She was dressed in a green housecoat with flounce sleeves of a lighter shade with vertical stripes. On her head she wore a white, lace-trimmed domestic's cap, tied in a bow beneath her chin. But despite the disparity of apparel, Fillmore recognized her immediately.

It was Ruth.

Chapter Three

Prison. A home away from home, Fillmore mused bitterly. First, the *Pinafore* brig. Then the Fleet. Now the Fleet again. Three times incarcerated since buying the blasted umbrella. Before then, never a serious brush with the law. (He didn't count the abortive undergraduate party. At 8 p.m., no one had shown, so he glumly went out to get himself a steak sandwich. When he got back, the place was teeming with uninvited guests and a coterie of irate campus cops who, fortunately, had no idea who the host was.)

He huddled in a corner for warmth but did his best to avoid bodily contact with the lice-ridden sot next to him. In a far corner, a man with a broken nose and a piercing stare watched Fillmore every second of the time.

At least they'd let him keep the umbrella for the time being. After the trial, the authorities might well confiscate his property and then the scholar would be stuck here for good.

Stuck where? It was obviously Dickensian London, but it took Fillmore quite a few hours to figure out the weirdly altered names of Holmes and Watson. When the answer came, it naturally disturbed him, but at least he began dimly to perceive the principle of universal economy.

Sherrinford Holmes. Ormond Sacker. These were names Arthur Conan Doyle toyed with before settling on "Sherlock" and "John H. Watson." Fillmore had landed himself smack in the middle of an incomplete *draft* of *A Study in Scarlet*. An *incomplete* draft. After all, what had Sacker said Holmes was busy doing? Investigating the Edwin Drood mystery—a notoriously unfinished masterpiece . . .

"That damned Ruth," the scholar muttered, clutching his

umbrella close and trying to ignore the fixed gaze of the man with the broken nose. "Must have been trying to bring charges against me for breach of promise."

Nothing else made sense. It was apparent he'd inherited the "sequence" from the earlier cosmos, because he was in the Fleet awaiting such a trial. Mrs. Bardell, though astonishingly similar in face and form to Ruth, was really Sacker and Holmes' landlady . . . the very same Mrs. Bardell who sued Mr. Samuel Pickwick and landed him in prison in *The Pickwick Papers*.

"Well, at least the old boy did me a favor, and now, it appears I'm doing him one, whether he ever learns it or no." It worried the scholar. The outrageously comic trial of Bardell vs. Pickwick is the dramatic focal point of that Dickens tome. But some bounder that resembled Fillmore apparently once jilted Mrs. B., and as a result, the hapless alien seemed to be usurping the breach-of-promise trial that ought to—

"There I go again!" Fillmore grumbled to himself. "Confusing fictional events with what takes place in these strange places I end up in. Do they follow the stories I read on 'normal earth'? Do they branch off wherever they wish? Maybe this is just an earlier trial and Pickwick's is yet to come here. *Or* maybe this is also a *draft* stage of *The Pickwick Papers* ms. Then how do I—?"

He could not even finish the thought. It was too complicated. As hard to define as the identical looks of Mrs. Bardell and Ruth. Perhaps, he pondered, the entire cosmic system is a network of interlinking puzzle boxes, one heartwall economically doubling, tripling in alternative dimensions, and each soul, in sleep, shares identities across the gaps of space and relative times.

"Bah," he murmured. "Einstein notwithstanding, Time is a concurrency."

But his philosophic gum-chewing was disturbed by a sharp poke in the ribs. It was the shifty-eyed ferret seated by him in the corner of the cell. " 'ere now," he whispered to Fillmore, "that's a peculiar thing ye've got there. Where'd ye fetch it?"

Fillmore tried to ignore him, but the ferret exchanged the poke for a pinch. "Ow!" the scholar yelped. "Stop that!"

"I asked ye a question," the ferret whispered. "And keep yer voice low, if ye value living!"

The scholar faced his tormentor squarely, an angry retort on his lips, but the impulse stopped when he beheld the other's expression. The ferret's face was strained, each muscle tensed to the stretching point. His eyes rolled independent of the fixed head, and they moved in the direction of the sinister individual on the other side of the cell. The man with the broken nose.

Fillmore did not look at him. He regarded the ferret anxiously, and replied as quietly as his questioner.

"I bought my umbrella far from here. What matter is it?"

" 'im. Don't ye see how he stares at it? I never saw one to covet something so much. Never takes 'is eyes off it."

"I thought he was staring at me."

The ferret shook his head. "Last night, when ye slumbered, 'e crept near to examine it. Mutterin' to 'isself. Thought he'd snatch it then." The ferret shrugged. "But then, where'd 'e go with it?" The beady eyes narrowed, glinting with an eager urgency. "Ye want advice, man? If he asks for it, don't argue. Sell it, or make it a gift. Don't cross 'im!"

Fillmore shook his head. "Impossible. I *can't* part with my umbrella!"

"I tell ye, man, 'e's half-mad! Don't cross 'im! They'll 'ave 'im out in a day or two and then 'e'll wait for ye, and 'e'll 'ave 'is cane."

What in all good hell is he babbling about? Fillmore wondered. The man has no cane. In fact, he walks perfectly well. Look at him—

The man with the broken nose was standing. He turned his gaze briefly on the little ferret, and that person shrank away from Fillmore and cowered in a corner of the cell.

What kind of a crazy sequence is this, anyway? If this is the Bardell trial, why should I worry about strange men with umbrella fixations? Even if he is dangerous, and even if he gets out of prison and tries to wait for me, my trial will keep me here indefinitely. And then? Damn, I may *never* escape!

"Permit me to introduce myself." The tall, sinister man proffered his card.

Fillmore stood. He was startled at the meek civility of the

other's mien. From a distance, he appeared so menacing. But now, he must rectify his mistake. A toff, doubtless, confined for some minor infraction of the peace. He was well dressed, dark suit, ruffled shirt, a thin tie which might have passed muster a century later on campus.

The card told him nothing. It bore nothing but a name, "A. I. Persano."

"I trust my reputation is not unknown to you?" he asked. His face was smiling in a way that might suggest a double meaning to the question. But Fillmore knew no one intimately in this peculiar world of confused beginnings, so he could certainly not identify the stranger by reputation.

"I have been admiring that odd instrument which you have over your arm," Persano remarked. "May I examine it more closely?"

Fillmore found it hard to deny the reasonable request, so mildly was it made, and yet, something warned him to refuse. From the corner of his eye, he saw the ferret urgently motioning him to comply. With considerable reluctance, the scholar relinquished the instrument.

The tall man minutely inspected the umbrella, turning it this way and that, pausing to push back the cloth folds and read the partially obliterated inscription on the handle. As he did, Fillmore studied the lean, hard face. The eyes never blinked. The mouth was set in a half-grin that could easily be assessed as cruel. The nose, too, at close scrutiny, was even more disturbing than it first appeared. It was not broken after all. Rather it had been *sliced*, as if by some sharp edge. A deep lateral furrow creased the bridge, so that it resembled an ill-set fracture. But Persano was not the kind to indulge in violent roughhouse, Fillmore was sure. He was too contained, too deceptively calm. He might deal in rapier, never in bludgeon.

Persano returned the umbrella without comment. Then, apparently satisfied, he asked what Fillmore was doing in jail. The scholar outlined the details of his case, and the other clucked in doleful sympathy.

"Who defends you?" the tall man asked.

"Myself."

"And who represents the Bardell interests?"

Fillmore shuddered. He knew who Martha Bardell's barristers *must* be. "Messrs. Dodson and Fogg, I do presume."

"What? Then you're a fool, man. You have no choice but to raise capital sufficient to fee attorneys as crooked as those pettifoggers!"

"I haven't the money," Fillmore demurred. He refused to petition Pickwick. That might be an action which would mire him in the mishmosh-world he'd stumbled into. The best course was to maintain a detached air from the circumstances afflicting him.

"Since you are destitute," Persano said, smiling, "I have a suggestion."

Silence.

Fillmore knew what the other was about to say.

"Sell me your umbrella. I will pay handsomely for it."

"Why?"

"It . . . amuses me."

Fillmore shook his head. To his relief, the other did not press his request.

Persano merely smiled more broadly. "Very well," he murmured. "There are other ways."

The following day, A. I. Persano was released from prison.

Two days later, a warder unlocked the door of the cell.

"Fillmore." He jerked his thumb to the door. "Out."

"Is it time for my trial?"

The warder shook his head. "Won't be one. Ye're free."

"*Free?*"

The ferret clucked in warning. "I told ye."

"How *can* I be free?" the scholar demanded, amazed, puzzled, overjoyed—and simultaneously uneasy.

"Plaintiff's counsel dropped charges. No estate worth speaking of to cover the expense."

"Estate? What are you talking about?"

The warder drew one finger across his throat in a gesture as meaningful in one world as another. "Bardell," he said. "Last night. Someone cut 'er throat."

Chapter Four

For once, he was not anxious to get out of prison. He dragged his footsteps along the last corridor before the outside gate and cudgeled his brains to make out what sort of dreadful sequence he'd landed in.

It *could* be the grimmer side of Dickens, he thought. Perhaps the only way to terminate one's existence here is to die. He shuddered.

At the front gate, he entreated the constable accompanying him to protect him, but the other merely grunted, "Oh, ye'll be noted, right enough," then turned and left Fillmore to the mercy of the streets.

What did he mean by that? the scholar wondered. Then, with a shock of dismay, he realized that he must be considered gravely suspect in the eyes of the police. "Bah!" he snapped, loud enough to be heard: "If I couldn't hire an attorney, what makes them think I could afford an assassin to murder Mrs. Bardell?"

He peered about nervously, but there was no trace of the sinister Persano anywhere. It was early, but the sickly pall of London mist obscurred the sun. Few foot passengers traversed the section of thoroughfares near the Fleet.

Fillmore walked aimlessly for a time, trying to work out the problem of the cosmic block of action he was expected to participate in. Since the breach-of-promise trial had come to naught, he could only presume that the uncompleted sequence with Ruth in G&S land had finally run its course. But a new situation appears to have taken up, the scholar mused, worriedly. A dreadful situation, very like.

He was just crossing Bentinck Street at the corner of Oxford when he heard a sudden clatter of hooves and the rumble of a large vehicle. He swerved in his tracks and paled. A two-horse van, apparently parked at a nearby curb, was in furious motion, bearing directly down on him. Fillmore uttered a lusty yell and leaped a good six or seven feet onto the curb. Without stopping; he ducked down behind a lamppost and did not rise until the carriage rolled into the distance and was lost to sight and sound.

He rose, puffing mightily. The jump was the heartiest exercise he'd undergone since trying to run away from Katisha weeks earlier. His heart pounded against his ribcage. Fillmore glanced right and left, but the few pedestrians in view went about their business, oblivious to the near-accident which had just occurred.

But was it an accident?

He continued his journey, but did not allow himself the luxury of abstracted thought. Instead, Fillmore looked right and left, backwards and forwards, fearful of another attack. And yet the street seemed deserted. He was practically the only foot passenger traversing the avenue.

His very solitariness made him even more anxious. He was an easy target for anyone who might be following just beyond the curtain of the fog. At the next corner, he looked down the cross street and decided to take it, in hopes of coming to a more populous quarter of town.

There was a constable in the middle of the block. Fillmore breathed a sigh of relief. At least he was safe for a few steps . . .

The constable turned and regarded him. The man's face turned ash-white. He stuck his whistle to his lips and blasted it, at the same time thrusting an arm directly at the professor. Fillmore, astonished, hopped back a step, and wondered whether he ought to run.

At the same instant, a huge brick smashed with tremendous impact upon the pavement directly in front of him. One more step and the brick would have crushed his skull.

Fillmore and the officer regarded each other for a second or two, too relieved to speak. Then Fillmore stepped far out into the street—looking carefully both ways—and walked over to the other, thanking him with great earnestness.

"I pride myself," said the constable, "on a quick reaction time. Fortunate for you, right enough."

"Yes . . . but who dropped that deuced brick?" Fillmore squawked.

The other's eyes widened. "Never occurred to me it wasn't an accident! Come, then! Better be brisk!"

Without another word, the constable dashed into the doorway of the large, cold tenement house from which the missile had apparently been impelled. Fillmore accompanied him, preferring to be in the company of the law at that moment than to be left waiting defenseless in the street.

They climbed dark, interminable stairs, redolent of cabbage and other less tolerable reeks. At length they found the skylight, which was reachable only by means of an iron ladder stapled with great brackets against the wall. It was a sheer vertical climb and Fillmore did not relish it.

At last they stood upon the roof, a good four or five stories above the street (Fillmore had lost count of how many flights they'd taken in the ascent). There was a large chimney stack off to one side, and the remnants of a clothesline, evidently blown down by a gust of wind. By the street edge of the roof lay a pile of shingles, slate and brick, the flotsam of some antique building venture.

"There's your accident," the officer said, jerking his head towards the pile of construction leavings. "Wind must've worked one loose. Bit of a hazard. I'd best move 'em."

Fillmore, after thanking the policeman once more, left him laboring on the roof. He doubted it was an accident, and if it was not, then he was in danger from the assailant, who must still be in the neighborhood. He wanted to cling to the protection of the law, but his conscience would not permit him to endanger the officer who saved his life—and proximity to J. Adrian (what a beastly name!) Fillmore might do just that.

On the stairwell, he tried the catch of the umbrella, but it would not open. The sequence was far from finished.

Just as he was turning the corner of the last landing leading to the street level and the doorway out, he thought he heard a slight noise below, in the corner of the corridor leading alongside the first approach of the stairwell. He peered down the side of the banister, but it was dark and he could see nothing.

He paused, unsure of what to do, whether to go back or forward. To rejoin the policeman would only prolong the danger. With a sudden burst of nerve, Fillmore leaped the railing and, umbrella pointed downward, dropped to the floor below.

A thud and a moan. A burly body broke his fall. He lugged the lurker into the moted dustlight and saw a feral visage, rich in scars and whiskers. A life-preserver—the British equivalent of a blackjack—was still clutched in the assailant's hand, but the man was unconscious.

Fillmore slumped against the wall, almost nauseous with fear. In the past half-hour, his life had been attempted three times, and, what may have been worse, he'd met the dangers with expedition and a physical courage all unsuspected in his makeup. It worried him as much as the danger.

Maybe *that's* what got me stuck in this damned place! Fillmore shook his head to clear it of the vertigo that the fall brought about. No time for cosmic trepidations. Probably more danger, any moment, any second . . .

He quickly turned out the pockets of the man on the floor, but found nothing incriminating or enlightening. The life-preserver he stuck into his own back pocket.

Slowly, fearfully, Fillmore cracked open the front door. The street was no longer sparse of population. A knot of people milled about the middle of the street, shouting, giving unobeyed orders; one person was busily engaged in retching on the sidewalk.

The professor hurried down the front steps and peered through the press of people. There was a body smeared along the street, a bloody rag of flesh and dislocated bone.

It was the policeman. Someone must have shoved him from the roof, Fillmore realized, horrified.

"The chimney! The bastard must have been behind it!"

Angry for the first time since the game of stalk-and-attack started, Fillmore wanted to punish the killer who'd destroyed a man who'd saved his own life. He trotted to the middle of the street, shielding his eyes from the glare of hidden sun shining through blanched clouds. Was there someone still on the roof? Could he take him, too, like the thug in the stairwell?

For answer, a fierce face suddenly appeared at the edge of the building top. An odd weapon quickly swiveled into position and pointed straight at the scholar.

He ran zigzag, hoping to evade the inevitable shot. But the other was a crack marksman. Even with the difficulty of hitting a moving target, the villain managed to lodge one shot in Fillmore's shoulder.

The professor staggered. What did that character say in the

Fredric Brown novel? "If you are killed here, you will be dead . . . in every world." Fillmore stumbled to his feet. The strange weapon—which made no noise—was already in position for another shot.

My God! It's an air-rifle!

The horrible universe suddenly fell into place. Terror overcame Fillmore and gave him the strength of mad desperation. He shot out across the street, waving the umbrella in huge, confusing arcs, changing direction every few seconds. He headed for the juncture of streets again, and as he did, shouted and screamed for help. Some of the denizens of the neighborhood huddled about the constable's body stared at the crazy fellow and decided instantly that it was he who must have murdered the officer. No one advanced to Fillmore's aid.

Oddly enough, there was no second bullet. Fillmore reached the intersection safely. He saw a hansom slowly rumbling down the middle of the avenue. "I must look a fearful sight," he thought, "shoulder bleeding, weird umbrella waving about like a Floradora girl's prop . . ."

Fillmore took no chances. He ran straight into the path of the hansom shouting for it to stop. At the last instant, remembering the dreadful attempt of the two-horse van to run him down, he experienced an awful qualm. But the cab pulled to a stop.

"Baker Street," Fillmore gasped, jumping in and slamming the door. "Number 221."

The cab rattled off slowly. The scholar gasped for sufficient breath, then pounded the sides and shouted for the driver to make haste, but to no avail. The hansom lumbered sluggishly along, neither creeping nor hurrying. Fillmore stuck his head out of the window and surveyed the street behind. There were no vehicles in pursuit.

He leaned back against the wall of the cab and panted. "Safe for a time, at least," he murmured. "I just hope that Sherrinford—"

Before he could even complete the thought, the cab lurched to a stop. Fillmore stuck his head out the window. "Here, what is this? This isn't Baker Street!"

"No, sir," the cabbie said, dismounting. He walked to

Fillmore's door and stood by it, preventing it from opening. "Taking on another passenger, we are, sir."

Fillmore regarded him blankly. Then he swung around in his seat, hoping to get out the other way. But that door was already opening.

The new passenger rested his cane against the seat and closed the door behind himself. He settled comfortably into the place opposite Fillmore.

"You've caused us a deal of trouble this morning." A. I. Persano remarked mildly.

Chapter Five

The cabbie whipped the horse to a froth. The hansom rattled along at breakneck speed. Fillmore braced himself to keep from bouncing straight through the flimsy ceiling. He gritted his teeth at the ache in his shoulder.

Persano, riding as skillfully as if mounted on a thoroughbred, was quite amiable. He regarded the other's persecution as a tiresome necessity, to be managed with swift expedition, but utterly without malice. *Not* to be discussed in polite company. The Code, by all means!

"Had you been reasonable," he stated mildly, "all this pother might have been eclipsed."

"Meaning I should have given you the umbrella?"

Persano gravely inclined his head.

"Rubbish!" Fillmore said with great asperity. "You are in a frenzy to get this instrument. Therefore, you must know its function. It follows, then, that you know I couldn't part with it at any price."

Persano clucked disapprovingly. "I could tell the authorities that the umbrella was stolen from my employer."

"You are blathering nonsense! Anyone with a shred of sense must deduce your employer has no desire to see this instrument's astonishing properties made public. You could have reported it stolen in prison. Instead, two people are dead because of it, and I have a bullet in my shoulder."

"An unfortunately staged episode," Persano agreed, stifling a yawn. "The Colonel has no idea of how to achieve maximum effect with minimal effort. His aggression grows in inverse proportion to his waning manhood.''

Suddenly, the puzzle, nearly solved, all clicked into place. The ferocious Colonel Sebastian Moran! (''The second most dangerous man in London, Watson!'') And the kindly sorcerer, John Wellington Wells, admitted to spying on *a master mathematician*, from whom he stole the umbrella. The instrument must be the brainchild of the brilliantly evil kingpin of London crime, Professor Moriarty! And then, another thought: Holmes once spoke of two especially dangerous members of the Moriarty gang. One was Moran. Persano must be the other.

Fillmore, shuddering, commented on Persano's remark. ''You are of course, referring to Colonel Moran.''

For a split-second, the mask of indifference dropped, and the other subjected Fillmore to a deadly scrutiny. Then his eyes clouded over again and Persano propped his cane by his chin and chuckled.

''Cards on the table, eh?'' He nodded approvingly. ''Very well, then, an end to games-playing: you, sir, are either an agent or a fool.''

''What do you mean?'' Fillmore stanched the wound in his throbbing shoulder with a handkerchief.

''It cannot be that you are with the Yard,'' Persano mused. ''A *provocateur* would not allow a fellow constable to blindly face an unseen foe without ample warning. Nor, for that matter, would Sherrinford Holmes stick someone else's neck on the chopping block. No. You did not lure me into an imminent trap. You are engaged in a lone game against the greatest organization of its type in the world. You are, therefore, a colossal fool.''

''In a word, you refer to Professor Moriarty's organization.''

''*Who?*'' Persano asked, pretending perplexity.

There was a lengthy silence.

''I do *not* know to whom you refer,'' Persano said, ''but I might amend what I said before. I called you a fool. I suspect you are worse: a veritable lunatic. But the tense soon shall alter . . .''

Fillmore clutched the umbrella tight, his thoughts racing. His life was in great danger. In whichever world he blundered, he ended up a victim. In this clime, he might well end his sequence *permanently*.

"This needs no further discussion, I think," Fillmore said airily, attempting an ease of manner which he hoped might match his opponent's. He shifted in the uncomfortable carriage seat. "You will steal the umbrella and there's an end of it."

Persano shook his head, an earnest expression on his face. "Really that is not possible. Don't you see? You, an independent agent, are somehow privy to details that my employer would not like bruited about. You are able to set my face and name to several recent incidents of dubious merit. You carry a pellet in you from an airgun and there are many unsolved crimes connected with such a weapon. What is worse, you know the Colonel's last name. No, no, it's quite impossible, surely you see my position?"

His eyebrows raised quizzically. He really seemed concerned lest Fillmore fail to comprehend and sanction the deplorable step that must be taken.

It did not fool Fillmore. Persano had never taken pains to cover his involvement in the "incidents." What was worse, he freely volunteered information about Moran's association with other atrocities. Persano evidently never at all intended to let the scholar survive.

"Look," he blurted, "I have a different suggestion. Come with me someplace else so that I am no longer in this world. I'll go back to my own cosmos! Then you can take the damned umbrella and return here!"

Persano shook his head again. "I can't do that. How do I know how long it will take before that thing decides to work again? If it could work now, you wouldn't be here at this moment. But even if you could waft us elsewhere immediately, you know I could not use the umbrella for long afterwards, and I have no time to wait."

"Why couldn't you use it?" Fillmore asked.

Persano eyed him curiously, "I think you actually don't know."

"Know *what*?" His shoulder still hurt. The carriage had decelerated to a more bearable rate, but he still was unable to sit comfortably.

Persano reached over and took the umbrella. Fillmore tried to hold tight, but the other easily plucked it from his grasp. Persano pushed aside the hood folds, and put his thumb on the catch.

"Observe." He pushed the button.

Nothing happened.

"It is imprinted with your brain pattern. It will take a long time to readjust. Unless . . ."

He let the thought dangle in the air, drumming his fingertips on the central pole of the bumbershoot.

A long while passed. They stared at one another without speaking.

Then the horse slowed to a walk.

"We are almost there," Persano said in a low voice.

"Where?"

"A warehouse. Prepare to disembark."

Persano looked out the window. As he did, Fillmore suddenly realized why he was having so much trouble sitting comfortably. There was something in his back-pocket—

The life-preserver!

Carefully, carefully, he reached his hand around to get the sapping tool. His fingers crept. Persano stared out the window.

Good! Teeth clenched, a cold perspiration bespangling his brow, the pedant strained for the ersatz blackjack. *Another quarter-inch . . .*

It snagged in a fold of his pocket, and he could not yank it free. Fillmore tugged, but his arm was in an awkward position and he hadn't ample leverage to twist out the thing cleanly.

The carriage shuddered to a stop.

"End of the line," Persano announced, turning. His eyes narrowed. "What *are* you doing?" he asked, his tone suggesting the indulgent displeasure of a kindly schoolteacher towards a wayward urchin.

Fillmore frantically pulled at the cosh. The whole back pocket of his pants ripped off. At last, he had it in his hand.

But the quick movement triggered Persano. Swiftly, soundlessly, he shot forward and clutched Fillmore's throat in a steel grip. He was not angry, only methodical. Whatever Fillmore was trying to do, Persano immediately recognized it

as a last-ditch effort and knew he must bring it to naught.
Though the business was clearly beneath him—throttling was
the preserve of brutal underlings—he squeezed Fillmore's
windpipe quite efficiently, nonetheless.

The scholar once read that it only takes a professional killer
seven seconds to choke someone to death. Already the lights
of life danced dimly and dwindled. He knew he only had
strength in his arm for a single assault—

He cracked the preserver against the base of Persano's
neck. (Gesture derived from countless spy and war films.)
Persano slumped for a second, only a second; the quick mind
analyzed the extent of danger with incredible celerity and
marshaled strength for a new attack.

But Fillmore only needed the one respite. He heaved Persano
off and simultaneously raked one hand upwards over the
other's face from jaw to nose (a trick out of *Shane*) while the
other hand slammed the life preserver into the throat thus
presented for the blow (*Bad Day at Black Rock*).

Persano gagged and doubled up.

Dropping the cosh, Fillmore wrested free the umbrella and
jumped out the opposite side of the carriage from that which
he'd entered. Just then, the driver pulled the other door open;
seeing he was gone, he cursed at Fillmore, slammed the door
and started after him. Fillmore threw his weight against the
hansom, hoping to tip it over onto the driver, but the effort
drew fresh pain from his shoulder wound and only earned
him a good jarring butt.

He saw the feet of the driver rounding the carriage, so he
started the other way. An idea struck him and he vaulted onto
the driver's seat ("Thanks to Gene Autry!") and slapped the
reins.

The horse ambled forward two inches and stopped.

"Damn! It always looks so *easy!*"

The driver came up on him. A sinewy, saturnine thug he
was, with a dagger in his hand. He hauled himself onto the
seat, slashing at Fillmore, but the professor administered a
stunning blow to the chest with the whip handle ("courtesy
Lash LaRue") and the rascal landed on his back in the street,
roaring.

The horse, mistaking the bellow for an order, reared up.

"*Whoa!*" Fillmore yelled. The animal, unfamiliar with the western idiom, interpreted the word as a seconding motion and immediately adopted the measure by dashing forth. The cab careened to one side, righted itself and lurched behind the crazed beast.

The jolt pitched Fillmore backwards. He nearly lost his grip on the umbrella, but clutched frantically, regained his hold, and simultaneously squirmed onto his face so he could embrace the cab roof with arms spread wide.

The horse stormed down the cobbled thoroughfare, which was a road that directly paralleled the river. Warehouses sped past; a confusion of disappearing drydocks. Cursing dock-wallopers sprang out of the path of the runaway.

Fillmore hugged the roof, too winded and frightened to move. But suddenly, the blade of a sword swiftly emerged from the roof one-sixteenth of an inch in front of his nose. He decided to budge after all.

While the blade was withdrawing for another thrust, he scrambled into the driver's seat and fished for the reins. No use; they hung over the lip and jounced in the roadbed; he strained but could not reach them. Next thing he knew, the furious pitch of the ride bumped his teeth together so he bit his tongue and shoved him straight back against the cab housing. He instantly pushed forward, narrowly avoiding the sword point which emerged at the place where his body had made impact.

He ran his hand down the umbrella and tried to snap it open. *No go!* Then he saw a new danger up ahead. About two blocks in the distance, the street curved sharply; where it turned, the embankment terminated and there was a sheer unprotected drop into the river.

Two thoughts, born of desperation and an acquaintanceship with Hopalong Cassidy and screen versions of *The Three Musketeers*, popped into his head. He peered ahead—*yes!* Just before the turn there was a custom house with empty flagpole jutting from the second-story . . . .

He sprang forward onto the traces and grabbed the link-pin with the handle of the umbrella. Fillmore seized the shaft of the bumbershoot and hauled up until the pin was almost free.

He stood up, balancing wobbily, squinting to gauge the correct angle and distance, waiting for the vital precise second.

"Now!"

Jumping as high as he could, he latched onto the flagpole with one hand, at the same time tugging on the umbrella so the link-pin disengaged. The carriage-top smartly smacked his ankle and, with a tremendous effort, Fillmore hooked the umbrella over his other arm and got a second purchase on the pole with his left hand. The carriage rumbled past beneath him. A bolt of pain struck his shoulder, but he endured it, watching with grim approval the event happening in the street below.

The cab lost speed and the steed, no longer shackled to it, pulled on ahead. It negotiated the bend, but the carriage lumbered straight to the edge, teetered for a fraction of a second, then plummeted into the icy Thames with a colossal splash.

"And that," Fillmore observed with satisfaction "is the last anyone will see of Mr. A. I. Persano!"

His pleasure was short-lived. Now that the immediate danger was over, it occurred to him that he hadn't the foggiest idea of how to get down from the flagpole without breaking his neck. But it didn't take him long to devise a course of action.

"Help!" Fillmore shouted. *"Get me the hell off of here!"*

Chapter Six

Sacker shook his head incredulously. "That is the strangest story I have ever heard, sir. Either you are up to something nefarious, or you are mad."

"I tell you that I am not lying!" Fillmore protested. "Would I mention Professor Moriarty if I were part of his gang?"

The argument had been going on for several minutes, and the professor was beginning to despair of ever convincing the good doctor that he was anything but a raving lunatic. Had it not been for his shoulder wound, Sacker probably would not have permitted him entry into Sherrinford Holmes' flat, half convinced as he was that Fillmore was indirectly responsible for Mrs. Bardell's murder.

The doctor shook his head slowly. "You come to me with wild tales about dimensional transfers—whatever that means—and worlds where I only exist in an unpublished manuscript and Holmes is not Holmes! The least marvelous portion of your romance is that which you claim happened this morning: runaway hansoms, customs clerks hauling you off flagpoles, brickbats and dead policemen! Surely, sir, you do not find it marvelous that I have some difficulty swallowing all this?"

Fillmore nodded wearily. It had been a most exhausting day, and his bandaged shoulder still throbbed dully. The night was drawing on and he wanted nothing more dramatic than sleep. But duty was duty, in whatever world he inhabited. If the Moriarty gang were so bent on attaining the umbrella, it could only follow that the infamous professor had some awful scheme in mind.

But Sacker was adamant. "Holmes only mentioned this pedagogue of yours once, and that recently. Whatever he did, I do not know. For Holmes only alluded to him on that one occasion at the time of his disappearance."

"His disappearance?!"

Sacker nodded. "Yes. I *do* recall Holmes' relief. *And* his perplexity. One day, he said, Moriarty was in London, the next he was nowhere on the face of the earth. 'And good riddance, Sacker!' he remarked, and there was an end of the conversation. I never heard Moriarty's name again until you brought it up tonight."

"Well, well," Fillmore said impatiently, "whatever may be the status of the professor, he has a strong and wicked organization which still carries on his works. It must be quashed. And since its lieutenants know about my umbrella, it is imperative that I speak to Sherrinford Holmes immediately!"

"Well, as for that," Sacker suggested, "I suppose you could come along with me tonight. Holmes has communicated from Cloisterham, where that business is all but wrapped up. He needs some final service pertaining to one Mr. Sapsea, and I am to perform it." Sacker chuckled. "Holmes rarely asks me to tackle anything histrionic. It must be a goose, indeed, to whom I must play the poker!"

Fillmore's brows knit. It sounded familiar . . . ah, yes, the

"Sapsea" fragment found in Dickens' study after his death, an enigmatic portion of the *Edwin Drood* manuscript that remained unpublished for many years. The rough-draft aspect of the present world still held. It occurred to the scholar that in a place composed of unfinished or half-polished literary concepts, it might not be *possible* to complete a sequence and get free. He nervously tapped his fingers against the curved grip of the umbrella and tried to follow the thought, but Sacker spoke again.

"I must ask you not to interfere with the progress of the case, or attempt to communicate with Holmes until he gives me leave to bring you forward. If you can agree to that, then you may accompany me on the 10:40 out of Charing Cross."

"Very well," Fillmore replied reluctantly. "But perhaps I might be able to give you a note to pass on to Holmes when we arrive. Time *may* be of the essence!"

The doctor nodded. "And now, since we can do nothing until it is time to entrain, I suggest we follow my friend's habit of tabling all talk of hypothetical crises until we have detabled. I will send round for an amiable Bordeaux and ask Mrs. Raddle, our new landlady, to set out supper. Does that seem agreeable?"

"Oh, of course," Fillmore concurred, dimly wondering where he'd heard of Mrs. Raddle before. "I take it you have decided not to regard me as an imminent threat."

"Well, sir," Sacker chuckled, "I must admit that is an odd angle for a man to shoot himself as a piece of corroborative evidence. I still cannot accept the wild history you related, but if you are mad, sir, at least it is an engaging malady. Besides, I detect a man of learning in you, and a scholar is by no means the worst of dinner companions."

Fillmore thanked the doctor for his courtesy and mentally noted that Sacker/Watson certainly matched the old Holmesian observation (was it first made by Christopher Morley?) that a man might be honored to meet the Great Detective, but it would be Watson with whom a wintery evening, a cold supper and brandy would be most enjoyed.

While the good physician stepped downstairs to talk to Mrs. Raddle (she's in *Pickwick Papers*, too, isn't she?), Fillmore busied himself looking about the drawing room/

library. It was easy to tell which portion of the bookshelves belonged to Holmes and which to Sacker. One half, or better, was cram full of standard references and albums of clippings of criminous activity. The other side of the room was devoted to a broad assortment of escape literature—tales of early English battles, ghost stories, high romance on the seas, an occasional sampler of sentimental poetry and (perhaps in deference to Holmes' profession) a tattered copy of the lurid *Newgate Calendar*, a volume destined for ignominy in another world.

Sacker had one book open on a table by his easy chair and the professor walked over to inspect what it was. "Ah! A man of similar tastes in fantasy," he murmured. "Benson's *The Room in the Tower* and other ghastly tales." He turned the book around and flipped through it, holding Sacker's place. The doctor evidently had just begun reading a short story, "Caterpillars." Fillmore remembered it with a shudder.

The doctor reentered the room and made a courteous remark concerning escapist literature, the likes of which Fillmore held in his hand. "Yes, yes, the Bensons *are* rather a dynasty," Sacker agreed. "I have another one, by Edward's brother, Robert Hugh. *The Mirror of Shallot*. Odd. Excellent."

Fillmore checked himself. He had been about to comment on the finding of the identical volume years later on the day he purchased the umbrella, but it occurred to him that the doctor would regard the assertion as further evidence that his wits weren't all in working order.

Supper was sumptuous, if simple fare. A roast beef, rare and huge. A brace of game. Trifle, coffee and brandy. The only disappointment was the Bordeaux, which was temporarily out of stock. In apology, Mrs. Raddle sent up a cherished tawny port, which Sacker set aside for post-dessert, if the professor so desired. The doctor clearly had no enthusiasm for the stuff. Fillmore, however, had not dined well since sharing supper with Mr. Pickwick, and he availed himself of all there was to be had, including the landlady's prize port, the effect of which was to lull him into a much-needed sleep.

He awoke with a start. It was dark in the room, and there wasn't a sound. He reached out, encountered a nightstand with a box of matches on it. He fumbled for one, lit it, noted the box to be one of those cheap cardboard pillboxes into which matches had been crammed. Perhaps it belonged to Holmes; it sounded like his brand of freeform adaptation, Persian slippers used to hold shag tobacco, knives stuck to the mantel to fix correspondence in place . . .

There was a lamp nearby. Fillmore lit it and turned up the key so he could better determine what surroundings he had. It was a small bed chamber, plain, with a wardrobe and a low table with mirror behind it where Holmes assuredly put on his disguises. There was a piece of paper affixed to the mirror in a place where Fillmore could not help but notice. He rose and took the lamp with him so he could read what was written thereon.

"My dear Fillmore," it said, "I had no idea your injury had so exhausted you. It was impossible to rouse you, and considering this as a physician, I am not so sure it will be wise for you to spend the better part of the night on a drafty railway train. Your resistance is low and you may do yourself an injury by coming, susceptible as you may be to sundry ills and fevers. I have put you in Holmes' bed, mine being uncharacteristically untidy and his having had the benefits of Mrs. Raddle's ministrations, and am off to catch the 10:40. If you do not sleep the night, you may wish to read; I will leave the drawing-room lights on for you. You are, of course, welcome to whatever fare you can find, and you may also use my toilet articles, shaving brush, etc. We shall return in a few days. If you feel the urgent need to see Holmes as soon as possible, you may, of course, join us in Cloisterham. The decision is yours. But, pertaining to the dangers you rehearsed, I must say, on your behalf, that a hasty perusal of Holmes' files shows that there is indeed in London one "Is. Persano," an athlete, duelist and singlestick competitor of awesome accomplishment. His card is checked in red ink, which Holmes employs for particularly dangerous criminals. If this is the same individual whom you claim to have dogged you, it may be wisest to stay at Baker Street and to not set foot out of doors until we get back. But I must not miss the train. Farewell. O.S."

Fillmore was too drowsy to clear his head and recall the reference that was bumping about in the back of his brain. He still felt logy. Rubbing his eyes, yawning, he walked to the door connecting with the drawing room/library. At least sleep had refreshed his memory on the matter of Mrs. Raddle. She was Bob Sawyer's landlady in Dickens, and a contributory vexation to Mr. Pickwick. A low, spiteful shrew who might do anything for money.

Roused from sleep, Fillmore's appetite had also returned. He wondered whether any of the beef was still left, or if it was all put away.

And what about the umbrella?

Certainly Sacker would have left it behind, yet Fillmore experienced a few qualms until he opened the door and saw the instrument propped in the same corner where he'd left it. That was reassuring; even more so was the sight of the unconsumed food still waiting, covered, on the table.

"The benevolent Dr. Sacker-alias-Watson," Fillmore beamed, stepping forward to lift the cover on the plate of beef. And then his warm sense of well-being plummeted and died.

There was a man seated in the doctor's easy chair by the fireside, a book on his lap; he was reading intently.

"By all means, sit and eat," Persano invited. "I have a few pages yet to go."

The man with the sliced nose did not even deign to look at Fillmore. He seemed possessed by the Benson volume in his hands.

Fillmore dashed over to the umbrella, and got a grip on it. He pushed aside the drapery that encloaked the left front window. The street outside was empty.

Should I smash through the glass, make a bit of a vault into the street? But a thought occurred to him concerning air-guns. He peered at the dark edifice directly opposite. A sudden glint of reflected light shone and was instantly gone, but it was enough to inform Fillmore that someone lurked behind one of the windows of Camden House, which must be the empty home across Baker Street from 221. (It was in Camden House that Colonel Moran lurked when he attempted to assassinate Sherlock in "The Adventure of the Empty House.")

There was no point in trying a dash for it. Unless there was a back way, Fillmore was trapped with Persano.

"In case you are in a gymnastic mood," Persano remarked, "allow me to advise you that the house is entirely surrounded. Now pray wait a moment longer. I have but a single page to complete."

Fillmore stood rooted to the spot, his appetite gone, waiting for the villainous Persano to come to the end of the tale in which he was engrossed.

Persano perceptibly shuddered as he closed the book. "That was indeed a horror!" he remarked. "I have always been a devotee of the fantastic. Are you familiar with the genre?"

Fillmore said nothing.

"Oh, come," said the other, "the mere matter of the umbrella and your inevitable demise can surely wait. There is nothing more soothing in this world than to contemplate something truly dreadful, such as Benson's 'Caterpillars,' and then come safely back to this mundane world where the only atrocities are the humdrum stuff of daily business. The tale is not up to 'The Room in the Tower,' but then, what is? Still, the idea of ghastly crablike caterpillars, giant ghostly creatures and their miniature daylight counterparts that scuttle about with their excrescent bodies and infect those that they bite with cancer—such is no ordinary *cauchemar*. It almost makes the idea of ordinary death-by-violence drab and comfortable."

Persano flashed his mirthless smile at Fillmore. Then, in a leisurely fashion, he extracted a thin cigar, bit off the end, spat it and requested a light from the scholar. Numbly, Fillmore tossed the pillbox to the other, who caught it, took out a match, struck it and lit the cigar.

Persano regarded the matchbox momentarily. "A box like this figures in the tale. Do you know it? An artist captures a miniature crablike caterpillar and keeps it in the box until he changes his mind and treads on the insect, which seals his doom." His shoulders went up and he shivered in fear. "I believe if I found such a creature in this box, my mind would snap. I have seen the ravages of the disease." He regarded his cigar with melancholy dissatisfaction. "That is the curse of all earthly endeavor, is it not? We bargain and bully and bludgeon for our own ends, but in no wise can we crush the microbes that infest us from within. I should *hope* I should go mad and do terminal injury to myself rather than undergo such a horror as I once witnessed and have just read about." He regarded the professor darkly, then his wicked smile reappeared. "But I wax melancholy. Shall we proceed to brighter matters?"

"How did you get in?" Fillmore asked hoarsely.

"Ah, that's the spirit! Ask questions, buy time, my friend. Since you ask, the Raddle's holdings were recently purchased by our interests and we set her up here after the death of Mrs. Bardell. She was instructed to inform us if anyone of your description and peculiar appurtenances"—he indicated the umbrella—"should appear to Dr. Sacker. I presume that you are an agent of Holmes, after all, in which case the dear boy is grown uncommon careless."

"I thought you'd drowned," Fillmore accused sullenly.

"Sorry for the disappointment. But be assured, sir, I hold no grudge for your maneuver. It was cleverly executed. But I am no mean swimmer. And as for tracking you down again, our system of surveillance is so thorough that you would have been found out in any event within a mere matter of hours. I confess, though, I did suspect this is where you would probably go. The only thing that at all bothered me was the possibility that the umbrella might function once more. But it does not appear to be in any hurry to remove you from this unlucky world, does it?"

"One must finish a sequence," Fillmore grumbled.

"I beg your pardon?"

The scholar briefly explained the necessity of participating in some basic block of action correspondent to the base literary form of the cosmos in which one was deposited by the parasol.

Persano nodded. "I see. That explains why the Professor has not yet returned. But what a deuced unpleasant condition! Imagine, for instance, ending up in Stoker's Hungaria and having no other way out but to combat Count Dracula. A horror, this umbrella, if one were carried by it into a world of night."

"Yes," Fillmore observed, stalling for time, "but no one who knows how it works would deliberately choose such a place."

"Well, no matter," Persano said, extinguishing his cigar, "the time has come to terminate this disagreeable matter. You will give me the umbrella."

"I will not!"

Weariness etched lines on Persano's face as he contemplated a struggle. "Come, come, man, bow to the inevitable. You cannot escape, and you know it perfectly well. Moran has a bead drawn on the front of the house, and there are thugs in front and back." He consulted a pocket watch. "It lacks two or three minutes of midnight. My men have been told to wait until twelve. If I have not returned by then with the umbrella, they are to forcibly enter and destroy you on sight. I'm afraid they would be rather messy about it."

Persano rose, picked up his cane, which had been resting on the floor, and withdrew the sword from its innermost depths. "Permit me to dispatch you swiftly and mercifully, while there is still time. It is the least I can do for so innovative and tenacious an opponent."

"*Have at you, then!*" Fillmore shouted, suddenly lofting the umbrella. Swinging it in both hands, he swept it at Persano in the manner of an antique broad sword.

Persano appeared rather disappointed in Fillmore as he dodged the blow. "As a gentleman, I waited until you woke. Perhaps, after all, I should have slain you in your sleep." He parried an umbrella-swash with a neat turn of the wrist. "Didn't you read Sacker's message? I am expert at this. Your form is barely passable academy, and rusty at that."

Fillmore, not wasting energy replying, panted and puffed as he tried to hack Persano to pieces. But the other met each attack with easy indifference, not deigning to attempt getting under Fillmore's guard with his own stroke.

When, at last, the scholar collapsed, breathless, back against the wall, Persano clucked dolefully. "You expend precious time needlessly. There is but a scant minute ere the clock chimes twelve, and then there will be tedious butchery. For the love of order, sir, I entreat you to accept an easy death!"

Fillmore lowered the umbrella. "Well, then," he gasped, still winded, "I suppose I must recognize the inevitability of my mortality. But it's hard." He nodded for the stroke that would end his life.

Persano reached across the table and, seizing the tawny port, poured a measure into a wine glass. He approached Fillmore, sword in one hand, the glass in the other. He held out the wine for the professor to take. "Drink this. It contains a potent sleeping-draught. When the doctor called for Bordeaux, The Raddle, following my instructions, brought this instead. It works quickly. I will withhold the *coup de grace* until you slumber."

Fillmore took the wine. The clock began to chime midnight as he raised the glass to his lips . . .

No!

The instinct for survival was too strong. He tried to dash the liquor into Persano's eyes, but the villain, half-expecting the gesture, ducked; the wine spattered his shirt. Persano's hand shot out. He grabbed the umbrella and wrenched it around, but Fillmore desperately resisted.

The two struggled fiercely, silently. But the exertions of the day were too much for Fillmore and he finally collapsed beneath the weight and superior strength of the other. Persano, pulled off balance, toppled onto his opponent, but even as he did, he jammed his elbow against Fillmore's throat.

"You *do* believe in last-minute heroics! You can't say I didn't try to bring you a painless death."

He stood up, planting a foot hard against Fillmore's chest, pinioning him. A pounding noise at the street door. The landlady shot the bolt. Coarse voices, the sound of many feet pounding up the stairs.

"My men," said Persano, mildly regretful. "Farewell." He poised the sword in the air, ready to plunge it into Fillmore's throat.

The scholar braced himself. A wave of hatred for Persano supplanted what fear he might have felt. He clutched the umbrella, wishing he could wield it one more time. His thumb brushed against the release catch.

The tip of the sword started down for Fillmore's jugular. But as it did, something unexpected happened.

The umbrella snapped open with a click.

Chapter Seven

There were dark, rolling clouds overhead, and in the air the heavy, oppressive sense of thunder. Slowly the darkness fell, and as it did, Fillmore felt a strange chill overtake him, and a lonely feeling.

Of Persano, there was no trace. He'd fallen off somewhere during the flight of the umbrella, his sword flailing wildly as he fell, screaming, to whichever earth Fillmore's distracted imagination dictated.

A dog began to howl in a farmhouse somewhere far down the road—a long, agonized wailing, as if from fear. The sound was taken up by another dog, and then another and another, till, borne on the wind which sighed along the dark and lonely mountain road, a cacophony of howling tormented his ears. In the sound, too, there was a deeper chuckling menace—that of wolves.

An arch of trees hemmed in the road, which became a kind of tunnel leading somewhere that he dreaded to contemplate. But there was no use trying to avoid a sequence, that was one fact he'd finally learned. The professor trudged on in the darkness, shivering at the icy air of the heights. The trees were soon replaced by great frowning rocks on both sides; the rising wind moaned and whistled through them and it grew colder and colder still. Fine powdery snow began to fall, driving against his pinched face, settling in his eyebrows and on the rims of his ears.

The baying of the wolves sounded nearer and nearer. Off a ways to the left, Fillmore thought he could discern faint flickering blue flames, ghost-lights that beckoned to him, but he fearfully ignored them.

How long he trod the awful lightless road, he could not tell. The rolling clouds obscured the moon and he could not read the crystal of his watch, nor could he strike a match. Persano had never returned them.

The path kept ascending, with occasional short downward respites. Suddenly the road emerged from the rock tunnel and led across a broad, high expanse into the courtyard of a vast ruined castle, from whose tall black casements no light shone.

Against the moonlit sky, Fillmore studied the jagged line of broken battlements and knew instinctively where he was.

A bit worse than Persano, he mused, approaching the great main door, old and studded with large iron nails, set in a projecting arch of massive stone. There was no bell or knocker, but he had no doubt that soon the tenant would sense his presence and admit him.

Perhaps it would be better to flee. But he did not relish the thought of another minute on the freezing road with the wolves constantly drawing nearer. True, he'd heard them to be much maligned animals, gentle and shy, but somehow he found it hard to believe at that moment.

The occupant of the castle was fiercer than wolves, but Fillmore guessed it was his destiny to meet him, and if so, it would be better to do so face to face rather than hide and wait for *him* to seek Fillmore out.

The matter was settled when he heard a heavy step approaching behind the door. A gleam of light appeared through the chinks. Chains rattled, huge bolts clanged back, a key turned in a seldom-used lock and the rusty metal noisily protested. But at last, the portal swung wide.

An old man stood there, clean-shaven but for a white mustache, dressed in black from head to toe. He held an old silver lamp in his hand; it threw flickering shadows everywhere. He spoke in excellent English, tinged, however, with the dark coloration of a middle-European accent.

"I bid you welcome. Enter freely and of your own will." He did not move. But neither did Fillmore. A frown creased the old man's brow. He spoke again. "Welcome to my house. Come freely. Go safely; and leave something of the happiness you bring!"

A bit better, Fillmore thought, stepping across the threshold. As he did, the host grasped his hand in a cold grip strong enough to make him wince.

Fillmore started to speak, but the tall nobleman held up his hand for silence until the howling of the wolves had died away.

"Listen to them," he beamed. "Children of the night! What music they make!"

Damn Persano! Fillmore swore to himself *I'm right! He*

would *have to put such a notion into my head just before the umbrella opened!*

He followed his host upstairs. Enroute, he had to tear a passage through a gigantic spiderweb.

The tall man smiled, and Fillmore knew what he was about to say. "The spider—" he began, but the professor finished it for him.

"—spinning his web for the unwary fly. For the blood is the life, eh?"

The Count frowned. "How did you know what was in my mind?"

Fillmore shrugged. "Bit of a fey quality, I fancy."

Some 500 miles distant from the castle is a town, Sestri di Levante, situated on the Italian Riviera. Near it stands the Villa Cascana on a high promontory overlooking the iridescent blue of the Ligurian Sea.

It was the latter part of a glorious afternoon in spring. The sun sparkled on the water, dazzling the eye so the place where the chestnut forest above the villa gave way to pines could not easily be discerned.

A *loggia* ran about the pleasant house, and outside a gravel path threaded past a fountain of Cupid through a riot of magnolias and roses. In the middle of the garden there suddenly appeared a stranger, walking with a cane. He seemed bewildered.

"I've lost him temporarily," Persano murmured. "But he must be in this world, and if he is, I'll find him and finish him at last. Then I'll take the umbrella and go home. Meantime, there are far less pleasant places where I have might have ended up."

He gazed about, noting with pleasure the marble fountain playing merrily nearby. He drank in the salty freshness of the sea wind and decided it would be a good place to sit and devise a scheme of action. Persano strolled the gravel-path and stopped at a bench near the Cupid fountain. He sat down and lit a cigar with the last match remaining in the pillbox he'd secured from Fillmore. He tossed away the empty box. It arced high and landed in the fountain.

Overhead, a bird twitted in the chestnuts. Someone seated

in the villa—spying Persano and wondering who he was—hailed the stranger, but the shouted greeting received no answer. Persano was staring at the pillbox bobbing on the surface of the water. An awful presentiment overtook him, and the blood drained from his face.

Slowly, reluctantly, step by step, he dragged himself to the fountain and stared, horrified, at the floating pillbox, which had landed open, like a miniature boat braving the crests of the fountain freshet.

A small caterpillar had crawled into the cardboard box and was scuttling this way and that. It was most unusual in color and loathsome in appearance: gray-yellow with lumps and excrescences on its rings, and an opening on one end that aspirated like a mouth. Its feet resembled the claws of a crab.

Persano's eyes bulged as the creature, sensing his presence, began to crawl out of the box and swim in his direction . . .

"I admit you are an unusual visitor," said Dracula. "An interesting fellow, if that is the slang these days. Try some of the wine. It is very old."

"No thank you," Fillmore demurred, having had his fill of soporifics in disguise. "I must say that you are an excellent host. The chicken was excellent, if thirsty."

"Perhaps you would prefer beer?" the vampire asked, anxious to please.

"If I can open the bottle myself."

Dracula shook his head. "You do me wrong. There are ancient customs which no host may defy, even if he be—how do the peasants call it?—*nosferatu!*"

"Yes, but I seem to recall the case of one Johnathan Harker—"

"Harker?" Dracula echoed surprised. "How do you know him? He is at this moment on the way from England to conduct some business for me."

"And you have no intention of letting him leave here *not* undead," Fillmore accused Dracula.

"You wrong me, young sir. When the formula I repeated below is stated by a host and a nobleman, it dare not be violated. *I* will do nothing to prevent Harker's departure."

"Except lock the doors and ring the castle with wolves," Fillmore countered sarcastically.

The vampire shrugged. "If I did not lock the doors, the wolves might get in . . ."

"Well, at any rate, you can see why I do not trust your wine."

"Yes," Dracula nodded, "you seem totally cognizant of my identity, nature and intentions. But knowing all this, why would you enter here of your own free will?"

"Well, it's a long story."

Dracula smiled icily. "I have until sun-up."

So Fillmore told the story of the umbrella yet again, omitting only the references to Mrs. Bardell's cut throat and the near-skewering of his own jugular by Persano . . . details that he was afraid might disagreeably excite the Count.

"Hah! Can such things be?" the vampire mused once the tale was done. His piercing eyes shone with an unholy crimson light. "Long ago, what arcane researches I carried on, seeking things beyond the mundane world in which I felt trapped. And the things I discovered only proved a far worse incarceration for me. But this—this umbrella—what opportunity lies within its mystic compass!"

Fillmore began to grow uneasy. He'd spun out the history till close to daybreak, figuring that the coming dawn would enable him to escape while Dracula slept. Even more to the point, he mentally punned, he might be able to rid the place of the vampire with a stroke of the point of his umbrella and, in such wise, complete the sequence and get out of this world of horror into which his fight with Persano had unluckily plunged him.

It escaped him until that moment that Dracula might look on the parasol as a far greater tool for spreading the brood of the devil than the original plan he'd devised to purchase Carfax Abbey from John Harker and move to England and its teeming millions. But how could London compare with the available necks of countless billions in worlds without number?

Fillmore stole a nervous glance towards the casement, hoping that dawn might shine through it soon. By no means could he allow the umbrella to fall into Dracula's hands!

"The night is nearly ended," the caped nobleman said, rising. His eyes fixed Fillmore's in a hypnotic stare. "I must sleep the day. Let me show you your room."

"The octagonal one, I know. Never mind, I'll find it." Fillmore strode across the large chamber and opened the door to his bedchamber. It was just where Stoker said it would be. At the door, he paused and fixed the vampire with a stern gaze that he hoped would command respect.

"I depend on you, Count, to be as good as your word. A vampire may lie—but a nobleman, never."

"We understand each other perfectly well," Dracula smiled, bowing his head gravely. "I have given my word, and I will repeat it. No harm to you shall come from *me*."

And he strode from the room, slamming the door shut behind him. Fillmore hurried to the portal and tried it, but it was securely locked.

The professor was worried. Dracula could not be trusted, and yet he had given his word as a patrician. Could he go against it, evil though he was? Fillmore did not think so.

He walked back to his room and stretched out on the bed, exhausted from the perils of the umbrella's flight and the terrible walk through the Carpathian forest. He began to sink into a delicious lassitude.

No, no, no, no, no, no! his mind repeated over and over, a still, small voice protesting a fact out of joint, a snag in logic, an unforeseen menace.

"*I have given my word, and I will repeat it. No harm to you shall come from* me."

Dracula did not say Fillmore would be unharmed. He said *he* would not *personally* hurt him.

Fillmore tried to get up, but his limbs were leaden. Above him, not far away, a dancing swirl of dustmotes pirouetted in a beam of moonlight. In the middle of the mist shone two mocking golden eyes, like those of an animal.

He tried to groan, but no sound emerged. He had forgotten Dracula's three undead mistresses who lived (?) with him in the vaults beneath the castle.

The fairest and most favored of the three was in the coffin-shaped room with Fillmore, baring her teeth for the inevitable bite.

He fell into a merciful swoon.

Chapter Eight

Some days, it is nigh onto impossible to get out of bed. The body, filled with a not altogether unpleasant lassitude, refuses to function. Too weak to protest, the mind feebly struggles to rouse the limbs, but to no avail, so weak is the will, so sapped the corporeal being. Easier to capitulate, to drift in that half-state between slumber and waking.

And so Fillmore remained in a condition of wan enthrallment for the greater part of the day. Only as the autumnal gloom began to draw in, signaling the approach of evening, did his torpid brain make an effort to gather in those wandering fantasies which possessed it and pack them away. Very deep within, clawing at the prison-door of consciousness, a voice urged him to wake.

He pushed himself up unwillingly and sat on the edge of the soft bed, head dangling, trying to recollect where he was.

A wolf greeted the oncoming sunset.

With a start, he sat bolt upright, remembering everything. He peered across the room with nervous dread, but to his surprise, the umbrella was still there. Getting to his feet, swaying from unexpected weakness, he lurched over to it and tried pressing the catch, but as he anticipated, it did not open. He turned this way and that, seeking a mirror, finally recalling that Dracula did not keep any such reminders of his vampiric status about the house.

When Fillmore put a hand to his neck, he knew he needed no glass to confirm what his fingers felt. He winced at the two tender spots, the tiny punctures that still felt tacky.

Luckily, according to Bram Stoker, vampires rarely finish off a victim in one night. But Fillmore felt so enervated that he very much doubted whether he could survive a second attack.

And the sun was going down.

He ran to the large casement in the dining room and stared out. The castle was built on a rocky precipice. The valley, spread out far below and threaded with raging torrents, was such a great distance straight down that if he fell, only a parachute could save him.

But how did Harker escape in *Dracula*? He emulated the Count, creeping from rugged stone to stone, crawling down the side of the castle like a great lizard to the courtyard underneath. But this drop was sheer, with no apparent footholds or niches for the hands to grasp. Nor was there a courtyard; only cruel and jagged rocks . . .

He ran to his room and pushed open the narrow aperture. The same vista—exit was impossible from either window!

Then how did Harker scale the walls? He beat his fists against his temples, thinking, thinking. He remembered that in the novel, the solicitor walked out the dining-room door into the corridor and explored the vast pile. Somewhere on the castle's south side must be the window that permitted access to the lower floors and the courtyard.

But the door to the corridor was locked.

Fillmore tore about like a madman, trying the door at the end opposite the octagonal room, but it, too, was locked. He set his back to the main door and bumped it, but the only thing that gave was his back.

Darting to the window a second time, he watched in fascinated horror as the sun dipped beneath the ridges and crests of the mountains. Only a thin slice of the golden rim remained on the horizon.

Figure another five or six minutes' worth of sunlight, and perhaps an equal time of afterlight. Another minute for the vampires to rouse themselves and come up here. Then, at the most generous estimate I have an unlucky thirteen minutes to—

"Well, say it!" he snapped at himself, aloud. "To save myself from a fate worse than death. Literally."

The teacher sat upon the edge of his bed and applied his mind to his predicament. Panic would accomplish nothing, he realized, so he might as well employ the residue of time in seeing whether there were any way out at all.

A chorus of wolves shivered on the rising wind.

He shuddered.

"There's enough of that, damn it!" he told himself. "It's about time I stopped behaving like a victim everywhere I fly to. Let's see now: can't get out the doors, windows are too high up, no way to safely climb down the wall. I'd probably dash my brains out, anyway, even if I tried it."

And then a new and startling notion flashed into his mind. He jumped to his feet and nervously paced the room.

"No time to follow it all up," he declaimed aloud like the actor he once aspired to be, "but some of it *must* be scanned! Is there an alternative reason? Quick—work out a chain of logic!"

He ticked off propositions on his fingertips. "*One:* a sequence has to be completed wherever one goes with the umbrella. *Two:* I am no longer in the Holmesian rough-draft world. *Hence:* I completed the sequence there. But how? Some of the literary works on which that place is based were unfinished in *my* original earth. Could it be that my adventure with Persano stopped just because it isn't over?!"

Fillmore shook his head. "Too many paradoxes. *The Pickwick Papers* was completed by Dickens, and that was— is—a part of Persano's world. So events cannot be dictated by literature that I know, at least not entirely. Which is confusing, but forget philosophy for now; ask Holmes, if I live to meet him!" He put the issue behind him with a flourish of one hand, a gesture he often used when confronting an adamantly incorrect student. "The vital question now is—*why did the umbrella open?*"

Only one answer fit. When Persano aimed his sword at Fillmore's throat, the scholar's life in that world was, for all practical purposes, terminated. Therefore, the sequence had to be at an end, and the umbrella finally worked.

Therefore, in a world of horror, where there are victims galore, all one must do to escape is . . . die.

He certainly hoped he was right.

Picking up the umbrella, Fillmore strode purposefully to the window and tried opening it. But the rusty latch would not budge. He spied an immense pewter candelabra, seized it and hurled the thing forcibly. It bumped the glass and clattered to the floor.

"*Hell!*" Exasperated, he stuck his face against the window and saw that it was doubly thick. He also perceived that the last sliver of sun was gone and the afterlight was fading swiftly.

Then, from far below in the very bowels of the castle, he heard a metallic grating noise, followed by an iron thunder-

ous clang, like a great door slammed open. Deperately he
wrestled with one of the Count's chairs. It was incredibly
heavy, and took a tremendous effort of the will for him to loft
it at all, let alone swing it. But swing it he did, and the
window shattered most gratifyingly. The massive piece of
furniture tumbled after the raining shards down, down into
the depths of the valley.

Fillmore scrambled onto the window seat, umbrella in
hand, thumb on the catch. Gazing out at the panoramic vista,
he felt queasy. Heights terrified him. If he was wrong, and
the umbrella did not open, he would be crushed on the rocks and
then—since he had been bitten by the vampire woman—he
might have to join the legions of the undead.

There was the sound of a heavy tread in the corridor
outside. Screwing up his courage, Fillmore forced himself to
look out at the landscape and conquer his fear of falling. He
saw the valley cloaked in shadow, and very far off, the glint
of rushing water, a distant cataract.

The cataract strong then—

"NO!" he admonished himself."No other literature this
time, just Sherlock Holmes!"

—cataract strong then plunges along—

"Sherlock Holmes!"

—striking and raging as if a war waging—

"Sherlock Holmes, Sherlock Holmes, Sherlock Holmes!"

—its caverns and rocks among—

"SHERLOCK HOLMES!" Fillmore shouted, jumping out the
window.

Behind him, in the room, the doors flung wide. The blond
fiend raced to the window, snarling.

"Gone!" she howled, turning to accuse her mate. "How
did you dare permit this? You might have taken the umbrella
while he slept!"

The Count, entering with a swirl of his cape, coldly replied, "I pledged my word I would not harm him. I may be a
vampire, but I am a nobleman first, and a *boyar* does not
break his word." In truth, Dracula had realized that transport-
ing fifty boxes of native soil across the dimensions would be
a grueling project. London was quite good enough . . .

The woman told him precisely what she thought of his

aristocratic airs. "Your precious blue blood," she snapped
spitefully, "is tainted with the plasma of the lowest village
peasants."

"And yours isn't?" he sneered, staring haughtily down his
long aquiline nose at her.

"The least you could have done would have been to hide
the thing so I could have supped again!"

"As for that," said Dracula, waving his hand with grand
disdain, "you are already more plump than is seemly."

"*Plump*?!" she screamed. "You told me that's the way
you like me best!"

The matter proceeded through a great many more ex-
changes and retorts, but it is perhaps indelicate to dwell at
length on the secrets of patrician domestic life, and so it were
good to draw the present chapter to a close.

Chapter Nine

Fillmore wanted to throw up, but he was too terrified to
move. Below, the ferocious cataract raged. A needle-spritz of
foam slashed up through the curtain of mist created by the
falls, occasionally spattering droplets on his face. The long
sweep of green water whirled and clamored, producing a kind
of half-human shout which boomed out of the abyss with the
spray.

"Miserable damned umbrella!" he grumbled. "I said 'Sherlock Holmes' time and again—NOT *The Cataract of Lodore*!"

The shelf on which the umbrella had deposited him was
barely big enough for his posterior. Fortunately, it (the shelf)
was cut high and deep enough so he could arch his back
against the black stone. There was just enough space to stand
the umbrella upright next to him along the vertical axis of the
niche, but otherwise there was no room to move or turn.
Eventually, he supposed, he would either fall into the chasm
or else figure a way to get down safely.

His feet dangled precariously over the edge. Below them,
the cliff bellied out so he could not see straight down. But to
the right, he spied a footpath that looked as if it ought to pass
directly beneath his perch. Yet to the left there was a sheer

drop into the torrent, so he could not be certain that the path extended all the way to the point just south of where he sat. If it did, he might be able to slide down the cliffside and land on the narrow walkway. It looked about a yard wide, surely large enough to break the momentum of his fall.

But what if the path stopped before it got to where he was sitting? Then he'd plummet right down the mountain.

Well, sooner or later I'll have to risk it. Unless—

Unless the umbrella had whisked him back to his own world, where Southey's cataract was situated. Sequence rules did not seem to apply to one's home cosmos (or else the bumbershoot could not have operated in the first place, or so Fillmore reasoned).

He pushed the button halfheartedly. Nothing happened. He was still stuck on the meager rocky mantel.

He glanced above him and saw, too far to reach, a bigger niche, covered with soft green moss. He looked down and was seized by vertigo. He shut his eyes and shoved his back against the eroded cliff wall, wishing he could sink inside it.

"Get hold of yourself! If you have to drop, you'd better be in full control of your muscles!" he told himself, wishing that he could somehow find a way to shut off the sound of the cascading flood—a strange, melancholy noise like lost souls lamenting in the deep recess of the pool into which the churning streams poured.

He tried to reestablish his equilibrium by turning his attention to the expanse of blue sky above him. The weather was mild and there was a pleasant breeze that he wished, all the same, would stop tugging and flapping his sleeve like insistent child-fingers begging him to come play in the rapids below. There were few clouds, and none obscured the sun, which shone high and bright.

Gazing nervously into the heavens, squinting to minimize the glare, Fillmore suddenly opened his eyes wide in surprise. A fact popped into his head, something he'd read in the rubric to *The Cataract of Lodore* in the textbook he used to teach English Romantic Fiction.

"Tourists who make special jaunts to view the site which inspired Southey's famous exercise in onomatopoeia are generally disappointed because—"

Because why? How did the rest of the rubric read?

Before the thought could be brought to mind, Fillmore was distracted by the sound of approaching footsteps . . . a rapid, yet heavy tread.

He sighed with relief. *Maybe it'll be someone who can help me get down from here!*

The footsteps neared. Fillmore stared down at the footpath curving around the mountainside to his right. A long moment passed, during which the footfalls grew louder, but slowed to a walk. And then a man rounded the bend and emerged into the professor's angle of vision.

The newcomer was extremely tall and thin. Clean-shaven, with a great dome of forehead and eyes sunk deep in his skull, the stranger was pale and ascetic in cast. Chalk dust clung to his sleeves and his shoulders were rounded and his head protruded forward as if he had spent too much time in closet study of abstruse intellectual problems.

Stopping in the middle of the narrow path, he peered with puckered, angry eyes at a place some steps in front of him. He spoke in an ironical tone of voice.

"Well, sir," he said, "as you are wont to quote, 'Journeys end in lovers meeting.' "

For a brief, disoriented second, Fillmore thought he himself was being addressed. Then there was a murmur from a spot directly beneath the ledge where he was dizzily balanced, and he realized that someone had been waiting all the while right under him, hidden by the bellying rock-swell that the mountainside described just below his feet.

"I warned you I would never stand in the dock," the tall man said in a dry, reprimanding voice. "Yet you have persevered in your attempts to bring justice upon my head."

The unseen man murmured a laconic reply.

"In truth," the other continued, "I doubted that you could so effectively quash the network of crime it took me so long to build up. But you have outstripped your potential, and I underestimated you, to my cost." As he spoke, his head was never still, but moved in a slow oscillating pattern from side to side, like some cold-blooded reptile. "However," he went on, "you have also underestimated me. I said if you were clever enough to bring destruction on me, I would do the same for you. I do not make idle threats."

Another murmur Fillmore could not hear—more protracted this time—and then the tall one grimly nodded. "Yes, I will wait that long. He who stands on the brink of world's-end rarely objects to the delay of a second or two before time stops."

Crossing his arms patiently, he waited silently, staring fixedly at the person Fillmore could not see.

But by then, of course, the teacher knew the identity of both antagonists, seen and unseen. With the knowledge came the recollection of the forgotten detail pertaining to the cataract of Lodore.

"Tourists who make special jaunts to view the site which inspired Southey's famous exercise in onomatopoeia," said the rubric, "are generally disappointed because the falls dry up by the time they visit in summer. The Lodore falls are best seen in colder weather."

The sky and sun and the breeze told Fillmore it must be late spring. Therefore, the cascading waters below could not be Lodore.

It had to be Reichenbach Falls, instead.

Reichenbach Falls . . . scene of the dramatic final meeting between Sherlock Holmes and his arch enemy, Professor Moriarty . . . perfectly logical considering that Fillmore simultaneously thought of Holmes and a waterfall. The umbrella took him precisely where it had been told.

All the same, he mused grumpily, *it might have picked a less disagreeable ringside seat!*

And yet, for all his fearful giddiness, Fillmore felt a bit like an Olympian looking down on the petty squabbling of puny mortals. The analogy was furthered by the fact that he knew both what was taking place and that which was about to happen.

Right now, he thought, *Holmes is writing a farewell message to Watson. When he finishes it, he'll put it on top of a boulder close by and anchor the paper by placing his silver cigarette case upon it.*

Fillmore had read "The Final Problem" several times. It was a bitter tale, the one in which Arthur Conan Doyle tried to kill off his famous detective; Fillmore often wondered what it must have been like to read it when it first appeared in print, not knowing that Holmes would be resurrected ten years later in "The Adventure of the Empty House." (Fillmore grinned to himself, thinking of the heresy his mind had just committed: referring to Conan Doyle as the author of the Holmes tales. "Are ye mad, man?" his pals at the local branch of the Baker Street Irregulars would say. "Watson wrote those *factual* accounts. Doyle was just the good Doctor's literary agent!")

Fillmore finally knew what he was going to do: simply wait until the adventure ran its course. Holmes would finish the message, rise and walk to the edge of the footpath. Moriarty, disdaining weaponry, would fling himself upon his enemy and the pair would struggle and tussle on the very edge of the falls. At the last, Holmes' superior knowledge of baritsu ("the Japanese system of wrestling, which has more than once been very useful to me") would win the day and Moriarty would take the horrible, fatal plunge alone. Then Fillmore could hail Holmes, who would surely help him to get down.

After that, I'll warn him that Colonel Moran is skulking about here someplace and—

And?

There was no point in making any other plans just yet. If Holmes were unable to rescue him from the awful ledge, there would be no future for J. Adrian (Blah!) Fillmore!

At that moment, Moriarty unfolded his arms.

"If the message is done, sir," he said, "then I presume we may proceed with this matter?"

A murmur and then footsteps.

He's walking to the end of the path. Now Moriarty will follow him and suddenly try to push Holmes off balance.

Moriarty did not move. A mirthless trace of humor tilted up the corner of his mouth.

Fillmore was suddenly seized by the chill premonition that something extremely unpleasant was about to take place.

"You surprise me at the last," the evil Professor remarked. "Had you expected some gentleman's Code of Honor, sir? My foolish lieutenant Persano might subscribe to such nonsense, but then again, he would be better suited physically to grapple with a man thoroughly skilled in singlestick. *And* baritsu."

"*What*?!" It was the first time Fillmore heard the crisp voice beneath him.

"Come, come," said Moriarty, drawing a revolver out of his coat, "I keep files on my enemies, too, you know."

No! This is wrong! Fillmore was stunned. *This isn't how the story turns out!*

"I am vexed," Moriarty stated. "You have twice underestimated me, sir." He raised the pistol and aimed.

Fillmore had no time to wonder whether direct interference might change the texture of the world he was in—it was *already* different. He did not concern himself, either, with the dangers of subsumption or, for that matter, the more immediate risk that he might break his neck.

Transferring the umbrella to his right hand, he shoved himself off the perch with a yell to warn the detective below. As he descended, he flailed the umbrella in Moriarty's direction.

The Professor immediately raised his arm and snapped off a shot at Fillmore, but he was aiming at a moving target and the bullet ricocheted harmlessly off a boulder. Before he could fire a second time, Holmes grasped his arm in an iron grip and instantly afterwards, Fillmore landed on the path in a heap.

The arch-antagonists struggled violently scant inches from the end of the walkway. Fillmore did his best to get out from underfoot, but elbows poked his ribs and feet trod his toes. He was an integral part of the melee.

The detective grunted. The criminal cursed. They swayed on the very lip of the precipice. Then Holmes unexpectedly and slickly slipped out of Moriarty's grip. The movement set the Professor off balance. With a cry of fear, he flailed, both hands clawing the air. One touched the grip of the umbrella and, instinctively, Moriarty clutched at it, wrenching it from Fillmore's grasp.

Forgetting all danger, Fillmore lurched forward and tried to get the umbrella back, but Moriarty, uttering one long terrified scream, pitched over backwards into the abyss.

Fillmore scrambled on his hands and knees to the edge and, with Holmes, watched the Napoleon of Crime falling, falling, the umbrella wildly waving. He vanished from view in the scintillating curtain of spray.

For a long while they watched, but they could not discern any movement in the maelstrom. Still, Fillmore thought he could hear Moriarty's cry of terror eternally intermingled with the half-human roar of the falls.

Rousing themselves, they walked down the path a ways. Then the tall, thin man with the well-remembered face addressed Fillmore good-humoredly.

"In the past," he chuckled, "I have been skeptical of the workings of Providence, but nevermore shall I doubt the efficacy of a *deus ex machina,* no matter what guise it descends in!"

Fillmore would have replied but they were all at once interrupted by a barrage of rocks from above.

"That would be Colonel Moran," Fillmore remarked. "He's just about on schedule."

Holmes looked at him curiously but decided to forestall all questions until after they escaped from the assiduous administrations of Moriarty's sole surviving lieutenant.

Explication and Epilogue

Late that evening, two men sat drinking ale in a pothouse in Rosenlaui. For a long while, only one of them spoke, but at last, he ended his narrative.

"That is certainly the most singular history I have ever heard," said the other, taller one, signaling to the waiter for more brew. "It is more surprising to me than that awful business at Baskerville and, at least to you, quite as harrowing."

"And now," said Fillmore, "I suppose you are going to suggest I consult a specialist in obscure nervous diseases?"

"Not at all, old chap," the lean detective grinned. "There is an internal cohesion that I should be prompted to trust in, to begin with. But knowing all that I do about the late Professor Moriarty, your tale makes considerable sense."

"It *does*?"

"Moriarty himself prefigured the possibility of a dimensional-transfer engine in his brilliant paper on *The Dynamics of an Asteroid.* Not in so many words, you understand, but the concept was buried within if one had the comprehension and the philosophical tools to prize it forth. The Professor certainly foresaw the ramifications of his theory, at least in this interesting—and rather distressing—side-channel of his research. I shudder to think what might have happened had he manufactured enough of them to arm his entire army of villains! Criminal justice in England (perhaps in the entire cosmos, eventually) would be totally unworkable.'' Holmes tapped his fingers against the frosted stein which the waiter set down before him. "Of course, I suppose it would have then been up to me to devise a similar engine and make it available to society at large.'' He shook his head, smiling ruefully.''I wish you could have held onto it. I should have been most interested in examining it.''

"I'm extremely disappointed myself,'' Fillmore said. "I came here specifically to ask you about the umbrella, and now it's gone!''

"You wanted to find out how it worked?''

"No,'' he replied, shaking his head. "I wanted to learn *why* it works so strangely.''

Holmes laughed. "Oh, you are referring, I suppose, to the business of its taking you to so-called 'literary' dimensions?''

Fillmore nodded. He had a sudden inkling of what Holmes was about to say.

"That, my dear Fillmore, is quite elementary! The physics and mathematics of space strongly imply the coexistence of many worlds in other dimensions. What are these places like? Surely, space is so infinite that there must be an objective reality to planets of every conceivable kind, variances and patterns mundane and fantastic.''

"Yes, yes, but why *literary* permutations?''

"You have been going about the problem backwards,'' said Holmes. "These places do not exist because people on your earth dreamed them up. I should say rather the reverse was more likely.''

"Meaning?''

"Meaning the 'fiction' of your prosaic earth must be borrowed, in greater or lesser degree, from notions and conceptions that occur across the barriers of the dimensions. Have you not heard writers (though surely not Watson) protest that they do not know from what heaven their inspirations descend? Even my good friend the doctor's agent, Conan Doyle, has sometimes told me that he invents characters in his historical romances that 'write themselves.' Does this not suggest that these artists may be unwittingly tapping the logical premises of other parallel worlds?''

"Then, in my case—'' Fillmore began, but Holmes already knew.

"Of course! You are an instructor in literature and drama. Your mind is evidently psychically attuned to the alternative earths which the literature of your world has told you of—and succeeded in captivating your imagination with.''

Fillmore nodded and sipped his ale. They sat in silence for a few moments before he spoke again.

"Your theory makes a great deal of sense, and yet—''

"And yet?''

"It does not totally explain why it has been necessary for me to complete a sequence of action in each world I visit.''

Holmes nodded. "That, I should say, is a three-pipe problem. But it will have to be left for a time when we can breathe more freely. Colonel Moran will surely pick up our trail before the night is over. We must proceed swiftly, and you must stay close by. Since he may have observed your role in the death of his chief, you may well be marked for extermination.''

"I don't mind at all sticking with you,'' Fillmore admitted as they rose from the table, "especially since I have no recourse now but to be subsumed.''

"I am not positive that subsumption is an inevitable function of the umbrella,'' said Holmes, insisting on taking the check, "but you are right to the extent that the instrument is now out of reach of our human resources.''

They walked out of the tavern and inhaled the clear, cold air of evening.

"I suppose you do not intend to get in touch with Watson, under the circumstances?''

"No,'' Holmes shook his head, "it would involve him in too great a risk. The dear boy is an innocent when it comes to dissembling. Moran will reason my path lies homeward, but if I do go to London, there will be danger for all and sundry. Moran might kidnap Watson to flush me out. No, I must stay away from England for a time.''

"And therefore you will change your name to Sigerson and—"

"How the devil did you know that?!" Holmes snapped, his brows beetling. Then his face cleared and he nodded merrily. "Of course! You have a contemporaneous awareness of certain likely events in this world. But I pray, sir, if we are to be travel companions, please refrain from casting yourself too often in the role of a Nostradamus. There is a piquancy to quotidian unawareness of one's Fate."

Fillmore agreed and they walked on for a time in silence. Then Holmes suggested that the professor ought to consider what role he might want to assume in the present world.

"Why, no one knows me here," the other said in some amazement. "Why should I need to be anyone but myself?"

"Because you will bring us into rather risky focus during our travels abroad if you insist on remaining a man without a background and point of origin. First thing we must do is purchase a good set of false papers. You will need a well-worked-out history—"

"And a new name!" Fillmore said suddenly and decisively.

"What on earth for? What's wrong with the one you have?"

"I thoroughly detest it!"

"Yes, yes, but you are apt to slip up if you stray too far from your original nomenclature. If you *must* pick a new name, choose one close enough to the present one so it won't take long to get used to it."

"Very well," Fillmore agreed, lapsing into thoughtful silence. *I'll get rid of that hateful middle name and call myself by my original first one, the one my aunt didn't like because it belonged to my father.* A bitter memory crossed his mind, and he determined to be done entirely with the painful past. *The hell with the surname, too! I'll go back to the old spelling.*

They stumped along for another quarter-hour and at last Holmes suggested they take shelter in the barn he saw upon the rise and stay there until the morning came. Fillmore agreed.

A few minutes later, they stretched out in straw and prepared to slumber. A peculiar idea occurred to the scholar at that moment, and he smiled.

"Something amusing?" Holmes asked.

Fillmore nodded. "It just crossed my mind . . . if your theory is correct and artists in my world really do unwittingly borrow from the events of alternative earths, then it is possible that I am already figuring in some work of literature back where I came from!''

Holmes chuckled. ''I do not think I am going to dwell on that thought just now. My poor tired brain has had enough of metaphysics for one day!''

With that, the Great Detective said good night and went to sleep.

His companion lay there for a long time, thinking about the morrow when he would take on his new name and identity and start a new life. The professor gazed into the darkness and pondered the perilous perplexities of the stars.

In his cozy Victorian study, the doctor gazed down on the new manuscript. The thing was more fun, he thought, if he could think of the perfect name.

There was already evidence that his readers enjoyed the wry device of Watson's ''stories-yet-to-be-told.'' It was a clever method of injecting humor into the often grim tales: tease the readers with promises of outlandish-sounding stories not yet written up by Watson.

For instance, there was the adventure of the Grice-Pattersons in the Isle of Uffa (wherever that was!) or the Repulsive Tale of the Red Leech, or—among the most outrageous—''the strange case of Isadora Persano, the well-known duelist, who was found stark staring mad with a matchbox in front of him which contained a remarkable worm said to be unknown to science . . .''

But this name now: J. Adrian Fillmore. It didn't have quite the properly quaint tone he was seeking. It was a trifle stuffy and stolid. Perhaps it was the middle name . . . try eliminating it. And what might the initial stand for? John? James? (He chortled as he thought of the printer's error that caused Watson's wife to call him James by mistake. What a tizzy of pseudo-scholastic comment that had provoked!)

James it would be then, he decided finally. And perhaps an older and quainter spelling of the surname . . .

And Arthur Conan Doyle wrote:

''. . . the incredible mystery of Mr. James Phillimore, who, stepping back into his own house to get his umbrella, was never more seen in this world . . .''

TWEEN

by J. F. Bone

"Leonard," Mr. Ellingsen said, "what on earth are you doing to your hair?"

"Nothing," Lenny said uncomfortably. He glared at Mary Ellen and she looked at him with eyes of greenest innocence. Damned witch, Lenny thought. What Mr. Ellingsen should have said was what in hell is happening to your hair. At least his geography would be more accurate.

"Hmm," Mr. Ellingsen said. "For a moment, it looked as though unseen hands were ruffling it. It was a thoroughly unpleasant sight. I have learned to endure long hair on young men, but I cannot stand watching it rise and fall like waves on a windy beach."

The class laughed and Mary Ellen looked smugly virtuous.

"I didn't do anything," Lenny protested.

"Please don't do it again," Mr. Ellingsen said.

The class giggled and Lenny wished that he was miles away, or that Mary Ellen was—preferably the latter. Just why did she have to pick on him? He wished that he had never dated her last summer. All he'd done was kiss her a couple of times. And he wouldn't have done that if Sue Campbell hadn't been in California with her parents. But the way she'd acted when Sue came back was like they'd been making out ever since Sue left.

It wasn't true. He'd only tried to go further once, and she froze like an icicle. She turned off just like she'd turned a switch. He shrugged. If she wanted to be a cold tomato, that was her bag, but she needn't have acted like she owned him. He dropped her like a hot potato and went back to Sue almost

97

with relief. That was when she started hanging around and being obnoxious. But Sue didn't like Mary Ellen, and that kept the witch away until the end of winter term. Jealousy was strong medicine against witches, Lenny guessed, but it wasn't perfect because Sue and Mary Ellen were talking to each other now.

That wasn't good. Sue was impressionable, and she believed that crap Mary Ellen dished out. Mary Ellen wasn't too truthful when she got going. In fact, she was a goddam liar. But Sue didn't know that. Mary Ellen sure knew how to get Sue worked up.

A guy would be safer with a rattlesnake. At least the snake gave warning before it struck. And its poison was no worse than Mary Ellen's—now she was making cold chills run up and down his spine. They really ran, leaving icy little footprints on his vertebrae. His skin tingled and he shivered uncontrollably.

Mr. Ellingsen looked at him again. A grimace of annoyance twisted the teacher's pallid face.

Lenny began to itch. The urge to scratch was almost uncontrollable.

"Miss Jones," Mr. Ellingsen said.

Mary Ellen shifted her eyes to the teacher. The itching promptly stopped, although the cold spots remained.

"What is there about the back of Leonard's head that demands such intense scrutiny?" Mr. Ellingsen asked.

Mary Ellen blushed.

Lenny felt a mild satisfaction; it served her right. She didn't like being the center of attention. Witches never do. When things began to happen to him a month ago, he'd been suspicious, and after some reading of books in the school and public library he had become certain. He was bewitched. It wasn't something he could talk about, and there wasn't much he could do about it. After all, killing witches was no longer a public service, especially not when they were as pretty as Mary Ellen Jones. Anyway, she was more an annoyance than a danger. She couldn't really harm him now that he was carrying a clove of garlic in his pocket and wore a cross, and a St. Christopher medal. And in three weeks he'd be graduating from dear old John Tyler High and that would be the last of Mary Ellen. He was going to join the Air Force and volunteer for foreign service.

Mary Ellen eyed Mr. Ellingsen with distaste. He didn't *have* to call attention to her. He was typical of all that was wrong with male high school teachers, Mary Ellen thought moodily. Possibly he would have turned out better if he had more body and less brains, but slight, balding, nearsighted Mr. Ellingsen, with his high precise voice and quick birdlike movements, was a distinct washout. He was almost as bad as Lenny Stone. She shook her head. No—that wasn't being fair to Mr. Ellingsen, Lenny was unique. Nobody could be as bad—as ugly—as inconsiderate—as horrid as Leonard Joseph Stone. Lord! How she disliked him! It was an emotion that might well develop into a first-class hatred. After all, Mr. Ellingsen was intelligent in a stupid sort of way, which made him different from Lenny. Still, that hardly compensated for his defects. He wasn't human—but then what teacher is? And he was awfully mean to poor Miss Marsden. Everyone knew Anna Marsden was in love with him, but Mr. Ellingsen never gave her a break. He didn't sit with her at the faculty table or walk with her in the hall. He was too wrapped up in Physics to even see a mere English teacher. He was absolutely insufferable. Mary Ellen eyed Ellingsen speculatively. He just might lose some of his offensive superiority if one of his experiments went sour, but nothing ever went wrong with an Ellingsen demonstration. They always went off like clockwork and always proved their point. Mary Ellen sighed. She wished she could do something for Miss Marsden, or do something to Mr. Ellingsen. Either alternative would be more pleasant than just sitting here and listening to things she didn't want to understand. She settled back into a comfortable daydream of experiments going wrong, to the complete frustration of Mr. Ellingsen. . . .

"The object of this demonstration," Mr. Ellingsen said, "is to show that the force of gravity is, to all intents and purposes, a constant when substances of relatively small mass are involved, and that under these conditions, objects will fall at the same velocity regardless of their size and weight. Of course, this is within reasonable limits. I suppose that if you dealt with something as large as the moon, compared with something as small as a steel ball bearing, you would find that the moon would reach the earth sooner because it would attract the earth to it more than the steel ball would, but insofar as the earth's attraction to the moon is concerned, the speeds of attraction would be the same, roughly about 16 feet per second, per second.

"What I'm going to do is show you that a Ping-Pong ball and a steel ball bearing of equal size will fall at the same speed."

"Wouldn't the steel ball hit the ground a lot sooner if you dropped them off a real high place like the top of the clock tower?" Bill Reichart asked. Bill was an honor student and always asked questions. Mr. Ellingsen liked it because it gave him a chance to explain.

"Of course it would, but there are other factors involved."

"Like air resistance?" Lenny asked.

"Exactly. The air would slow the Ping-Pong ball. But if you dropped the two balls through a vacuum they'd fall at the same speed."

"Exactly the same speed?" Reichart persisted.

"Theoretically no—actually yes. The steel ball should attract the earth toward it more than the Ping-Pong ball, but their relative masses are so infinitesimally small as compared with the mass of the earth that the difference is calculable only mathematically and would be expressed in a fractional skillionth of a nanosecond. At any rate, there is no instrument in this school that can measure the difference." Mr. Ellingsen was sidestepping the issue. Actually, he wasn't as sure of himself as he had been a few minutes ago. There was something about gravity nibbling at the edges of his memory, but he consoled himself with the thought that if he didn't know, neither did the members of the class. He thought wryly that this was probably why he was teaching high school rather than working for a Nobel prize in physics. He simply didn't know enough.

Bill Reichart nodded. "You wouldn't want to bring up Einstein's math?" he asked.

"Not now," Ellingsen said. The class looked relieved. "I'll try to explain," he continued, ignoring the collective subliminal sigh from the students, "but I'll do it with this apparatus. You see, all I want to show at this time is that within practical limits the earth's attraction is a constant. Indeed, it is enough of a constant that Sir Isaac Newton used it as a base for his theory of gravitation and to develop a mathematics that is still useful, despite later discoveries. From a practical viewpoint, we have no need for an analysis of gravity that is more accurate than Newton's, unless we become astronomers or astronauts.

"Now let us examine the demonstration apparatus," Mr. Ellingsen pointed to the two clear plastic tubes behind him that reached from the floor almost to the high ceiling.

"These tubes contain a reasonably hard vacuum," Mr. Ellingsen said. "This will eliminate air resistance. They also contain two dissimilar objects—a Ping-Pong ball and a steel ball bearing, and some electronic apparatus to measure time. The left-hand tube contains the ball bearing and the right-hand tube contains the Ping-Pong ball. The Ping-Pong ball has a few iron filings glued to its surface. Both balls are held in the top of the tubes by electromagnets and there is a sensing device in the bottom of each tube. When I touch this button it will cut the current to the magnets and both balls will be released simultaneously. Now watch what happens. . . ."

Mr. Ellingsen pushed the button.

The Ping-Pong ball smacked against the bottom of the right-hand tube but the steel ball remained at the top of its container. With an exclamation of annoyance Mr. Ellingsen punched the button a second time. "Apparently the magnet didn't release," he said uncomfortably. "Well—we'll try again. It's no trouble to reset the balls. All we have to do is turn on the current and invert—" His voice stopped and his eyes bulged. For the steel ball was floating hesitantly down the inside of the tube—moving an inch at a time, pausing occasionally as though to determine whether it was safe to descend another inch. As Mr. Ellingsen peered at the ball, it shivered coyly and retreated to the top of the tube.

"I think I am going mad!" Mr. Ellingsen muttered. "This simply cannot happen. It repeals the Law of Gravity."

Mary Ellen giggled. The sound held a triumphant note.

The whole tube quivered, rose slowly from its metallic

base and floated toward the ceiling. Mr. Ellingsen made a
frantic grab for the plastic column—and missed.

The class giggled.

Beads of sweat dotted Ellingsen's forehead as he watched
the tube snuggle against the ceiling.

"That's a good trick, sir," Bill Reichart said. "How do
you do it?"

"I don't," Mr. Ellingsen said unhappily. "It's doing it all
by itself."

"I'll bet you do it with wires," Mary Ellen offered helpfully.

"Why should I?" Mr. Ellingsen said in a harassed voice.

"I don't know. Maybe it's a teaching device."

"I intended to teach you about the Law of Gravity—not to
repeal it," Mr. Ellingsen replied pettishly. "Both you and I
know perfectly well that a thing like this can't happen. It's a
physical impossibility. Yet there it is." He gestured hope-
lessly at the ceiling. "It should be down here."

"But it isn't, sir," Reichart said. "We can all see that.
What makes it stay up there?"

"If I knew, do you think I'd be here?" Mr. Ellingsen said.
"I'd be so busy patenting the process I wouldn't have time to
teach. What you're looking at is antigravity." He looked up
at the tube accusingly. "Come down this instant!" he ordered.

The tube dropped on Mr. Ellingsen's head. He went down
as though he had been poleaxed—and mixed with the horrified gasp from the class, Lenny could hear Mary Ellen's
gloating giggle. . . .

Later, when Mr. Hardesty, the vice-principal, tried to establish the cause of the accident that put Mr. Ellingsen in the
hospital with a mild concussion, he came to the conclusion
that everyone in Physics 3 was stark, raving mad—including
Mr. Ellingsen. The matter was quickly dropped and everyone
tried to forget it. Of course, no one did, and it was a six days'
wonder until it was replaced with something else. In Home
Ec class, about a week later and for no reason at all, plates
and glassware sailed across the room and shattered against the
wall. Mrs. Albritton, the teacher, was put under the doctor's
care, suffering from nervous collapse. Mr. Hardesty told
reporters from the school paper that Mrs. Albritton hadn't

been feeling well prior to the incident and that everyone
hoped she would be better soon. There was no truth in either
statement.

The high school baseball team, with worse material than it
had the previous year, when it had a 0-10 season, won games
with depressing regularity, and by lopsided scores. The ball,
no matter who hit it, went for extra bases. And the pitching
was uncanny. The only games the team lost were ones a long
distance from home, and those losses were by almost as
nightmarish scores as the wins near at hand.

"I can't explain it," Mr. Curtis said, as he flexed his Mr.
America muscles, "unless we've got a friendly gremlin. I've
never coached a team like this. At home we can't do a thing
wrong, and on the road we can't do a thing right. If I didn't
know better, I'd swear that there's a sorcerer in the stands
casting spells for our side. I saw one pitch last night change
directions twice. I can't figure it." Curtis's muscles were
fine, but his eyes were a bit weak or were playing tricks on
him. At least that was what most people figured after listening. And after Mr. Hardesty talked to him it was noticeable
that he didn't talk so much about the antics of his baseball
team.

Lenny figured it was Mary Ellen's doing. Mr. Curtis was
wrong only in the matter of sex. It wasn't a sorcerer. It was a
witch. Mary Ellen liked baseball. And she liked to win.
Lenny would have bet his last dime that Mary Ellen had
hexed the entire baseball team as well as being responsible
for everything that went wrong in school . . . and he would
have been right.

As Mary Ellen saw it, Anna Marsden was well on her way
to becoming an old maid. Even though she was pretty and
intelligent, she was twenty-five, which was on the downhill
side toward thirty. And everyone knew that thirty was *ancient*! That was mainly because she had to fall in love with
that awful stick of a Mr. Ellingsen. Now Mr. Curtis, the
baseball coach, was much nicer. Not only did he have hair
and muscles, but he had been hanging around the English
class for weeks. He said it was because one of his players
was having trouble with English Comp, but it was obvious
that he liked Miss Marsden. Miss Marsden never gave him a

break, which was silly. All she could see was that skinny Mr. Ellingsen—and he never noticed her at all. Miss Marsden would do a lot better with Mr. Curtis. Now if . . .

The scandal erupted two nights later when Mr. Ellingsen broke into Mr. Curtis's apartment and found Miss Marsden. It was only because Mr. Ellingsen was just out of the hospital that Curtis was still alive. Ellingsen had hit him with a bronze table lamp which should have fractured his skull, but due in equal parts to the hardness of Curtis's head and Ellingsen's lack of strength, all the baseball coach suffered was a split scalp. Ellingsen apparently had cause for his actions, since he had been married to Anna Marsden for nearly two months.

"Damned homewrecker!" Mr. Ellingsen snapped from his cell in the city jail. "Casanova! Wife stealer! I hope he's crippled for life. But he won't be," he added gloomily. "I hit the oaf on the head!"

"I never knew she was married, and she never told me," Mr. Curtis explained. "I asked her to come up to my place to look at my Hogarth engravings. She could have refused if she wanted to, but she didn't."

"I don't know what happened. I can't explain it at all," Miss Marsden said wildly. "I love Reggie. I always will. We were going to keep our marriage a secret this year because of this silly school board rule about married couples working in the same school, and earn the down payment on a house. Everything was wonderful until Bill Curtis began chasing after me. I didn't like it and I wanted to tell him so, but I couldn't. I didn't want to go to his apartment, but when he asked me, I said yes. I tried to tell him I was married, but the words wouldn't come. It was like I was sitting outside myself watching something move me like a puppet. It was horrible!"

Sue Campbell ran off with Bill Reichart and got married, and their families were squabbling about an annulment. Bill didn't seem worried about it and Sue had forgotten about becoming a medical missionary and decided to become a mother instead. Somehow she developed an appalling domesticity that made Lenny oddly grateful that things turned out as they did, although for a couple of days he despised Sue and hated Bill. Fortunately it was close enough to graduation that the happy couple were assured of getting their degrees. After that it wouldn't matter. Reichart was going to college and Sue would go with him.

The baseball team won the remainder of its games by lopsided scores, went to the state tournament and was eliminated. Mary Ellen was home in bed with the flu.

Old Mr. Dodds took the wraps off his English History course the last two weeks before finals and gave his students enough details about the Regency Period to arouse a burning love for scatology in the breasts of students who had never cared for history at all. He also gave the class a blanket "A." He was promptly suspended for conduct unbecoming a teacher and went chortling into retirement.

"I've been wanting to do that for thirty years," he chuckled as he made his way through a crowd of admiring students after his last session with the School Board. "For thirty years I've taught emasculated pap for children and I finally got tired of it. This time I gave them the facts."

"What do you intend to do now?" a reporter asked. "The Board can't allow you to continue teaching. They've got you labeled as a menace to society. In Socrates' time they'd have fed you a hemlock cocktail."

"I couldn't care less," Dodds said. "It makes no difference what they do. I'm six months past retirement, so they can't take away my pension. That was my last class. I stayed on only because I was asked." Mr. Dodds chuckled. "I guess I have finally become too old to be worried about anything. I was tired of distorting the truth. Put it down to senile dementia if you wish."

"Your diagnosis may be correct," the reporter said, "but I doubt it."

"You might be right," Dodds replied. "That could have been the only sane act of my entire life."

And while this was going on and the staid order of John Tyler High School was being destroyed, things were happening to Lenny. His shoelaces came untied. His books disappeared. Drinks spilled on him. He stumbled and fell in empty corridors, and suffered embarrassing rips in his trousers. Things were constantly getting in his way. Accidents clung to him as though he was their patron saint. He developed alertness and a sixth sense of impending disaster that enabled him to dodge things like falling fire axes and flower pots. Lenny was certain that Mary Ellen was behind the trouble. He was always conscious of her presence. And gradually, his feeling of resentment and persecution turned from fear to a growing anger. Enough was enough. He had no desire to become a statistic, but he was damned if he'd spend the rest of the school year looking over his shoulder or listening for things that went bump in the dark. He was damned if he was going to duck every time a bird flew over his head. He'd see Mary Ellen alone and settle this once and for all.

It took two days to corner her in a deserted corridor.

"I've taken all I'm going to," Lenny told her fiercely. "Now get off my back and stay off."

"You just think you have, Lenny Stone," Mary Ellen replied. "I haven't even started on you!" Her eyes widened and her slim body tensed. "You're going to regret the day you jilted me!"

"I never—" Lenny began.

"Don't lie! You kissed me last summer, and then went right over to Sue Campbell."

"Good grief—did you think I meant anything? That was just common courtesy. You girls expect to be kissed. I've known that from junior high."

"No boy ever kissed me before. You lied to me and you'll pay for it."

"The way you're overreacting, a guy would think we made out," Lenny said. "I wouldn't touch you with tongs. You're a weirdo of the worst kind. And if you're worrying about me kissing you—don't. It won't happen again. Just lay off, that's all I ask. I don't want any part of you, anytime. Get out of my life and stay out of it. I don't give a damn what you do to anyone else, even though I know you're responsible for everything that's wrong around here. I don't know how you do it, but so help me, if you try to put the whammy on me again I'll—"

"You'll what?"

"I don't know—but it'll be something drastic." '

Mary's body tensed and Lenny felt an overwhelming weight settle on his shoulders. His knees buckled under the strain and his body sagged as it was forced toward the floor. "I'd

love to see you crawl!'' Mary Ellen gritted. ''You snake!''—
and he was a snake, complete with skin and scales. He
wanted to slither away from here. An empty high school
corridor was no place for a snake. He shivered and straightened. This was wrong! He wasn't a snake; he was a man!
Sweat poured from his face as he forced his sagging body
erect, hands clawing at the air for support. One hand struck
Mary Ellen's shoulder, and as it did, a sharp gasp came from
the girl. The weight on his back was gone, his scales vanished. Volition rushed back to his muscles—and Mary Ellen
writhed on her back on the corridor floor looking up at him
with hate-filled eyes. ''You pushed me!'' she gasped. ''You
knocked me down!''

''I told you I'd do something if you tried any more fancy
tricks,'' Lenny said heavily. ''So long Mary—see you around.''
He turned from her and walked away, slowly at first. Then he
began to run. He skidded around a corner and disappeared.

Mary Ellen rose to her feet. Rage radiated from her. He
had made a fool of her again. The window beside her exploded
in a burst of flying glass. Two girls coming down the corridor
were slammed against the wall. Mary stood in the center of
a whirlpool of fury. The floor heaved, a crack appeared in
the ceiling, chunks of plaster fell, and a rain of fine gray
dust drifted down in crazy patterns through the tortured air.

Mary gasped at the ruin surrounding her. Was *she* doing
this? The thought that Lenny might be right crossed her mind,
followed by a wave of terror. For if he *was* right, she'd be
expelled—maybe even sent to jail! But on the heels of her
terror came another thought. If Lenny was right, and she did
have this kind of power, there must be a way of controlling
it—Mary Ellen's lips curled in a peculiar half smile that was
hard and unpleasant. Lenny Stone would whistle a different
tune when she got through with him! Meantime, she'd better
do something about those two girls. They had seen her and
the wreckage that surrounded her, and they would talk. They'd
cackle like hens. She'd make them forget—make them forget
everything! She began walking slowly toward them. . . .

Emily Jones intruded into her husband's martini with the
expertise of nearly two decades of marriage. ''John,'' she

said, "this can't go on much longer. Mary Ellen's already damaged the Ellingsens' marriage, got poor Mr. Curtis beat up, put Mrs. Albritton in the hospital, ruined Mr. Dodd's reputation, interfered with the lives of Bill Reichart and Susan Campbell, and made amnesiacs of Ellen Andress and Tami Johnston." Emily eyed her husband accusingly. "You're her father," she said. "Do something! You should have known she'd be a tween before we were done here."

"You're overreacting," Jones said. "Just what can I do? Who can do anything with a tween?"

"We should have watched her more closely. It's our fault."

"For heaven's sake, stop acting like the natives. It's not our fault. Tweens are as old as history. Can't you remember what you were like?"

Emily blushed. "I can," she said, "and that's what worries me."

"Damn it!" Jones said. "It's bad enough living in this crazy breast-beating society without adopting its attributes. I figure we have at least another six months. Kids grow up fast in this environment, but not that fast. We'll be in the Arizona desert working with the Navaho by June and after that phase is over we can go home. I suppose living around sexually mature youngsters fourteen or fifteen years old has some effect but it'll wear off once we get into a more stable environment. However, I'll put your data into the matricizer and run it out."

"What good will that do? What we need is a way to handle Mary Ellen right now. We aren't going to be able to carry this bag of worms by ourselves. You know that."

"We're not going to do a thing as long as they don't suspect her; we're going to keep our hands off. I'm in the final phase of this study and if I abort it now we'll wind up in Limbo, or on the backside of the moon, or some other misbegotten place where we'd be conveniently forgotten. We'd spend the rest of our lives scratching flea bites and shaking dust out of our clothing. We simply have to stick it out."

Emily shook her head. "I think you're wrong, John. There are three weeks left, and by that time—if she keeps growing—Mary Ellen can destroy the school. I don't even want to think of what can happen to the graduation ceremony if she comes to it in as foul a mood as she was in this afternoon. She uprooted a whole row of petunias along the front walk as she came in. Didn't leave a speck of earth on the roots and she never came within three feet of them! I don't think she noticed the damage that followed her from the bus and no one was on the street. No, John, we simply must leave."

"We can't. I can't even pack my records in a week."

"Call a moving company."

"Are you mad? One of those people might be intelligent enough to know what he was packing. Do you want to blow our cover?"

"I want to get out of here."

"Why? No one has accused us of anything. No one suspects Mary Ellen. We can hold out another two or three weeks."

"I suppose you want to wait until she kills someone. Do you want your daughter to be a murderess?"

"She isn't going to kill anyone. She's been raised to respect life."

"And how much does that mean to a tween in the middle of an emotional storm?"

"Damn it, Emily! I'm not going to blow fifteen years' work just to keep an adolescent from acting like an idiot!"

"I wasn't thinking of us—or even of Mary Ellen." Emily said, "I was thinking of the people around us. They're nice inoffensive folks, but they don't really understand what children can do. They take a dim view of vandalism, mayhem, and murder, and they have absolutely no experience handling tweens. If Mary Ellen is discovered as the cause of all this, they might even try to restrain her."

Jones gulped. He had a mental picture of what might happen, and it wasn't pleasant. A chilly grue squiggled down his spine. He shivered, and not entirely from the cold. Once the plaster stopped falling and the bodies were removed from the wreckage, his cover would be blown wide open. And naturally, people would draw the wrong conclusions, and a century of study and preparation would go down the drain. The prospect was appalling. "They'd think we were spies," he said. "They might even think we were a prelude to invasion."

"Well—aren't we?"

"Not that way. We want to open trade, not war. We want to exchange technology."

"Doesn't it amount to the same thing in the end? We'll eventually make an economic conquest, and that can be just as bad as a military one."

"No one gets killed."

"Not directly. But the inferior culture doesn't survive. It gets replaced. And in the end we conquer as surely as if we came with bombs and blasters."

John shrugged. "That's not our affair. We have nothing to do with the economics of empire. We simply collect demographic and sociopolitical data."

"You're being awfully narrow-minded. Can't you remember what happened to Enserala? Or won't you think of what happened to the primitive societies here when they came into contact with Europe? The primitive society always dies except for a few taboos and inconsequential customs."

Jones sighed. He couldn't forget it even though he tried. The path of empire was strewn with the corpses of civilizations and cultures. It was inevitable. One could take some comfort in the thought that nothing could be done to a Class B culture that was half as bad as the things the culture did to itself if it developed in the direction of nation-states. This world had a fairly poor prognosis. Indeed it was a miracle that it had lasted as long as it had. But there was a hard streak of self-preservation in its peoples. At least they'd never started a nuclear war. Somehow despite their mass hysterias, their irrationality, their uncontrolled appetites, their overbreeding, their prides, ideologies, and bigotry, they never took that catastrophic final step. It had aroused Imperial curiosity several decades ago after the first surveys gave the planet a potential lifespan of about fifty standard years. The world had already lasted almost a hundred and seemed in no particular haste to exterminate itself. Yet the inhabitants were to all intents and purposes a nonsurvival type. They were hardly more than tweens without psi—children masquerading as adults. And their continued existence drew the attention of Empire. They might be useful.

"They need to trade with us," Jones said. "We can educate them in the ways of peace and self-control."

"You don't mention that trade is the lifeblood of our society," Emily said. "Without it, we'd have died long ago."

"It gives us a reason for existence," he admitted.

"And increases our power and prestige, and gives our people places to go and things to do."

"It's not our fault that our ancestors overpopulated our world."

"I won't argue that. We're stuck with a demographic fact, and we have learned to live with it, but I don't like thinking that this beautiful world will become another Lyrane."

"Emily—we need this world. The Council has it on first priority. Even though I like these people and don't want to see them hurt, I can't scrap my own loyalties. The survey and investigation *must* go on. Without data we can accomplish nothing."

"They're not going to forgive us if Mary Ellen runs wild," Emily answered.

Jones shrugged. It was a rotten little problem. "Does she hate anyone?" he asked. "Or is she behaving in a reasonably normal tween fashion?"

"I think she doesn't like Lenny Stone, but mainly she's peaking and bottoming out emotionally."

"Is Stone that kid who was hanging around most of last summer? The one whose parents work in the city?"

Emily nodded.

"I can't see why she'd hate him. He's not worth that much thought."

"She's a tween."

"Poor Lenny. I should warn him. It might be well if he left town."

"He'd think you were crazy." Emily said.

"Hey! what's going on here? Are you two plotting something?" Mary Ellen's voice preceded her into the room. "I come down for a glass of milk and find you two whispering over martinis like a pair of spies. What's up?"

Jones looked at his daughter and choked back a reply that sprang to his lips. She was a very satisfactory tween, leggy, elf-faced, with eyes of clearest green that were almost too large. Her bones were good and her body was beginning to mature. Odd that he hadn't noticed—but he'd been busy the last few months. She was tween all right. There was something fey, alien, and appealing about her, like a Keane painting come to life. "It's grown-up talk, sprout," he said. "None of your business."

"We were talking about your future," Emily said.

"Maybe you ought to let me in on it," Mary Ellen said.

"We will, in due time," Emily said blandly. "This talk was about college and money and a career—the kind of background data we have to talk about before we put the savings account on the line."

Such a magnificent liar, John thought with admiration. The diplomatic service lost a star performer when Emily married and went with him on this mission.

"After all, dear, you're our only child and we are concerned about you. The way time passes and the way you kids grow nowadays it's almost no time before you're adults. You'll even be able to vote this fall, and chances are you'll be away from home and in college."

"I don't think I want to go to college."

"Why not?"

"Oh, I don't know. I'm sort of tired of school. It's getting to be a real drag. I think I'd like to get a job, like maybe with the paper, the U.N. or the Peace Corps."

"You're old enough, but you'd be better off in school."

"As usual, you don't understand," Mary Ellen said. "I have to get out. It's—you know—a drag. Irrelevant."

"Stop mouthing," John said. "In the first place I don't know, and in the second there's nothing more relevant to a modern technological society than education."

"You sound like a teacher, Daddy."

"Oh—I won't stop you if you want to get a job. You'll learn a lot from the experience. And besides, if you earn money you can pay board, which will help our budget."

"Mercenary," Mary Ellen said.

Jones grinned. The conversation was safely sidetracked. He hoped that neither the strain nor the relief showed in his face. It had taken a genuine effort to keep from blurting it out when Mary Ellen had wanted a straight answer badly enough to push for it. If it hadn't been for Emily, he might have done just that. He thought bitterly that life had some damnably unpleasant episodes during its passage. This was going to be one of them. There was no question that the girl was dangerous. . . . He'd have to warn Lenny. . . . And he'd have to be prepared to brainwash the kid if he wouldn't listen to reason. . . .

John Jones leaned over the table in the back of McGonigle's Pizza Parlor and looked at the skinny kid with the shock of black hair who sat on the base of his spine and eyed a half-consumed Idiot's Delight pizza and an empty Coke bottle. The boy's face was moody and introspective.

"Are you Lenny Stone?" Jones asked.

"Yeah—that's me."

"I'm Mary Ellen's father."

"I remember you from last summer. And if Mary Ellen's said anything about me, she's lying."

"It's not that. I want to talk with you."

"No way. I don't want anything to do with you—or your daughter. Anything related to Mary Ellen is bad news."

"I don't care what you want. I must warn you. Your life is in danger. Mary Ellen is capable of destroying you. I'm trying to do you a favor."

Lenny shook his head. "Naw—she can't hurt me. All she can do is hurt my friends."

"That's not very charitable."

"Who said I was charitable? Look, Mr. Jones, I hate her guts. She pesters me. She broke up my thing with Sue Campbell. She louses up my classes. The only favor you could do me would be to move far away and take Mary Ellen with you."

"I've considered that," Jones said. He would have been amused if he weren't so worried. Lenny and Emily had the same solution, and the same objections still applied. He couldn't move—not now. It was Lenny who'd have to go. Mary Ellen would murder him! Lenny was a poor innocent idiot playing with the trigger of a loaded machine gun. "The only trouble is that I can't move right now. But maybe you could. I'll pay the expenses."

"No way," Lenny said. "No girl is going to run me out of

town, and besides, my folks wouldn't let me go." He eyed
Jones with a mixture of suspicion and curiosity. He felt
drawn to the man. There was none of the strangeness about
him that marked his daughter.

"I wish I could do this easily," Jones said, "but I can't.
Somehow I have to make you understand that my daughter
can kill you, and that she'll probably do just that if you stay
around. She has powers most people don't possess."

"You're telling me? She's a witch." Lenny nodded.. "I've
known that for weeks, but nobody believes me when I tell
them. She hexed Mr. Ellingsen. She whammied the baseball
team. She— "

"She's not a witch. She's perfectly normal."

"Ha!" Lenny eyed Jones speculatively and wondered if
he'd gone too far. Fathers weren't noted for tolerating kids
who bad-mouthed their daughters. But, oddly enough, Mr.
Jones wasn't affected. He might love Mary Ellen, although
Lenny couldn't see why, but the love didn't affect his temper.
"Look, sir," Lenny said, "I took Mary Ellen out last summer. I kissed her a few times, but we didn't do anything else,
no matter what she says."

"She hasn't said anything except that she hates you. Why
did you stop dating?"

"She got too possessive. Acted like she owned me. I
didn't like it very much, so I dropped her. A week or so later
she chewed me out and told me she hated me."

"When was that?"

"Last September." Lenny shrugged. "She kept telling me
all fall and winter term. Kept saying, 'Just you wait, Lenny
Stone. I'll fix you!' "

Jones shivered. "Get out of town, Lenny. I know what I'm
talking about. You haven't got a chance."

"But she can't really hurt me. She's tried."

"She hasn't got her full powers yet," Jones said. "The
best thing you can do is get away while you still can. Get
lost. Vanish. Visit relatives. Don't come back until we're
gone. I'm leaving in June—by the tenth I'll be far from here
and so will Mary Ellen. You'd be safe then."

"Hey—you're really worried."

"You damn well know I am." Jones stared at Lenny as

though he could force his fears and concern into the young man's mind. The light from the window fell on Lenny's face. It had a stark quality not normally found in an adolescent.

Lenny shook his head. "It's my graduation as much as hers," he said. "I belong there as much as she does. I'm staying."

Jones sighed. "All right, Lenny, let's do it the hard way."

"What do you mean by that?"

"This." Jones said. His face hardened and Lenny watched him with mild uneasiness. He was going to get mad after all.

"Are you mad at me for calling Mary Ellen a witch? Are you—hey—leggo—you can't—" Lenny's voice ran down and stopped as he sat with glassy eyes clamped in a fixed stare on Jones's tense face.

This has to be fast, Jones thought. He had perhaps a minute before one of Pop McGonigle's teenage customers was going to notice that Lenny was somewhere on cloud nine. He marshaled what he thought were the most important things for Lenny's safety, gave the necessary instructions, planted the posthypnotic suggestions, and awakened Lenny.

"Goodbye, Lenny, and good luck," he said.

"Sorry, sir, but I couldn't leave anyway. My parents would object, and I don't have any relatives."

Jones smiled. "Well—you've been warned. I guess that's all I can do. . . ." He walked out of the store feeling reasonably happy. By tomorrow, Lenny should be a hundred miles or more from here. . . .

Mary Ellen faced her father across the dinner table. "What were you talking about with Lenny Stone down at McGonigle's?" she asked. "And don't say you weren't because I saw you. I want to know."

"Now Mary—" Emily protested.

"*I want to know!*"

"That's no way to talk to your father."

"I don't care—you can't touch me. I've got something that makes me bigger than either of you. I've found out all about it."

"Is the high school still standing?" Jones asked. Sweat broke out on his forehead. He was conscious of a horrid compulsion to tell everything. He clenched his teeth. Mary had a last arrived at control of her powers. She was strong—as strong as Emily had been. He was right when he told Lenny that he couldn't control her—but he hadn't dreamed how right he was. He'd thought he could deny her. That was his worst mistake.

Suddenly he was suspended in midair looking down at the tight angry face of his daughter. The thought that she had learned a lot in a very short time dominated his brain. He had a reasonable certainty that he wasn't going to be hurt physically, even though his position was ridiculous. Adults simply didn't levitate. That was kid stuff.

"Mary! Put your father down this minute!" Emily ordered. She couldn't resist the wry thought that she would love to be in her daughter's place right now. But of course she wasn't, and after all, she couldn't have done a thing like this to John. Still, he *was* a stubborn, opinionated, and unreasonable man at times, and a good shaking would do him a world of good.

"I want to know what he was talking to Lenny about," Mary Ellen said, "and I'm not going to let him down till I do." She smiled a tight, hard, smug little smile. "I've found out what I can do—and how to do it," she said. "I'm maybe the most powerful person in the world. And you're going to tell me what I want to know and do what I want you to do—or—I'll—"

"You'll what?" Lenny asked. He stood in the kitchen door, looking at the suddenly frozen tableau. There was a solid thump as Jones's buttocks made contact with the floor, followed by three lesser thumps as heels and head followed the example of his behind. He scrambled to his feet, his face a study in anger and embarrassment.

"You!" Mary Ellen screeched at Lenny. "Go away! Get out of here!"

"Why?"

"Thanks," Jones said. "I'm glad you showed up, but you should be running for your life."

"Mom said you did a pretty good job for a quickie," Lenny said. "You left only a couple of loose ends. But those were enough. You gave me no motivation that would stand probing. I don't know that I told you, but I can't hide anything from Mom. Anyway, it lookes as though I came just in time.''

''You did. I'm too old to appreciate being the centrum of a psi effect.''

''I told you to get out of here,'' Mary Ellen said, glaring at Lenny.

''Get lost,'' Lenny said.

Jones shuddered. In about ten seconds there would be bloodshed.

''I am going to wring you out and hang you up to dry,'' Mary Ellen said. ''I am going to smash you and shred the pieces. I am going to break you into little bits. I know what I can do!''

''Big talk,'' Lenny said. He stood in front of her, his face twisted into a mocking grin. ''There's a lot of hot air in you that ought to be let out,'' he said. ''You're all puffed up. Your hubris is showing. You need deflating.''

Mary Ellen ground her teeth and her face turned livid with anger.

''Run!'' Emily gasped. ''You've gone too far! She'll kill you!''

The air in the room thickened and writhed and became a gelid something that wasn't air. Forces gathered, poised, pulsed, and as Mary Ellen paused to focus the effect, Lenny reached out and touched her. Something snatched Mary Ellen, spun her through the air and bounced her off the floor! The room shook, the walls creaked, plaster fell, and a dead calm descended upon the Jones kitchen.

Emily's eyes opened with a mixture of amazement and realization. Jones grinned, and Mary Ellen looked at Lenny with hate-filled eyes. ''You did it again!'' she said. ''Damn you!''

''It's a good thing you have a well-padded behind,'' Lenny said. ''That was quite a wallop.''

''It hurts,'' Mary Ellen said.

''Maybe it'll teach you not to act stupid,'' Lenny said. ''I told your dad that you couldn't hurt me. You can't. You and I—we're complements. We cancel out. You're a psi positive. I'm negative. It's a defense mechanism our race has had from the beginning. We'd never have survived if a bunch of nutty tweens could damage each other and everyone else because they had no self-control. Of course, psi effects were useful to discourage predators and other big terrifying things. But except for telepathy they're no good to help the race become civilized. When you can't lie you've gotta be honest. But psychokinetics such as you have are no good for anything nowadays."

"What are you talking about? I don't get it."

"Don't worry, you will as soon as your mom gets through talking to you. My mom told me about it before she sent me over here. And I guess it's a good thing she did. You were making an idiot out of yourself and you might have done something real bad. You can't help being a tween any more than I can—it's part of growing up. But you can help being stupid."

Mary Ellen got slowly to her feet. It dawned on her that she was abysmally ignorant, and from the expressions on her parents' faces she realized that she was the only one who was. Her parents knew exactly what Lenny was saying. It wasn't fair, she thought. And from the relaxed smile on her father's face she was certain that whatever had happened, it was something that took a monkey off his back. The thought was ambivalent.

"Just keep a hand on her, Lenny," Jones said. "Emily's bound to have her bracelets around somewhere. She never throws anything away." Jones sighed with relief. "I suppose I should have guessed. You practically told me down at McGonigle's, but I wasn't thinking very well. I had a mental picture of you on a marble slab."

"Don't worry about the bracelets," Lenny said. "Mom gave me hers. She figured you might need them." He reached into his jacket pocket and took out a plain gold bracelet. There wasn't anything unusual about it except that it locked with a final-sounding click when he closed it around Mary Ellen's wrist. "I'm wearing the mate to it," Lenny said, pushing back the left sleeve of his jacket to show an identical bracelet around his lean wrist. "She can't do anything now. As long as I'm around, she's neutralized."

"It's a miracle!" Emily said. "To think that there was a complementary—why the odds against it are in the millions!"

"Not quite," Lenny said. "You see, Mrs. Jones, my folks were transferred from Chicago because my psych profile and Mary Ellen's were almost identical. The—the Council?" He paused and Jones nodded. "The Council," Lenny continued, "thought Mary Ellen would go tween earlier on this world than on Lyrane— something to do with the kind of sunlight and the shortness of the years. Since my pattern fitted hers to four decimal points, they figured I was almost certainly complementary, so they sent my parents here. I guess you have a higher research priority than Dad. Anyway, I don't know much about these things."

"I expect we should have told Mary Ellen," Emily said.

"You should have," Lenny said. "Tweens aren't really stupid or uncooperative, we're merely young."

"Have you learned the standing rules?" Jones asked.

"No, but Mom said that was why we never got in touch. We were ready if needed, but we weren't supposed to contact you. That was why she broke me off with Mary Ellen last summer. I kinda liked her, but Mom brainwashed it out of me. It might have been better if she hadn't. Besides, she thinks you're crazy to bring a girl here."

"Mary Ellen was born here," Emily said.

"You're going to stay with us, of course," Jones said.

"Naturally. Your assignment's about over and Mom wants me to go home for advanced training. I think I'd like to be a psychologician, and you can't get that sort of education on this world. My folks say it's all right if I go with you to Arizona. They'll both be interested in financial operations this summer. And when you're done I can go home with you."

"Good!" Emily said.

Mary Ellen shook her head. "I won't stand for this," she said. "If Lenny comes into this house, I'm leaving!"

"You're not going anywhere," Lenny said, "or doing anything except graduate from dear old John Tyler High. After that, you and I and your parents are going to take a long trip to a place called Lyrane. And when the people there get through with us, we'll be adults. And maybe then I won't look so much like a louse to you, and you won't look so much like a witch to me."

"Mom!"—*do* something!"

Emily shrugged. Her pleasant face wore a tight Gioconda smile, half loving, half cruel. Looking at her, Jones wondered if the Mona Lisa had been a Lyranian. It was hardly possible, but there was more than a passing resemblance. "Dear," Emily said, "I can't do a thing about it. You'll simply have to grow up and become decently inhuman."

THE BOY WHO BROUGHT LOVE

by Edward D. Hoch

On Crucis Two, the second planet of the sun Alpha Crucis, men still talk of the boy Serov. Some say he possessed magic powers, while others claim his only power was the ability to speak to the people and to lead them. Whatever the truth, it was Serov who caused the downfall of the evil King Hapan. And he did it with a gift of love.

It had been a century of troubles for the people of Crucis Two, when solar storms buffeted the planet and space pirates from other worlds landed by night to kill and burn. Such conditions had caused the rise of the great King Hapan, and the fact that he was an evil man was overlooked in the struggle for survival. Hapan ruled with an iron fist, crushing the space pirates and even calming the solar storms with the aid of great reflecting mirrors. But in the process he doomed many of his own people, many of the loyal citizens of Crucis Two.

It was in such a time that the boy Serov was first seen, wandering with the other orphans among the endless desert camps where those without families lingered and often died. He was no more than ten or eleven years old, and the clothes hung loosely from his frail body. But when he spoke, the older men and women listened.

"Some say he is a wizard," his advisers told Hapan. "He talks in words too wise for one so young."

Hapan, whose title was Ruler of the Suns, glowered at those around him. "You tell me that I can defeat the space pirates and tame the sun itself and yet a ten-year-old boy

121

can upset my people with his talk? What does he tell them?''

"He speaks of freedom and beauty," they said.

Hapan was an old man at that time, tired and unwell. But he still ruled his people with unyielding force, and he was not ready to see his power diminished by the words of a mere boy. "Arrest him," he ordered. "Bring him to me!"

The boy Serov was seized in the marketplace as he spoke to the people, and brought before the ruler in chains. "Well," King Hapan said, staring down at the boy before him. "You have given me a great deal of trouble in recent days."

The boy lifted his chained hands. "I come in peace. I am no wizard. I only speak to the people of love and beauty!"

"You spread uncertainty and distrust. You spread the germs of rebellion where before there dwelt only the healthy seeds of loyalty. I have ruled here many years on Crucis Two, and you do not win my kingdom so easily."

"I bring only love," the boy insisted. "Do you fear that?"

Hapan did not fear love, and yet as he stared down at the face of the chained boy, he knew there was a danger here. This was not an ordinary boy to be won over with trips to the space zoo or the hologram theater. The face of Serov held kindness and love, but it held something else too. Perhaps it held a vision of all the forces King Hapan had repressed during the years of his rule.

"If I had you tortured or killed, would you respond with love?" he asked.

"Yes." The boy smiled. "Sometimes love can be a powerful weapon. Sometimes love can even destroy."

The king only laughed. "You can destroy me with love?"

"Yes." The boy spread out his chained hands. "I could send you a gift of love that would kill as surely as a laser beam, and yet I think you would die happy."

King Hapan at last grew fearful of this talk, and he ordered the guards to abandon Serov in the wilderness, where the boy might wander and finally perish from lack of food.

That was the last anyone saw of the boy for many months, and Hapan assumed that he had indeed perished. In time the memory of him passed, and the king began to make preparations for the annual Festival of Welcome.

For as long as anyone on Crucis Two could remember, the coming of spring had been the occasion for great rejoicing. The celebration centered about the Festival of Welcome, at which all the people of the area were invited to pay their respects to the king. Hapan would stand at the gate of his great chrome palace, touching hands with all who came, and sometimes the line would stretch for miles. It was the custom that he remained at the gate until all had been greeted, and in earlier, happier days the ruler often stood there through half the night—until the very last of his subjects had departed for home. Now he was lucky if a few hundred came to touch his hand.

So the day of the Festival dawned, sunny and warm, as were all spring days on the planet. He walked to the palace gate and was pleased to see that the line had already formed to greet him. It seemed longer than last year's line had been, and his heart was gladdened. Perhaps it was a sign that the people were accepting the necessary harshness of his rule at last. He touched the first man's hands and murmured the traditional words of greeting.

By the time the fifth hour had passed, he knew there would be more to greet him than in previous years. Some were the familiar faces of his palace staff, but there were many strangers too. By their dusty garments he could see they had traveled far to see him this day, and he gave them an extra word of greeting and a squeeze of the hand.

By evening the line ahead seemed no shorter, and only the pleasure of it all kept him from tiring. Word of the event had spread throughout the kingdom, and an amazing thing was beginning to happen. Men and women who had never in their lives come to the Festival of Welcome began now to appear in the line. Some he even recognized as former enemies, and he wondered what had brought them to pay tribute to him.

When dawn came, the line at the palace gate was still nearly a mile long, and through his bleary old eyes Hapan began to suspect that some of the strangers were coming through twice. He considered calling a halt to the Festival of Welcome, but to do such a thing would only be a sign of weakness and age. He would last for a few more hours, till noon at least, and certainly by then all would have passed by him.

But once again, as the line dwindled to only a dozen or so men, and King Hapan began to dream of sleep, others came from the countryside. Men and women working on the big synthetic farms put down their tools to join the line. Noon passed, and the heat of the day was upon his head.

Hapan licked his parched lips and sent for wine. It refreshed him, and soon he returned to the touching of hands.

On the morning of the third day he was barely able to stand, and still they came. He recognized more of his old enemies, and wondered why they had joined the line. He saw children from the space schools, and marveled at what brought them here. Toward nightfall he had a chair brought to the palace gate because he could no longer stand.

Yet still they came.

He was weaker on the fourth day, and now he knew with a certainty that he must call an end to this madness. Yet they came on, and he touched them all. Now even his own palace guards and household joined in the procession, lengthening it once again.

On the fifth day, toward noon, he could no longer hold up his head. He slumped in the chair and would have slept, except for the persistence of those who touched his hand.

Toward evening on the fifth day he opened his old eyes for the last time, and he saw before him the familiar face of the boy Serov, standing now at the head of the line.

"When?" Hapan managed to ask. "When will this all end?"

And the boy answered, "Never, my king. This line goes on forever, because it is made up not of your friends but of your enemies. This is the gift of love I promised you. Love from your enemies. A love to destroy you."

And the old king closed his eyes forever, slumping lower in his chair, and the people praised the boy who had freed them.

THE VACATION

by Ray Bradbury

It was a day as fresh as grass growing up and clouds going over and butterflies coming down could make it. It was a day compounded of silences of bee and flower and ocean and land, which were not silences at all, but motions, stirs, flutters, risings, fallings, each in their own time and matchless rhythm. The land did not move, but moved. The sea was not still, yet was still. Paradox flowed into paradox, stillness mixed with stillness, sound with sound. The flowers vibrated and the bees fell in separate and small showers of golden rain on the clover. The seas of hill and the seas of ocean were divided, each from the other's motion, by a railroad track, empty, compounded of rust and iron marrow, a track on which, quite obviously, no train had run in many years. Thirty miles north it swirled on away to farther mists of distance, thirty miles south it tunneled islands of cloud shadows that changed their continental positions on the sides of far mountains as you watched.

Now, suddenly, the railway track began to tremble.

A blackbird, standing on the rail, felt a rhythm grow faintly, miles away, like a heart beginning to beat.

The blackbird leaped up over the sea.

The rail continued to vibrate softly until at long last around a curve and along the shore came a small workman's handcar, its two-cylinder engine popping and spluttering in the great silence.

On top of this small four-wheeled car, on a double-sided bench facing in two directions and with a little surrey roof above for shade, sat a man, his wife and their small seven-year-old son. As the handcar traveled through lonely stretch after lonely stretch, the wind whipped their eyes and blew their hair, but they did not look back but only ahead. Sometimes they looked eagerly, as a curve unwound itself, sometimes with great sadness, but always watchful, ready for the next scene.

As they hit a level straightaway, the machine's engine gasped and stopped abruptly. In the now-crushing silence, it seemed that the quiet of the earth, sky and sea itself, by its friction, brought the car to a wheeling halt.

"Out of gas."

The man, sighing, reached for the extra can in the small storage bin and began to pour it into the tank.

His wife and son sat quietly looking at the sea, listening to the muted thunder, the whisper, the drawing back of huge tapestries of sand, gravel, green weed and foam.

"Isn't the sea nice?" said the woman.

"I like it," said the boy.

"Shall we picnic here, while we're at it?"

The man focused binoculars on the green peninsula ahead.

"Might as well. The rails have rusted badly. There's a break ahead. We may have to wait while I set a few back in place."

"As many as there are," said the boy, "we'll have picnics!"

The woman tried to smile at this, then turned her grave attention to the man. "How far have we come today?"

"Not ninety miles." The man still peered through the glasses, squinting. "I don't like to go farther than that any one day, anyway. If you rush, there's no time to see. We'll reach Monterey day after tomorrow, Palo Alto the next day, if you want."

The woman removed her great shadowing straw hat which had been tied over her golden hair with a bright yellow ribbon, and stood perspiring faintly, away from the machine. They had ridden so steadily on the shuddering rail car that the motion was sewn in their bodies. Now, with the stopping, they felt odd, on the verge of unraveling.

"Let's eat!"

The boy ran with the wicker lunch basket down to the shore.

The boy and the woman were already seated by a spread tablecloth when the man came down to them, dressed in his business suit and vest and tie and hat as if he expected to meet someone along the way. As he dealt out the sandwiches and exhumed the pickles from their cool green Mason jars, he began to loosen his tie and unbutton his vest, always looking around as if he should be careful and ready to button up again.

"Are you all alone, Papa?" said the boy, eating.

"Yes."

"No one else, anywhere?"

"No one else."

"Were there people before?"

"Why do you keep asking that? It wasn't that long ago. Just a few months. You remember?"

"Almost. If I try hard, then I don't remember at all." The boy let a handful of sand fall through his fingers. "Were there as many people as there is sand here on the beach? What *happened* to them?"

"I don't know," the man said, and it was true.

They had wakened one morning and the world was empty. The neighbor's clothesline was still strung with blowing white wash, cars gleamed in front of other seven-A.M. cottages, but there were no farewells, the city did not hum with its mighty arterial traffics, phones did not alarm themselves, children did not wail in sunflower wildernesses.

Only the night before he and his wife had been sitting on the front porch when the evening paper was delivered and, not even daring to open to the headlines, he had said, "I wonder when He will get tired of us and just rub us all out?"

"It has gone pretty far," she said. "On and on. We're such fools, aren't we?"

"Wouldn't it be nice"—he lit his pipe and puffed it—"if we woke tomorrow and everyone in the world was gone and everything was starting over?" He sat smoking, the paper folded in his hand, his head resting back on the chair.

"If you could press a button right now and make it happen, would you?"

"I think I would," he said. "Nothing violent. Just have everyone vanish off the face of the earth. Just leave the land

and the sea and the growing things like flowers and grass and fruit trees. And the animals, of course, let them stay. Everything except man, who hunts when he isn't hungry, eats when full, and is mean when no one's bothered him."

"Naturally," she smiled, quietly, "we would be left."

"I'd like that," he mused. "All of time ahead. The longest summer vacation in history. And us out for the longest picnic-basket lunch in memory. Just you, me and Jim. No commuting. No keeping up with the Joneses. Not even a car. I'd like to find another way of traveling, an older way . . . then, a hamper full of sandwiches, three bottles of pop, pick up supplies where you need them from empty grocery stores in empty towns, and summertime forever up ahead . . ."

They sat a long while on the porch in silence, the newspaper folded between them.

At last she spoke.

"Wouldn't we be *lonely*?" she said.

So that's how it was the morning of the first day of the new world. They had awakened to the soft sounds of an earth that was now no more than a meadow, and the cities of the earth sinking back into seas of saber grass, marigold, marguerite and morning-glory. They had taken it with remarkable calm at first, perhaps because they had not liked the city for so many years and had had so many friends who were not truly friends, and had lived a boxed and separate life of their own within a mechanical hive.

The husband arose and looked out the window and observed very calmly, as if it were a weather condition, "Everyone's gone . . ." knowing this just by the sounds the city had ceased to make.

They took their time over breakfast, for the boy was still asleep, and then the husband sat back and said, "Now I must plan what to do."

"Do? Why, why you'll go to work, of course."

"You still don't believe it, do you?" he laughed. "That I won't be rushing off each day at 8:10, that Jim won't go to school again ever. School's out for all of us! No more pencils, no more books, no more boss' sassy looks! We're let out, darling, and we'll never come back to the silly damn dull routines. Come on!''

And he had walked her through the still and empty city streets.

"They didn't die," he said. "They just . . . went away."

"What about the other cities?"

He went to an outdoor phone both and dialed Chicago, then New York, then San Francisco.

Silence. Silence. Silence.

"That's it," he said, replacing the receiver.

"I feel guilty," she said. "They gone and we here. And . . . I feel happy. Why? I *should* be unhappy."

"Should you? It's no tragedy. They weren't tortured or blasted or burned. It went easily and they didn't know. And now we owe nothing to anyone. Our only responsibility *is* being happy. Thirty more years of happiness, wouldn't that be good?"

"But then we must have more children!"

"To repopulate the world?" He shook his head slowly, calmly. "No. Let Jim be the last. After he's grown and gone let the horses and cows and ground squirrels and garden spiders have the world. They'll get on. And someday some other species that can combine a natural happiness with a natural curiosity will build cities that won't even look like cities to us, and survive. Right now, let's go pack a basket, wake Jim and get going on that long thirty-year summer vacation. I'll beat you to the house!''

He took a sledge hammer from the small rail car and while he worked alone for half an hour fixing the rusted rails into place, the woman and the boy ran along the shore. They came back with dripping shells, a dozen or more, and some beautiful pink pebbles, and sat and the boy took schooling from the mother, doing homework on a pad with a pencil for a time; and then at high noon the man came down, his coat off, his tie thrown aside, and they drank orange pop, watching the bubbles surge up, glutting, inside the bottles. It was quiet. They listened to the sun tune the old iron rails. The smell of hot tar on the ties moved about them in the salt wind, as the husband tapped his atlas map lightly and gently:

"We'll go to Sacramento next month, May, then work up toward Seattle. Should make that by July first, July's a good month in Washington, then back down as the weather cools, to Yellowstone, a few miles a day, hunt here, fish there . . ."

The boy, bored, moved away to throw sticks in the sea and wade out like a dog to retrieve them.

The man went on: "Winter in Tucson, then, part of the winter, moving toward Florida, up the coast in the spring, and maybe New York by June. Two years from now, Chicago in the summer. Winter, three years from now, what about Mexico City? Anywhere the rails lead us, anywhere at all, and if we come to an old offshoot rail line we don't know anything about, what the hell, we'll just take it, go down it to see where it goes. And some year, by God, we'll boat down the Mississippi, always wanted to do that. Enough to last us a lifetime. And that's just how long I want to take to do it all . . ."

His voice faded. He started to fumble the map shut, but before he could move, a bright thing fell through the air and hit the paper. It rolled off into the sand and made a wet lump.

His wife glanced at the wet place in the sand and then swiftly searched his face. His solemn eyes were too bright. And down one cheek was a track of wetness.

She gasped. She took his hand and held it tight.

He clenched her hand very hard, his eyes shut now, and slowly he said, with difficulty:

"Wouldn't it be nice if we went to sleep tonight and in the night, somehow, it all came back. All the foolishness, all the noise, all the hate, all the terrible things, all the nightmares, all the wicked people and stupid children, all the mess, all the smallness, all the confusion, all the hope, all the need, all the love. Wouldn't it be nice?"

She waited and nodded her head once.

Then both of them started.

For standing between them, they knew not for how long, was their son, an empty pop bottle in one hand.

The boy's face was pale. With his free hand he reached out to touch his father's cheek where the single tear had made its track.

"You," he said. "Oh, Dad, you. You haven't anyone to play with, either . . ."

The wife started to speak.

The husband moved to take the boy's hand.

The boy jerked back. "Silly! Oh, silly! Silly fools! Oh, you dumb, dumb!" And, whirling, he rushed down to the ocean and stood there crying, loudly.

The wife rose to follow, but the husband stopped her.

"No. Let him."

And then they both grew cold and quiet. For the boy, below on the shore, crying steadily, now was writing on a piece of paper and stuffing it into the pop bottle and ramming the tin cap back on and taking the bottle and giving it a great glittering heave up in the air and out into the tidal sea.

What, thought the wife, what did he write on the note? What's in the bottle?

The bottle moved out in the waves.

The boy stopped crying.

After a long while he walked up the shore to stand looking at his parents. His face was neither bright nor dark, alive nor dead, ready nor resigned; it seemed a curious mixture that simply made do with time, weather and these people. They looked at him and beyond to the bay where the bottle, containing the scribbled note, was almost out of sight now, shining in the waves.

Did he write what *we* wanted? thought the woman; did he write what he heard us just wish, just say?

Or did he write something for only himself? she wondered, that tomorrow he might wake and find himself alone in an empty world, no one around, no man, no woman, no father, no mother, no fool grownups with fool wishes, so he could trudge up to the railroad tracks and take the handcar motoring, a solitary boy, across the continental wilderness, on eternal voyages and picnics?

Is that what he wrote in the note?

Which?

She searched his colorless eyes, could not read the answer; dared not ask.

Gull shadows sailed over and kited their faces with sudden passing coolness.

"Time to go," someone said.

They loaded the wicker basket onto the rail car. The woman tied her large bonnet securely in place with its yellow ribbon, they set the boy's pail of shells on the floor boards, then the husband put on his tie, his vest, his coat, his hat, and they all sat on the bench of the car looking out at the sea where the bottled note was far out, blinking on the horizon.

"Is asking enough?" said the boy. "Does wishing work?"

"Sometimes . . . *too* well."

"It depends on what you ask for."

The boy nodded, his eyes faraway.

They looked back at where they had come from, and then ahead to where they were going.

"Goodbye, place," said the boy, and waved.

The car rolled down the rusty rails. The sound of it dwindled, faded. The man, the woman, the boy dwindled with it in the distance, among the hills.

After they were gone, the rail trembled faintly for two minutes and ceased. A flake of rust fell. A flower nodded.

The sea was very loud.

THE ANYTHING BOX

by Zenna Henderson

I suppose it was about the second week of school that I noticed Sue-lynn particularly. Of course, I'd noticed her name before and checked her out automatically for maturity and ability and probable performance the way most teachers do with their students during the first weeks of school. She had checked out mature and capable and no worry as to performance so I had pigeonholed her—setting aside for the moment the little nudge that said, "Too quiet"—with my other no-worrys until the fluster and flurry of the first days had died down a little.

I remember my noticing day. I had collapsed into my chair for a brief respite from guiding hot little hands through the intricacies of keeping a Crayola within reasonable bounds and the room was full of the relaxed, happy hum of a pleased class as they worked away, not realizing that they were rubbing "blue" into their memories as well as onto their papers. I was meditating on how individual personalities were beginning to emerge among the thirty-five or so heterogeneous first graders I had, when I noticed Sue-lynn—really noticed her—for the first time.

She had finished her paper—far ahead of the others as usual—and was sitting at her table facing me. She had her thumbs touching in front of her on the table and her fingers curving as though they held something between them—something large enough to keep her fingertips apart and angular enough to bend her fingers as if for corners. It was something pleasant that she held—pleasant and precious. You could tell that by the softness of her hold. She was leaning

133

forward a little, her lower ribs pressed against the table, and she was looking, completely absorbed, at the table between her hands. Her face was relaxed and happy. Her mouth curved in a tender half-smile, and as I watched, her lashes lifted and she looked at me with a warm share-the-pleasure look. Then her eyes blinked and the shutters came down inside them. Her hand flicked into the desk and out. She pressed her thumbs to her forefingers and rubbed them slowly together. Then she laid one hand over the other on the table and looked down at them with the air of complete denial and ignorance children can assume so devastatingly.

The incident caught my fancy and I began to notice Sue-lynn. As I consciously watched her, I saw that she spent most of her free time staring at the table between her hands, much too unobtrusively to catch my busy attention. She hurried through even the fun-est of fun papers and then lost herself in looking. When Davie pushed her down at recess, and blood streamed from her knee to her ankle, she took her bandages and her tear-smudged face to that comfort she had so readily—if you'll pardon the expression—at hand, and emerged minutes later, serene and dry-eyed. I think Davie pushed her down because of her Looking. I know the day before he had come up to me, red-faced and squirming.

"Teacher," he blurted. "She Looks!"

"Who looks?" I asked absently, checking the vocabulary list in my book, wondering how on earth I'd missed *where*, one of those annoying *wh* words that throw the children for a loss.

"Sue-lynn. She Looks and Looks!"

"At you?" I asked.

"Well—" He rubbed a forefinger below his nose, leaving a clean streak on his upper lip, accepted the proffered Klee-nex and put it in his pocket. "She looks at her desk and tells lies. She says she can see—"

"Can see what?" My curiosity picked up its ears.

"Anything," said Davie. "It's her Anything Box. She can see anything she wants to."

"Does it hurt you for her to Look?"

"Well," he squirmed. Then he burst out. "She says she saw me with a dog biting me because I took her pencil—she said." He started a pell-mell verbal retreat. "She *thinks* I took her pencil. I only found—" His eyes dropped. "I'll give it back."

"I hope so," I smiled. "If you don't want her to look at you, then don't do things like that."

"Dern girls," he muttered, and clomped back to his seat.

So I think he pushed her down the next day to get back at her for the dogbite.

Several times after that I wandered to the back of the room, casually in her vicinity, but always she either saw or felt me coming and the quick sketch of her hand disposed of the evidence. Only once I thought I caught a glimmer of something—but her thumb and forefinger brushed in sunlight, and it must have been just that.

Children don't retreat for no reason at all, and though Sue-lynn did not follow any overt pattern of withdrawal, I started to wonder about her. I watched her on the playground, to see how she tracked there. That only confused me more.

She had a very regular pattern. When the avalanche of children first descended at recess, she avalanched along with them and nothing in the shrieking, running, dodging mass resolved itself into a withdrawn Sue-lynn. But after ten minutes or so, she emerged from the crowd, tousle-haired, rosy-cheeked, smutched with dust, one shoelace dangling, and through some alchemy that I coveted for myself, she suddenly became untousled, undusty and unsmutched.

And there she was, serene and composed on the narrow little step at the side of the flight of stairs just where they disappeared into the base of the pseudo-Corinthian column that graced Our Door and her cupped hands received whatever they received and her absorption in what she saw became so complete that the bell came as a shock every time.

And each time, before she joined the rush to Our Door, her hand would sketch a gesture to her pocket, if she had one, or to the tiny ledge that extended between the hedge and the building. Apparently she always had to put the Anything Box away, but never had to go back to get it.

I was so intrigued by her putting whatever it was on the ledge that once I actually went over and felt along the grimy

little outset. I sheepishly followed my children into the hall,
wiping the dust from my fingertips, and Sue-lynn's eyes
brimmed amusement at me without her mouth's smiling. Her
hands mischievously squared in front of her and her thumbs
caressed a solidness as the line of children swept into the
room.

I smiled too because she was so pleased with having
outwitted me. This seemed to be such a gay withdrawal that I
let my worry die down. Better this manifestation than any
number of other ones that I could name.

Someday, perhaps, I'll learn to keep my mouth shut. I
wish I had before that long afternoon when we primary
teachers worked together in a heavy cloud of Ditto fumes, the
acrid smell of India ink, drifting cigarette smoke and the
constant current of chatter, and I let Alpha get me started on
what to do with our behavior problems. She was all raunched
up about the usual rowdy loudness of her boys and the eternal
clack of her girls, and I—bless my stupidity—gave her Sue-
lynn as an example of what should be our deepest concern
rather than the outbursts from our active ones.

"You mean she just sits and looks at nothing?" Alpha's
voice grated into her questioning tone.

"Well, I can't see anything," I admitted. "But apparently
she can."

"But that's having hallucinations!" Her voice went up a
notch. "I read a book once—"

"Yes." Marlene leaned across the desk to flick ashes in
the ash tray. "So we have heard and heard and heard!"

"Well!" sniffed Alpha. "It's better than *never* reading a
book."

"We're waiting," Marlene leaked smoke from her nostrils,
"for the day when you read another book. This one must
have been uncommonly long."

"Oh, I don't know." Alpha's forehead wrinkled with concentration. "It was only about—" Then she reddened and
turned her face angrily away from Marlene.

"Apropos of *our* discussion—" she said pointedly. "It
sounds to me like that child has a deep personality disturbance. Maybe even a psychotic—whatever—" Her eyes glis-
tened faintly as she turned the thought over.

"Oh, I don't know," I said, surprised into echoing her words at my sudden need to defend Sue-lynn. "There's something about her. She doesn't have that apprehensive, hunched-shoulder, don't-hit-me-again air about her that so many withdrawn children have." And I thought achingly of one of mine from last year that Alpha had now and was verbally bludgeoning back into silence after all my work with him. "She seems to have a happy, adjusted personality, only with this odd little—*plus*."

"Well, I'd be worried if she were mine," said Alpha. "I'm glad all my kids are so normal." She sighed complacently. "I guess I really haven't anything to kick about. I seldom ever have problem children except wigglers and yakkers, and a holler and a smack can straighten them out."

Marlene caught my eye mockingly, tallying Alpha's class with me, and I turned away with a sigh. To be so happy— well, I suppose ignorance does help.

"You'd better do something about that girl," Alpha shrilled as she left the room. "She'll probably get worse and worse as time goes on. Deteriorating, I think the book said."

I had known Alpha a long time and I thought I knew how much of her talk to discount, but I began to worry about Sue-lynn. Maybe this *was* a disturbance that was more fundamental than the usual run of the mill that I had met up with. Maybe a child *can* smile a soft, contented smile and still have little maggots of madness flourishing somewhere inside.

Or, by gorry! I said to myself defiantly, maybe she *does* have an Anything Box. Maybe she *is* looking at something precious. Who am I to say no to anything like that?

An Anything Box! What could you see in an Anything Box? Heart's desire? I felt my own heart lurch—just a little— the next time Sue-lynn's hands curved. I breathed deeply to hold me in my chair. If it was *her* Anything Box, I wouldn't be able to see my heart's desire in it. Or would I? I propped my cheek up on my hand and doodled aimlessly on my time schedule sheet. How on earth, I wondered—not for the first time—do I manage to get myself off on these tangents?

Then I felt a small presence at my elbow and turned to meet Sue-lynn's wide eyes.

"Teacher?" The word was hardly more than a breath.

"Yes?" I could tell that for some reason Sue-lynn was loving me dearly at the moment. Maybe because her group had gone into new books that morning. Maybe because I had noticed her new dress, the ruffles of which made her feel very feminine and lovable, or maybe just because the late autumn sun lay so golden across her desk. Anyway, she was loving me to overflowing, and since, unlike most of the children, she had no casual hugs or easy moist kisses, she was bringing her love to me in her encompassing hands.

"See my box, Teacher? It's my Anything Box."

"Oh, my!" I said. "May I hold it?"

After all, I have held—tenderly or apprehensively or bravely—tiger magic, live rattlesnakes, dragon's teeth, poor little dead butterflies and two ears and a nose that dropped off Sojie one cold morning—none of which I could see any more than I could the Anything Box. But I took the squareness from her carefully, my tenderness showing in my fingers and my face.

And I received weight and substance and actuality!

Almost I let it slip out of my surprised fingers, but Sue-lynn's apprehensive breath helped me catch it and I curved my fingers around the precious warmness and looked down, down, past a faint shimmering, down into Sue-lynn's Anything Box.

I was running barefoot through the whispering grass. The swirl of my skirts caught the daisies as I rounded the gnarled apple tree at the corner. The warm wind lay along each of my cheeks and chuckled in my ears. My heart outstripped my flying feet and melted with a rush of delight into warmness as his arms—

I closed my eyes and swallowed hard, my palms tight against the Anything Box. "It's beautiful!" I whispered. "It's wonderful, Sue-lynn. Where did you get it?"

Her hands took it back hastily. "It's mine," she said defiantly. "It's mine."

"Of course," I said. "Be careful now. Don't drop it."

She smiled faintly as she sketched a motion to her pocket. "I won't." She patted the flat pocket on her way back to her seat.

Next day she was afraid to look at me at first for fear I

might say something or look something or in some way remind her of what must seem like a betrayal to her now, but after I only smiled my usual smile, with no added secret knowledge, she relaxed.

A night or so later when I leaned over my moon-drenched windowsill and let the shadow of my hair hide my face from such ebullient glory, I remembered the Anything Box. Could I make one for myself? Could I square off this aching waiting, this outreaching, this silent cry inside me, and make it into an Anything Box? I freed my hands and brought them together, thumb to thumb, framing a part of the horizon's darkness between my upright forefingers. I stared into the empty square until my eyes watered. I sighed, and laughed a little, and let my hands frame my face as I leaned out into the night. To have magic so near—to feel it tingle off my fingertips and then to be so bound that I couldn't receive it. I turned away from the window—turning my back on brightness.

It wasn't long after this that Alpha succeeded in putting sharp points of worry back in my thoughts of Sue-lynn. We had ground duty together, and one morning when we shivered while the kids ran themselves rosy in the crisp air, she sizzed in my ear.

"Which one is it? The abnormal one, I mean."

"I don't have any abnormal children," I said, my voice sharpening before the sentence ended because I suddenly realized whom she meant.

"Well, I call it abnormal to stare at nothing." You could almost taste the acid in her words. "Who is it?"

"Sue-lynn," I said reluctantly. "She's playing on the bars now."

Alpha surveyed the upside-down Sue-lynn, whose brief skirts were belled down from her bare pink legs and half covered her face as she swung from one of the bars by her knees. Alpha clutched her wizened, blue hands together and breathed on them. "She sure looks normal enough," she said.

"She *is* normal!" I snapped.

"*Well*, bite my head off!" cried Alpha. "You're the one that said she wasn't, not me—or is it 'not I'? I never could remember. Not me? Not I?"

The bell saved Alpha from a horrible end. I never knew a person so serenely unaware of essentials and so sensitive to trivia.

But she had succeeded in making me worry about Sue-lynn again, and the worry exploded into distress a few days later.

Sue-lynn came to school sleepy-eyed and quiet. She didn't finish any of her work and she fell asleep during rest time. I cussed TV and drive-ins and assumed a night's sleep would put it right. But next day Sue-lynn burst into tears and slapped Davie clear off his chair.

"Why Sue-lynn!" I gathered Davie up in all his astonishment and took Sue-lynn's hand. She jerked it away from me and flung herself at Davie again. She got two handfuls of his hair and had him out of my grasp before I knew it. She threw him bodily against the wall with a flip of her hands, then doubled up her fists and pressed them to her streaming eyes. In the shocked silence of the room, she stumbled over to Isolation and seating herself, back to the class, on the little chair, she leaned her head into the corner and sobbed quietly in big gulping sobs.

"What on earth goes on?" I asked the stupefied Davie, who sat spraddle-legged on the floor fingering a detached tuft of hair. "What did you do?"

"I only said 'Robber Daughter,'" said Davie. "It said so in the paper. My mama said her daddy's a robber. They put him in jail cause he robbered a gas station." His bewildered face was trying to decide whether or not to cry. Everything had happened so fast that he didn't know yet if he was hurt.

"It isn't nice to call names," I said weakly. "Get back into your seat. I'll take care of Sue-lynn later."

He got up and sat gingerly down in his chair, rubbing his ruffled hair, wanting to make more of a production of the situation but not knowing how. He twisted his face experimentally to see if he had tears available and had none.

"Dern girls," he muttered, and tried to shake his fingers free of a wisp of hair.

I kept my eye on Sue-lynn for the next half hour as I busied myself with the class. Her sobs soon stopped and her rigid shoulders relaxed. Her hands were softly in her lap and I knew she was taking comfort from her Anything Box. We had our talk together later, but she was so completely sealed off from me by her misery that there was no communication between us. She sat quietly watching me as I talked, her hands trembling in her lap. It shakes the heart, somehow, to see the hands of a little child quiver like that.

That afternoon I looked up from my reading group, startled, as though by a cry, to catch Sue-lynn's frightened eyes. She looked around bewildered and then down at her hands again—her empty hands. Then she darted to the Isolation corner and reached under the chair. She went back to her seat slowly, her hands squared to an unseen weight. For the first time, apparently, she had had to go get the Anything Box. It troubled me with a vague unease for the rest of the afternoon.

Through the days that followed while the trial hung fire, I had Sue-lynn in attendance bodily, but that was all. She sank into her Anything Box at every opportunity. And always, if she had put it away somewhere, she had to go back for it. She roused more and more reluctantly from these waking dreams, and there finally came a day when I had to shake her to waken her.

I went to her mother, but she couldn't or wouldn't understand me, and made me feel like a frivolous gossipmonger taking her mind away from her husband, despite the fact that I didn't even mention him—or maybe because I didn't mention him.

"If she's being a bad girl, spank her," she finally said, wearily shifting the weight of a whining baby from one hip to another and pushing her tousled hair off her forehead. "Whatever you do is all right by me. My worrier is all used up. I haven't got any left for the kids right now."

Well, Sue-lynn's father was found guilty and sentenced to the state penitentiary and school was less than an hour old the next day when Davie came up, clumsily a-tiptoe, braving my wrath for interrupting a reading group, and whispered hoarsely, "Sue-lynn's asleep with her eyes open again, Teacher."

We went back to the table and Davie slid into his chair next to a completely unaware Sue-lynn. He poked her with a warning finger. "I told you I'd tell on you."

And before our horrified eyes, she toppled, as rigidly as a

doll, sideways off the chair. The thud of her landing relaxed her and she lay limp on the green asphalt tile—a thin paper doll of a girl, one hand still clenched open around something. I pried her fingers loose and almost wept to feel enchantment dissolve under my heavy touch. I carried her down to the nurse's room and we worked over her with wet towels and prayer and she finally opened her eyes.

"Teacher," she whispered weakly.

"Yes, Sue-lynn." I took her cold hands in mine.

"Teacher, I almost got in my Anything Box."

"No," I answered. "You couldn't. You're too big."

"Daddy's there," she said. "And where we used to live."

I took a long, long look at her wan face. I hope it was genuine concern for her that prompted my next words. I hope it wasn't envy or the memory of the niggling nagging of Alpha's voice that put firmness in my voice as I went on. "That's play-like," I said. "Just for fun."

Her hands jerked protestingly in mine. "Your Anything Box is just for fun. It's like Davie's cow pony that he keeps in his desk or Sojie's jet plane, or when the big bear chases all of you at recess. It's fun-for-play, but it's not for real. You mustn't think it's for real. It's only play."

"No!" she denied. *"No!"* she cried frantically, and hunching herself up on the cot, peering through her tear-swollen eyes, she scrabbled under the pillow and down beneath the rough blanket that covered her.

"Where is it?" she cried. "Where is it? Give it back to me, Teacher!"

She flung herself toward me and pulled open both my clenched hands.

"Where did you put it? Where did you put it?"

"There is no Anything Box," I said flatly, trying to hold her to me and feeling my heart breaking along with hers.

"You took it!" she sobbed. "You took it away from me!" And she wrenched herself out of my arms.

"Can't you give it back to her?" whispered the nurse. "If it makes her feel so bad? Whatever it is—"

"It's just imagination," I said, almost sullenly. "I can't give her back something that doesn't exist."

Too young! I thought bitterly. Too young to learn that heart's desire is only play-like.

Of course the doctor found nothing wrong. Her mother dismissed the matter as a fainting spell and Sue-lynn came back to class the next day, thin and listless, staring blankly out the window, her hands palm down on the desk. I swore by the pale hollow of her cheek that never, *never* again would I take any belief from anyone without replacing it with something better. What had I given Sue-lynn? What had she better than I had taken from her? How did I know but that her Anything Box was on purpose to tide her over rough spots in her life like this? And what now, now that I had taken it from her?

Well, after a time she began to work again, and later, to play. She came back to smiles, but not to laughter. She puttered along quite satisfactorily except that she was a candle blown out. The flame was gone wherever the brightness of belief goes. And she had no more sharing smiles for me, no overflowing love to bring to me. And her shoulder shrugged subtly away from my touch.

Then one day I suddenly realized that Sue-lynn was searching our classroom. Stealthily, casually, day by day she was searching, covering every inch of the room. She went through every puzzle box, every lump of clay, every shelf and cupboard, every box and bag. Methodically she checked behind every row of books and in every child's desk until finally, after almost a week, she had been through everything in the place except my desk. Then she began to materialize suddenly at my elbow every time I opened a drawer. And her eyes would probe quickly and sharply before I slid it shut again. But if I tried to intercept her looks, they slid away and she had some legitimate errand that had brought her up to the vicinity of the desk.

She believes it again, I thought hopefully. She won't accept the fact that her Anything Box is gone. She wants it again.

But it *is* gone, I thought drearily. It's really-for-true gone.

My head was heavy from troubled sleep, and sorrow was a weariness in all my movements. Waiting is sometimes a burden almost too heavy to carry. While my children hummed happily over their fun-stuff, I brooded silently out the window until I managed a laugh at myself. It was a shaky laugh that threatened to dissolve into something else, so I brisked back to my desk.

As good a time as any to throw out useless things, I thought, and to see if I can find that colored chalk I put away so carefully. I plunged my hands into the wilderness of the bottom right-hand drawer of my desk. It was deep with a hugh accumulation of anything—just anything—that might need a temporary hiding place. I knelt to pull out leftover Jack Frost pictures, and a broken beanshooter, a chewed red ribbon, a roll of cap gun ammunition, one striped sock, six Numbers papers, a rubber dagger, a copy of the Gospel According to St. Luke, a miniature coal shovel, patterns for jack-o'-lanterns, and a pink plastic pelican. I retrieved my Irish linen hankie I thought lost forever and Sojie's report card that he had told me solemnly had blown out of his hand and landed on a jet and broke the sound barrier so loud that it busted all to flitters. Under the welter of miscellany, I felt a squareness. Oh, happy! I thought, this *is* where I put the colored chalk! I cascaded papers off both sides of my lifting hands and shook the box free.

We were together again. Outside, the world was an enchanting wilderness of white, the wind shouting softly through the windows, tapping wet, white fingers against the warm light. Inside, all the worry and waiting, the apartness and loneliness were over and forgotten, their hugeness dwindled by the comfort of a shoulder, the warmth of clasping hands— and nowhere, nowhere was the fear of parting, nowhere the need to do without again. This was the happy ending. This was—

This was Sue-lynn's Anything Box!

My racing heart slowed as the dream faded—and rushed again at the realization. I had it here! In my junk drawer! It had been there all the time!

I stood up shakily, concealing the invisible box in the flare of my skirts. I sat down and put the box carefully in the center of my desk, covering the top of it with my palms lest I should drown again in delight. I looked at Sue-lynn. She was finishing her fun paper, competently but unjoyously. Now would come her patient sitting with quiet hands until told to do something else.

Alpha would approve. And very possibly, I thought, Alpha would, for once in her limited life, be right. We may need "hallucinations" to keep us going—all of us but the Alphas—but when we go so far to try to force ourselves, physically, into the Never-Neverland of heart's desire—

I remembered Sue-lynn's thin rigid body toppling doll-like off its chair. Out of her deep need she had found—or created? Who could tell?—something too dangerous for a child. I could so easily bring the brimming happiness back to her eyes—but at what a possible price!

No, I had a duty to protect Sue-lynn. Only maturity—the maturity born of the sorrow and loneliness that Sue-lynn was only beginning to know—could be trusted to use an Anything Box safely and wisely.

My heart thudded as I began to move my hands, letting the palms slip down from the top to shape the sides of—

I had moved them back again before I really saw, and I have now learned almost to forget that glimpse of what heart's desire is like when won at the cost of another's heart.

I sat there at the desk trembling and breathless, my palms moist, feeling as if I had been on a long journey away from the little schoolroom. Perhaps I had. Perhaps I had been shown all the kingdoms of the world in a moment of time.

"Sue-lynn," I called. "Will you come up here when you're through?"

She nodded unsmilingly and snipped off the last paper from the edge of Mistress Mary's dress. Without another look at her handiwork, she carried the scissors safely to the scissors box, crumpled the scraps of paper in her hand and came up to the wastebasket by the desk.

"I have something for you, Sue-lynn," I said, uncovering the box.

Her eyes dropped to the desk top. She looked indifferently up at me. "I did my fun paper already."

"Did you like it?"

"Yes." It was a flat lie.

"Good," I lied right back. "But look here." I squared my hands around the Anything Box.

She took a deep breath and the whole of her little body stiffened.

"I found it," I said hastily, fearing anger. "I found it in the bottom drawer."

She leaned her chest against my desk, her hands caught tightly between, her eyes intent on the box, her face white with the aching want you see on children's faces pressed to Christmas windows.

"Can I have it?" she whispered.

"It's yours," I said, holding it out. Still she leaned against her hands, her eyes searching my face.

"Can I have it?" she asked again.

"Yes!" I was impatient with this anticlimax. "But—"

Her eyes flickered. She had sensed my reservation before I had. "But you must never try to get into it again."

"Okay," she said, the word coming out on a long relieved sigh. "Okay, Teacher."

She took the box and tucked it lovingly into her small pocket. She turned from the desk and started back to her table. My mouth quirked with a small smile. It seemed to me that everything about her had suddenly turned upwards—even the ends of her straight taffy-colored hair. The subtle flame about her that made her Sue-lynn was there again. She scarcely touched the floor was she walked.

I sighed heavily and traced on the desk top with my finger a probable size for an Anything Box. What would Sue-lynn choose to see first? How like a drink after a drought it would seem to her.

I was startled as a small figure materialized at my elbow. It was Sue-lynn, her fingers carefully squared before her.

"Teacher," she said softly, all the flat emptiness gone from her voice. "Anytime you want to take my Anything Box, you just say so."

I groped through my astonishment and incredulity for words. She couldn't possibly have had time to look into the Box yet.

"Why, thank you, Sue-lynn," I managed. "Thanks a lot. I would like very much to borrow it sometime."

"Would you like it now?" she asked, proffering it.

"No, thank you," I said, around the lump in my throat. "I've had a turn already. You go ahead."

"Okay," she murmured. Then—"Teacher?"

"Yes?"

Shyly she leaned against me, her cheek on my shoulder. She looked up at me with her warm, unshuttered eyes, then both arms were suddenly around my neck in a brief awkward embrace.

"Watch out!" I whispered, laughing into the collar of her blue dress. "You'll lose it again!"

"No I won't," she laughed back, patting the flat pocket of her dress. "Not ever, ever again!"

A BORN CHARMER

by Edward P. Hughes

At sixteen, his father promoted Dafydd Madoc Llewelyn. *"Mab,"* said the *tad* casually, "I reckon as how you are old enough now to shoulder some responsibility. Owain and I have plenty to do about the farm. I want you to keep an eye on the sheep."

Dafydd scowled down at this boots to mask the disappointment. Guarding sheep was a dog's job. He had been hoping for real responsibility. He demurred. "If we are so short-handed, cannot the sheep manage without an eye on them?"

Unexpectedly, his father smiled. "Well, you won't only be watching sheep, will you? Doesn't the Bangor road go by the side of Moelfre? And would that not be the way the Raiders would likely come, if they wanted to get at Cwm Goch?" Then he punched Dafydd's shoulder proudly. "The Council has decided that Matty Price is getting too old for sentinel. They reckon you can take his place!"

Next morning, the *tad* unlocked the dining room cupboard and got out the twelvebore. Until then, Dafydd had handled the gun only under supervision. He watched his father thumb a shell into each chamber, then snap on the safety. "Two rounds should be enough, *mab*. One for 'Raiders sighted,' two for 'Help wanted quick!'" He proffered the gun to Dafydd, face serious. "Keep your eye on that road. Don't get personally involved. Let them take a sheep or two, if that is all they want."

Dafydd accepted the gun, hoping his father would not notice his hands trembling. He tucked it under his arm, muzzle down, as he had been taught. "I will be most careful, *tad*," he promised.

His father smiled again and patted his shoulder. "Go and get your dinner now from the *mam*. Then get up that hill as quick as you can. It is almost daylight."

The wind blew cold on the slopes of Moelfre. The black slate roof of Careg Ddu lay out of sight behind the gorse-clad shoulder he had just climbed. Dafydd pulled up the collar of his sheepskin coat, turned his back to the rising sun, and scanned the fields and road below. The long slopes were dark green in the mountain's shadow. Clusters of white dots showed where the sheep had spent the night. Nothing moved on the road.

He pulled a hand from his pocket and casually conjured up a shotgun shell. Easy when you had the knack. And the poor old *tad* economizing on ammo because it had become so hard to find! If only he knew that his younger son could produce shotgun shells at will! Dafydd thought of the charmer they had caught in the village and shivered at the gruesome memory. Sorry, *tad*—some things had to be kept secret!

Not that Dafydd had anything against charmers. There were hardly enough of them to worry about. One in each million people, he had heard. He could even call himself a charmer—if he dared do publicly what he practiced in private. But folk were queer. Still blaming the charmers for wrecking their daft old civilization, and the war finished thirty years ago. Still ranting on about things you had never seen—motion pictures, airplanes, oranges. But what you had never had, you never missed. And if some Russky really had charmed an H-bomb or two onto the English Houses of Parliament, more than likely the *Saesneg* had done it to the Russkies first. And why keep on about what happened years ago? The bombs had not touched Cwm Goch. Maybe a sprinkle of the fallout stuff blew over now and again, but, if you could not see it, taste it, nor smell it—how could you tell?

As he watched, the mist lifted from the humps of Yr Eifl and Moel Pen-Llechog. He saw the sea, and he grimaced. Gone for good now, he was willing to wager, would be the sailing trips with the village lads. Brother Owain would make sure that brother Dafydd did not neglect his sentineling and his mutton-watching on Moelfre. Brother Owain was rapidly becoming a pain in the neck. Dafydd hitched bow and quiver more comfortably across his back, tucked gun under his arm, grasped his crook firmly, and started downhill. There was an animal bleating below—probably stuck in a thorn bush. Dafydd sighed. Dealing with a Raider would be more fun.

He gained the road before he found the plaintive teg stuck, legs up, in a ditch. The sun was warm. He shed coat and accouterments, stooped to grasp a front and back leg. From the corner of his eye he saw a shadow move on the road. He flung himself sideways. A hand gripping a knife swept through the space vacated by his shoulder blades. He kicked out, catching a wrist, sending a knife flashing end over end. The aspiring assassin yelled and dived for the weapon. Dafydd dived after him and got him in a headlock before he reached the knife. The man was undernourished; Dafydd held him easily despite his struggles. What a sucker he had been! Caught out on his first day as sentinel! Angrily he forced the man's head down. "What's the idea, eh?"

"Ifor!" yelled his captive. "Help!"

Ifor emerged from the cover of the hedge, knife in hand. "Hold him still, Tum," he requested.

Dafydd hid his shock. "Come any closer," he warned, "and your pal is a corpse."

"Get his gun," wailed Tum, now bent almost double.

"I will do that," agreed Ifor. "If only to prevent him letting it off. We don't want the yokels warned, do we?"

He reached the twelvebore before Dafydd could hook his foot around it.

"Now, my bucko!" Ifor waved the gun encouragingly. "Suppose you let Tum go. Then we can discuss things reasonable like."

"I have warned you," panted Dafydd, not quite prepared to see if Tum's neck would actually break. "Bugger off, or your pal will suffer."

"You are being stubborn," persisted Ifor. "We haven't waited here all morning, listening to that blotty sheep, to be easy put off." He darted sideways without warning.

Dafydd swung his captive like a shield. "Tum," he gasped, "tell your mate to piss off before I break your neck!"

The man struggled ineffectually. "Ifor! He is killing me!"

"Swing the bastard round," counseled Ifor. "I can't get at him with you in the way."

Dafydd tensed his muscles to resist any effort his prisoner might make. Ifor stood barely a yard off, knife poised. Then Dafydd heard the sound of hooves. A horse and rider, followed by a pack pony, emerged from the shadow of trees overhanging the road.

"Help!" yelled Dafydd.

Ifor cursed fluently. Fifty yards away the horseman kicked his mount into a gallop. Ifor half turned, one eye on Dafydd, blade ready.

The rider swung under his knife, striking behind the shoulder. Ifor screamed and dropped the knife. His arm hung limp. He hoisted the shotgun one-handed and swung after the horseman, trying to thumb off the safety.

Dafydd hurled his captive away. There was a shotgun in his hands. He blasted shot into the tarmac at Ifor's feet.

"Drop it!"

Ifor stared, unbelieving. *"Duw!* A blotty charmer!" He let the gun fall. Tum cowered on the road, wordless.

The rider returned, leading his horse. He said in *Saesneg,* "You didn't need much help, friend."

Dafydd switched languages. "You spoiled his best arm. That was a good aid."

The *Sais* slapped a leather-covered sap on his palm and laughed. "What shall we do with 'em? Execute them here, or take them to your authorities?"

Dafydd glanced involuntarily from the gun in his hands to its twin on the road. "I do not think I want them to go to my village," he admitted.

"Mm." The *Sais* eyed both guns. "You must have quite a collection of those things."

Dafydd had not, but he did not wish the knowledge broadcast. The charmer who could get rid of things, besides producing them, was a very rare bird.

"I try to keep it quiet," he confessed.

"Better do 'em here, then," advised the *Sais*. "And quick. That shot will bring someone."

Dafydd nodded. "It is a signal. They will send scouts from Cwm Goch."

"Well, get on with it. Those villians have said their prayers."

Dafydd raised the gun. Ifor glared at him, nursing his shoulder. Tum sat uncaring in the road. Dafydd lowered the gun. "I cannot do it. The gun only came because I was angry, and I am no longer angry."

"Give it to me, then," said the *Sais*.

Dafydd handed him the weapon. The *Sais* aimed it at Ifor. "Which barrel did you fire?"

"They are both loaded. But there must be only one more shot. The father gave me but two shells."

The *Sais* snorted. "You are being greedy. You want two for the price of one. Now there are two guns we can justify as many shots as we wish. Your father doesn't know how many shells I carry." He brought the gun up to his shoulder.

Dafydd closed his eyes. Then the words burst from him. "Stop! I cannot let you murder them."

The *Sais* kept the gun steady. "I am not bothered. The rogues deserve to die. They would have done for you. Let me do for them."

Dafydd shook his head. "Let them go. They are both hurt. And we have suffered no harm."

The *Sais* frowned. "There are probably more of 'em down the road, waiting for these two to report back."

"I do not care. The village is warned now. They will go away."

The *Sais* lowered the gun. "If only all the Welsh were as soft as you!" He gestured to the captives. "Go on—scat! Before I change my mind."

They hesitated, incredulous.

The gun roared. Shot sprayed over their heads. They fled like guilty schoolboys.

The *Sais* tucked the duplicate gun inside his saddle roll. He nodded at the sheep bleating in the ditch. "Suppose you get that cuckoo out of its nest, while I find my pony?"

Dafydd had forgotten the trapped teg. He said, "I reckon my job will be easier than yours."

The *Sais* said, "I wouldn't bet." He put two fingers into his mouth and blew a shrill blast. "Sometimes he comes, sometimes he don't. Not always obedient like the horse." He whistled again, and the pony trotted from the shadow of the trees, where it had been cropping grass. The *Sais* laughed. "Just being awkward, you see!"

Dafydd grabbed the teg's legs and heaved. The animal came free, making more noise about it than when it had been born. Dafydd clapped it on the rump to send it squealing up the hillside. Then, grinning, he put two fingers into his mouth in imitation of the *Sais* and blew an echo of his whistle. The teg ignored him. The *Sais* applauded. "All you need now is a reliable horse."

"Or more cooperative sheep," Dafydd amended.

"My name," said the *Sais*, "if you are interested, is Long John Ledger. Of nowhere in particular."

Dafydd walked beside him, itching to take the horse's rein. The *Sais* was indeed long—well over six feet. Corduroy jacket and britches provided no clue to his origins. The moleskin cap was incongruous, but smart.

Dafydd introduced himself. *Saeson* were rare on the Lleyn since the collapse of the pre-bomb English tourist trade. There was novelty in strolling and chatting with someone from a different part of the world. He asked, "Are you traveling to Cwm Goch?"

The *Sais* halted while the horse voided a bladder. "I am making for Pwllheli. I have a date with the circus."

"Then you have plenty of time. The circus is not due for a month."

The *Sais* clapped hand to mouth. "A month in front of myself, am I? They must have sent me out early, without letting on."

"Who would they be?" asked Dafydd, curiosity vanquishing his politeness.

"House of Correction in Bangor. I usually arrange to spend the winter somewhere cozy. They must have grown tired of feeding me."

"What did you do?"

"Stole something—I forget what." The *Sais* shrugged, without embarrassment. "It doesn't matter."

"And what do you do for a living?"

The *Sais* doffed his cap and bowed. He extended a hand, fingers spread wide, made a fist, twirled his wrist, and fanned out a pack of cards.

"A charmer!" Dafydd could not believe his eyes.

The *Sais* laughed. "No, sir—a conjurer! Innocuous and entertaining. I do parlor tricks *ex tempore,* and more impressive productions, given time. I have a contract permitting me to set up a stall within the perimeter of the circus area at Pwllheli in June."

"Since you have a month to spare," Dafydd suggested, "you could put on a show in Cwm Goch."

"It is an idea," admitted the *Sais.* "Do you pay in money in Cwm Goch?"

"What is money?"

The *Sais* rummaged in his pocket. He brought out a couple of carved bone tokens the size of coat buttons. Dafydd examined them. Each had a face and a date cut into one side, and on the reverse, the larger showed the words *One Pound* and the smaller *Fifty Pence.* Dafydd returned them to the *Sais.* "What use are they?"

Long John Ledger laughed. "No use at all, Dai my innocent." He tossed the coins into the air, caught them, and showed Dafydd an empty palm. "Voilà! The quickness of the hand deceives the Dai! But they are used in London Town— which is where I got them. And sometimes I am able to persuade tradesmen here and there to accept them as payment, since they are carved from ivory and cannot be charmed."

Dafydd shook his head scornfully. In Cwm Goch you discharged a debt with your creditor, and there was the Arbiter to decide the value of a lamb—or a day's work—if you were not able to agree. The Arbiter would also hold IOUs until quarter day, if you wished.

He said, "We can carve our own bones, man. You would be lucky to get anyone I know to accept those things—although, strangely enough, we use the same words on our IOUs."

Long John allowed a fifty piece to reappear. It jumped from knuckle to knuckle across the back of his hand. "Pounds and pence are words that come from before the bombs, when everyone used tokens like these. They have been reintroduced in London to make trading easier."

Dafydd recalled illustrations in the *mam's* book. "I have seen pictures of London. Does the King still live there? We have our own King Rhys in Caernarvon, now, you know."

King Rhys of Ruthin was also Lord of the Lleyn Peninsula. Dafydd remembered being taken to Conway for the coronation.

Long John palmed the tokens. "You could call him 'king' I suppose. Most Londoners call him 'The Owner' because he owns the town. I am told he makes charmers welcome."

Dafydd made a face. "That would be a change. Perhaps, one day, I shall get to London and see if *I* am welcome."

Cwm Goch Defense Force were manning the roadblock at the junction for Pentre-bach. Dafydd greeted them. "It is all right. They have gone."

Blacksmith Idris Evans, Commander of the Cwm Goch Defence Force, called, "Stand easy, men!" Forty-odd assorted weapons were uncocked, forty-odd faces turned to Dafydd and his companion. In a quieter voice, Idris asked, "Who has gone, *mab?*"

Dafydd waved airily. "The Raiders—they ran away."

He heard the *tad's* voice from the hillside above the barricades. "How many shots did you fire, Dafydd?"

"One." He pointed to Long John. "He fired the other." Dafydd stopped hurriedly, fingering a nonexistent stone from his boot, hoping the *tad* would not notice the flush in his cheeks.

"I said there was two," commented an anonymous voice.

Emrys Jones the Buss, Senior Village Councillor and only man of Cwm Goch tall enough to match the *Sais* for height, said, "And who is this?"

Long John Ledger swept off his cap. He bowed. "A lone traveler who was able to give assistance to this stalwart youth in a time of need."

Forty-odd pairs of ears pricked at the sound of English. Emrys switched languages courteously. "And what are you doing here, stranger?"

Long John explained at length.

"And those Raiders? You are sure that they have gone?"

"Like rabbits before the reaper."

Emrys drew himself to his full six foot four. "We thank you, Englishman, for the assistance you gave our sentinel. Welcome to Cwm Goch!" He turned to Dafydd. "Well done, lad!"

Dafydd felt his chest swell. The ticklish part was over. Now he could enjoy himself.

Emrys made a sign to Idris. Commander Evans raised his voice. "Troops—form up!" Forty-odd pair of feet shuffled through an ill-practiced drill which eventually had them all in lines facing back toward Cwm Goch. "Forward march!"

The commander was now at the rear of his troops. He dropped back to chat with the *Sais*. Dafydd shouldered the twelvebore in Defense Force style and got into step. Maybe, after this, he would be permitted to go on the slate at Jones the Pub's tavern.

He heard the *tad's* voice from the head of the column. "*Mab! Who minds the sheep?*"

Dafydd sighed. Ten steps, and his glory was used up! He fell out of the column. From the slopes of Moelfre, he watched the Defense Force disappear into the dust.

"No," said his father. "You may *not* go on the slate at Jones the Pub. Not even if every lad in the village is on it already—which I do not believe. You are far too young to be drinking spirituous liquor.

"But—*tad!*" Dafydd bleated.

His father's eyebrows came down darkly, like a line squall. "But me no 'buts,' lad!" His eyes went to the window. "I see Ceinwen Thomas is taking the cow to be milked. If you care, you may go out immediately and talk to her. Otherwise you have my permission to stay and help your brother and me prepare the sheep dip for tomorrow."

Dafydd got himself through the doorway almost before his father had finished the sentence.

Ceinwen Thomas was not exactly pretty, but Dafydd liked her well enough. When the only alternatives were fat Blodwen Hughes, Gronwy Jones the Schoolmistress, or Mari Evans who resembled her *tad's* pigs—well, prettiness was not important. Besides, Ceinwen was a good sport—and, also, she had Dafydd's parents' approval. The Thomases lived in the largest house in the village. Before the bombs, the story went, they had run something called a teashop, supplying English holiday-makers with food and drink. The cow was all that remained of the business, but Tecwin Thomas and Arfon Llewelyn still honored a pre-bomb agreement by which Ceinwen's father pastured a cow on Llewelyn grass.

Dafydd caught up with her at the gate to the milking parlor. She said, "Where was you today, Dai? Howel and Gethyn was looking for you in the village."

He said nonchalantly. "I am sentinel, now. Taking over from Matty Price. And I have also to keep an eye on my sheep."

She cocked her head on one side. "Oh—it is important we are, now, is it? Well, did you hear about the *Sais?*"

Dafydd, who had spent his second day on Moelfre almost hoping the Anglesey Raiders might return to relieve the boredom, said, "What about the *Sais?*"

Ceinwen tethered the cow to a ring on the wall. She got a pail and a stool, then rinsed her hands at the yard pump. "He has been doing what he calls conjuring tricks. You know—making things come and go, without you spotting how."

He nodded. "I have seen him do it."

"Well, then, he has been fooling us all. Blodwen Hughes, who is helping Jones the Pub where your *Sais* is staying, went up to do his room. She found a Purdy twelvebore hidden in the wardrobe. It is the exact twin of your *tad's.*"

Dafydd felt the color rising in his face. "There are hundreds of twelvebores like my *tads,*" he objected.

Ceinwen sat down on the stool, pushed her head into the cow's flank, and began to stroke the teats. "With a mended trigger guard like your *tad's?* Remember when he broke it over the back of that fox, the day he ran out of shells? Blodwen got Idris to go and look. Idris said the repair was his own work—he would know it anywhere."

Dafydd flushed hotly. "Are you trying to say the *Sais* is a thief?"

The milk made ringing sounds as Ceinwen began to direct alternate streams into the pail. "Oh, no! We know you're still got your *tad's* gun. Your man is a charmer. They have him locked in the old Post Office. The Council are going to deal with him tomorrow. He is lucky none of King Rhys' men are in the village—they would not wait that long!''

Dafydd's throat felt tight. The last charmer taken in the village had died painfully. "What will they do to him?''

Ceinwen wiped the sweat from her forehead with the back of her hand. "Some of the Council wanted him put down straight off, but Pastor Roberts appealed for clemency. He said, if the *Sais* couldn't see, he wouldn't be able to charm—so they are putting out his eyes in the morning.''

Dafydd could not sleep. Around two o'clock, judging by the stars, he got up and quietly dressed. In the village below they had a man locked up for a charmer. He had only to open his mouth to put Dafydd Madoc Llewelyn in a similar predicament. Why had Long John not spoken out?

Dafydd eased up the sash and climbed through the window. It was an easy drop onto the roof of the unused chemical privy. He soft-footed across the yard, vaulted the fence, and was off down the hill, wet grass soaking his trousers. The moon provided enough light for him to reach the village without mishap.

Cwm Goch slept. Dafydd avoided the outpost sentinels, and found Willie Evans on watch before the Post Office door. Fleetest runner in the village, Willie, but not very bright. Dafydd shook him awake.

"Willie—I want a quiet word with the *Sais*. Go take a walk. I'll keep guard.''

Willie stumbled to his feet. "I've been wanting to go to the back.''

Dafydd gave him a push. "Now is your chance, boyo.''

The old Post Office was a converted wooden barn, unused for postal purposes since the bombs. An enormous wooden beam, doweled into position, barred the door. Shuttered windows were similarly fastened. The ex-barn had held charmers before. There was no way Dafydd could have released the *Sais* without rousing the village.

In English, he hissed, "Are you awake, Long John?''

The *Sais* whispered back. "Would you be sleeping under the circumstances? Who is it?''

"It is me, Dafydd. What are you going to do?''

"What can I do, friend? I was foolish to keep that gun. I

had thought to swap it for a few necessities in Pwllheli. See where it got me?"

"Why have you not told them who the real charmer is?"

He heard a rueful laugh. "Is that what you want, Dai?"

"*Duw!* No!"

"It wouldn't help, anyway. We would both finish up as suspects. And some of the tests for charmers can be fatal, even though you are innocent. What's the testing process in Cwm Goch?"

Dafydd choked. "They—they are not going to test you. The Council has already decided. They are going to blind you to make sure you never charm no more."

"Mm . . . how exactly do they plan to do that, little Welshman?"

Dafydd tried to recall what Ceinwen had said. "They will pluck out your eyes—I think." He hesitated. "I have heard that it is not very . . . painful."

Long John was silent. Dafydd said, "I am sorry."

"It is not your fault, lad. How exactly do they manage the job? Come on, little friend. I can take it."

Dafydd's voice trembled. "Last time they used a spoon. I can just remember. I was not very old. Afterwards, the soldiers chopped off his head."

"But I am to be spared the last indignity?"

"Pastor Roberts pleaded for your life. He said, if you was blind you could not be a charmer. And so they should not put an innocent man to death."

The *Sais'* voice was suddenly urgent. "Dai, can you get me out of here, now?"

Dafydd studied the old barn joylessly. Built entirely from timber, dowels—no nails, no charming could touch it. "There is nothing I could do that would not make a noise. And Willie Evans is watching from over the road."

"Damn Willie Evans! Can you set fire to this place?"

"Why—are you loose in there?"

"I am tied to a chair, hand and foot."

"Then it is too dangerous. I will try to think up something for after they bring you out tomorrow."

There was a tremor in the *Sais'* voice. "Think hard then, Dafydd. They are the only eyes I've got."

He was first up and dressed next morning. When his mother came down, he said, "Can I go to the village today?"

His *mam* said, "And who will watch the Bangor road?"

He fiddled with a coat button, avoiding her gaze. "Old Matty Price is still keeping an eye out. They have not told him yet that I am sentinel also. It is just that his eyes are not so good as they were. Can I go?"

"You had better ask your *tad.*"

"I only want to see what they do to the *Sais*. Then I will go up Moelfre."

The *mam* lit the ready-laid stove with a big Cardiff match. "I am surprised you should say that, *mab*. I am sure *I* should not like to watch what they do to him this morning."

"Do you not hate the charmers, then, *mam?*"

He found himself staring into a pair of placid gray eyes which made him feel vaguely uncomfortable. Suddenly he was glad that the *Sais* was his friend. She said, "*Mab*—it is wrong to hate anyone. This *Sais* has done us no harm."

"But may I go?"

"Ask your *tad.*"

His father said, "We had enough of you last time. Nightmares—waking up screaming. You get on up Moelfre as soon as you have finished breakfast."

Dafydd bit his lip. Unless he got to the village, Long John's eyes were forfeit. If only his father appreciated that.

"But *tad*—it is important!"

His father's eyebrows make a menacing line. "One Llewelyn at this morning's pantomime will be sufficient. Your brother is staying here. You will be upon Moelfre doing your duty. Is that understood?"

Dafydd nodded meekly.

Once over the gorsey shoulder, he dropped down to the road and worked his way back to the village. The sun was well up, and people were about by the time he reached the gate of the Thomas milking parlor. Ceinwen was closing the door of the cool house.

He hissed. "Ceinwen! Will you do us a favor?"

She came to the gate. "Shouldn't you be up on the hill?"

He nodded. "My *tad* thinks that is where I am." He hesitated only a moment. There was no time for cajoling. He had to take her into his confidence. "Listen—do you think that poor bloody *Sais* deserves to lose his eyes?"

She picked at the wood of the gate. "My *tad* says charmers should be destroyed like vermin, because of the damage they have done."

"I am asking you—not your *tad*."

"Don't shout at me, Dafydd Llewelyn. I am not your wife yet."

He held back a ready response. "I am sorry, Ceinwen. Will you help me to save the *Sais'* sight?"

"It might be dangerous. Why do you want to help him?"

"He saved my life. Surely I owe him a good turn."

"My *tad* says—"

"Sod your *tad!* I am talking about an innocent man's eyes."

"How do you know he is innocent?"

"Because—" He balled his fists in frustration. His mouth opened and shut. It came out in a rush. "Because *I* am the charmer! I charmed that spare gun."

"Dai!" Her eyes grew round, like big daisies.

"Look!" He laid his hand on the top of the gate, palm up. A shotgun shell appeared in it. "Now do you believe me?"

She grabbed the shell from his hand and flung it far into the grass. "Dai—you must not let them find out!"

"Don't worry—I won't," he reassured her. "But I've got to help the *Sais*."

She said, "What do you want me to do?"

The square in Cwm Goch was crowded by the time Dafydd climbed, crouching furtively, onto the roof of the schoolhouse. Owen Owen the carpenter had knocked out the security dowels holding the bar which closed the door of the old Post Office. Two helpers withdrew the great beam. Then they carried out the *Sais*, chair and all, and brought him to the war memorial. Six bowmen stood in a semicircle, arrows nocked. The porters loosed the *Sais* from his chair and bound him with hempen rope to the pillar of stone. They tied an extra ligature to hold his head immovable.

Pastor Roberts in full canonicals stood behind the archers. The voice of Emrys Jones, speaking English, carried clearly to the school roof.

"Englishman, you have betrayed yourself as a charmer, and it is useless to deny it. By the law of the land, you should die."

Pastor Roberts raised his voice. "Thou shalt not suffer a witch to live, Exodus, chapter twenty-two, verse eighteen."

Emrys ignored the interruption. "Sightless charmers cannot harm. *Ergo*, they are no longer charmers. Do you understand the need for you to be sightless, Englishman?"

Long John Ledger responded in a loud voice. "I have done you no harm. I intend you no harm. Let me go, and I will leave Cwm Goch."

Emrys Jones wagged his head. "Rhys of Ruthin would hardly accept that as a valid excuse for releasing you. And we are accountable to him."

"It is not the harm you do now," pointed out Tecwin Thomas. "It is the harm your kind have done in the past."

"The sins of the fathers—" began Pastor Roberts.

"Shut up, you old fool!" yelled Ceinwen's father.

"Keep me prisoner while I send an appeal to King Rhys," suggested Long John.

Again Emrys Jones wagged his head. "You are playing for time, Englishman, and we have none to spare. Executer!"

No one moved.

Emrys Jones turned round. "Where is Dylan Williams?"

A voice. "He is not here."

"Then who has the spoon?"

No one spoke.

Emrys Jones said, "I will get another."

In silence the Senior Councillor crossed the road, entered his house, and returned with a teaspoon. He called, "Stand forward who will do the job!"

No one moved. A voice called, "Find yourself a soldier!" Dafydd thought he recognized his father's laugh.

Emrys puffed out his cheeks, as he did when faced with knotty Council problems. "I am sorry that no one is prepared to undertake an honorable task. I suppose I must do my own dirty work." He turned back to the *Sais*. "If this hurts too much, Englishman, I apologize. But, consider: it is better to lose your sight than lose your life—and it will be over in a minute."

He approached the *Sais*, spoon raised.

Dafydd dared delay no longer. There was no chance, now, that Long John could talk himself out of this fix. Dafydd glared at the pillar to which the *Sais* was bound. He knew the war memorial as well as he knew his own front door: from the triangular apex, past the catalogue of names on its face, to the base—chipped by a Raider's bullet long before he was born.

He charmed, and the war memorial disappeared. The *Sais* stood free, bonds hanging loosely around him.

"Archers!" shrieked Emrys.

Dafydd charmed again, a picture from the *mam's* book clear in his mind. And, like some medieval knight, the *Sais* stood in a replica of the armor worn by Edward Plantagenet, Black Prince of England. The crowd fell back. A nervous finger twitched, and an arrow bounced harmlessly off the *Sais'* breastplate.

Dafydd put two fingers into his mouth and blew a shrill blast. Down at the tavern, Ceinwen Thomas opened a stable door to push out a horse and a pony.

Dafydd whistled again. The horse whickered and came up to the square at a smart trot, towing the reluctant pony.

The Black Prince had his sword out.

"Back!" he ordered. "I command you in the name of Sir John Ledger de Main!"

The bowmen retreated before him. On the far side of the square a man raised a shotgun, and pulled the trigger ineffectually.

Dafydd grinned.

He looked anxiously up the road towards Pastor Roberts' chapel. It was high time his diversion was showing. He glimpsed the unnoticed wisps of smoke trailing from the chapel windows. From the cover of the schoolhouse project, he yelled, "Fire! The chapel is on fire!"

He heard Pastor Roberts' high-pitched shriek. Other voices took up the warning. When he dared to look, the crowd was streaming up the road towards the burning building.

Sir John Ledger de Main stood alone in the square. His horse and loaded pack pony trotted up and halted, whinnying at the unfamiliar armor. The Black Night got leisurely onto his mount. He raised the sword in salute.

"Elegantly done, Dai! You did not need much help, that time!"

Dafydd glanced nervously up the street to where the chapel burned. The damp straw he had set smoldering in the chancel that morning was still producing enough smoke to hold the firefighters' attention. He stood up to wave at the Black Knight. "Time you were on your way, *Sais!*"

The Black Knight waved back. "Thanks for my eyes, little Welshman. Don't forget London when your luck runs out here!"

Then Long John Ledger sheathed his sword and was off down the street, like some lone Crusader on his way to war.

Dafydd waved until he was out of sight, then turned his attention to the burning chapel. Encouraged by Pastor Roberts, the population of Cwm Goch had formed bucket chains to drench the chapel through door and windows.

They appeared to have forgotten Long John. Dafydd sniffed scornfully. Without the backing of King Rhys' soldiers, Cwm Goch hadn't much stomach for charmer-baiting. They would probably make sure the fire was not out while there was a chance that the mail-clad menace was still in the village! Dafydd eyed the dense billows of smoke. He had piled the straw well clear of the wooden pews, so there was little chance of serious damage. Maybe Pastor Roberts would want some sooty stonework scrubbed later on: Dafydd Llewelyn would be pleased to volunteer.

The wind veered, sending smoke down the street to envelope the schoolhouse roof. Dafydd coughed amid the fumes and grinned. It had been a good charm—one the *mam* would surely approve of, if only he dared tell her. A full suit of armor, by damn—and only a picture to work from! And everyone convinced Long John Ledger was the culprit!

Everyone, that is, except—!

Dafydd launched himself down the incline, no slipperier nor steeper than some of the slopes on Moelfre. Time to go before his fellow conspirator arrived dying to blather on about the success of their plan. He dropped from the drain pipe, picked himself out of the dust. He saw her running up the street from Jones' tavern. Ceinwen who knew his secret. Ceinwen whose father would not see reason about charmers. Ceinwen who maybe now thought she had a hold on Dafydd Madoc Llewelyn. . . .

He shivered. He was in no mood to face his new ally. In any case, the firefighters would soon discover the fire was arson and come looking for the criminal. The *tad* among them. He could hear his father's voice. *"Dafydd—who minds the sheep?"*

He turned towards the square, concentrated, and restored Cwm Goch's war memorial, bullet chip and all. Then he started back up the hill towards the slopes of Moelfre. Ceinwen Thomas, and the future, could look after themselves for the time being. Dafydd Llewelyn now needed an alibi that only absence from the scene of the crime could provide. Let the *tad* tell him all about Long John's escape and how the chapel went on fire when he got home that night.

Dafydd smirked, tasting the wine of success. Too young to drink spirituous liquor, was he?

WHAT IF—

by Isaac Asimov

Norman and Livvy were late, naturally, since catching a train is always a matter of last-minute delays, so they had to take the only available seat in the coach. It was the one toward the front; the one with nothing before it but the seat that faced wrong way, with its back hard against the front partition. While Norman heaved the suitcase onto the rack, Livvy found herself chafing a little.

If a couple took the wrong-way seat before them, they would be staring self-consciously into each other's faces all the hours it would take to reach New York; or else, which was scarcely better, they would have to erect synthetic barriers of newspaper. Still, there was no use in taking a chance on there being another unoccupied double seat elsewhere in the train.

Norman didn't seem to mind, and that was a little disappointing to Livvy. Usually they held their moods in common. That, Norman claimed, was why he remained sure that he had married the right girl.

He would say, "We fit each other, Livvy, and that's the key fact. When you're doing a jigsaw puzzle and one piece fits another, that's it. There are no other possibilities, and of course there are no other girls."

And she would laugh and say, "If you hadn't been on the streetcar that day, you would probably never had met me. What would you have done then?"

"Stayed a bachelor. Naturally. Besides, I would have met you through Georgette another day."

"It wouldn't have been the same."

"Sure it would."

"No, it wouldn't. Besides, Georgette would never have introduced me. She was interested in you herself, and she's the type who knows better than to create a possible rival."

"What nonsense."

Livvy asked her favorite question: "Norman, what if you had been one minute later at the streetcar corner and had taken the next car? What *do* you suppose would have happened?"

"And what if fish had wings and all of them flew to the top of the mountains? What would we have to eat on Fridays then?"

But they *had* caught the streetcar, and fish *didn't* have wings, so that now they had been married five years and ate fish on Fridays. And because they had been married five years, they were going to celebrate by spending a week in New York.

Then she remembered the present problem. "I wish we could have found some other seat."

Norman said, "Sure. So do I. But no one has taken it yet, so we'll have relative privacy as far as Providence, anyway."

Livvy was unconsoled, and felt herself justified when a plump little man walked down the central aisle of the coach. Now, where had he come from? The train was halfway between Boston and Providence, and if he had had a seat, why hadn't he kept it? She took out her vanity and considered her reflection. She had a theory that if she ignored the little man, he would pass by. So she concentrated on her light-brown hair which, in the rush of catching the train, had become disarranged just a little; at her blue eyes, and at her little mouth with the plump lips which Norman said looked like a permanent kiss.

Not bad, she thought.

Then she looked up, and the little man was in the seat opposite. He caught her eye and grinned widely. A series of lines curled about the edges of his smile. He lifted his hat hastily and put it down beside him on top of the little black box he had been carrying. A circle of white hair instantly sprang up stiffly about the large bald spot that made the center of his skull a desert.

She could not help smiling back a little, but then she caught sight of the black box again and the smile faded. She yanked at Norman's elbow.

Norman looked up from his newspaper. He had startlingly dark eyebrows that almost met above the bridge of his nose, giving him a formidable first appearance. But they and the dark eyes beneath bent upon her now with only the usual look of pleased and somewhat amused affection.

He said, "What's up?" He did not look at the plump little man opposite.

Livvy did her best to indicate what she saw by a little unobtrusive gesture of her hand and head. But the little man was watching and she felt a fool, since Norman simply stared at her blankly.

Finally she pulled him closer and whispered, "Don't you see what's printed on his box?"

She looked again as she said it, and there was no mistake. It was not very prominent, but the light caught it slantingly and it was a slightly more glistening area on a black background. In flowing script it said, "What If."

The little man was smiling again. He nodded his head rapidly and pointed to the words and then to himself several times over.

Norman said in an aside, "Must be his name."

Livvy replied, "Oh, how could that be anybody's name?"

Norman put his paper aside. "I'll show you." He leaned over and said, "Mr. If?"

The little man looked at him eagerly.

"Do you have the time, Mr. If?"

The little man took out a large watch from his vest pocket and displayed the dial.

"Thank you, Mr. If," said Norman. And again in a whisper, "See, Livvy."

He would have returned to his paper, but the little man was opening his box and raising a finger periodically as he did so, to enforce their attention. It was just a slab of frosted glass that he removed—about six by nine inches in length and width and perhaps an inch thick. It had beveled edges, rounded corners, and was completely featureless. Then he took out a little wire stand on which the glass slab fitted comfortably.

He rested the combination on his knees and looked proudly at them.

Livvy said, with sudden excitement, "Heavens, Norman, it's a picture of some sort."

Norman bent close. Then he looked at the little man. "What's this? A new kind of television?"

The little man shook his head, and Livvy said, "No, Norman, it's *us*."

"What?"

"Don't you see? That's the streetcar we met on. There you are in the back seat wearing that old fedora I threw away three years ago. And that's Georgette and myself getting on. The fat lady's in the way. Now! Can't you see us?"

He muttered, "It's some sort of illusion."

"But you see it too, don't you? That's why he calls this 'What If.' It will *show* us what if. What if the streetcar hadn't swerved . . ."

She was sure of it. She was very excited and very sure of it. As she looked at the picture in the glass slab, the late-afternoon sunshine grew dimmer and the inchoate chatter of the passengers around and behind them began fading.

How she remembered that day. Norman knew Georgette and had been about to surrender his seat to her when the car swerved and threw Livvy into his lap. It was such a ridiculously corny situation, but it had worked. She had been so embarrassed that he was forced first into gallantry and then into conversation. An introduction from Georgette was not even necessary. By the time they got off the streetcar, he knew where she worked.

She could still remember Georgette glowering at her, sulkily forcing a smile when they themselves separated. Georgette said, "Norman seems to like you."

Livvy replied, "Oh, don't be silly! He was just being polite. But he is nice-looking, isn't he?"

It was only six months after that that they married.

And now here was that same streetcar again, with Norman and herself and Georgette. As she thought that, the smooth train noises, the rapid clack-clack of the wheels, vanished completely. Instead, she was in the swaying confines of the streetcar. She had just boarded it with Georgette at the previous stop.

Livvy shifted weight with the swaying of the streetcar, as did forty others, sitting and standing, all to the same monotonous and rather ridiculous rhythm. She said, "Somebody's motioning at you, Georgette. Do you know him?"

"At me?" Georgette directed a deliberately casual glance over her shoulder. Her artificially long eyelashes flickered. She said, "I know him a little. What do you suppose he wants?"

"Let's find out," said Livvy. She felt pleased and a little wicked.

Georgette had a well-known habit of hoarding her male acquaintances, and it was rather fun to annoy her this way. And besides, this one seemed quite . . . interesting.

She snaked past the line of standees, and Georgette followed without enthusiasm. It was just as Livvy arrived opposite the young man's seat that the streetcar lurched heavily as it rounded a curve. Livvy snatched desperately in the direction of the straps. Her fingertips caught and she held on. It was a long moment before she could breathe. For some reason, it had seemed that there were no straps close enough to be reached. Somehow, she felt that by all the laws of nature she should have fallen.

The young man did not look at her. He was smiling at Georgette and rising from his seat. He had astonishing eyebrows that gave him a rather competent and self-confident appearance. Livvy decided that she definitely liked him.

Georgette was saying, "Oh no, don't bother. We're getting off in about two stops."

They did. Livvy said, "I thought we were going to Sach's."

"We are. There's just something I remember having to attend to here. It won't take but a minute."

"Next stop, Providence!" the loudspeakers were blaring. The train was slowing and the world of the past had shrunk itself into the glass slab once more. The little man was still smiling at them.

Livvy turned to Norman. She felt a little frightened. "Were you through all that, too?"

He said, "What happened to the time? We *can't* be reaching Providence yet?'' He looked at his watch. ''I guess we are.'' Then, to Livvy, ''You didn't fall that time.''

''Then you *did* see it?'' She frowned. ''Now, that's like Georgette. I'm sure there was no reason to get off the street-car except to prevent my meeting you. How long had you known Georgette before then, Norman?''

''Not very long. Just enough to be able to recognize her at sight and to feel that I ought to offer her my seat.''

Livvy curled her lip.

Norman grinned, ''You can't be jealous of a might-have-been, kid. Besides, what difference would it have made? I'd have been sufficiently interested in you to work out a way of meeting you.''

''You didn't even look at me.''

''I hardly had the chance.''

''Then how would you have met me?''

''Some way. I don't know how. But you'll admit this is a rather foolish argument we're having.''

They were leaving Providence. Livvy felt a trouble in her mind. The little man had been following their whispered conversation, with only the loss of his smile to show that he understood. She said to him, ''Can you show us more?''

Norman interrupted, ''Wait now, Livvy. What are you going to try to do?''

She said, ''I want to see our wedding day. What it would have been if I had caught the strap.''

Norman was visibly annoyed. ''Now, that's not fair. We might not have been married on the same day, you know.''

But she said, ''Can you show it to me, Mr. If?'' and the little man nodded.

The slab of glass was coming alive again, glowing a little. Then the light collected and condensed into figures. A tiny sound of organ music was in Livvy's ears without there actually being sound.

Norman said with relief, ''Well, there I am. That's our wedding. Are you satisfied?''

The train sounds were disappearing again, and the last thing Livvy heard was her own voice saying, ''Yes, there *you* are. But where am *I*?''

*   *   *

Livvy was well back in the pews. For a while she had not expected to attend at all. In the past months she had drifted further and further away from Georgette, without quite knowing why. She had heard of her engagement only through a mutual friend, and, of course, it was to Norman. She remembered very clearly that day, six months before, when she had first seen him on the streetcar. It was the time Georgette had so quickly snatched her out of sight. She had met him since on several occasions, but each time Georgette was with him, standing between.

Well, she had no cause for resentment; the man was certainly none of hers. Georgette, she thought, looked more beautiful than she really was. And *he* was very handsome indeed.

She felt sad and rather empty, as though something had gone wrong—something that she could not quite outline in her mind. Georgette had moved up the aisle without seeming to see her, but earlier she had caught *his* eyes and smiled at him. Livvy thought he had smiled in return.

She heard the words distantly as they drifted back to her, "I now pronounce you—"

The noise of the train was back. A woman swayed down the aisle, herding a little boy back to their seats. There were intermittent bursts of girlish laughter from a set of four teenage girls halfway down the coach. A conductor hurried past on some mysterious errand.

Livvy was frozenly aware of it all.

She sat there, staring straight ahead, while the trees outside blended into a fuzzy, furious green and the telephone poles galloped past.

She said, "It was *she* you married."

He stared at her for a moment and then one side of his mouth quirked a little. He said lightly, "I didn't really, Olivia. You're still my wife, you know. Just think about it for a few minutes."

She turned to him. "Yes, you married me—because I fell in your lap. If I hadn't, you would have married Georgette. If she hadn't wanted you, you would have married someone else. You would have married *anybody*. So much for your jigsaw-puzzle pieces."

Norman said very slowly, "Well—I'll—be—darned!" He put both hands to his head and smoothed down the straight hair over his ears where it had a tendency to tuft up. For the moment it gave him the appearance of trying to hold his head together. He said, "Now, look here, Livvy, you're making a silly fuss over a stupid magician's trick. You can't blame me for something I haven't done."

"You would have done it."

"How do you know?"

"You've seen it."

"I've seen a ridiculous piece of—of hypnotism, I suppose." His voice suddenly raised itself into anger. He turned to the little man opposite. "Off with you, Mr. If, or whatever your name is. Get out of here. We don't want you. Get out before I throw your little trick out the window and you after it."

Livvy yanked at his elbow. "Stop it. *Stop it!* You're in a crowded train."

The little man shrank back into the corner of the seat as far as he could go and held his little black bag behind him. Norman looked at him, then at Livvy, then at the elderly lady across the way who was regarding him with patent disapproval.

He turned pink and bit back a pungent remark. They rode in a frozen silence to and through New London.

Fifteen minutes past New London, Norman said, "Livvy!"

She said nothing. She was looking out the window but saw nothing but the glass.

He said again, "Livvy! Livvy! Answer me!"

She said dully, "What do you want?"

He said, "Look, this is all nonsense. I don't know how the fellow does it, but even granting it's legitimate, you're not being fair. Why stop where you did? Suppose I *had* married Georgette, do you suppose *you* would have stayed single? For all I know, you were already married at the time of my supposed wedding. Maybe that's why I married Georgette."

"I wasn't married."

"How do you know?"

"I would have been able to tell. I knew what my own thoughts were."

"Then you would have been married within the next year."

Livvy grew angrier. The fact that a sane remnant within her clamored at the unreason of her anger did not soothe her. It irritated her further, instead. She said, "And if I did, it would be no business of yours, certainly."

"Of course it wouldn't. But it would make the point that in the world of reality we can't be held responsible for the 'what ifs.' "

Livvy's nostrils flared. She said nothing.

Norman said, "Look! You remember the big New Year's celebration at Winnie's place year before last?"

"I certainly do. You spilled a keg of alcohol all over me."

"That's beside the point, and besides, it was only a cocktail shaker's worth. What I'm trying to say is that Winnie is just about your best friend and had been long before you married me."

"What of it?"

"Georgette was a good friend of hers too, wasn't she?"

"Yes."

"All right, then. You and Georgette would have gone to the party regardless of which one of you I had married. I would have had nothing to do with it. Let him show us the party as it would have been if I had married Georgette, and I'll bet you'd be there with either your fiancé or your husband."

Livvy hesitated. She felt honestly afraid of just that.

He said, "Are you afraid to take the chance?"

And that, of course, decided her. She turned on him furiously. "No, I'm not! And I hope I *am* married. There's no reason I should pine for you. What's more, I'd like to see what happens when you spill the shaker all over Georgette. She'll fill both your ears for you, and in public, too. I know *her*. Maybe you'll see a certain difference in the jigsaw pieces then." She faced forward and crossed her arms angrily and firmly across her chest.

Norman looked across at the little man, but there was no need to say anything. The glass slab was on his lap already. The sun slanted in from the west, and the white foam of hair that topped his head was edged with pink.

Norman said tensely, "Ready?"

Livvy nodded and let the noise of the train slide away again.

*   *   *

Livvy stood, a little flushed with recent cold, in the the doorway. She had just removed her coat, with its sprinkling of snow, and her bare arms were still rebelling at the touch of open air.

She answered the shouts that greeted her with "Happy New Years" of her own, raising her voice to make herself heard over the squealing of the radio. Georgette's shrill tones were almost the first thing she heard upon entering, and now she steered toward her. She hadn't seen Georgette, or Norman, in weeks.

Georgette lifted an eyebrow, a mannerism she had lately cultivated, and said, "Isn't anyone with you, Olivia?" Her eyes swept the immediate surroundings and then returned to Livvy.

Livvy said indifferently, "I think Dick will be around later. There was something or other he had to do first." She felt as indifferent as she sounded.

Georgette smiled tightly. "Well, Norman's here. That ought to keep you from being lonely, dear. At least, it's turned out that way before."

And as she said so, Norman sauntered in from the kitchen. He had a cocktail shaker in his hand, and the rattling of ice cubes castanetted his words. "Line up, you rioting revelers, and get a mixture that will really revel your riots— Why, Livvy!"

He walked toward her, grinning his welcome. "Where've you been keeping yourself? I haven't seen you in twenty years, seems like. What's the matter? Doesn't Dick want anyone else to see you?"

"Fill my glass, Norman," said Georgette sharply.

"Right away," he said, not looking at her. "Do you want one too, Livvy? I'll get you a glass." He turned, and everything happened at once.

Livvy cried. "Watch out!" She saw it coming, even had a vague feeling that all this had happened before, but it played itself out inexorably. His heel caught the edge of the carpet; he lurched, tried to right himself, and lost the cocktail shaker. It seemed to jump out of his hands, and a pint of ice-cold liquor drenched Livvy from shoulder to hem.

She stood there, gasping. The noises muted about her, and for a few intolerable moments she made futile brushing gestures at her gown, while Norman kept repeating. "Damnation!" in rising tones.

Georgette said coolly, "It's too bad, Livvy. Just one of those things. I imagine the dress can't be very expensive."

Livvy turned and ran. She was in the bedroom, which was at least empty and relatively quiet. By the light of the fringe-shaded lamp on the dresser, she poked among the coats on the bed, looking for her own.

Norman had come in behind her. "Look, Livvy, don't pay any attention to what she said. I'm really devilishly sorry. I'll pay—"

"That's all right. It wasn't your fault." She blinked rapidly and didn't look at him. "I'll just go home and change."

"Are you coming back?"

"I don't know. I don't think so."

"Look, Livvy . . ." His warm fingers were on her shoulders—

Livvy felt a queer tearing sensation deep inside her, as though she were ripping away from clinging cobwebs and—

—and the train noises were back.

Something *did* go wrong with the time when she was in there—in the slab. It was deep twilight now. The train lights were on. But it didn't matter. She seemed to be recovering from the wrench inside her.

Norman was rubbing his eyes with thumb and forefinger. "What happened?"

Livvy said, "It just ended. Suddenly."

Norman said uneasily, "You know, we'll be putting into New Haven soon." He looked at his watch and shook his head.

Livvy said wonderingly, "You spilled it on me."

"Well, so I did in real life."

"But in real life I was your wife. You ought to have spilled it on Georgette this time. Isn't that queer?" But she was thinking of Norman pursuing her; his hands on her shoulders. . . .

She looked up at him and said with warm satisfaction, "I wasn't married."

"No, you weren't. But was that Dick Reinhardt you were going around with?"

"Yes."

"You weren't planning to marry him, were you, Livvy?"

"Jealous, Norman?"

Norman looked confused. "Of that? Of a slab of glass? Of course not."

"I don't think I would have married him."

Norman said, "You know, I wish it hadn't ended when it did. There was something that was about to happen, I think." He stopped, then added slowly, "It was as though I would rather have done it to anybody else in the room."

"Even to Georgette."

"I wasn't giving two thoughts to Georgette. You don't believe me, I suppose."

"Maybe I do." She looked up at him. "I've been silly, Norman. Let's—let's live our real life. Let's not play with all the things that just might have been."

But he caught her hands. "No, Livvy. One last time. Let's see what we would have been doing right now, Livvy! This very minute! If I had married Georgette."

Livvy was a little frightened. "Let's not, Norman." She was thinking of his eyes, smiling hungrily at her as he held the shaker, while Georgette stood beside her, unregarded. She didn't *want* to know what happened afterward. She just wanted this life now, this *good* life.

New Haven came and went.

Norman said again, "I want to try, Livvy."

She said, "If you want to, Norman." She decided fiercely that it wouldn't matter. Nothing would matter. Her hands reached out and encircled his arm. She held it tightly, and while she held it she thought: "Nothing in the make-believe can take him from me."

Norman said to the little man, "Set 'em up again."

In the yellow light the process seemed to be slower. Gently the frosted slab cleared, like clouds being torn apart and dispersed by an unfelt wind.

Norman was saying, "There's something wrong. That's just the two of us, exactly as we are now."

He was right. Two little figures were sitting in a train on

the seats which were farthest toward the front. The field was enlarging now—they were merging into it. Norman's voice was distant and fading.

"It's the same train," he was saying. "The window in back is cracked just as—"

Livvy was blindingly happy. She said, "I wish we were in New York."

He said, "It will be less than an hour, darling." Then he said, "I'm going to kiss you." He made a movement, as though he were about to begin.

"Not here! Oh, Norman, people are looking."

Norman drew back. He said, "We should have taken a taxi."

"From Boston to New York?"

"Sure. The privacy would have been worth it."

She laughed. "You're funny when you try to act ardent."

"It isn't an act." His voice was suddenly a little somber. "It's not just an hour, you know. I feel as though I've been waiting five years."

"I do, too."

"Why couldn't I have met you first? It was such a waste."

"Poor Georgette," Livvy sighed.

Norman moved impatiently. "Don't be sorry for her, Livvy. We never really made a go of it. She was glad to get rid of me."

"I know that. That's why I say 'Poor Georgette.' I'm just sorry for her for not being able to appreciate what she had."

"Well, see to it that *you* do," he said. "See to it that you're immensely appreciative, infinitely appreciative—or more than that, see that you're at least half as appreciative as I am of what *I've* got."

"Or else you'll divorce me, too?"

"Over my dead body," said Norman.

Livvy said, "It's all so strange. I keep thinking; 'What if you hadn't spilt the cocktails on me that time at the party?' You wouldn't have followed me out; you wouldn't have told me; I wouldn't have known. It would have been so different . . . everything."

"Nonsense. It would have been just the same. It would have all happened another time."

"I wonder," said Livvy softly.

* * *

Train noises merged into train noises. City lights flickered outside, and the atmosphere of New York was about them. The coach was astir with travelers dividing the baggage among themselves.

Livvy was an island in the turmoil until Norman shook her.

She looked at him and said, "The jigsaw pieces fit after all."

He said, "Yes."

She put a hand on his. "But it wasn't good, just the same. I was very wrong. I thought that because we had each other, we should have all the *possible* each others. But all the possibles are none of our business. The real is enough. Do you know what I mean?"

He nodded.

She said, "There are millions of other *what ifs*. I don't want to know what happened in any of them. I'll never say 'What if' again."

Norman said, "Relax, dear. Here's your coat." And he reached for the suitcases.

Livvy said with sudden sharpness, "Where's Mr. If?"

Norman turned slowly to the empty seat that faced them. Together they scanned the rest of the coach.

"Maybe," Norman said, "he went into the next coach."

"But why? Besides, he wouldn't leave his hat." And she bent to pick it up.

Norman said, "What hat?"

And Livvy stopped her fingers hovering over nothingness. She said, "It was here—I almost touched it." She straightened and said, "Oh, Norman, what if—"

Norman put a finger on her mouth. "Darling . . ."

She said, "I'm sorry. Here, let me help you with the suitcases."

The train dived into the tunnel beneath Park Avenue, and the noise of the wheels rose to a roar.

MILLENNIUM

by Fredric Brown

Hades was Hell, Satan thought; that was why he loved the place. He leaned forward across his gleaming desk and flicked the switch of the intercom.

"Yes, Sire," said the voice of Lilith, his secretary.

"How many today?"

"Four of them. Shall I send one of them in?"

"Yes—wait. Any of them look as though he might be an unselfish one?"

"One of them does, I think. But so what, Sire? There's one chance in billions of his making The Ultimate Wish."

Even at the *sound* of those last words Satan shivered despite the heat. It was his most constant, almost his only worry that someday someone might make The Ultimate Wish, the ultimate, *unselfish* wish. And then it would happen; Satan would find himself chained for a thousand years, and out of business for the rest of eternity after that.

But Lilith was right, he told himself.

Only about one person out of a thousand sold his soul for the granting of even a minor unselfish wish, and it might be millions of years yet, or forever, before the ultimate one was made. Thus far, no one had even come close to it.

"Okay, Lil," he said. "Just the same, send him in first; I'd rather get it over with." He flicked off the intercom.

The little man who came through the big doorway certainly didn't look dangerous; he looked plain scared.

Satan frowned at him. "You know the terms?"

"Yes," said the little man. "At least, I think I do. In

180

exchange for your granting any one wish I make, you get my soul when I die. Is that right?''

''Right. Your wish?''

''Well,'' said the little man, ''I've thought it out pretty carefully and—''

''Get to the point. I'm busy. Your wish?''

''Well . . . I wish that, without any change whatsover in myself, I become the most evil, stupid and miserable person on earth.''

Satan screamed.

DREAMS ARE SACRED

by Peter Phillips

When I was seven, I read a ghost story and babbled of the consequent nightmare to my father.

"They were coming for me, Pop," I sobbed. "I couldn't run, and I couldn't stop 'em, great big things with teeth and claws like the pictures in the book, and I couldn't wake myself up, Pop, I couldn't come awake."

Pop had a few quiet cuss words for folks who left such things around for a kid to pick up and read; then he took my hand gently in his own great paw and led me into the six-acre pasture.

He was wise, with the canny insight into human motives that the soil gives to a man. He was close to Nature and the hearts and minds of men, for all men ultimately depend on the good earth for sustenance and life.

He sat down on a stump and showed me a big gun. I know now it was a heavy Service Colt .45. To my child eyes, it was enormous. I had seen shotguns and sporting rifles before, but this was to be held in one hand and fired. Gosh, it was heavy. It dragged my thin arm down with its sheer, grim weight when Pop showed me how to hold it.

Pop said: "It's a killer, Pete. There's nothing in the whole wide world or out of it that a slug from Billy here won't stop. It's killed lions and tigers and men. Why, if you aim right, it'll stop a charging elephant. Believe me, son, there's nothing you can meet in dreams that Billy here won't stop. And he'll come into your dreams with you from now on, so there's no call to be scared of anything."

He drove that deep into my receptive subconscious. At the

end of half an hour, my wrist ached abominably from the kick of that Colt. But I'd seen heavy slugs tear through two-inch teakwood and mild steel plating. I'd looked along that barrel, pulled the trigger, felt the recoil rip up my arm and seen the fist-size hole blasted through a sack of wheat.

And that night, I slept with Billy under my pillow. Before I slipped into dreamland, I'd felt again the cool, reassuring butt.

When the Dark Things came again, I was almost glad. I was ready for them. Billy was there, lighter than in my waking hours—or maybe my dream-hand was bigger—but just as powerful. Two of the Dark Things crumpled and fell as Billy roared and kicked, then the others turned and fled.

Then I was chasing them, laughing, and firing from the hip.

Pop was no psychiatrist, but he'd found the perfect antidote to fear—the projection into the subconscious mind of a common-sense concept based on experience.

Twenty years later, the same principle was put into operation scientifically to save the sanity—and perhaps the life—of Marsham Craswell.

"Surely, you've heard of him?" said Stephen Blakiston, a college friend of mine who'd majored in psychiatry.

"Vaguely," I said. "Science fiction, fantasy . . . I've read a little. Screwy."

"Not so. Some good stuff." Steve waved a hand round the bookshelves of his private office in the new Pentagon Mental Therapy Hospital, New York State. I saw multicolored magazine backs, row on row of them. "I'm a fan," he said simply. "Would you call me screwy?"

I backed out of that one. I'm just a sports columnist, but I knew Blakiston was tops in two fields—the psycho stuff and electronic therapy.

Steve said: "Some of it's the old 'peroo, of course, but the level of writing is generally high and the ideas thought-provoking. For ten years, Marsham has been one of the most prolific and best-loved writers in the game.

"Two years ago, he had a serious illness, didn't give himself time to convalesce properly before he waded into writing again. He tried to reach his previous output, tending more and more towards pure fantasy. Beautiful in parts, sheer rubbish sometimes.

"He forced his imagination to work, set himself a wordage routine. The tension became too great. Something snapped. Now he's here."

Steve got up, ushered me out of his office. "I'll take you to see him. He won't see you. Because the thing that snapped was his conscious control over his imagination. It went into high gear, and now instead of writing his stories, he's living them—quite literally, for him.

"Far-off worlds, strange creatures, weird adventures—the detailed phantasmagoria of a brilliant mind driving itself into insanity through the sheer complexity of its own invention. He's escaped from the harsh reality of his strained existence into a dream world. But he may make it real enough to kill himself.

"He's the hero, of course," Steve continued, opening the door into a private ward. "But even heroes sometimes die. My fear is that his morbidly overactive imagination working through his subconscious mind will evoke in this dream world in which he is living a situation wherein the hero must die.

"You probably know that the sympathetic magic of witchcraft acts largely through the imagination. A person imagines he is being hexed to death—and dies. If Marsham Craswell imagines that one of his fantastic creations kills the hero—himself—then he just won't wake up again.

"Drugs won't touch him. Listen."

Steve looked at me across Marsham's bed. I leaned down to hear the mutterings from the writer's bloodless lips.

". . . We must search the Plains of Istak for the Diamond. I, Multan, who now have the Sword, will lead thee; for the Snake must die and only in virtue of the Diamond can his death be encompassed. Come."

Craswell's right hand, lying limp on the coverlet, twitched. He was beckoning his followers.

"Still the Snake and the Diamond?" asked Steve. "He's been living that dream for two days. We only know what's happening when he speaks in his role of hero. Often it's quite unintelligible. Sometimes a spark of consciousness filters through, and he fights to wake up. It's pretty horrible to watch him squirming and trying to pull himself back into reality. Have you ever tried to pull yourself out of a nightmare and failed?"

It was then that I remembered Billy, the Colt .45. I told Steve about it, back in his office.

He said: "Sure. Your Pop had the right idea. In fact, I'm hoping to save Marsham by an application of the same principle. To do it, I need the cooperation of someone who combines a lively imagination with a severely practical streak, hoss-sense—and a sense of humor. Yes—you."

"Uh? How can I help? I don't even know the guy."

"You will," said Steve, and the significant way he said it sent a trickle of ice water down my back. "You're going to get closer to Marsham Craswell than one man has ever been to another.

"I'm going to project you—the essential you, that is, your mind and personality—into Craswell's tortured brain."

I made pop-eyes, then thumbed at the magazine-lined wall. "Too much of yonder, brother Steve," I said. "What you need is a drink."

Steve lit his pipe, draped his long legs over the arm of his chair. "Miracles and witchcraft are out. What I propose to do is basically no more miraculous than the way your Pop put that gun into your dreams so you weren't afraid anymore. It's merely more complex scientifically.

"You've heard of the encephalograph? You know it picks up the surface neural currents of the brain, amplifies and records them, showing the degree—or absence—of mental activity. It can't indicate the kind or quality of such activity save in very general terms. By using comparison-graphs and other statistical methods to analyze its data, we can sometimes diagnose incipient insanity, for instance. But that's all—until we started work on it, here at Pentagon.

"We improved the penetration and induction pickup and needled the selectivity until we could probe any known portion of the brain. What we were looking for was a recognizable pattern among the millions of tiny electric currents that go to make up the imagery of thought, so that if the subject thought of something—a number, maybe—the instruments would react accordingly, give a pattern for it that would be repeated every time he thought of that number.

"We failed, of course. The major part of the brain acts as a unity, no one part being responsible for either simple or complex imagery, but the activity of one portion inducing activity in other portions—with the exception of those parts dealing with automatic impulses. So if we were to get a pattern we should need thousands of pickups—a practical impossibility. It was as if we were trying to divine the pattern of a colored sweater by putting one tiny stitch of it under a microscope.

"Paradoxically, our machine was too selective. We needed, not a probe, but an all-encompassing field, receptive simultaneously to the multitudinous currents that made up a thought pattern.

"We found such a field. But we were no further forward. In a sense, we were back where we started from—because to analyze what the field picked up would have entailed the use of thousands of complex instruments. We had amplified thought, but we could not analyze it.

"There was only one single instrument sufficiently sensitive and complex to do that—another human brain."

I waved for a pause. "I'm home," I said. "You'd got a thought-reading machine."

"Much more than that. When we tested it the other day, one of my assistants stepped up the polarity reversal of the field—that is, the frequency—by accident. I was acting as analyst and the subject was under narcosis.

"Instead of 'hearing' the dull incoherencies of his thoughts, I became part of them. I was inside that man's brain. It was a nightmare world. He wasn't a clear thinker. I was aware of my own individuality. . . . When he came round, he went for me bald-headed. Said I'd been trespassing inside his head.

"With Marsham, it'll be a different matter. The dream world of his coma is detailed, as real as he used to make dream worlds to his readers."

"Hold it," I said. "Why don't you take a peek?"

Steve Blakiston smiled and gave me a high-voltage shot from his big gray eyes. "Three good reasons: I've soaked in the sort of stuff he dreams up, and there's a danger that I would become identified too closely with him. What he needs is a salutary dose of common sense. You're the man for that, you cynical old whiskey-hound.

"Secondly, if my mind gave way under the impress of his imagination, I wouldn't be around to treat myself; and thirdly, when—and if—he comes round, he'll want to kill the man who's been heterodyning his dreams. You can scram. But I want to stay and see the results."

"Sorting that out, I gather there's a possibility that I shall wake up as a candidate for a bed in the next ward?"

"Not unless you let your mind go under. And you won't. You've got a cast-iron nongullibility complex. Just fool around in your usual iconoclastic manner. Your own imagination's pretty good, judging by some of your fight reports lately."

I got up, bowed politely, said: "Thank you, my friend. That reminds me—I'm covering the big fight at the Garden tomorrow night. And I need sleep. It's late. So long."

Steve unfolded and reached the door ahead of me.

"Please," he said, and argued. He can argue. And I couldn't duck those big eyes of his. And he is—or was—my pal. He said it wouldn't take long—just like a dentist—and he smacked down every "if" I thought up.

Ten minutes later, I was lying on a twin bed next to that occupied by a silent, white-faced Marsham Craswell. Steve was leaning over the writer adjusting a chrome-steel bowl like a hair drier over the man's head. An assistant was fixing me up the same way.

Cables ran from the bowls to a movable arm overhead and thence to a wheeled machine that looked like something from the Whacky Science Section of the World's Fair, A.D. 2,000.

I was bursting with questions, but the only ones that would come out seemed crazily irrelevant.

"What do I say to this guy? 'Good morning, and how are all your little complexes today'? Do I introduce myself?"

"Just say you're Pete Parnell, and play it off the cuff," said Steve. "You'll see what I mean when you get there."

Get there. That hit me—the idea of making a journey into some nut's nut. My stomach drew itself up to softball size.

"What's the proper dress for a visit like this? Formal?" I asked. At least, I think I said that. It didn't sound like my voice.

"Wear what you like."

"Uh-huh. And how do I know when to draw my visit to a close?"

Steve came round to my side. "If you haven't snapped Craswell out of it within an hour, I'll turn off the current."

He stepped back to the machine. "Happy dreams."

I groaned.

It was hot. Two high summers rolled into one. No, two suns, blood-red, stark in a brazen sky. Should be cool underfoot—soft green turf, pool-table smooth to the far horizon. But it wasn't grass. Dust. Burning green dust—

The gladiator stood ten feet away, eyes glaring in disbelief. All of six-four high, great bronzed arms and legs, knotted muscles, a long shining sword in his right hand.

But his face was unmistakable.

This was where I took a good hold of myself. I wanted to giggle.

"Boy!" I said. "Do you tan quickly! Couple of minutes ago, you were as white as the bedsheet."

The gladiator shaded his eyes from the twin suns. "Is this yet another guise of the magician Garor to drive me insane—an Earthman here, on the Plains of Istak? Or am I already—mad?" His voice was deep, smoothly modulated.

My own was perfectly normal. Indeed, after the initial effort, I felt perfectly normal, except for the heat.

I said: "That's the growing idea where I've just come from—that you're going nuts."

You know those half-dreams, just on the verge of sleep, in which you can control your own imagery to some extent? That's how I felt. I knew intuitively what Steve was getting at when he said I could play it off the cuff. I looked down. Tweed suit, brogues—naturally. That's what I was wearing when I last looked at myself. I had no reason to think I was wearing—and therefore to be wearing—anything else. But something cooler was indicated in this heat, generated by Marsham Craswell's imagination.

Something like his own gladiator costume, perhaps.

Sandals—fine. There were my feet—in sandals.

Then I laughed. I had nearly fallen into the error of accepting his imagination.

"Do you mind if I switch off one of those suns?" I asked politely. "It's a little hot."

I gave one of the suns a very dirty look. It disappeared.

The gladiator raised his sword. "You are—Garor!" he cried. "But your witchery shall not avail you against the Sword!"

He rushed forward. The shining blade cleaved the air towards my skull.

I thought very, very fast.

The sword clanged, and streaked off at a sharp tangent from my G.I. brain-pan protector. I'd last worn that homely piece of hardware in the Argonne, and I knew it would stop a mere sword. I took it off.

"Now listen to me, Marsham Craswell," I said. "My name's Pete Parnell, of the Sunday *Star*, and—"

Craswell looked up from his sword, chest heaving, startled eyes bright as if with recognition. "Wait! I know now who you are—Nelpar Retrep, Man of the Seven Moons, come to fight with me against the Snake and his ungodly disciple, magician and sorceress, Garor. Welcome, my friend!"

He held out a huge bronzed hand. I shook it.

It was obvious that, unable to rationalize—or irrationalize—me, he was writing me into the plot of his dream! Right. It had been amusing so far. I'd string along for a while. My imagination hadn't taken a licking—yet.

Craswell said: "My followers, the great-hearted Dok-men of the Blue Hills, have just been slain in a gory battle. We were about to brave the many perils of the Plains of Istak in our quest for the Diamond—but all this, of course, you know."

"Sure," I said. "What now?"

Craswell turned suddenly, pointed. "There," he muttered. "A sight that strikes terror even into my heart—Garor returns to the battle, at the head of her dread Legion of Lakros, beasts of the Overworld, drawn into evil symbiosis with alien intelligences—invulnerable to men, but not to the Sword, or to the mighty weapons of Nelpar of the Seven Moons. We shall fight them alone!"

Racing across the vast plain of green dust towards us was a horde of . . . er . . . creatures. My vocabulary can't cope fully with Craswell's imagination. Gigantic, shimmering things, drooling thick ichor, half-flying, half-lolloping. Enough to say I looked around for a washbasin to spit in. I found one, with soap and towels complete, but I pushed it over, looked at a patch of green dust and thought hard.

The outline of the phone booth wavered a little before I could fix it. I dashed inside, dialed "Police H.Q.? Riot squad here—and quick!"

I stepped outside the booth. Craswell was whirling the Sword round his head, yelling war cries as he faced the onrushing monsters.

From the other direction came the swelling scream of a police siren. Half a dozen good, solid patrol cars screeched to a dust-spurting stop outside the phone booth. I don't have to think hard to get a New York cop car fixed in my mind. These were just right. And the first man out, running to my side and patting his cap on firmly, was just right, too.

Michael O'Faolin, the biggest, toughest, nicest cop I know.

"Mike," I said, pointing. "Fix 'em."

"Shure, an' it's an aisy job f'the bhoys I've brought along," said Mike, hitching his belt.

He deployed his men.

Craswell looked at them fanning out to take the charge, then staggered back towards me, hand over his eyes. "Madness!" he shouted. "What madness is this? What are you doing?"

For a moment, the whole scene wavered. The lone red sun blinked out, the green desert became a murky transparency through which I caught a split-second glimpse of white beds with two figures lying on them. Then Craswell uncovered his eyes.

The monsters began to diminish some twenty yards from the riot squad. By the time they got to the cops, they were man-size, and very amenable to discipline—enforced by raps over their horny noggins with nightsticks. They were bundled into the squad cars, which set off again over the plains.

Michael O'Faolin remained. I said: "Thanks, Mike. I may have a couple of spare tickets for the big fight tomorrow night. See you later."

"Just what I was wantin', Pete. 'Tis me day off. Now, how do I get home?"

I opened the door of the phone booth. "Right inside." He stepped in. I turned to Craswell.

"Mighty magic, O Nelpar!" he explained. "To creatures of Garor's mind you opposed creatures of your own!"

He'd woven the whole incident into his plot already.

"We must go forward now, Nelpar of the Seven Moons—forward to the Citadel of the Snake, a thousand lokspans over the burning Plains of Istak."

"How about the Diamond?"

"The Diamond—?"

Evidently, he'd run so far ahead of himself getting me fixed into the landscape that he'd forgotten all about the Diamond that could kill the Snake. I didn't remind him.

However, a thousand lokspans over the burning plains sounded a little too far for walking, whatever a lokspan might be.

I said: "Why do you make things tough for yourself, Craswell?"

"The name," he said with tremendous dignity, "is Multan."

"Multan, Sultan, Shashlik, Dikkidam, Hammaneggs or whatever polysyllabic pooh-bah you wish to call yourself—I still ask, why make things tough for yourself when there's plenty of cabs around? Just whistle."

I whistled. The Purple Cab swung in, perfect to the last detail, including a hulking-backed, unshaven driver, dead ringer for the impolite gorilla who'd brought me out to Pentagon that evening.

There is nothing on earth quite so unutterably prosaic as a New York Purple Cab with that sort of driver. The sight upset Craswell, and the green plains wavered again while he struggled to fit the cab into his dream.

"What new magic is this! You are indeed mighty, Nelpar!"

He got in. But he was trembling with the effort to maintain the structure of this world into which he had escaped, against my deliberate attempts to bring it crashing round his ears and restore him to colorless—but sane—normality.

At this stage, I felt curiously sorry for him; but I realized that it might only be permitting him to reach the heights of creative imagery before dousing him with the sponge from the cold bucket that I could jerk his drifting ego back out of dreamland.

It was dangerous thinking. Dangerous—for me.

Craswell's thousand lokspans appeared to be the equivalent of ten blocks. Or perhaps he wanted to gloss over the mundane near-reality of a cab ride. He pointed forward, past the driver's shoulder: "The Citadel of the Snake!"

To me, it looked remarkably like a wedding cake designed by Dali in red plastic: ten stories high, each story a platter half a mile thick, each platter diminishing in size and offset to the one beneath so that the edifice spiraled towards the glossy sky.

The cab rolled into its vast shadow, stopped beneath the sheer, blank precipice of the base platter, which might have been two miles in diameter. Or three. Or four. What's a mile or two among dreamers?

Craswell hopped out quickly. I got out on the driver's side. The driver said: "Dollar-fifty."

Square, unshaven jaw, low forehead, dirty-red hair straggling under his cap. I said: "Comes high for a short trip."

"Lookit the clock," he growled, squirming his shoulders. "Do I come out and get it?"

I said sweetly: "Go to hell."

Cab and driver shot downward through the green sand with the speed of an express elevator. The hole closed up. The times I've wanted to do just that—

Craswell was regarding me open-mouthed. I said: "Sorry. Now I'm being escapist, too. Get on with the plot."

He muttered something I didn't catch, strode across to the red wall in which a crack, meeting place of mighty gates, had appeared, and raised his sword.

"Open, Garor! Your doom is nigh. Multan and Nelpar are here to brave the terrors of this Citadel and free the world from the tyranny of the Snake!" He hammered at the crack with the sword-hilt.

"Not so loud," I murmured. "You'll wake the neighbors. Why not use the bell-push?" I put my thumb on the button and pressed. The towering gates swung slowly open.

"You . . . you have been here before—"

"Yes—after my last lobster supper." I bowed. "After you."

I followed him into a great, echoing tunnel with fluorescent walls. The gates closed behind us. He paused and looked at me with an odd gleam in his eyes. A gleam of—sanity. And there was anger in the set of his lips. Anger for me, not Garor or the Snake.

It's not nice to have someone trampling all over your ego. Pride is a tiger—even in dreams. The subconscious, as Steve had explained to me, is a function or state of the brain, not a small part of it. In thwarting Craswell, I was disparaging not merely his dream, but his very brain, sneering at his intellectual integrity, at his abilities as an imaginative writer.

In a brief moment of rationality, I believe he was strangely aware of this.

He said quietly: "You have limitations, Nelpar. Your outward-turning eyes are blind to the pain of creation; to you the crystal stars are spangles on the dress of a scarlet woman, and you mock the God-blessed unreason that would make life more than the crawling of an animal from womb to grave. In tearing the veil from mystery, you destroy not mystery—for there are many mysteries, a million veils, world within and beyond worlds—but beauty. And in destroying beauty, you destroy your soul."

These last words, quiet as they sounded, were caught up by the curving walls of the huge tunnel, amplified then diminished in pulsing repetition, loud then soft, a surging hypnotic echo: "Destroy your SOUL, DESTROY your soul. SOUL—"

Craswell pointed with his sword. His voice was exultant. "There is a Veil, Nelpar—and you must tear it lest it become your shroud! The Mist—the Sentient Mist of the Citadel!"

I'll admit that, for a few seconds, he'd had me a little groggy. I felt—subdued. And I understood for the first time his power as a word-spinner.

I knew that it was vital for me to reassert myself.

A thick, gray mist was rolling, wreathing slowly towards us, filling the tunnel to roof-height, puffing out thick, groping tentacles.

"It lives on Life itself," Craswell shouted. "It feeds, not on flesh, but on the vital principle that animates all flesh. I am safe, Nelpar, for I have the Sword. Can your magic save you?"

"Magic!" I said. "There's no gas invented yet that'll get through a Mark 8 mask."

Gas-drill—face-piece first, straps behind the ears. No, I hadn't forgotten the old routine.

I adjusted the mask comfortably. "And if it's not gas," I added, "this will fix it." I felt over my shoulder, unclipped a nozzle, brought it round into the "ready" position.

I had only used a one-man flame-thrower once—in training—but the experience was etched on my memory.

This was a deluxe model. At the first thirty-foot oily, searing blast, the Mist curled in on itself and rolled back the way it had come. Only quicker.

I shucked off the trappings. "You were in the Army for a while, Craswell. Remember?"

The shining translucency of the walls dimmed suddenly, and beyond them I glimpsed, as in a movie close-up through an unfocused projector, the square, intense face of Steve Blakiston.

Then the walls re-formed, and Craswell, still the bronzed, naked-limbed giant of his imagination, was looking at me again, frowning, worried. "Your words are strange, O Nelpar. It seems you are master of mysteries beyond even my knowing."

I put on the sort of face I use when the sports editor queries my expenses, aggrieved, pleading. "Your trouble, Craswell, is that you don't want to know. You just won't remember. That's why you're here. But life isn't bad if you oil it a little. Why not snap out of this and come with me for a drink?"

"I do not understand," he muttered. "But we have a mission to perform. Follow." And he strode off.

Mention of drink reminded me. There was nothing wrong with my memory. And that tunnel was as hot as the green desert. I remembered a very small pub just off the streetcar depot end of Sauchiehall Street, Glasgow, Scotland. A ginger-whiskered ancient, an exile from the Highlands, who'd listened to me enthusing over a certain brand of Scotch. "If ye think that's guid, mon, ye'll no' tasted the brew from ma own private deestillery. Smack yer lips ower this, laddie—" And he'd produced an antique silver flask and poured a generous measure of golden whisky into my glass. I had never tasted such mellow nectar before or since. Until I was walking down the tunnel behind Craswell.

I nearly envisaged the glass, but changed my mind in time to make it the antique flask. I raised it to my lips. Imagination's a wonderful thing.

Craswell was talking. I'd nearly forgotten him.

". . . near the Hall of Madness, where strange music assaults the brain, weird harmonies that enchant, then kill, rupturing the very cells by a mixture of subsonic and supersonic frequencies. Listen!"

We had reached the end of the tunnel and stood at the top of a slope which, broadening, ran gently downward, veiled by a blue haze, like the smoke from fifty million cigarettes, filling a vast circular hall. The haze eddied, moved by vagrant, sluggish currents of air, and revealed on the farther side, dwarfed by distance but obviously enormous, a complex structure of pipes and consoles.

A dozen Mighty Wurlitzers rolled into one would have appeared as a miniature piano at the foot of this towering music machine.

At its many consoles which, even at that distance, I could see consisted of at least half a dozen manuals each, were multilimbed creatures—spiders or octopuses or Polilollipops—I didn't ask what Craswell called them—I was listening.

The opening bars were strange enough, but innocuous. Then the multiple tones and harmonies began to swell in volume. I picked out the curious, sweet harshness of oboes and bassoons, the eldritch, rising ululation of a thousand violins, the keen shrilling of a hundred demonic flutes, the sobbing of many 'cellos. That's enough. Music's my hobby, and I don't want to get carried away in describing how that crazy symphony nearly carried me away.

But if Craswell ever reads this, I'd like him to know that he missed his vocation. He should have been a musician. His dream music showed an amazing intuitive grasp of orchestration and harmonic theory. If he could do anything like it consciously, he would be a great modern composer.

Yet not too much like it. Because it began to have the effects he had warned about. The insidious rhythm and wild melodies seemed to throb inside my head, setting up a vibration, a burning, in the brain tissue.

Imagine Puccini's "Recondita Armonia" reorchestrated by

Stravinsky then rearranged by Honegger, played by fifty symphony orchestras in the Hollywood Bowl, and you might begin to get the idea.

I was getting too much of it. Did I say music was my hobby? Certainly—but the only instrument I play is the harmonica. Quite well, too. And with a microphone, I can make lots of nice noise.

A microphone—and plenty of amplifiers. I pulled the harmonica from my pocket, took a deep breath, and whooped into "Tiger Rag," my favorite party-piece.

The stunning blast-wave of jubilant jazz, riffs, tiger-growls and tremolo discords from the tiny mouth organ crashed into the vast hall from the amplifiers, completely swamping Craswell's mad music.

I heard his agonized shout even above the din. His tastes in music were evidently not as catholic as mine. He didn't like jazz.

The music machine quavered, the multilimbed organists, ludicrous in their haste to escape from an unreal doom, shrank, withered to scuttling black beetles; the lighting effects that had sprayed a rich, unearthly effulgence over the consoles died away into pastel, blue gloom; then the great machine itself, caught in swirl upon wave of-augmented chords complemented and reinforced by its own outpourings, shivered into fragments, poured in a chaotic stream over the floor of the hall.

I heard Craswell shout again, then the scene changed abruptly. I assumed that, in his desire to blot out the triumphant paean of jazz from his mind, and perhaps in an unconscious attempt to confuse me, he had skipped a part of his plot and, in the opposite of the flashback beloved of screen writers, shot himself forward. We were—somewhere else.

Perhaps it was the inferiority complex I was inducing, or in the transition he had forgotten how tall he was supposed to be, but he was now a mere six feet, nearer my own height.

He was so hoarse, I nearly suggested a gargle. "I . . . I left you in the Hall of Madness. Your magic caused the roof to collapse. I thought you were—killed."

So the flash-forward wasn't just an attempt to confuse me. He'd tried to lose me, write me out of the script altogether.

I shook my head. "Wishful thinking, Craswell old man," I said reproachfully. "You can't kill me off between chapters. You see, I'm not one of your characters at all. Haven't you grasped that yet? The only way you can get rid of me is by waking up."

"Again you speak in riddles," he said, but there was little confidence in his voice.

The place in which we stood was a great, high-vaulted chamber. The lighting effects—as I was coming to expect— were unusual and admirable—many colored shafts of radiance from unseen sources, slowly moving, meeting and merging at the farther end of the chamber in a white, circular blaze which seemed to be suspended over a thronelike structure.

Craswell's size-concepts were stupendous. He'd either studied the biggest cathedrals in Europe, or he was reared inside Grand Central Station. The throne was apparently a good half-mile away, over a completely bare but softly resilient floor. Yet it was coming nearer. We were not walking. I looked at the walls, realized that the floor itself, a gigantic endless belt, was carrying us along.

The slow, inexorable movement was impressive. I was aware that Craswell was covertly glancing at me. He was anxious that I should be impressed. I replied by speeding up the belt a trifle. He didn't appear to notice.

He said: "We approach the Throne of the Snake, before which, his protector and disciple, stands the female magician and sorceress Garor. Against her, we shall need all your strange skills, Nelpar, for she stands invulnerable within an invisible shield of pure force.

"You must destroy that barrier, that I may slay her with the Sword. Without her, the Snake, though her master and self-proclaimed master of this world, is powerless, and he will be at our mercy."

The belt came to a halt. We were at the foot of a broad stairway leading to the throne itself, a massive metal platform on which the Snake reposed beneath a brilliant ball of light.

The Snake was—a snake. Coil on coil of overgrown python, with an evil head the size of a football swaying slowly from side to side.

I spent little time looking at it. I've seen snakes before.

And there was something worth much more prolonged study standing just below and slightly to one side of the throne.

Craswell's taste in feminine pulchritude was unimpeachable. I had half expected an ancient, withered horror, but if Flo Ziegfeld had seen this baby, he'd have been scrambling up those steps waving a contract, force shield or no force shield, before you could get out the first glissando of a wolf-whistle.

She was a tall, oval-faced, green-eyed brunette, with everything just so, and nothing much in the way of covering—a scanty metal chest protector and a knee-length, filmy green skirt. She had a tiny, delightful mole on her left cheek.

There was a curious touch of pride in Craswell's voice as he said, rather unnecessarily: "We are here, Garor," and looked at me expectantly.

The girl said: "Insolent fools—you are here to die."

Mm-m-m—that voice, as smooth and rich as a Piatigorski 'cello note. I was ready to give quite a lot of credit to Craswell's imagination, but I couldn't believe that he'd dreamed up this baby just like that. I guessed that she was modeled on life; someone he knew; someone I'd like to know—someone pulled out of the grab bag of memory in the same way as I had produced Mike O'Faolin and that grubby-chinned cab driver.

"A luscious dish," I said. "Remind me to ask you later for the phone number of the original, Craswell."

Then I said and did something that I have since regretted. It was not the behavior of a gentleman. I said: "But didn't you know they were wearing skirts longer, this season?"

I looked at the skirt. The hem line shot down to her ankles, evening-gown length.

Outraged, Craswell glared at his girlfriend. The skirt became knee-length. I made it fashionable again.

Then that skirt-hem was bobbing up and down between her ankles and her knees like a crazy window blind. It was a contest of wills and imaginations, with a very pretty pair of well-covered tibiae as battleground. A fascinating sight, Garor's beautiful eyes blazed with fury. She seemed to be strangely aware of the misbecoming nature of the conflict.

Craswell suddenly uttered a ringing, petulant howl of anger

and frustration—a score of lusty-lunged infants whose rattles had been simultaneously snatched from them couldn't have made more noise—and the intriguing scene was erased from view in an eruption of jet-black smoke.

When it cleared, Craswell was still in the same relative position but his sword was gone, his gladiator rig was torn and scorched, and thin trickles of blood streaked his muscular arms.

I didn't like the way he was looking at me. I'd booted his superego pretty hard that time.

I said: "So you couldn't take it. You've skipped a chapter again. Wise me up on what I've missed, will you?" Somehow it didn't sound as flippant as I intended.

He spoke incisively. "We have been captured and condemned to die, Nelpar. We are in the Pit of the Beast, and nothing can save us, for I have been deprived of the Sword and you of your magic.

"The ravening jaws of the Beast cannot be stayed. It is the end, Nelpar. The End—"

His eyes, large, faintly luminous, looked into mine. I tried to glance away, failed.

Irritated beyond bearing by my importunate clowning, his affronted ego had assumed the whole power of his brain, to assert itself through his will—to dominate me.

The volition may have been unconsicous—he could not know why he hated me—but the effect was damnable.

And for the first time since my brash intrusion into the most private recesses of his mind, I began to doubt whether the whole business was quite—decent.

Sure, I was trying to help the guy, but . . . but dreams are sacred.

Doubt negates confidence. With confidence gone, the gateway is open to fear.

Another voice, sibilant. Steve Blakiston saying ". . . unless you let your mind go under." My own voice ". . . wake up as a candidate for a bed in the next ward—" No, not—". . . not unless you let your mind go under—" And Steve had been scared to do it himself, hadn't he? I'd have something to say to that guy when I got out. If I got out . . . if—"

The whole thing just wasn't amusing anymore.

"Quit it, Craswell," I said harshly. "Quit making goo-goo eyes, or I'll bat you one—and you'll feel it, coma or no coma."

He said: "What foolish words are these, when we are both so near to death?"

Steve's voice: ". . . sympathetic magic . . . imagination. If he imagines that one of his fantastic creations kills the hero—himself—he just won't wake up again."

That was it. A situation in which the hero must die. And he wanted to envisage my death, too. But he couldn't kill me. Or could he? How could Blakiston know what powers might be unleashed by the concept of death during this ultramundane communion of minds?

Didn't psychiatrists say that the death urge, the will to die, was buried deep, but potent, in the subconscious minds of men? It was not buried deep here. It was glaring, exultant, starkly displayed in the eyes of Marsham Craswell.

He had escaped from reality into a dream, but it was not far enough. Death was the only full escape—

Perhaps Craswell sensed the confusion of thought and speculation that laid my mind wide open to the suggestions of his rioting, perfervid, death-intent imagination. He waved an arm with the grandiloquent gesture of a Shakespearean chorus introducing a last act, and brought on his monster.

In detail and vividness it excelled everything that he had dreamed up previously. It was his swan song as a creator of fantastic forms, and he had wrought well.

I saw, briefly, that we were in the center of an enormous, steep-banked amphitheater. There were no spectators. No crowd scenes for Craswell. He preferred that strange, timeless emptiness which comes from using a minimum number of characters.

Just the two of us, under the blazing rays of great, red suns swinging in a molten sky. I couldn't count them.

I became visually aware only of the Beast.

An ant in the bottom of a washbowl with a dog snuffling at it might feel the same way. If the Beast had been anything like a dog. If it had been anything like *anything*.

It was a mass the size of several elephants. An obscene hulking gob of animated, semitransparent purple flesh, with a gaping, circular mouth or vent, ringed inside with pointed beslimed tusks, and outside with—eyes.

As a static thing, it would have been a filthy envenomed horror, a thing of surpassing dread in its mere aspect; but the most fearsome thing was its nightmarish mode of progression.

Limbless, it jerked its prodigious bulk forward in a series of heaves—and lubricated its path with a glaucous, viscid fluid which slopped from its mouth with every jerk.

It was heading for us at an incredible pace. Thirty yards—Twenty—

The rigidity of utter fear gripped my limbs. This was true nightmare. I tried desperately to think . . . flame-thrower . . . how . . . I couldn't remember . . . my mind was slipping away from me in face of the onward surging of that protoplasmic juggernaut . . . the slime first, then the mouth, closing . . . my thoughts were a screaming turmoil—

Another voice, a deep, drawling, kindly voice, from an unforgettable hour in childhood—"There's nothing in the whole wide world or out of it that a slug from Billy here won't stop. There's nothing you can meet in dreams that Billy here won't stop. He'll come into your dreams with you from now on. There's no call to be scared of anything." Then the cool, hard butt in my hand, the recoil, the whining irresistible chunk of hot, heavy metal—deep in my subconscious.

"Pop!" I gasped. "Thanks, Pop."

The Beast was looming over me. But Billy was in my hand, pointing into the mouth. I fired.

The Beast jerked back on its slimy trail, began to dwindle, fold in on itself. I fired again and again.

I became aware once more of Craswell beside me. He looked at the dying Beast, still huge, but rapidly diminishing, then at the dull metal of the old Colt in my hand, the wisp of blue smoke from its uptilted barrel.

And then he began to laugh.

Great, gusty laughter, but with a touch of hysteria.

And as he laughed, he began to fade from view. The red suns sped away into the sky, became pin points; and the sky was white and clean and blank—like a ceiling.

In fact—what beautiful words are "in fact"—in fact, in sweet reality, it *was* a ceiling.

Then Steve Blakiston was peering down, easing the chromium bowl off the rubber pads round my head.

"Thanks, Pete," he said. "Half an hour to the minute. You worked on him quicker than an insulin shock."

I sat up, adjusting myself mentally. He pinched my arm. "Sure—you're awake. I'd like you to tell me just what you did—but not now. I'll ring you at your office."

I saw an assistant taking the bowl off Craswell's head.

Craswell blinked, turned his head, saw me. Half a dozen expressions, none of them pleasant, chased over his face.

He heaved upright, pushed aside the assistant.

"You lousy bum," he shouted. "I'll murder you!"

I just got clear before Steve and one of the others grabbed his arms.

"Let me get at him—I'll tear him open!"

"I warned you," Steve panted. "Get out, quick."

I was on my way. Marsham Craswell in a nightshirt may not have been quite so impressive physically as the bronzed gladiator of his dreams, but he was still passably muscular.

That was last night. Steve rang this morning.

"Cured," he said triumphantly. "Sane as you are. Said he realized he'd been overworking, and he's going to take things easier—give himself a rest from fantasy and write something else. He doesn't remember a thing about his dream-coma—but he had a curious feeling that he'd still like to do something unpleasant to a certain guy who was in the next bed to him when he woke up. He doesn't know why, and I haven't told him. But better keep clear."

"The feeling is mutual," I said. "I don't like his line in monsters. What's he going to write now—love stories?"

Steve laughed. "No. He's got a sudden craze for Westerns. Started talking this morning about the sociological and historical significance of the Colt revolver. He jotted down the title of his first yarn—'Six-Gun Rule.' Hey—is that based on something you pulled on him in his dream?"

I told him.

So Marsham Craswell's as sane as me, huh? I wouldn't take bets.

Three hours ago, I was on my way to the latest heavy-weight match at Madison Square Garden when I was button-holed by an off-duty policeman.

Michael O'Faolin, the biggest, toughest, nicest cop I know.

"Pete, m'boy," he said. "I had the strangest dream last night. I was helpin' yez out of a bit of a hole, and when it was all over, you said, in gratitude it may have been, that yez might have a couple of spare tickets f'the fight this very night, and I was wondering whether it could have been a sort of tellypathy like, and—"

I grabbed the corner of the bar doorway to steady myself. Mike was still jabbering on when I fumbled for my own tickets and said: "I'm not feeling too well, Mike. You go. I'll pick my stuff up from the other sheets. Don't think about it, Mike. Just put it down to the luck of the Irish."

I went back to the bar and thought hard into a large whiskey, which is the next best thing to a crystal ball for providing a focus of concentration.

"Tellypathy, huh?"

No, said the whiskey. Coincidence. Forget it.

Yet there's something in telepathy. Subconscious telepathy—two dreaming minds in rapport. But I wasn't dreaming. I was just tagging along in someone else's dream. Minds are particularly receptive in sleep. Premonitions and what-have-you. But I wasn't sleeping either. Six and four makes minus ten, strike three—you're out. You're nuts, said the whiskey.

I decided to find myself, a better-quality crystal ball. A Scotch in a crystal glass at Cevali's club.

So I hailed a Purple Cab. There was something reminiscent about the back of the driver's head. I refused to think about it. Until the pay-off.

"Dollar-fifty," he growled, then leaned out. "Say—ain't I seen you some place?"

"I'm around," I said, in a voice that squeezed with reluctance past my larynx. "Didn't you drive me out to Pentagon yesterday?"

"Yeah, that's it," he said. Square unshaven jaw, low forehead, dirty red hair straggling under his cap. "Yeah—but there's something else about your pan. I took a sleep between cruises last night and had a daffy dream. You seemed to come into it. And I got the screwiest idea you already owe me a dollar-fifty.''

For a moment, I toyed with the idea of telling him to go to hell. But the roadway wasn't green sand. It looked too solid to open up. So I said, "Here's five," and staggered into Cevali's.

I looked into a whiskey glass until my brain began to clear, then I phoned Steve Blakiston and talked. "It's the implications," I said finally. "I'm driving myself bats trying to figure out what would have happened if I'd conjured up a few score of my acquaintances. Would they all have dreamed the same dream if they'd been asleep?"

"Too diffuse," said Steve, apparently through a mouthful of sandwich. "That would be like trying to broadcast on dozens of wavelengths simultaneously with the same transmitter. Your brain was an integral part of that machine, occupying the same position in the circuit as a complexus of recording instruments, keyed in place with Craswell's brain—until the pickup frequency was raised. What happened then I imagined purely as an induction process. It was—as far as the Craswell hookup was concerned, but—"

I couldn't stand the juicy champing noises any longer, and said: "Swallow it before you choke." The guy lives on sandwiches.

His voice cleared. "Don't you see what we've got? During the amplification of the cerebral currents, there was a backsurge through the tubes and the machine became a transmitter. These two guys were sleeping, their unconscious minds wide open and acting as receivers; you'd seen them during the day, envisaged them vividly—and got tuned in, disturbing their minds and giving them dreams. Ever heard of sympathetic dreams? Ever dreamed of someone you haven't seen for years, and the next day he looks you up? Now we can do it deliberately—mechanically assisted dream telepathy, the waves reinforced and transmitted electronically! Come on over. We've got to experiment some more."

"Sometimes," I said, "I sleep. That's what I intend to do now—without mechanical assistance. So long."

A nightcap was indicated. I wandered back to the club bar. I should have gone home.

She hipped her way to the microphone in front of the band, five-foot-ten of dream wrapped up in a white, glove-tight gown. An oval-faced, green-eyed brunette with a tiny, delightful mole on her left cheek. The gown was a little exiguous about the upper regions, perhaps, but not as whistle-worthy as the outfit Craswell had dreamed on her.

Backstage, I got a double shot of ice from those green eyes. Yes, she knew Mr. Craswell slightly. No, she wasn't asleep around midnight last night. And would I be so good as to inform her what business it was of mine? College type, ultra. How they do drift into the entertainment business. Not that I mind.

When I asked about the refrigeration, she said: "It's merely that I have no particular desire to know you, Mr. Parnell."

"Why?"

"I'm hardly accountable to you for my preferences." She frowned as if trying to recall something, added: "In any case—I don't know. I just don't like you. Now if you'll pardon me, I have another number to sing—"

"But, please . . . let me explain—"

"Explain what?"

She had me there. I stumble-tongued, and got a back view of the gown.

How can you apologize to a girl when she doesn't even know that you owe her an apology? She hadn't been asleep, so she couldn't have dreamed about the skirt incident. And if she had—she was Craswell's dream, not mine. But through some aberration a trickle of thought waves from Blakiston's machine had planted an unreasonable antipathy to me in her subconscious mind. And it would need a psychiatrist to dig it out. Or—

I phoned Steve from the club office. He was still chewing. I said: "I've got some intensive thinking to do—into that machine of yours. I'll be right over."

She was leaving the microphone as I passed the band on my way out. I looked at her hard as she came up, getting every detail fixed.

"What time do you go to bed?" I asked.

I saw the slap coming and ducked.

I said: "I can wait. I'll be seeing you. Happy dreams."

THE SAME TO YOU DOUBLED

by Robert Sheckley

In New York, it never fails, the doorbell rings just when you've plopped down onto the couch for a well-deserved snooze. Now, a person of character would say, "To hell with that, a man's home is his castle and they can slide any telegrams under the door." But if you're like Edelstein, not particularly strong on character, then you think to yourself that maybe it's the blonde from 12C who has come up to borrow a jar of chili powder. Or it could even be some crazy film producer who wants to make a movie based on the letters you've been sending your mother in Santa Monica. (And why not; don't they make movies out of worse material than that?)

Yet this time, Edelstein had really decided not to answer the bell. Lying on the couch, his eyes still closed, he called out, "I don't want any."

"Yes you do," a voice from the other side of the door replied.

"I've got all the encyclopedias, brushes and waterless cookery I need," Edelstein called back wearily. "Whatever you've got, I've got it already."

"Look," the voice said, "I'm not selling anything. I want to give you something."

Edelstein smiled the thin, sour smile of the New Yorker who knows that if someone made him a gift of a package of genuine, unmarked $20 bills, he'd still somehow end up having to pay for it.

"If it's *free*," Edelstein answered, "then I *definitely* can't afford it."

"But I mean *really* free," the voice said. "I mean free that it won't cost you anything now or ever."

206

"I'm not interested," Edelstein replied, admiring his firmness of character.

The voice did not answer.

Edelstein called out, "Hey, if you're still there, please go away."

"My dear Mr. Edelstein," the voice said, "cynicism is merely a form of naïveté. Mr. Edelstein, wisdom is discrimination."

"He gives me lectures now," Edelstein said to the wall.

"All right," the voice said, "forget the whole thing, keep your cynicism and your racial prejudice; do I need this kind of trouble?"

"Just a minute," Edelstein answered. "What makes you think I'm prejudiced?"

"Let's not crap around," the voice said. "If I was raising funds for Hadassah or selling Israel bonds, it would have been different. But, obviously, I am what I am, so excuse me for living."

"Not so fast," Edelstein said. "As far as I'm concerned, you're just a voice from the other side of the door. For all I know, you could be Catholic or Seventh-Day Adventist or even Jewish."

"You knew," the voice responded.

"Mister, I swear to you—"

"Look," the voice said, "it doesn't matter, I come up against a lot of this kind of thing. Goodbye, Mr. Edelstein."

"Just a minute," Edelstein replied.

He cursed himself for a fool. How often had he fallen for some huckster's line, ending up, for example, paying $9.98 for an illustrated two-volume *Sexual History of Mankind*, which his friend Manowitz had pointed out he could have bought in any Marboro bookstore for $2.98?

But the voice was right. Edelstein had somehow known that he was dealing with a goy.

And the voice would go away thinking, *The Jews, they think they're better than anyone else.* Further, he would tell this to his bigoted friends at the next meeting of the Elks or the Knights of Columbus, and there it would be, another black eye for the Jews.

"I do have a weak character," Edelstein thought sadly.

He called out, "All right! You can come in! But I warn you from the start, I am not going to buy anything."

He pulled himself to his feet and started toward the door. Then he stopped, for the voice had replied, "Thank you very much," and then a man had walked through the closed, double-locked wooden door.

The man was of medium height, nicely dressed in a gray pinstripe modified Edwardian suit. His cordovan boots were highly polished. He was black, carried a briefcase, and he had stepped through Edelstein's door as if it had been made of Jell-O.

"Just a minute, stop, hold on one minute," Edelstein said. He found that he was clasping both of his hands together and his heart was beating unpleasantly fast.

The man stood perfectly still and at his ease, one yard within the apartment. Edelstein started to breathe again. He said, "Sorry, I just had a brief attack, a kind of hallucination—"

"Want to see me do it again?" the man asked.

"My God, no! So you *did* walk through the door! Oh, God, I think I'm in trouble."

Edelstein went back to the couch and sat down heavily. The man sat down in a nearby chair.

"What is this all about?" Edelstein whispered.

"I do the door thing to save time," the man said. "It usually closes the credulity gap. My name is Charles Sitwell. I am a field man for the Devil."

Edelstein believed him. He tried to think of a prayer, but all he could remember was the one he used to say over bread in the summer camp he had attended when he was a boy. It probably wouldn't help. He also knew the Lord's Prayer, but that wasn't even his religion. Perhaps the salute to the flag. . . .

"Don't get all worked up," Sitwell said. "I'm not here after your soul or any old-fashioned crap like that."

"How can I believe you?" Edelstein asked.

"Figure it out for yourself," Sitwell told him. "Consider only the war aspect. Nothing but rebellions and revolutions for the past fifty years or so. For us, that means an unprecedented supply of condemned Americans, Viet Cong, Nigerians, Biafrans, Indonesians, South Africans, Russians, Indians, Pakistanis and Arabs. Israelis, too, I'm sorry to tell you. Also, we're pulling in more Chinese than usual, and just recently, we've begun to get plenty of action on the South American market. Speaking frankly, Mr. Edelstein, we're overloaded with souls. If another war starts this year, we'll have to declare an amnesty on venial sins."

Edelstein thought it over. "Then you're really not here to take me to hell?"

"Hell, no!" Sitwell said. "I told you, our waiting list is longer than for Peter Cooper Village; we hardly have any room left in limbo."

"Well. . . . Then why are you here?"

Sitwell crossed his legs and leaned forward earnestly. "Mr. Edelstein, you have to understand that hell is very much like U.S. Steel or I.T.&T. We're a big outfit and we're more or less a monopoly. But, like any really big corporation, we are imbued with the ideal of public service and we like to be well thought of."

"Makes sense," Edelstein said.

"But, unlike Ford, we can't very well establish a foundation and start giving out scholarships and work grants. People wouldn't understand. For the same reason, we can't start building model cities or fighting pollution. We can't even throw up a dam in Afghanistan without someone questioning our motives."

"I see where it could be a problem," Edelstein admitted.

"Yet we like to do something. So, from time to time, but especially now, with business so good, we like to distribute a small bonus to a random selection of potential customers."

"Customer? Me?"

"No one is calling you a sinner," Sitwell pointed out. "I said *potential*—which means everybody."

"Oh. . . . What kind of bonus?"

"Three wishes," Sitwell said briskly. "That's the traditional form."

"Let me see if I've got this straight," Edelstein said. "I can have any three wishes I want? With no penalty, no secret ifs and buts?"

"There is one but," Sitwell said.

"I knew it," Edelstein said.

"It's simple enough. Whatever you wish for, your worst enemy gets double."

Edelstein thought about that. "So if I asked for a million dollars—"

"Your worst enemy would get two million dollars."

"And if I asked for pneumonia?"

"Your worst enemy would get double pneumonia."

Edelstein pursed his lips and shook his head. "Look, not that I mean to tell you people how to run your business, but I hope you realize that you endanger customer goodwill with a clause like that."

"It's a risk, Mr. Edelstein, but absolutely necessary on a couple of counts," Sitwell said. "You see, the clause is a psychic feedback device that acts to maintain homeostasis."

"Sorry, I'm not following you," Edelstein answered.

"Let me put it this way. The clause acts to reduce the power of the three wishes and, thus, to keep things reasonably normal. A wish is an extremely strong instrument, you know."

"I can imagine," Edelstein said. "Is there a second reason?"

"You should have guessed it already," Sitwell said, baring exceptionally white teeth in an approximation of a smile. "Clauses like that are our trademark. That's how you know it's a genuine hellish product."

"I see, I see," Edelstein said. "Well, I'm going to need some time to think about this."

"The offer is good for thirty days," Sitwell said, standing up. "When you want to make a wish, simply state it—clearly and loudly. I'll tend to the rest."

Sitwell walked to the door. Edelstein said, "There's only one problem I think I should mention."

"What's that?" Sitwell asked.

"Well, it just so happens that I don't have a worst enemy. In fact, I don't have an enemy in the world."

Sitwell laughed hard, then wiped his eyes with a mauve handkerchief. "Edelstein," he said, "you're really too much! Not an enemy in the world! What about your cousin Seymour, who you wouldn't lend five hundred dollars to, to start a dry-cleaning business? Is he a friend all of a sudden?"

"I hadn't thought about Seymour," Edelstein answered.

"And what about Mrs. Abramowitz, who spits at the mention of your name, because you wouldn't marry her Marjorie? What about Tom Cassiday in apartment 1C of this building, who has a complete collection of Goebbels' speeches and dreams every night of killing all of the Jews in the world, beginning with you? . . . Hey, are you all right?"

Edelstein, sitting on the couch, had gone white and his hands were clasped tightly together again.

"I never realized," he said.

"No one realizes," Sitwell said. "Look, take it easy, six or seven enemies is nothing; I can assure you that you're well below average, hatewise."

"Who else?" Edelstein asked, breathing heavily.

"I'm not going to tell you," Sitwell said. "It would be needless aggravation."

"But I have to know who is my worst enemy! Is it Cassiday? Do you think I should buy a gun?"

Sitwell shook his head. "Cassiday is a harmless, half-witted lunatic. He'll never lift a finger, you have my word on that. Your worst enemy is a man name Edward Samuel Manowitz."

"You're sure of that?" Edelstein asked incredulously.

"Completely sure."

"But Manowitz happens to be my best friend."

"Also your worst enemy," Sitwell replied. "Sometimes it works like that. Goodbye, Mr. Edelstein, and good luck with your three wishes."

"Wait!" Edelstein cried. He wanted to ask a million questions; but he was embarrassed and he asked only, "How can it be that hell is so crowded?"

"Because only heaven is infinite," Sitwell told him.

"You know about heaven, too?"

"Of course. It's the parent corporation. But now I really must be getting along. I have an appointment in Poughkeepsie. Good luck, Mr. Edelstein."

Sitwell waved and turned and walked out through the locked solid door.

Edelstein sat perfectly still for five minutes. He thought about Eddie Manowitz. His worst enemy! That was laughable; hell had really gotten its wires crossed on that piece of

information. He had known Manowitz for twenty years, saw
him nearly every day, played chess and gin rummy with him.
They went for walks together, saw movies together, at least
one night a week they ate dinner together.

It was true, of course, that Manowitz could sometimes open
up a big mouth and overstep the boundaries of good taste.

Sometimes Manowitz could be downright rude.

To be perfectly honest, Manowitz had, on more than one
occasion, been insulting.

"But we're *friends*," Edelstein said to himself. "We *are*
friends, aren't we?"

There was an easy way to test it, he realized. He could
wish for $1,000,000. That would give Manowitz $2,000,000.
But so what? Would he, a wealthy man, care that his best
friend was wealthier?

Yes! He would care! He damned well would care! It would
eat his life away if a wise guy like Manowitz got rich on
Edelstein's wish.

"My God!" Edelstein thought. "An hour ago, I was a poor
but contented man. Now I have three wishes and an enemy."

He found that he was twisting his hands together again. He
shook his head. This was going to need some thought.

In the next week, Edelstein managed to get a leave of absence
from his job and sat day and night with a pen and pad in his
hand. At first, he couldn't get his mind off castles. Castles
seemed to *go* with wishes. But, on second thought, it was not
a simple matter. Taking an average dream castle with a
ten-foot-thick stone wall, grounds and the rest, one had to
consider the matter of upkeep. There was heating to worry
about, the cost of serveral servants, because anything less
would look ridiculous.

So it came at last to a matter of money.

I could keep up a pretty decent castle on $2000 a week,
Edelstein thought, jotting figures down rapidly on his pad.

But that would mean that Manowitz would be maintaining
two castles on $4000 a week!

By the second week, Edelstein had gotten past castles and
was speculating feverishly on the endless possibilties and

combinations of travel. Would it be too much to ask for a cruise around the world? Perhaps it would; he wasn't even sure he was up to it. Surely he could accept a summer in Europe? Even a two-week vacation at the Fontainebleau in Miami Beach to rest his nerves.

But Manowitz would get two vacations! If Edelstein stayed at the Fontainebleau, Manowitz would have a penthouse suite at the Key Largo Colony Club. Twice.

It was almost better to stay poor and to keep Manowitz deprived.

Almost, but not quite.

During the final week, Edelstein was getting angry and desperate, even cynical. He said to himself, I'm an idiot, how do I know that there's anything to this? So Sitwell could walk through doors; does that make him a magician? Maybe I've been worried about nothing.

He surprised himself by standing up abruptly and saying, in a loud, firm voice, "I want twenty thousand dollars and I want it right now."

He felt a gentle tug at his right buttock. He pulled out his wallet. Inside it, he found a certified check made out to him for $20,000.

He went down to his bank and cashed the check, trembling, certain that the police would grab him. The manager looked at the check and initialed it. The teller asked him what denominations he wanted it in. Edelstein told the teller to credit it to his account.

As he left the bank, Manowitz came rushing in, an expression of fear, joy and bewilderment on his face.

Edelstein hurried home before Manowitz could speak to him. He had a pain in his stomach for the rest of the day.

Idiot! He had asked for only a lousy $20,000. But Manowitz had gotten $40,000!

A man could die from the aggravation.

Edelstein spent his days alternating between apathy and rage. That pain in the stomach had come back, which meant that he was probably giving himself an ulcer.

It was all so damned unfair! Did he have to push himself into an early grave, worrying about Manowitz?

Yes!

For now he realized that Manowitz was really his enemy and that the thought of enriching his enemy was literally killing him.

He thought about that and then said to himself, Edelstein, listen to me; you can't go on like this, you must get some satisfaction!

But how?

He paced up and down his apartment. The pain was definitely an ulcer; what else could it be?

Then it came to him. Edelstein stopped pacing. His eyes rolled wildly and, seizing paper and pencil, he made some lightning calculations. When he finished, he was flushed, excited—happy for the first time since Sitwell's visit.

He stood up. He shouted, "I want six hundred pounds of chopped chicken liver and I want it at once!"

The caterers began to arrive within five minutes.

Edelstein ate several giant portions of chopped chicken liver, stored two pounds of it in his refrigerator and sold most of the rest to a caterer at half price, making over $700 on the deal. The janitor had to take away 75 pounds that had been overlooked. Edelstein had a good laugh at the thought of Manowitz standing in his apartment up to his neck in chopped chicken liver.

His enjoyment was short-lived. He learned that Manowitz had kept ten pounds for himself (the man always had had a gross appetite), presented five pounds to a drab little widow he was trying to make an impression on and sold the rest back to the caterer for one third off, earning over $2000.

I am the world's prize imbecile, Edelstein thought. For a minute's stupid satisfaction, I gave up a wish worth conservatively $100,000,000. And what do I get out of it? Two pounds of chopped chicken liver, a few hundred dollars and the lifelong friendship of my janitor!

He knew he was killing himself from sheer brute aggravation.

He was down to one wish now.

And now it was *crucial* that he spend that final wish wisely. But he had to ask for something that he wanted desperately—something that Manowitz would *not* like at all.

Four weeks had gone by. One day, Edelstein realized glumly that his time was just about up. He had racked his brain, only to confirm his worst suspicions: Manowitz liked everything that he liked. Manowitz liked castles, women, wealth, cars, vacations, wine, music, food. Whatever you named, Manowitz the copycat liked it.

Then he remembered: Manowitz, by some strange quirk of the taste buds, could not abide lox.

But Edelstein didn't like lox, either, not even Nova Scotia.

Edelstein prayed: Dear God, who is in charge of hell and heaven, I have had three wishes and used two miserably. Listen, God, I don't mean to be ungrateful, but I ask you, if a man happens to be granted three wishes, shouldn't he be able to do better for himself than I have done? Shouldn't he be able to have something good happen to him without filling the pockets of Manowitz, his worst enemy, who does nothing but collect double with no effort or pain?

The final hour arrived. Edelstein grew calm, in the manner of a man who had accepted his fate. He realized that his hatred of Manowitz was futile, unworthy of him. With a new and sweet serenity, he said to himself, I am now going to ask for what I, Edelstein, personally want. If Manowitz has to go along for the ride, it simply can't be helped.

Edelstein stood up very straight. He said, "This is my last wish. I've been a bachelor too long. What I want is a woman whom I can marry. She should be about five feet, four inches tall, weigh about 115 pounds, shapely, of course, and with naturally blond hair. She should be intelligent, practical, in love with me, Jewish, of course, but sensual and fun-loving—"

The Edelstein mind suddenly moved into high gear!

"And *especially*," he added, "she should be—I don't know quite how to put this—she should be the *most*, the *maximum*, that I want and can handle, speaking now in a purely sexual sense. You understand what I mean, Sitwell? Delicacy forbids that I should spell it out more specifically than that, but if the matter must be explained to you . . ."

There was a light, somehow *sexual* tapping at the door. Edelstein went to answer it, chuckling to himself. Over twenty thousand dollars, two pounds of chopped chicken liver and now this! Manowitz, he thought, I have you now: Double the most a man wants is something I probably shouldn't have wished on my worst enemy, but I did.

GIFTS...

by Gordon R. Dickson

The paper boy, cutting across soft spring grass of the front lawn in the bright sunshine of a late May afternoon, was so full of bubbling expectations that he did not see Jim and almost threw the newspaper into Jim's face.

"Oh, here, Mr. Brewer," he said, checking and handing it up the height of the three concrete steps. He squinted against the sun up at the chunky, adult body in blue wash slacks and T-shirt and the square-boned face under short red hair. "We're having a P.T.A. carnival at school, tonight. You coming?"

"I guess not tonight, Tommy," said Jim.

"They're going to have a shooting gallery," said Tommy, and hurried on to the neighbors.

Jim, turning, went back through the screen door into the living room.

"Something?" called Nancy, from the kitchen. He went on into her, still carrying the paper. She was standing by the sink, peeling potatoes for the casserole of a Friday dinner, the transparent, tight-tied apron making her look slimmer and blonder and younger—like a new bride just beginning to play housewife.

"What?" Jim asked.

"I heard you talking." She looked aside and up at him.

"Just the paper boy," he said. "Wanted to know if we're going to a P.T.A. party at the school, tonight."

She laughed cheerfully.

"Tell him to wait until Joey's old enough for school. Then we'll go to all the P.T.A. parties."

"If we can afford it." Jim batted the paper idly against the

216

refrigerator. "It's a fund-raising deal, of course. You have to spend—nickels and dimes, but it adds up."

She watched him.

"Worrying, hon?" she asked. He shook his head; then grinned at her.

"Just thinking. A week of filling prescriptions and selling home permanent wave kits doesn't add up to much. A two-year-old house like this—a three-year-old car—and what's left over? A lot of running just to stand still."

"You'll have your own drugstore someday."

"Someday is right."

She finished off the potato in her hands without taking her eyes off him.

"You're hungry," she said. "Go sit down. Dinner'll be ready soon."

"All right." He went back into the living room, opening the paper as he went. He was just sitting down in the green armchair across from the television when the doorbell chimed.

"I'll get it," he called to the kitchen. Nancy did not answer. Just as he had called, Jim had heard the back door slam, and the noise of their son, Joey, and Pancho, the family cocker, was filling the kitchen air.

Jim approached the front door and saw through the screen the dark faces of two slim, middle-aged men, tall in business suits. The Community Fund, thought Jim, remembering suddenly that this was the week of their drive for a new hospital.

"May we come in?" asked the taller of the two.

"Sure, come on in," Jim opened the screen for them and led the way to the living room. He was turning over in his head the possible amounts he would have to subscribe. "Sit down." The two men sat side by side on the sofa. "What can I do for you?"

"My name is Long," said the taller one. "And this is White."

"Pleased to meet you." Jim half-rose from his own chair to shake hands with both of them. They looked enough alike, he thought, to be brothers.

"Mr. Brewer," said Long, "you have a dog in the house."

"Why, yes," answered Jim. He looked at them, suddenly frowning, and then a slight scraping noise, as of claws on a polished floor, caught his ear and he turned his head to see Pancho standing in the entrance to the kitchen, head and tail up, staring at the strangers. The cocker spaniel was perfectly still and rigid, leaning forward, nose extended, almost in point. Then, slowly, with the delicate care with which he approached birds in cover, the dog began to advance. Step by slow step he came up before the two men, who had not moved, but sat watching with patient eyes. Before them he halted. Then, equally slowly, he began to back away from them, step by step, until he came up hard against Jim's legs, pressing sideways against them with hip and flank, his head still turned to the two on the couch. Through the thin material of his slacks, Jim felt Pancho's whole body trembling.

"Easy, boy," said Jim, automatically, putting his hand on the furry head. "Easy." He stared at the two; and then suddenly a coldness ran down the narrow line of his spine and he felt the fine hairs on his own neck begin to rise as his body tensed in the chair. He was watching the two faces, so much alike, and he saw them now as motionless and impersonal as masks.

"Yes," said the one called Long. "You see that we aren't human."

Jim said nothing. But he could hear the sound of Nancy and Joey's voices in the kitchen and he was slowly, as slowly as Pancho had moved, shifting the weight of his body forward in the chair, so that it would be over the bone and muscle springs of his knees.

"Please," said the one introduced as White. "There's nothing for you to be afraid of. We won't harm you. And you can't harm us. We only want to talk to you."

Jim was poised now. He was thinking that he could leap forward and yell at the same time. But there was the danger that Nancy and Joey would only be bewildered by his shout and come instead into the living room to see what was the matter.

"What about?" said Jim.

"You've been chosen," said Long, "at random. Not entirely at random, but mainly so, to answer a question for us. That's all there is to it." He looked into Jim's eyes; and Jim had the impression that he smiled suddenly and warmly,

although Long's lips did not move, or any part of his face.
"It's a question that concerns your interests, only, not ours.
Only you ought to get over being afraid of us. Here—"

He extended his hand toward Pancho. He did not snap his
fingers or beckon in any way, but merely held out his fingers,
waiting. And after a slow, still movement, the dog began to
move, step by step away from the comfort of Jim's legs and
toward the stranger. He approached the hand as he might
approach a new dog in the neighborhood, stiffly and with
caution. For a long second, with neck outstretched, he sniffed
at the fingers—and then, with a change as dramatically sudden as the snapping of a violin string, his tail wagged and he
shoved his head forward onto the hand of Long.

Long brought forward his other hand and scratched Pancho
between the ears. He looked up at Jim.

"You see?" he said.

"That's a dog," said Jim; but he had relaxed, nonetheless. Not completely, but relaxed. "Well, what is it?"

"Did you ever think much about ethics, Mr. Brewer?"
said Long, still petting Pancho.

"Ethics?" Jim looked from one to the other of them.

"Perhaps you might call it morality," said White. "The
duty of morality. The duty to your neighbor."

"We get a lot of that here," said Jim, thinking of the
P.T.A. and the Community Fund and all the many other
drives and collections.

"You have a lot," said White. "But did you ever think
much about it?"

"You don't think about things like that," said Jim, still
watching them. "You just do them."

"But," said White, "there are two sides to that coin. The
coin called charity."

"What do you mean?" said Jim. He looked from White to
Long, who was still holding Pancho's head in one slim palm,
and stroking between Pancho's ears now, with the other. The
dog's eyes were closed in an ecstasy of pleasure.

"We're talking," said Long, suddenly, "about the ethics
of Charity. If your dog here were lost far from your home,
and trying to find his way back—if he were obviously hun-

gry, you'd think someone else was a good person, if he or she fed him?''

"Certainly," said Jim.

"And what if the dog were interested only in getting back to you? Would it still be a kindness to tie him up until he did eat? And perhaps force him to stay, in an effort to feed him up again?''

"That's what we'd call a mistaken kindness," said Jim. "Look, what's the point of all this?"

"The point is the ethics of Charity," said Long, "and that we feel the same way about them you do. Charity isn't a kindness when the one receiving it doesn't really want it. It's an instinct among civilized people to give help—but the instinct can be mistaken.''

"I still don't get what you're driving at," said Jim.

Long let go of Pancho, who shoved a furry head forward onto his knee. He reached into his right-hand suitcoat pocket and took out something small enough to be hidden in his hand.

"Mr. Brewer," he said, "when you were very young, did you ever dream of having something—something magical that could grant all your wishes?''

Jim frowned at him.

"Doesn't everybody?"

"Everybody does," said Long. He turned his hand over and opened it out. Lying in his palm was what looked like a child's marble, a glassy small globe of swirled color, green, and rust, and white. He half-stood and passed it into Jim's automatically receiving hand. "There you are.''

"There I am, what?" demanded Jim, staring at it.

"There you have your wish-granter," said Long.

Jim looked back up into the dark face of the slim man and smiled a little.

"No," said Long. "It's quite true. Close your hand on it and wish.''

Jim looked back at the marble. The others waited. Long had gone back to petting Pancho.

"No, I don't think so," said Jim, handing the marble back. Long accepted it, put it back in his pocket. They both stood up, and went toward the door.

"Wait," said Jim, getting up himself. "You're going?"

"We took it you had answered us," said White.

"No, wait—" said Jim. "Come on back. Let me see that again."

The two of them returned to the couch and sat down. Long passed over the marble. Jim took it, sitting back down himself, and turned it over curiously in his fingers."

"Anything?" he said.

Once more Jim had the impression of a smile from the unmoving countenance of Long.

"Almost anything," he said. "The almost doesn't have to concern you."

Slowly, Jim closed his hand over the marble. He squeezed his eyes shut and thought. He opened them again.

He was standing in the drugstore where he worked. A middle-aged woman customer was just walking out past him, filling his nostrils with an invisible cloud of her cologne. Behind the drugs and toiletries counter Dave Hogart, the owner, was looking up at him, his face wrinkled in surprise.

"Jim. I didn't see you come in. What're you doing back down here?" he said.

"Uh . . . aspirin," said Jim. "Fifty of the kid aspirin, Dave. Joey's got a slight cold."

Dave turned and reached to an upper shelf, turned back and handed Jim the bottle. He rang it up on the charge key of the cash register, the fingers of his left hand resting swollen and hunched on the bare counter beside the register.

"How's the arthritis?" Jim found himself asking, suddenly.

Dave jerked his head up with a grin.

"Not bad enough to make me want to retire yet," he said. "Want to buy the store?"

"Wish I could," said Jim.

"I guess we're going to be ready to make that deal about the same time," said Dave. "Hope Joey's all right in the morning—" Another customer was coming into the store. "See you, Jim." He moved off.

Both their backs were turned. Jim closed his hand on the marble and wished again.

He was back in his own living room. He sat down again in his chair and noticed the small transparent bottle of orange-colored tablets was still in his hand. He set it carefully down on the coffee table by his chairside and looked up. Long and White were still sitting, watching him.

"I don't understand," said Jim. "I just don't understand."

Long pointed to the hand of Jim's that still held the marble.

"That," he said, "isn't important. We only wanted something to show you, something to convince you with. The whole story's much bigger."

Jim glanced suddenly toward the kitchen entrance and the voices of Joey and Nancy coming through it.

"Don't worry," said White. "They won't think to come in until we're through here."

"You see," said Long. "We don't come from anywhere near the family of worlds that go around your sun. But we couldn't help discovering you people, when you started doing things. We've been watching you for some years now. You people are like we were—a long time back on our own world. You have the same troubles, the same sorrows, much the same hopes. You remind us very much of us, in the beginning."

"You're that much like us?" said Jim, dazedly.

"Well, not so much as you might think just by looking at us—and again, much more so than you would realize in ways you've yet to learn about," said Long. "The point is, we look at you—with your conflicts, your diseases, your pains and famines—all your lacks. And many of them are things we can do something about. We could heal your sick, we can give you longer and more useful lives. We can help you to go out among the stars and find more living room. We could open up great new fields of opportunity for you."

"Well," said Jim, looking from one to the other, "why tell me about this? Why don't you?"

"Because we're not sure it would be right," said White. "We're not sure you want our help."

"For those things?" said Jim. "Are you crazy? Of course we do."

"Are you sure?" said Long.

They sat watching him; and Jim stared back at them. The moment stretched out long between them.

"Of course I'm sure," said Jim at last.

"I hope so," said White. "Because the decision is up to you."

Jim jerked his gaze suddenly over to look at White.

"Us?" he said.

"No," answered White, knitting his long fingers together in his lap. "Just you, you alone."

"Me?" cried Jim, and then checked his voice to hold it down below a level that would carry into the kitchen. He stared at them. "Just me? Why? Why, *me?*"

"We picked you at random and on purpose," said White. "We think you are most likely to give us the truest answer."

"But you don't want me!" said Jim, turning to Long. "I'm nobody to make a decision for the whole world! Look, there's the President. Or the United Nations—"

"You see," said Long, patiently, "the question isn't a logical one. It isn't an intellectual one, to be investigated by charts and speeches and discussions. It's an emotional question, dealing with deep and basic instincts. It isn't *what* help we can give you, it's—do you *want* help? Any help? Help of any kind?"

He stopped speaking and waited. Jim did not say anything.

"Are you still so sure?" asked White, gently.

Jim sagged slowly back in his chair. He turned his head slowly and looked at the aspirin bottle. Beyond it, the window was just beginning to tint with the first translucency of twilight. Slowly, he shook his head.

"I don't know," he said, in a low voice. "I don't know."

"You can think it over," said White. "Take tonight and think about it. We can come back for your answer, tomorrow."

"I'm not the man," said Jim, weakly. "I'm not the man to ask—something like that."

"You are the man," said Long, as they got up, "because we picked you to be the man."

Jim rose also. The faces of all three of them were very close together. He felt their alienness now, more strongly than at any earlier moment since they had come in.

"Let me help you with a little advice," said Long. "Forget that you're deciding for a world. Don't try to think of how all the rest will feel. Decide only for yourself. I promise you, what you sincerely feel, the great and lasting part of your people, those who work and marry and have children and endure, will feel the same.''

They turned away from him and went through the screen door into the strong glare of the sunset. Jim heard the screen door slam quietly behind them.

"Dinner's ready!" called Nancy, from the kitchen.

Incredibly, he actually forgot about it during the general chatter and excitement of dinner. It was only later, after Joey had been put to bed and he and Nancy were sitting in the living room watching television, that it all came back to him. He waited until the western they happened to be watching came to its noisy climax and then got up from his chair.

"I've got some letters to write," he told Nancy.

He went into the extra bedroom, that they called the office, and shut the door. He sat down in the chair before the card table that did service as a desk and turned on the lamp. Its light shone warmly at the bookcases and secondhand over-stuffed chair that had been their first furniture purchase for the apartment he and Nancy had moved into after their honeymoon. He got out his fountain pen, the notepaper and envelopes—and then took the marble once more from his pocket and laid it on the white sheet of paper before him. It glowed back up at him, reflecting the lamplight.

"I've got to think this thing out," he told himself.

But no thoughts came. Once he closed his hand around the marble hesitantly, but then let go of it again without using it. He tried to imagine what the world would be like if he should tell Long and White that his answer was yes. No hospitals, different kinds of cars, he supposed—he was not very good at this kind of imagining. If everybody had everything they needed, what about money—and jobs.

He checked suddenly. Funny it had not occurred to him before. Of course, his own job would be one of the first to go. Well people wouldn't need medicine. And as for all the rest of the stuff a drugstore sold, beauty aids and the rest, there would probably be new versions that would last for a lifetime. Magazines would probably be left, candy, ice cream, toys . . . What would happen to Nancy and Joey if he had no job? What would eventually happen to him?

But he was forgetting. Under the new set-up they wouldn't want for things they needed. No need to worry there. But what would he do? He couldn't just sit around for the rest of his life. Or could he? There were things he'd always wanted to do, like deep-sea fishing and places he'd always wanted to go. But would that be enough?

On second thought, there would probably be thousands of new jobs opening up. Long and White obviously belonged to a people who had work to do. Perhaps there would be something he would like better than pharmacy, something that would give him a feeling of really getting somewhere, making progress . . .

After some while, he glanced at his watch. It was almost eleven; he had been sitting here close to two hours. And nothing was decided. He stood up, feeling the weight and weariness of his own body. His eyes smarted from staring at the light reflected from the blank white paper before him. He put everything away, turned out the lamp and went to his and Nancy's bedroom.

Nancy was already in bed and reading the newspaper. She looked up as he came in.

"What time do you go in the morning?" she asked.

"Not until noon," he said. "Dave's opening up tomorrow." He took off his shirt and went about the business of getting ready for sleep. Nancy put the paper away on the shelf underneath the night table beside their double bed. She yawned and slid down under the covers.

"I've got to take Joey shopping tomorrow," she said. "He's just bursting out of his socks."

"Yes," he said. He turned out the light and got into bed. The peaceful darkness washed in around him. He lay there, slowly breathing. There was a movement under the covers and he felt Nancy's hand touch gently upon his arm.

"What's wrong?" she asked softly.

He sighed, deeply and gustily; and, turning toward her, he told her, the whole story about White and Long, and all that they had said and done.

Nancy always had been a good listener. She listened now, without interrupting him with questions, her face a pale blur in the little light filtering in around the edges of the window shades. Toward the end of it they were both sitting up in bed; and Jim got up to turn on the light and retrieve the marble from his pants' pocket. He brought it back to her and got into bed again.

She took it from his hand and turned it over in her own fingers. The light from their bedstand lamp caught and glinted from its surface, making the three colors seem to flow as she turned it, as if they were being stirred about within a transparent shell. She looked at Jim.

"Could I?" she said. "Do you suppose—"

"Go ahead," said Jim.

She closed her fingers about the marble and closed her eyes. A fur stole appeared on the blanket before them. Nancy opened her eyes again.

"Oh!" she said, on a little intake of breath. She reached and touched the fur with a feather touch, stroking it almost imperceptibly with the ends of her fingers. She got up suddenly, climbing over Jim, who was on the outside of the bed, carrying the stole, and went to the mirror of her dressing table. She put the stole around her neck and held it there with both hands, gazing into the mirror. Watching her, standing there in her nightgown with the fur around her, Jim felt a sudden ridiculous tightening in his throat.

"Nancy," he said.

She turned about and came back to the bed, climbing in again and reaching for the marble. As her hand closed about it, the fur vanished.

"Nancy!" said Jim. "You didn't have to do that. You can keep it."

"If you decide, I'll get it back," she said. Without warning she kissed him on the cheek. "Thank you, darling."

"I didn't do anything," said Jim.

"Thank you for saying I could keep it."

He squeezed her hand in his; but he still frowned at the marble lying before them on the blanket.

"What'll I do? What'll I do?" he murmured.

He felt the light touch of her hand on his shoulder.

"Why don't you sleep on it," she said. "You'll think better in the morning."

"All right," he sighed. "I'll try. Only I don't think I can."

But he did sleep. He had not known how tired he was and unconsciousness had flooded in on him almost in the moment in which he closed his eyes. Only with sleep came the dreams, a multitude of them—vast confused fantasies of enormous ships that sailed above cities under hothouse domes. And houses unroofed to the ever-present air, beneath the domes. And people at work with shining machines whose purpose he could not comprehend.

Then, later on, the dreams changed back to the ordinary world; and there came the only one that he was ever to remember clearly afterward. In it he stood on the customer's side of a counter in the drugstore where he worked; and facing him on the counter's other side was Joey, in a white pharmacist's jacket. Joey, grown to a man now. A young man, but with the hair already receding on his forehead and tired lines of premature age on his face; and the drugstore about him was dingier and shabbier than Jim remembered. Joey handed him a bottle filled with small, pink children's aspirin.

"Take this to my boy," Joey was saying. "It's not much, but it's the best we have."

Jim took it from him; and as Jim did so, he noticed that Joey's fingers had swollen, arthritic joints as Dave's hand had. Joey saw his eyes fall on them, and took the hand away, hiding it under the counter.

"I'm sorry, Joey!" cried Jim, suddenly.

"It's not your fault," said Joey. But he had turned his head away; and would not look at his father.

Jim woke, sweating.

He lay flat on his back on his side of the bed. Beside him, Nancy slept sweetly, breathing silently, with her face pressed against her pillow. Pale lines of beginning dawnlight were marking the windows around the edges of the pulled window shades.

Jim breathed deeply; and slowly, quietly, got up out of the bed. He dressed while Nancy continued to sleep, looking over at the alarm clock on the night table. Its white hands stood at the black numerals that told him it was five-thirty, an hour and a half before the alarm was due to go off. Dressed at last in slacks and shirt, he went out through the silent living room to the front door, opened it, and went down the steps onto the front walk.

He stopped, breathing in the fresh morning air and looking at the sky. It was as cloudless as clear water and the new rays of the morning sun made it scintillate as if it was possessed of a light of its own. The lawns up and down the block on either side of him and across the street glittered greener than ever with the night's dew. The other houses all seemed sleeping; but as he watched Chuck Elison came out of his kitchen door five doors down on the street's other side and climbed into his panel truck with "Elison Plumbing" painted on its side. Chuck's wife, Jean, came out the kitchen door to stand in her apron and wave at him as he backed down his driveway, turned the truck up the street, and drove off. She went back into their house.

Jim turned, slowly from his gazing at the street, to look at his own house. The yellow trim around the screens and windows was beginning to flake a little. He should repaint before the heat of the summer months really got under way. And the grass would need cutting, soon—by Sunday, anyway.

Under the picture window of the living room the early tulips were in bloom, the yellow tips of their scarlet petals forming neat, scallop-edged cups. He reached out a forefinger, bemused, to touch one. He could not remember, just now, seeing any flowers in his dreams of the domes and ships. Undoubtedly they had been there, but—never had he felt before how beautiful these small plants were. . . .

A slight sound of shoes on the sidewalk behind him made him straighten and turn. Long stood there alone, the morning sun lighting up his strange, dark face. For a moment they merely looked at each other saying nothing. Then Long spoke.

"Do you want more time?" he asked.

Jim sighed. Once more he looked around the street on both sides of him.

"No," he said. Slowly he put his hand into the right-hand pocket of his slacks. The marble was there. He took it out and handed it over to Long.

Long took it and put it back in his own pocket.

"You're sure?" he asked, looking closely at Jim.

"I think," said Jim, and sighed again, "we ought to get it for ourselves."

Long nodded, thoughtfully. He was turning to go when Jim stopped him.

"Was that the right answer?" Jim asked.

Long hesitated. For a second there seemed to be something strange and sad, but at the same time warm and friendly behind his eyes; but it was gone too quickly for Jim to pin it down.

"That's not for me to say," he said. And then, astonishingly, he did smile—for the first and only time; and the smile lit up his face like sunset after a storm has blown away. "But ask your grandson."

And, suddenly, as shadow, he was gone.

I WISH I MAY, I WISH I MIGHT

by Bill Pronzini

He sat on a driftwood throne near the great gray rocks by the sea, watching the angry foaming waves hurl themselves again and again upon the cold and empty whiteness of the beach. He listened to the discordant cry of the endlessly circling gulls overhead and to the sonorous lament of the chill October wind. He drew meaningless patterns in the silvery sand before him with the toe of one rope sandal and then erased them carefully with the sole and began anew.

He was a pale, blond young man of fourteen, his hair close-cropped, his eyes the color of faded cornflower. He was dressed in light corduroy trousers and a gray cloth jacket, and his thin white feet inside the sandals were bare. His name was David Lannin.

He looked up at the leaden sky, shading his eyes against its filtered glare. His fingers were blue-numb from the cold. He turned his head slowly, bringing within his vision the eroded face of a steep cliff, with its clumps of tule grass like patches of beard stubble, rising from the beach behind him. He released a long, sighing breath and turned his head yet again to look out at the combers breaking and retreating.

He stood and began to walk slowly along the beach, his hands buried deep in the pockets on his cloth jacket. The wind swirled loose sand against his body, and there was the icy wetness of the salt spray on his skin.

He rounded a gradual curve in the beach. Ahead of him he could see the sun-bleached, bark-bare upper portion of a huge timber half-buried in the sand, some twenty yards from the water's edge. Something green and shiny, something which had gone unnoticed as he passed earlier, lay in the wet sand near it.

A bottle.

He recognized it as such immediately. It was resting on its side with the neck partially buried in the sand, recently carried in, it seemed, on the tide. It was oddly shaped, the glass an opaque green color—the color of the sea—very smooth, without markings or labelings of any kind. It appeared to be quite old and extremely fragile.

David knelt beside it and lifted it in his hands and brushed the clinging particles of sand from its slender neck. Scarlet sealing wax had been liberally applied to the cork guarding the mouth. The wax bore an indecipherable emblem, an ancient seal. David's thin fingers dexterously chipped away most of the ceration, exposing the dun-colored cork beneath. He managed to loosen the cork—and the bottle began to vibrate almost imperceptibly. There was a sudden loud popping sound, like a magnum of champagne opening, and a microsecond later an intense, blinding flash of crimson phosphorescence.

David cried out, toppling backward on the sand, the bottle erupting from his hands. He blinked rapidly, and there came from very close to him high, loud peals of resounding laughter that commingled with the wind and the surf to fill the cold autumn air with rolling echoes of sound. But he could see nothing. The bottle lay on the sand a few feet away, and there was the timber and the beach and the sea; but there was nothing else, no one to be seen.

And yet, the hollow, reverberating laughter continued.

David scrambled to his feet, looking frantically about him. Fright kindled inside him. He wanted to run, he tensed his body to run—

All at once, the laughter ceased.

A keening voice assailed his ears, a voice out of nowhere, like the laughter, a voice without gender, without inflection, a neuter voice: "I wish I may, I wish I might."

"What?" David said, his eyes wide, vainly searching. "Where are you?"

"I am here," the voice said. "I am here on the wind."

"Where? I can't see you."

"None can see me. I am the king of djinns, the ruler of genies, the all-powerful—unjustly doomed to eternity in yon flagon by the mortal sorcerer Amroj." Laughter. "A thousand years alone have I spent, a millennium on the cold dark empty floor of the ocean. Alone, imprisoned. But now I am free, you have set me free. I knew you would do thus, for I know all things. You shall be rewarded. Three wishes shall I grant you, according to custom, according to tradition. I wish I may, I wish I might. Those be the words, the gateways to your fondest dreams. Speak them anywhere, anytime, and I shall hear and obey. I shall make each of your wishes come true."

David moistened his lips. "*Any* three wishes?"

"Any three," the voice answered. "No stipulations, no limitations. I am the king of djinns, the ruler of genies, the all-powerful. I wish I may, I wish I might. You know the words, do you not?"

"Yes! Yes, I know them."

The laughter. "Amroj, foul sorcerer, foul mortal, I am avenged! Avaunt, avaunt!"

And suddenly, there was a vacuum of sound, a roaring of silence, the presence of which hurt David's ears and made him cry out in pain. But then the moment passed, and there was nothing but the sounds of the tide and the wind and the scavenger birds winging low, low over the sea.

He gained his feet and stood very still for perhaps a minute. Then he began to run. He ran with wind-speed, away from the timber half-buried in the sand, away from the smooth, empty green bottle; his sandaled feet seemed to fly above the sand, leaving only the barest of imprints there.

He fled along the beach until, in the distance, set back from the ocean on a short bluff, he could see a small white house with yellow warmth shining through its front window. He left the sand there, running across ground now more solid, running toward the white house on the bluff.

A wooden stairway appeared on the rock, winding skyward. As he neared it, a woman came rushing down the stairs. She ran toward him and threw her arms around him and hugged him close to her breast. "Oh, David, where have you been! I've been frantic with worry!"

"At the beach," he answered, drinking great mouthfuls of the cold salt air into his aching lungs. "By the big rocks."

"You know you're not supposed to go there," the woman said, hugging him. "David, you know that. Look at the way you're dressed. Oh, you mustn't ever, ever do this again. Promise you won't ever do it again."

"I found a bottle by the big timber," David said. "There was a genie inside. I couldn't see him, but he laughed and laughed, and then he gave me three wishes. He said that all I have to do is wish and he'll make my wish come true. Then he laughed some more and said some things I didn't understand, and then he was gone and my ears hurt."

"Oh, what a story! David, where did you get such a story?"

"I have three wishes," he said. "I can wish for anything and it will come true. The genie said so."

"David, David, David!"

"I'm going to wish for a million-trillion ice cream cones, and I'm going to wish for the ocean to always be as warm as my bathwater so I can go wading whenever I want, and I'm going to wish for all the little boys and girls in the world to be just like me so I'll never-ever be without somebody to play with."

Gently, protectively, the mother took the hand of her retarded son. "Come along now, dear. Come along."

"I wish I may, I wish I might," David said.

THREE DAY MAGIC

by Charlotte Armstrong

Do you believe in magic? Old-fashioned magic? That which can twang the threads of cause and effect, take a swipe right across the warp and woof of them, and alter the pattern?

If you ask George this question, he will get a look on his face, a certain look, as if he were remembering a time, an hour, maybe only a certain feeling that once he had. He'll answer, yes, he believes in magic. But he won't explain.

You'll concede he has the right to mean whatever he means by that. You'll like George.

The Casino at the Ocean House, up in Deeport, Maine, was a long room with windows to the sea. Its tables and soft lights, the dance music, gave the hotel's guests something to do in the evening. It was a huge success. Even the village oldsters were proud of it. "Beth'z down to the Casino, last night," they'd say. "George'z got a new trumpet. Fellow from Bath. Ayah. Pretty good, she says."

George Hale and his band played in the Casino every summer, but George, himself, belonged to Deeport, as had his Pa and Grandpa and many other Hales before him. Tourists exclaimed over the old Hale house, up on the slope, when they saw it glimmering behind the lilacs, under the elms. But George always thought it was most beautiful in the winter when the flounces and ruffles of green fell away and it stood forth, bared and exquisite, etched by delicate shadow, white on white.

Here, also, lived his mother and two of her sisters, all three of them widows, all three doting on George, but each pretending, with a native instinct towards severity, that this was not so. Nor did Nellie Hale, Aunt Margaret or Aunt Liz ever admit that the way he earned a living was ''work'' at all. George had too much fun. George knew he had fun and he knew the Casino was a success. But he did not suspect what a huge sucess *he* was.

He was perfect for the Casino. For George felt he was in the middle of a party, any night; therefore, when he took up his saxophone as if he *had* to join, something better than the seabreeze blew across the floor. George's music may have been a little bit corny. He liked all kinds, George did, but whatever he, himself, touched, came out with a jig quality, a right foot, left foot, whirl-me-around-again ta-ra-ra-boom-de-ay effect. But he was right for the Casino. He kept the customers remembering that here they were, up on the coast of Maine, breathing deeper than they breathed in town, and in touch for two weeks, more or less, with some simple source of joy.

The Casino paid George well, in fact, enough to last him a frugal winter. But it never occurred to George to push onward. Winters, he went right on enjoying himself. Then the band, and at local fees, would play for the Elks, or the High School prom. In fact, for some miles around, wherever people gathered together for fun and society, George was usually right there, beating out the festive rhythm of their mood. Deeport was proud of him, for in the winter, like the streets and the shore, he was theirs alone.

George was nearly 29, and unmarried. The neighbors speculated about this, sometimes. But his mother and the Aunts, if they speculated, said nothing. Aunt Liz darned his socks exquisitely. Aunt Margaret ironed his shirts to perfection. And his mother, without seeming to do so, based the menus on his preferences.

Naturally George had his secrets. For one thing, he played some pretty highbrow records when he was alone. For another, he believed in true love. He wasn't so naïve as to think it happened to everybody, but he did hope it was going to happen to him. There were certain volumes of English poetry, never caught off the shelves in the old Hale house, which grew, nevertheless, dog-eared and loose at the bindings. Oh, George had his secrets.

One evening in August, George was leading the boys through a waltz, when a red-haired girl in a white dress floated out of the dimness in somebody's arm. Something about the line of her back, the tilt of her head as she took the turns (George played a fast bright waltz, nothing dreamy) pleased him very much for no reason he could trap by taking thought. When later, she danced by with John Phelps 3rd, an old-timer among the summer people, George gave the baton to his second fiddle, climbed down, and sought Phelps out.

She was sitting at a table with an elderly bald-headed man, who had a long sour face and cold gray eyes over which horny lids fell insolently. She was Miss Douglas. He was Mr. Bennett Blair. George didn't know who Bennett Blair was and didn't care. He invited Miss Douglas to dance.

The music happened to be another waltz. George held her off, the prettiest way to waltz, and somehow, on the crowded floor there was plenty of room. They flew along, dipping like birds. Her long white skirt fanned and flared. Her bright hair swung. Her brown eyes smiled at George and he smiled gently down.

She had no "line." Neither did George, of course. They exchanged a little information. They told each other where they lived. She lived in New York with Mr. Blair who was no kin but her guardian. She liked Maine very much. George said he'd been to New York twice and he liked it very much. It was a wonderful city. She said it was wonderful up here, she thought. And they waltzed.

When it was over, there was a small warm spot, somewhere under George's dress shirt, a little interior glow, perhaps in the heart.

The next morning George was hanging around the drugstore when she came in. It wasn't much of a coincidence, because all the summer people went to the drugstore at least twice every day. She came in alone. She wore a blue dress that was solid in the middle. He'd known she wouldn't come down to the drugstore with her ribs bare. He felt very close to her, having known this in advance as he had.

Her name was Kathleen. After she accepted his invitation to a Coke so graciously, it seemed all right to ask her.

She said she was called Kathy. He said there wasn't any nickname for George, except Georgie, but he'd outgrown that of course, by the time he was six. Then he was telling her about his mother and the Aunts. Pretty soon, George and Kathy were walking up High Street towards the old Hale house, and inside, against their coming, Aunt Liz was wiping the pink hobnail pickle dish, Aunt Margaret was straightening the antimacassars in the sitting room, and Nellie Hale was adding just a little more milk to the chowder.

Kathy stopped at the gate and said the exact right thing. She said, "It must be just beautiful in the wintertime!" George's hand on the gate shook a little as he opened it. There was a meaning to the time. It would be remembered, this moment in which Kathy Douglas stepped through his front gate.

Nellie Hale and the Aunts, for all one could tell, were absolutely hardened to George's well-known habit of bringing strange and beautiful red-haired girls home for dinner. They thought nothing of it at all. But in a little while they began to unbend from this stiff proud nonchalance. For Kathy talked about old things and she understood them, too. Old things that had belonged here a long long time. She asked about Captain Enos Gray, whose cherry table they sat around. And about Captain Mark, who'd brought the china home. She listened, bemused, while the ships went out again and some went down . . . the tales were spun . . . the worn rosary of family legend was told out, bead by bead.

It was after three o'clock before George took her back to the Ocean House. They laughed a lot, skipping along the afternoon streets, her hand in his arm.

They were a little giddy, both of them.

Phelps 3rd was on the veranda, looking concerned. Mr. Blair, in a formidable beach outfit, was waiting in the lobby. He shooed Kathy upstairs. He looked at George from under his horny lids and grunted and walked away.

George came, blinking, out on the veranda again, and now, too late, Phelps 3rd told him.

Kathy Douglas had as her inheritance about $5,000,000 of her own. Bennett Blair had about $10,000,000 of his own and was a power in the land. Also, upright and cold, he was a guardian who really guarded. Nobody would get Kathy except the crème de la crème in blood, character, business ability and financial standing.

She was a flower, a lovely lovely flower, but not a wild flower, nor one that had grown under amateur culture in a suburban garden. No, delicately and expensively nurtured, precious and unobtainable was Kathy. She was not, admitted Phelps 3rd, for such as he, who was heir to only half a million from Phelps 1st, toothpaste.

She was not . . . oh, heavens, never! . . . for such as George!

For a dashed moment or two, it seemed to George that he must give her up. But then his vision cleared. By definition it was no solution to give her up. So he dismissed the notion from his mind.

The aroma of millions clung to Mr. Blair and around Kathy, too. It wafted along the harsh Maine sand to the beach, where Kathy and her Fräulein spent most of the day. Naturally, George took to the beach. Afternoons, he would greet Mr. Blair, back from his morning golf to stretch his knobby white knees to the sun. But George couldn't for the life of him dig up any mutual interests. Mr. Blair looked wearily down from an eminence of age and experience and nothing George had to offer seemed worth his response. Yet George knew he was not ignored. He felt, in the afternoons, the weight of that cold glance. He felt himself being labeled and filed in some compartment of that shrewd old brain. Mr. Blair was a guardian who really guarded. Phelps 3rd had known what he was talking about, all right.

But, somehow, seeing Kathy every day, the problem postponed itself and hung suspended in a golden time. For Kathy wasn't discouraging at all.

A golden week went by and then, one morning, Kathy came running to tell him. "George, we're leaving. We have to go!" Clouds fell over the day. "Mr. Blair had planned another week, but something has come up."

"Gosh," said George from the bottom of his heart, "I'm sorry to hear that." And yet, somewhere inside his head a little lick of triumph told him that nothing had come up at all.

George folded himself up and sat down where he was and Kathy knelt beside him. "When, Kathy?" he asked bleakly.

"This afternoon." She was frankly full of woe.

George bit his lip thoughtfully. "Back to New York?"

"Yes."

George looked at the ocean and something closed in his mind. Something said goodbye to it. "Me, too," he said. "Right after Labor Day, when the Casino closes, I'm coming down."

"Oh, George! You'll come to see me!" She was all vivid and glad. Her hand moved on the sand towards his.

"I can't say anything, Kathy. I can't ask you anything, yet."

"Ask me what?" Her eyes were shining.

But George, in the bottom of his soul, agreed with Mr. Blair. Nothing was too good for Kathy. Of course, she was infinitely precious and she must have the best, the very best of everything. So he put his lips on her hand, just once, and let it go. "I'm going to be able to ask Mr. Blair," he said grimly, "the very same day."

Yet, here on the beach in the sunshine, with Kathy near and the dark blue sea and the whole world sparkling around them, the future cleared before him. He'd go down to New York and settle himself and make about a million dollars in some sound respectable way and then he'd ask her. It seemed not only clear and simple, but certain that all this must come to pass.

For Kathy wasn't discouraging at all.

George's decision was the result of a marching logic. Now, in the blood and character departments, George was fine. What he lacked was in the success department. So he must abandon this easygoing life. He must acquire the proof, that is to say, the money. Nothing he could do in Deeport would lead to the kind of money Mr. Blair probably had in mind. So . . .

The boys in the band were disconsolate. The manager of the hotel set up such a pained and frantic howl that George fled his office, with bitter reproaches of ingratitude, pleas for mercy, predictions of the Casino's ruin, ringing in his ears. George thought this was shock. He was sorry.

He arranged to leave the bulk of his earnings in the bank for his mother and the Aunts where it would, as it always had, take them nicely through the winter. "So you see," George explained to them hopefully, "it's not going to make any difference to you."

The three ladies tightened their mouths and agreed. Aunt Margaret, although plump, was the one who tended to fear the worst, but, of course, she didn't weep. Aunt Liz, tiny and angular, chose to look on the bright side, and smiled mysteriously to herself as if she'd been tipped off by a private angel. Nellie Hale, a blend of both temperaments, simply tightened her mouth. "George is grown," she said, and that was all she would say.

So, darned and mended, cleaned and pressed, and fed to the utter limit, George, with $200 in his pocket and his saxophone in his hand, took the train one September evening, without the faintest conception of the gap his departure tore in the whole fabric of the town's life. All hints of this he took for kindliness and so he was spared. He suffered only the wrench of his own homesickness.

New York received George and his saxophone with her customary indifference. Yet he was lucky in the first hour, for he walked by Mrs. McGurk's four-story brownstone on West 69th Street just as her hand in the front window hung up the vacancy sign.

George, trained all his life to pretend that only cleanliness mattered, saw that the square ugly room on the fourth floor was clean and so said he'd take it. Mrs. McGurk sniffed. Take it, indeed! She said she'd take him. Rent by the month, in advance. That was her rule. George paid and looked about him. The room had no charm, but George, although he had always lived in the most charming surroundings, knew not the word or its definition. The place felt queer. He imagined, however, that it was only strange.

Mrs. McGurk was a widow, 40-odd, toughened by her career. The poor woman had a nose that took, from head-on, the outline of a thin pear, and was hung, besides, a trifle crookedly on her face. Her character, though scrupulously honest, was veiled by no soft graces. Like the room, she was clean but she had no charm.

What other roomers might hole up, two to a floor, below him in this tall narrow house, George did not know. He tried to say "Good day" to a man who seemed about to emerge from the other door on his landing, but he got no answer. All he saw was a brown beard, a narrow eye, and the door, reversing itself, closing softly to wait till he had gone by.

George shrugged. He had other matters on his mind. First, he had to get a job. This was not very difficult, since he was a member of the union in good standing. Pretty soon George had hired himself and saxophone out to Carmichael's Cats, a small dance band, playing in a small nightclub. It wasn't such a wonderful job, but George felt that in this great city first one got a toehold and then one took the time to look around.

His first night off, he called on Kathy. She lived only just across the Park in Bennett Blair's gray stone house that looked to George exactly like a bank building. He was received in a huge parlor, stuffed full of ponderous pieces, dark carving, stifled with damask in malevolent reds and dusty greens, lit by lamps whose heavy shades were muddy brown.

Kathy was glad to see him. Bennett Blair was not.

George walked home through the Park, and on its margins the tall buildings glittered, high and incredible in the dark. " 'Tisn't going to be so darned easy!" George thought to himself. And he tightened his mouth.

George, from his toehold, had no time to look around because the toehold gave way. Carmichael's Cats were sorry but they couldn't use him. He wasn't right.

George had to stir himself and get another job with Barney and his Bachelors. They played, as had the Cats, a jagged and stylized kind of music, full of switches and turns. Barney liked to ambush himself, to leap on a sweet passage with an odd blue interruption, to fall from a fast blare to a low whimper with shock tactics. These tricks were no ingredient of George's bag. It wasn't that he didn't like the effect. He admired it. But he couldn't do it. Barney could jerk and shake up the whole band, but not George. George would try, but first thing he knew, there he'd be, tootling along in his own jig time, following one note with the probable next at the probable interval. Being obvious! Barney was disgusted!

So George left the Bachelors, unhappily, and approached Harry and his Hornets.

Each new month, Mrs. McGurk waited for dawn to crack, but no longer. Pay in advance was her rule and her system had no flaws. Rarely, indeed, did the sun go down upon a deficit, or a roomer escape to carry his debt unto the second day.

On the fourth floor, George, occupationally a late riser, was just getting up when she sang out, "First of the month, Mr. Hale." Her initial assault was always blithe and confident.

"Why, sure," drawled George. "Come in a minute." He fumbled under his handkerchiefs in the top drawer. "Hey," cried George in honest surprise, "I don't seem to have much money!"

The landlady's nostrils quivered, scenting battle.

"Gosh," said George reasonably, "I can't give you all of this!" In the midst of turmoil, changing jobs, George had not noticed how low his capital funds were getting. He stared at calamity. He had been here a month and a half, now, and he had not only had made no progress toward his million dollars, he dared not pay the November rent!

Mrs. McGurk was nagging monotonously. "Month in advance. Told you my rule. Took the room, didn't you?"

Up in Deeport, of course, money lay in the bank. But it was not his.

"Rent's due," shrilled Mrs. McGurk. "You've got it!"

George pulled himself together. "How about taking half of it?"

She looked at the bills he offered and on her lopsided face there was no recognition. "Half of it now," urged George. "I've just got a new job. All I want to do is see the man and get an advance." George was not going to let next week's meals out of his fingers. He couldn't. This crisis had sneaked up on him, but his instinct was to meet it with caution and compromise. There was a sense, here, in which Greek met Greek.

Mrs. McGurk snorted. "Why don't you pay me and *then* go get this advance?"

"Because I'd rather do it the other way around," said
George.

"Nope," said Mrs. McGurk.

"Yup."

"Nope."

"Do you think I'm trying to cheat you?" George was
really curious.

"I got my rules, young man, and nobody's talked me out
of them for twenty years."

George sat down on the bed and ran his hand through his
hair. "I wish a little bird would tell me where the money's
gone," he said ruefully.

"Either pay up or get out!" Mrs. McGurk wanted no
persiflage. "I'll take two weeks' notice money. You want it
like that? Eh?"

George said, "The first of the month lasts till midnight.
Take half. If I bring you the rest before midnight, it's my rent
on time. If I don't, then this is notice money." Her face, if
possible, hardened. "That's fair," said George.

"That's not the way I do business."

"But it's fair," he insisted.

"You got it, right there, and I want it!"

"You're not going to get it," said George quietly. He put
the bills on the bed.

Mrs. McGurk was wild. George swung around. "Of course,
there's another way that's just as fair. Give me back a half,
tonight, if things go wrong. Want *me* to trust *you?*" George
smiled. "O.K."

Head down, she glowered at him. Her hand snatched at the
money on the bed and stuffed it furiously into her old brown
handbag. Mrs. McGurk was fit to be tied. During the years of
shortages, what with rent ceilings and rising costs, she had
not grown rich and avarice was not her trouble. But she had
acquired a taste for power, and she was not going to be
jockeyed out of position. "You gimme the rest before midnight," she cried, "or I'll rent the room out from under you
tomorrow." She flung herself out the door and pounded
across the hall. "Mr. Josef! Mr. Josef!"

George closed his door gently. He had to think, what to
do. As a matter of fact, Harry, the bandleader, hadn't been

absolutely definite about taking George on. And no use looking for Harry this early. George sat down on the bed and
removed all artificial props from under his spirits. Promptly
they sank, way down. This ugly room was more unfriendly,
uglier than ever.

But the mood was one George had been taught to cast off.
He thought he'd go across the Park and see Kathy for a
minute.

Kathy came in a little girl's hop down the great stairs,
seeming, as always, glad to see him. But she said, "Oh,
George, Mr. Blair is home. He wants to have a talk with you
and I promised . . ." George felt a chill of foreboding.
"Maybe," she added hopefully, "he's too busy."

But Mr. Blair was not too busy. George was taken from
Kathy's side and ushered through the high rooms to the
library where Mr. Blair, entrenched behind his desk, frostily
received him.

Mr. Blair was old and cold and his past lay around him
here in this sanctum, relics of past enthusiasms, the accumu-
lations of his mind. The total effect was overwhelming. There
was so much, and everywhere each single item in the mass
reeked of its expense. The smell of money rose like dust.
George nearly choked.

Mr. Blair massaged the vague arthritic pains in his knuckles. "Mr. Hale," he said crisply, "am I correct in guessing
that your reason for transplanting yourself to this city is your
interest in my ward?"

"Correct," croaked George.

A faint sigh came out of Mr. Blair. It seemed to set the
dust dancing. "I envy your youth," he said in his rusty
voice. George thought of the knobby old knees that had never
tanned, in all that Maine week, though he had held them so
faithfully to the sun, and felt, oddly in this place, a brief pang
of pity. "But," the tough old lids lowered, "I must ask you
to consider my point of view."

"I recognize your point of view, sir. I wouldn't think of
asking for Katby . . . yet."

Mr. Blair pushed out his lower lip. George had jumped the
interview several steps ahead. "You expect to be in a position to ask for her, ever?"

"Yes, sir. I do."

Mr. Blair went into a fast rhythm. "What is your work?" He barked.

"I . . . uh . . ."

"You play a saxophone." Mr. Blair knew the answers, too. "How much do you earn?"

"Uh . . ."

"Not very much. What prospects for the future?"

"Well . . ."

"Few," said Blair. "As a matter of fact, you are just floundering. And even if you had a job, at this moment, what prestige, what standing in the community are you aiming for?"

"But . . ."

"When can you hope to ask for Kathleen?"

George wilted. "I don't know," he admitted.

Mr. Blair took another tack. "Now, if," he purred, "you point out to me that Kathleen already has enough mere money, I would agree with you. But I'll ask you this. Have you had any business training? Have you the slightest idea how to watch over and guard her estate?"

"I intend to learn," said George desperately.

Mr. Blair let his lids fall in pure disdain. "Let me speak plainly. If you were to defy my expressed opinion, I am empowered to divert her estate into charitable channels . . ."

"No, sir," said George promptly. "That won't happen."

Bennett Blair's lids lifted and he stared a moment. "I don't accuse you of fortune hunting," he said stiffly. "I merely say that since it will take you many years to achieve the standing I consider necessary, will you ask her now to fix her affections on you? Can't you see that's unfair?"

George leaned back. "It certainly is," he answered steadily. "I shouldn't even risk her liking me, now. Somebody better for *her* than I am might be shut out. That's what you mean, sir, isn't it?" Mr. Blair's fish mouth remained a little open. "It does me a lot of good to see her," said George wistfully. "But I'll have to get along without that."

"Quite right," snapped Mr. Blair. "You realize what it means?"

"Yes," said George sadly.

"I cannot," said Mr. Blair crossly, "be so swayed by my admiration for your handsome attitude that I will forget to insist upon a strict accord between your principles and your actions."

"Did you think I was just talking?" asked George forlornly. He got up. "Is there some back way out?"

Mr. Blair caught his tongue between his teeth and around this physical arrangement crept a reluctant grimace verging on a smile. "Oh, no, no, no," he waved a hand. "You may speak to Kathleen, of course. You might tell her," he added ruthlessly, "how we agree."

Kathy was waiting in the parlor. George took her hands. "Goodbye," he said.

She scrambled out of the chair in alarm.

"Mr. Blair's been explaining some things and he's right, Kathy. I'd better not see you any more. Until maybe . . . someday."

Kathy's hair gleamed as if it brightened with her temper. "I won't be seeing you at all? Because Mr. Blair says you mustn't?"

"But he's right, Kathy. Maybe you don't realize . . ."

"You haven't asked me what I realize."

"I know *you* never think about money or success or things like that," groaned George. "But they have a meaning, just the same. I . . . I have a lot to do." He stepped away from her. "In the meantime, don't wait."

"What!"

"Don't . . . don't wait . . ." said George, ready to bawl.

Kathy flung out her hands in a gesture that might have been despair.

"There's only one thing to do," babbled George.

Kathy cocked her head. "Are you sure you know what it is, George?"

George's eyes were storing up the sight of her.

"I haven't any intention of waiting for you!" said Kathy boldly.

George was beyond heeding. "Then . . . Kathy, goodbye," he groaned. She looked so lovely, so tempting, so perfect, George felt he couldn't bear it another minute. He blurted out, "I hope I'll be seeing you . . . but if I never do, it was wonderful to have seen you at all. Goodbye. Goodbye."

He turned and fled.

Kathy began to breathe very quickly, in angry little gasps. She ran after him. She cried out, to the door that had already closed behind him, "Aren't you going to ask me what I mean?" The last word went up in an outraged wail. But Kathy took her hand from the door and drew away.

It was a black morning. George walked along, staggering under a succession of blows. He was about as far down as he could get. But, gradually, the bottom began to feel solid under his feet.

He wouldn't be seeing Kathy, so he must use every moment to claw and fight his way back to her. Definitely, he must kick away the toehold of his musical background. That meant no Hornets. That meant no advance! That meant raising the rest of his rent some other way.

Well, he'd sell his saxophone. So much was settled. George's spirits began to bounce. He would close his mind to what Kathy had said. Whether she waited or not, nothing could keep him from hoping, from *trying*.

By sheer luck, he caught the landlady off guard and ran up the long stairs. On the last flight he overtook the bearded figure of his fourth-floor-mate. "Pardon," said George. The man flattened himself against the wall, palms in, head turned, eyes furtive. He stood as if he felt himself to be invisible against the protective coloration of the wallpaper.

George paid him no mind. He knew what he had to do. When his hand went cozily around the handle of his instrument case, he beat down the sentimental pang. He reconnoitered. Mrs. McGurk's voice was raised, back in her kitchen regions, so he fled past the last newel post and escaped.

He tramped along the street, west, his mind busy solidifying plans. Sell the sax, pay the rent, read the ads, go to employment agencies, poke and pry, wedge himself in somewhere. His imagination glanced off miracles of one kind or another, bouncing, steadying.

There probably weren't going to be any miracles, George reminded himself. He mustn't expect any magic.

He didn't believe in magic, at this time.

Something told him to stop walking. He saw that he stood before a pawnshop, looking into a very dirty window at a jumble of stuff that gleamed in the dust, whether jewelry or junk he couldn't tell. But deeper within he could discern the dim shapes of larger objects, among them the unmistakable curve of a violin. Musical instruments? Well, he could ask.

George opened the door and went in. A bell made a flat clank over his head. Out of the shadowy back regions, the proprietor approached, a very small man, humped and tele-scoped with age, his face netted with a million wrinkles. He had a dark eye, this little man, dark, liquid and gleaming.

"Yess?" he said.

George lifted his case. "How much for this?" he asked, speaking distinctly in case these ancient ears were deaf.

The proprietor fluttered back of the counter. He moved silently and somehow weightlessly. "Sixteen dollarsss," he said in a dry wisp of sound.

"Not enough," said George's Yankee blood promptly.

The old man moved his shoulders in light indifference. But the dark eyes swam to look up, as if to suggest a hesitation. So George stood still, although his urgency, the glow of his resolution, the steam George had up, tumbled and churned around him.

The old man said, "I've got things I give you to boot."

"What things?" said George. "Look, I don't want to swap, you know. I want . . ."

"Yesss . . . but come. . . ." The whole little man was nodding, now.

George followed him along a dark lane that led to the darkest interior corner. The proprietor paused in a clearing in the jungle of objects, picked up something and set it on a low table. "If you wish," said the proprietor, "sixteen dollarsss and thisss. . . ." "Thisss" was an old carpet bag.

"What's in it?"

"See . . ."

George pulled at the double handle. "Nuh-uh. What would I want with . . . ? Hey, what's that?" He reached in. There was an old sword wedged diagonally in the bag. George had a fancy for old things and a small-boyish love for swords. He fondled the hilt of this one. The scabbard was some worn crimson stuff.

George waked himself out of a dream. The old man's bright eyes were avid and sly. "No, no," said George.

"Maybe isss antique. . . ."

"Looks antique, all right," George fished into the bag and found a small carved box. The lid opened by sliding. There was nothing in it but a flower. A rose. Artificial, he supposed. He dropped the box and rummaged again. There were soft cloth masses. There was a piece of flat metal, framed with a wrought design, burnished in the center. Old, very old. There was a small dark leather pouch. "What's this?"

"Open," said the proprietor softly.

George pulled the thong fastenings. Inside, he found a single piece of metal. Flat, lopsided, with some worn engraving on it, perhaps it was gold. "Hey," said George, "did you know this was in here?" The old man made his butterfly shrug. "Is it a coin? Is it gold?"

"Maybe . . ."

"This might be worth something," George said honestly. "Old coins, y'know."

"May be . . ." said the proprietor indifferently. "You take?"

"Wait a minute," said George, "how do you know this isn't gold? How do you know it isn't worth a lot of money?"

"I am tired," said the old man.

George looked dubious. He chewed on his lip. The whole thing was queer. Queer shivery feeling to this place. "I certainly don't want this bagful of junk. Give me $25 and the coin. How about that?"

"I give twenty and all thisss. So no more, not less." The sibilants sighed on the dusty air.

"You seem to want to get rid of it," murmured George. His imagination was jumping. Maybe the coin was worth a lot. Maybe the sword would sell for something to a man who knew about swords.

"I am going," said the proprietor softly, "to California."

Ah! George relaxed. He had a sense of satisfaction, and clearing of confusion. Of course! Anyone who was going to California flung off the winter garments of old caution. *He* wouldn't want to bother, this old fellow whose bones were promised to the sun!

But George was young and full of beans, and George could spare the energy that lurks at the bottom of most strokes of luck. George said, "It's a deal."

The old man's hands came up as if he would rub them together, but cautiously, he did not. He simply nodded, all over, as before, and fluttered towards his till.

When George lugged his new property out into the street, he felt perhaps he'd been had. One thing led him to hope he'd done well. The queer stark look with which the old man's eyes clung to the carpet bag, there at the last . . . as if there were something . . . something unusual . . . about this carpet bag.

As a matter of fact, it was old-fashioned, ungainly, mis-shapen, distended ridiculously at one bottom corner because the sword inside was really too long, and it made George feel foolishly conspicuous. The only thing to do was dump it in his room.

Even as he gained the second floor, he heard a henlike flutter in the lower hall. He went up fast, anyway, shut himself in and began to empty the carpet bag out on his bed. Might as well see what he had here.

Across the hall, Mr. Josef held his ear against the inside panel of his own door. His eyes rolled, relishing this pose. His fat hand, on which the nails were chewed away, caressed the inner knob with delicious stealth.

Down below, Mrs. McGurk muttered to herself and began to climb.

Outside, the city roared.

George looked at what he had here. There was the pouch. He tossed it aside. The box that held a rose, the sword . . . George balanced it a moment in his hand and it felt alive. He had a terrible suspicion that he could never sell it.

There was that flat metal oval. Then there was a strange object, in metal that resembled a teapot and yet was not a teapot. Baffled, George put it down. He fished out a queer old flask. It seemed to be made of pinkish stone, with a stony stopper, the whole bound in an intricate metal lattice. Something swished inside. George could not get the stopper out to sniff at whatever was in there. He put it down and delved deeper.

Now he came to the fabric. First, he drew out an odd garment, made of a black, rather porous cloth that was opaque and yet so soft it seemed to melt under his fingertips. The thing was designed to be worn. The top of it was cut, obviously, to fit around one's shoulders. George blinked and put it by.

He certainly did not understand what kind of person packed this bag, nor of what kind of household these things could be the relics. There must be some rhyme or reason to this conglomeration. True, all these things were old. But what other quality they had in common he couldn't . . . at this time . . . imagine.

Rolled tightly at the bottom of the bag there now remained a small thin, old, and shabby Oriental rug. As George extracted it, something else dropped. The last object of all in the bag was a ring.

Very old. Not gold, however. Perhaps it was blackened silver. On a plain band, a wrought setting in the same dark metal held an uncut lumpish stone of a bluish-gray color. This stone was curiously filmed over. George put his thumb on it. It wasn't dusty. Nothing rubbed off. It was certainly a queer-looking ring. He held it in his palm, thinking suddenly of Kathy.

Mrs. McGurk rapped sharply, opened the door, and stepped in. She loosened the set of her mouth long enough to let out a "Well?"

George dropped the ring and felt for the coin in his pocket. "It's not midnight yet," he said mildly. It occurred to him that he had better hunt up an old coin man as soon as possible.

"Lying, weren't you?" she sneered. "You got no new job, and no man to see!"

George didn't answer. He just met her steady glare with a steadier look of patience and regret. Mrs. McGurk's eyes fell away. They spied the bed. "I'd thank you to keep that junk off my bedspread," she snapped.

"Sorry," said George gently. "I've got to go out again now."

Mrs. McGurk said venomously. "Don't hurry. I've decided not to accept your full month's rent. I'm giving *you* notice, Mr. Hale."

"All right," said George patiently. "Excuse me." He went out, past her, leaving her there.

He felt stiff and sad. There was no need for such unpleasantness. It served no purpose except to sadden and embitter the innocent day.

Mr. Josef stood in the hall. When George appeared, he turned his back and pretended to be entering his room. George started downstairs. He looked back. Mr. Josef was in a ridiculous position. He seemed to be staring into the blank wood, a foot and half from his face. He was not, of course. His eyes, sidewise, were watching George.

"Who," wondered George, "does he think he is, anyway?"

Mrs. McGurk, having been rude, ugly and unjust, was of course furious. She stalked about George's room, looking for something to pin her fury on. George, however, kept his things clean and orderly as effortlessly as he breathed. There was nothing for his landlady to pounce on, except the bed and its array of strange objects.

Mrs. McGurk approached it then, with nostrils dilated. But, dusty and old as many of these things appeared, nothing, no dust of any kind, had been transferred to the bedspread. Mrs. McGurk's fury began to give way to sheer curiosity.

The cloak she made nothing of. It couldn't belong usefully to a personable young man like George. The metal things she shook her head over. Junk. She wouldn't, she huffed to herself, give them houseroom.

What quiet there was, existing under the constant flow of sound from the city, was being broken hideously by a cat, down below. He was a displaced feline who lived by his wits in the deep yards in the heart of the block. He was sitting on a fence, wailing his heart out. Mrs. McGurk winced at the piercing pain of his cries.

She picked up the pinkish stone flask and shook it, but she couldn't get the stopper out, either. She opened the pouch and drew her mouth down at the sight of the flattened lump of gold that lay within in. She could not know that George, even now, was taking a similar coin out of his pocket to show it to a man behind a counter, two blocks south. Nor could she know that George had not the slightest idea of the existence of this second coin. No thief, she merely drew the thongs tight and cast the pouch down, impatiently.

The cat wailed as if the world's end were at hand. Mrs. McGurk moved to the window and joined the neighbors in a lively exchange of shouted despair. The cat had no mind for the troubles of humans. It wailed on.

Shaking her head, Mrs. McGurk drew it into the room again. She picked up the ring. A curious piece of work. She slipped it on her finger, where it fit with a pleasant weight to it and looked, for all its queerness, rather well on her work-bitten hand.

The cat thought of something particularly outrageous and screamed in an ecstasy of self-pity. "I wish to goodness," said Mrs. McGurk out loud, "that cat would stop its yowling!"

On her hand, the dull bluish lump of stone in the ring began to catch light. For a brief moment, it gleamed. The dusty look of it seemed to burn away.

The cat stopped it. Abruptly. His current yowl, in fact, was cut off in the middle and never finished. Silence poured down like water and extinguished the noise.

Mrs. McGurk blinked. The precipitate quiet was just a trifle uncanny. She listened with a curious eagerness for the cat to resume, but it did not. She tok off the ring and dropped it back on the bed, vaguely sorry, in an inexplicable way, that she had ever touched it.

For just a moment, the things lying on the bed up here in George's room were more than queer. Their antiquity was worse than puzzling.

"Fifty?" said the old coin man, casually. His thumb came up in a caressing pinch. His junior clerk wasn't breathing.

George made a low mirthful sound. "You've certainly been helpful," he said cheerfully. "May I see your classified directory?"

"One hundred dollars," said the man.

"Two hundred," said George gaily.

"It's a deal," snapped the man and now George staggered.

In a tense silence, the junior took the coin, the money was fetched and George signed something.

Then the little office bloomed with three wide smiles.

"I'm satisfied, you know," said George. "But I wish you'd tell me . . ."

"Rare!" babbled the man. "Rare? Not even listed. And indisputably genuine. The inscriptions, the feel of the gold . . ." he rubbed his fingers, "greasy with time . . ." He slapped the counter jubilantly. "Now tell me. Where *did* you get it?"

"Found it, like I told you," said George cheerfully. "I'm certainly glad you liked it. Tell you what, if I ever run across another one, I'll let you know. So long."

George went off jauntily. The boss's mouth curled. "He'll bring us another one! Ha!"

"Ha ha!" echoed the clerk.

Mrs. McGurk had shaken off her funny feeling. She went on examining this queer collection, and at last she picked up the little carved box with the sliding lid and looked sourly at the rose inside. Artificial, she presumed. Yet . . . no . . . or, if it was, it was a marvel! Her woman's eye could see as much. She touched it and the petals were sweet and cool. Mrs. McGurk raised the box to her crooked nose. To her senses came the unmistakable fresh rich fragrance of the living rose.

Just then, George opened his door.

Rose to nose, Mrs. McGurk looked full at him.

Until this day, Mrs. McGurk's impression of George had been mild. Her trained gaze had gone over him and not finding the mark of the complainer, or the destroyer of rented property, or the innocent stare of the deadbeat, she had looked no more.

This morning, however, he had offered her good faith and fair play and she had been obliged to turn them down. Under her tough protective crust still existed an uneasy heart that knew and recognized her losses. George had what she had no more . . . the capacity for trusting. Something about him was sweet to the core and it hurt! So, of course, she had been stubbornly angry.

But now, as the perfume of the rose penetrated her senses,

something very strange happened to Mrs. McGurk. This crust of hers seemed suddenly and for no cause to dissolve. Her bosom swelled as if some withered seed, lying dormant in her heart, had been touched by magic moisture so that it sprang into life and began to grow. Looking full at George, the light in her eye grew suddenly tender. How was it she had not noticed before the gentleness of his eyes, the sweetness of his smile? This was such a boy as one could be fond of, as if he were one's own, almost. Mrs. McGurk had the sensation of melting. She swayed a little. She put the rose, in its box, down on the bed and she smiled.

Even in its best day, Mrs. McGurk's smile had been rather terrifying, involving her long teeth bared to the upper gums and somehow the illusion that the bulbous end of her nose had taken a sudden twitch farther off center. "I'm sorry, Mr. Hale," said she contritely. And her inner being swooned and swam in the luxury of this humility. "I was rude and unjust to you and I'm terribly sorry."

George realized at last what she thought she was doing with her face. However, to him a kindly feeling was the most natural thing in the world and he accepted it immediately. "That's all right, Mrs. McGurk. I was probably irritating. I've got the money, now," he added gently. "Do I owe you anything?"

"My dear boy!" cried Mrs. McGurk, "of course not! You paid me for two full weeks ahead! And you must stay! This room is yours. I want you to feel at home!"

It was the first time the sweet sense of home had come to her mind for years and years. Mrs. McGurk's eyes filled. She wanted to do more for George. She felt a compelling urge to make him happy. "Please let me show you my second floor front," she snuffled. "Such a lovely room it is, Mr. Hale. It would just suit you! Only one flight up and a private bath."

"That's mighty nice of you," said George, somewhat bewildered. "But you know I can't afford . . ."

"Same price!" cried she. "And handy to the phone!"

"Well, I . . . uh . . . if you say so," said George weakly. "It's very nice of you. But I want to pay my full month ahead. Please. I know it's your rule."

"One has to have rules, Mr. Hale. The people I meet . . ."

"Sure. I know. I don't bla—"

"But I should have *seen*," said his landlady, "that *you* are *different!*"

George realized, with some dismay, that Mrs. McGurk was trying to be charming. There she stood, in her shapeless print dress, with her hair piled up in the usual slapdash coiffure, the same woman . . . and yet . . . The head was cocked, now, in a kind of old-fashioned coquetry, the curled lip bared the long teeth; the glance came sideways from under arched brows, with the left eye not quite in focus. It was a formidable sight!

George swallowed. But, being George, he gave her full marks for effort. He thanked her.

"Oh, you will stay?" cried she. "I'll go right down. And freshen up the room a bit. Don't bother about your things. I'll move them. It's no trouble. I feel," said Mrs. McGurk "so happy to have someone like you in the house, I can't tell you . . . !" The brows ached with sweetness. She went out with a bob and a flirt of her skirt.

George sank down on the bed. He rubbed the back of his head. The money was in his hand. He stared down at it. It occurred to him that this was one of the strangest days of his life.

But here was $200, here in his hand. He began to wonder if there was more, disguised in the heap of stuff beside him. He shoved the money into a pocket and reached for that flat oval . . . But his thoughts drifted off to Kathy. Now that he had $200, was he any nearer? When would he see her again, her sweet pretty face, the red-gold of her hair, the enchanting lights in her tawny eyes?

Kathy was standing in the middle of a dainty bedroom . . . on a thick white rug . . . near a soft green chair . . .

George inhaled a great gasp.

He *was* seeing her!

He had been looking absently into the burnished metal and now it was acting like a mirror but what it reflected was not here! He could see Kathy!

He lifted the thing in both trembling hands. The vision did not go. It trembled a little, but the tiny Kathy began to fumble at the fastenings of her dress!

George's hair rippled on the back of his neck. He'd heard there were people who could see things in a crystal ball. Now he, George Hale, of Deeport, Maine, was seeing things! Why, the strength of his love was so great . . . !

Kathy began to wiggle out of her dress. She stood in her slip, bare-shouldered, adorable. Another figure crossed the little reflected scene. Fräulein!

Now, George knew darned well he wasn't in love with Fräulein!

He breathed. He had to. The image in the Magic Mirror shook with his body but did not fade.

Magic?

Kathy pushed the straps of her slip down and took hold of it at the hem. She was going to take it off. No doubt of it. Right now, across the Park, Kathy was undressing!

But George, in spite of his state of absolute astonishment, was yet a gentleman, and, above all, he adored her. So he tore his gaze away from the enchanted bit of metal, turned it over, dull side up, and slid it away from him, under the pillow.

He put his reeling head in his hands.

In a little while, he lifted his face. It was rather white. Not every day does a man run into old-fashioned magic! Slowly, he drew the pouch to him, opened it, and observed with only a dull thud of verified suspicion the presence therein of another golden coin. He took this out and put it in his pocket, drew the thongs together for a moment, and looked inside again. Sure enough. There lay the third coin. George left it there. This was the Magic Purse that never stayed empty!

Here? On 69th St.?

But what else? Suddenly he was in a frenzy to know what else. That carpet. Well, of course! He had no doubt it was the one that could fly! He got up and began to paw over his strange loot. He took up the soft black cloak, put it over his shoulders, and vanished.

That is, of course, George remained standing right where he was, but when he looked down along his body, he couldn't see it! This was the Cloak of Darkness! The very one!

He shuddered out of the thing. Cold chills were racing in

his spine. He hung the Cloak in his closet, aimlessly, without thought.

Ah, the thing like a teapot! He recognized it now! He'd seen it drawn, in a hundred illustrations. It was the Lamp, the only Lamp that could qualify for this collection! Aladdin's! Must be! Must be! But George wasn't going to rub it. Not now. He didn't want to meet the Slave of the Lamp! Not this afternoon!

George inched it aside. He was excited and he was scared. He daren't stop and think. That ring? Ah, but all the old tales were full of rings, with one magic property or another. He slipped it on his finger, where it seemed to fit comfortably. Nothing happened.

His eye lit on the pink stone flask and he picked it up. He was convinced, now, that this, too, was magically endowed. Somehow, he had here the strangest of all collections.

(The little old proprietor must have known! How old? How old was that man? A thousand? Five thousand? He'd said he was tired! George trembled. Never mind. Don't think of it!)

Oh yes, everything here, logic insisted, must be magical.

The pink flask was heavy in his right hand. He rubbed his head. "I wish," he murmured,"murmured, "a little bird would tell me what's in here."

In the Ring, forgotten on his left hand, and back of his head, the dull stone brightened. It lit, like an eye that saw, suddenly.

"Water from the Fountain of Youth." This sentence came into the air. It was like a line of music, high and full of flats. George turned his head in sharp alarm. Had he heard it? Or thought it? No sound now, certainly. Only beyond the window sill, the flutter of wings . . . some sparrow . . .

Water from the Fountain of Youth! George loosened his fingers. He wanted none of that! Suddenly, he wanted none of any of it! He stripped off the Wishing Ring and threw it down. He understood that one might wish to get rid of these things.

It wasn't . . . well, it wasn't right! He wanted to crawl back within the safety of the possible, the steadiness and order of the natural world, the sane and simple world of splitting atoms, of nebulae, of radar and penicillin.

It is not so easy to believe in magic.

George paced up and down, conquering his fright, assimilating his wonder.

There remained the Rose and the Sword. He mistrusted the Rose. He had a shadowy recollection of the Rose and the tale of the Rose. He picked up the Sword and drew it from the scabbard.

It leaped in his hand. What a piece it was! George swung his wrist over and sliced off the top of the bedpost. The hard brass separated, clean and sharp. The upper six inches fell off on the floor.

It was impossible not to take another swipe at something. George brought his arm around. The Sword leaped and flashed down through the back, the seat, the springs of his tough, hard-cushioned leather chair. Clattering, it fell apart in two perfectly neat sections. Wood, fabric, metal, anything! Lord, lordy, what a sword! The Sword of Swiftness, or maybe Excalibur itself! He whirled the blade around his head. Whistling sweetly, it descended and cleaved the washbasin as if it were butter. A chunk of the hard porcelain came clean away and dropped with a bang on the floor. Lucky he'd missed the plumbing, for heaven's sakes! George realized he'd better restrain himself. This thing was dangerous! Much, much too dangerous to play with.

He flicked the Sword at the window sill, cutting a swift notch with the bare tip. He took a neat triangle delicately out of the mirror. He fought temptation. Sweating, he made himself take up the crimson scabbard and insert therein the wicked and utterly fascinating blade.

(Outside, in the hall, Mr. Josef stood quivering. His beard was agitated. His eye yearned for George's keyhole.)

But George sheathed the Sword and put it away from him. He puffed out his breath. What to do now? Anybody else might have run for a good stiff drink, but to George came the thought that he'd had no lunch! No wonder he felt queer. Besides, he'd think better on a full stomach.

Oh, he hadn't forgotten what he was really after. It would take more than a bag of magic to make George forget what he'd wrapped his whole life around. Now, somehow, he was

going to be able to ask for Kathy! All he had to do was calm
himself, and think it out!

He shoved all the stuff back into the carpet bag, or thought
he did. He hadn't counted the nine objects. He was too
excited to check. He forgot the Mirror, still under his pillow,
and the Cloak, in his closet.

The rest he packed and then he shoved the bag under the
bed with the instinct to hide it. He felt of his money. He was
whistling a Georgish version of *Tonight We Love* as he
slammed out of his door, and went downstairs with swift
heels beating out the jig time of his tune.

No sooner did George depart, in the very backwash of the
sound of his going, Mr. Josef oozed across the hall. His ears
shadowed George out the door far below, checked the finality
of its slam. Then, softly, he put his own key into George's
lock. It yielded. Mr. Josef poured himself around the edge of
the door and inside.

He stared at the empty room as if he would hypnotize this
space to remain empty. The closet door was half-open. Mr.
Josef went slinking along the wall towards it, his right hand
in his pocket. Finally, he took a leap and a whirl and brought
himself up sharp with the closet door wide open and him
confronting and threatening George's blue serge and other
garments.

Mr. Josef watched the blue serge closely for a moment.
Then he took his hand out of his pocket, arranged the muscles
around his eyes, and began to rake the place methodically
with a narrowed glance. When he spied the chair, lying so
absurdly in two pieces, his eyes rounded. In fact, they popped.

But he moved coolly to examine it. He saw the washstand
and blinked incredulously at the thick raw edge where George
had sliced it, at the hunk of the outer curve that lay like a
piece of melon on the floor. As he crept over and touched it,
gingerly, there came from deep in the house the thump of feet
on the stairs.

It was, in fact, Mrs. McGurk, coming up.

Mr. Josef rolled himself a glance of dark warning, via the
mirror. He took long crouching steps across to the door. He
skated down the hall.

When Mrs. McGurk, humming *My Wild Irish Rose* in a gay wobbly soprano, had gone into George's room, Mr. Josef slipped like a shadow in soft pell-mell down the stairs to the telephone.

"X?"

"Y."

"Z!" breathed Mr. Josef. "Listen, I have stumbled on something terrific! I must have help at once! Something bigger even than A. You know what I mean?"

"Frankly, no," said Y, wearily.

"A, I say!"

"A for apple?"

"No, no, no. Nuclear Fission," hissed Mr. Josef. "Send Gogo, At once! I tell you, they have a secret weapon!"

"Yeah?"

"I saw results with my own eyes, you fool! This is of desperate importance! *Mother must know!*"

"Hm? Oh, yeah," mumbled Y. "Mother Country, that is."

"Stupid!" Mr. Josef spat into the phone. "Send Gogo. At all costs, I will secure for us this secret!"

"O.K." said Y. "Keep your shirt on. O.K. O.K."

"I will expect him here in five minutes," said Mr. Josef silkily. He hung up, silkily.

Y looked across the plain office toward the other desk. "Josef. That clown. He's got a spy complex."

"His *is* a spy," said the other man, placidly. "We all are, I suppose." He wrote down a neat numeral.

"I'd better send somebody around, if only to keep an eye on him. It's embarrassing. Why doesn't the FBI pick him up?" frothed Y. "We've betrayed him, six times over."

The other man shook his head, went on totaling some figures, compiling information received.

Y got on the phone again, angrily.

Mrs. McGurk stopped humming for a moment, when she saw the broken chair, the washbasin, the bedpost. But the warm flood of happy activity on which (under the spell of the Rose) she was floating bore her right by such details. If George had done the damage, he, being George, would of course make it right. They would talk it over, once he was snug downstairs.

She found his empty suitcase under the bed, beside an old carpet bag, already packed. Mrs. McGurk opened George's dresser drawers and began to fill the suitcase. At last, staggering a little, she lugged both pieces to the top of the stairs and started down.

The second floor front was a room of pleasing proportions. Mrs. McGurk felt proud of it. Into the clean paper-lined drawers of her best dresser she put George's clothing, fussing daintily with the arrangement. She was an absolutely happy woman. She was creating, with love. She was Making a Home.

She closed the drawers. The top of the dresser was bare. Ah, but his own things . . . all the little touches . . . She dove into the carpet bag. This flask, now, was a pretty thing. But the metal lattice work seemed dull. Mrs. McGurk fetched a rag and some scouring paste. Snatches of old tunes came humming out of her as she worked. Her fingers felt tireless. She was so light of heart that she wondered, intermittently, if she was not coming down with something.

At last the flask shone as bright as she could make it and she set it on the dresser and cocked her head. It looked well, but certain artistic instincts were stirring in Mrs. McGurk today. It needed balancing. She dug into the carpet bag and came out with the lamp.

Naturally, at the first swipe of her cleaning rag across its surface, the Genie materialized. It seemed for a moment that steam was pouring out of the spoutlike protuberance on the lamp, but the cloud fell away rapidly to reveal a rather pleasant-looking man, whose skin was on the dark side, and who wore, of course, an Oriental costume of Aladdin's day. He was standing in the air about a foot above the floor.

Mrs. McGurk leapt. She screamed! The lamp rolled off her lap. Before the Genie had time to make his set speech about being the Slave of the Lamp and so forth (which perhaps he delayed in the process of translating it from the Arabic) Mrs. McGurk cried, "Eek! Go away!"

The Slave of the Lamp, of course, obeyed her.

Mrs. McGurk stood trembling in an empty room. Then she fled that place. Ricocheting from wall to wall, blindly, she raced for the sanctuary of her kitchen.

* * *

George munched his lunch, considering ways and means. The thing was, he concluded, to show the old man that Kathy would be safe and sound as George's wife, even without her inheritance. That George, all by himself, with his own resources, could take care of her.

At last, George rose and paid for his meal and sloped his course towards Mrs. McGurk's, stepping jauntily, trying to beat down a persistent little twinge of uneasiness. He told himself that with the Lamp, with the bottomless Purse, all *must* be magically smooth. There was a legless man, begging in the street. George put two fingers on the old gold coin in his pocket, tossed it into the cup and went swiftly on. It made him feel a trifle better to do this.

He had forgotten about his new quarters. He proceeded up the stairs, as usual, put his key in the lock of the door, and waltzed blithely in. Something hard jabbed him in the ribs. A thousand motion pictures, from childhood on, had conditioned him to know, at once, exactly what it was. His arms began to go up.

The voice behind him said, "My dear Mr. Hale, won't you . . . sit down?"

George saw the mocking eye of Mr. Josef, gleaming with pleasure. A second man came from behind the door, a large creature with a flat impassive face. George recognized the type. A henchman!

"Close the door," hissed Mr. Josef. The henchman kicked it shut.

George let the tail of his eye explore the room. The bedspread had been flung up over the pillow. He could see the curls of dust on the bare floor under the bed. The carpet bag was not where he had left it.

"Now, if you please," said Josef sternly, "the secret, and quickly!"

"What secret?"

"Come now, Mr. Hale. Surely we needn't pursue the childish course of torture?"

"I don't know what you're talking about," said George. "My money's in my pocket." He pointed with his elbow.

Mr. Josef put his head to one side. "Gogo, he is going to be stubborn."

"What did *that?*" said Gogo suddenly in a reasonable tone of curious inquiry.

"Did what? Oh . . ." George saw that he meant the cut up the washbasin. "Why . . . uh . . ." He swallowed hard. "Accident," he croaked. It did not seem possible to answer this question. George realized he was in quite a spot. The fourth floor was well removed from a policeman. The house had been so quiet, no help could be in it. And there were two of them.

"What kind of accident?" asked Gogo skeptically.

Josef shoved himself between them. The gun looked wicked and unsafe in his gloved hand. "Mr. Hale, naturally you are loyal to your government. But we will, you know, by one means or another, possess this new ray."

"Huh?" said George.

Mr. Josef chuckled. "So it *is* a ray!" he purred triumphantly.

"Ray!" said George in perfect astonishment.

"You would never," teased Mr. Josef, "make your fortune on the stage."

George simply goggled.

"Can we bribe you, Mr. Hale?" inquired Josef suddenly.

"Bribe me to do what?"

"Oh, give us specifications. We wish to know the source of this ray's power, how it is controlled, all about it. Come now."

"There is no such thing!"

Mr. Josef smiled.

"I don't know what you mean!" cried George.

Mr. Josef's eyebrows rose, pityingly.

George knew, now, he had to get away. There wasn't anything he could say. They had in their heads an explanation for the damage in his room that was just about as preposterous as the real one. They weren't going to listen to his old-fashioned stuff. And torture wasn't going to get anybody anywhere, especially George. He said, in an artful whimper, "Don't hurt me." He stumbled back a little farther. "I can't tell you anything."

"A hero," said Mr. Josef regretfully. "Ah, well, we have our little ways. No one regrets these necessities more than I do," cried Mr. Josef, frothing a bit at the mouth, "but we must know what you know, and know it now! And if we pay eventually with our lives for what we do . . . be it so!" The gun quivered with his fervor.

George made up his mind and leaped backward into the closet. He wound himself into the Cloak and leaped out again as the gun in Mr. Josef's startled hand went off. The bullet got George's blue serge in the heart, but George, in his gray, invisible and whole, slid along the wall away from danger.

"A secret passage!" screeched Mr. Josef, tearing his beard. He staggered towards the closet, eyes bulging. George lifted an invisible foot and kicked Gogo hard on the seat. The shock on the toe of his shoe felt wonderful. He only wished it had been Mr. Josef.

His visitors did not notice the door apparently open by itself, for Gogo was growling in his throat, looking on all sides for what had hit him. And Mr. Josef, with his eyes so narrowed that he could hardly see at all, was frantically clawing the inside closet wall.

George, still in the Cloak, flitted down to the second floor. The carpet bag was there, all right. He had deduced as much. Furthermore, it had been opened. George spotted the Flask. Then he saw the Lamp, on the floor. When he also saw the cleaning rag, where Mrs. McGurk had let it fall, George deduced the rest.

He sighed. He supposed the poor lady had been frightened out of her wits. He hated to sneak out on her now, especially since she had been so kind. But he could not stay in the same house with Mr. Josef's obsession. And his new plans involved leaving here, anyhow.

So George scribbled a note. "Enclosed please find a full month's rent . . . also what I hope will pay for the damages. . . . Many thanks for your kindness. . . . All best wishes . . ."

Then he listened to the house. There was a muted, though furious buzzing still going on upstairs. He guessed he was safe here for a few more minutes.

George slid out of the Cloak and packed it. He took up the Lamp. Gently and somewhat fearfully, he brought his palm to its side and rubbed.

When the Genie appeared, George, having been braced for this, found himself unalarmed. This Genie looked like a nice fellow. Nothing ferocious about him. Little bit up in the air, of course, George smiled cordially.

"I am the Slave of the Lamp," said the Genie slowly. "What are your commands?" He used the broad A, George noticed.

"Uh, how about getting me a reservation at the Waldorf for the night?" asked George a bit nervously. "Single room, with bath, of course. Name of Hale."

The Genie bowed his turbaned head. "I hear and obey," he murmured.

"Wait a minute," said George, more easily. "As long as you're here, listen. You could build me a house, I suppose? A real nice house, furnished, and with pretty grounds? Fix it, with servants and all, so I could invite some people, say, to lunch?"

The Genie bowed.

"Lessee," said George. "About how long would it take you? Could I count on that by the middle of November?" The Genie looked simply scornful. "By next week then?" The Genie's expression remained haughty. "Tomorrow!" cried George joyfully.

The Genie drew air whistling in through his teeth. "I hear and obey," he said, as before.

"Wait a minute. Don't be in a hurry," George wished this fellow would relax and chat. "Fix it up . . . say . . . uh . . . in one of the nice parts of Westchester County. I want it to look rich, you know. Maybe there should be a swimming pool. But everything the best quality. Nothing flashy. How will I know my address?" demanded George, who liked things clear.

"I will return, Master."

"Call me . . . uh . . . Mr. Hale," said George, shuddering. "And, by the way, the servants should be regular. Not . . . uh . . . slaves, y'know. O.K.? Then, tomorrow morning, I'll be seeing you."

The Genie appeared to shimmer in the air. George didn't say any more. The Genie quietly vanished. George took up the Lamp and packed it. He felt exhilarated, with something of the sensation of one who defies the laws of gravity on a tight rope and walks on the wings of mere balance. Things were moving fast all right.

He got out of the house without any trouble. The spies must have still been rooting around in the upstairs closet, and poor Mrs. McGurk was nowhere to be seen. George hefted the carpet bag and set off down the street. Whatever way he was going, he knew he was headed for Kathy.

He went by way of the Waldorf. George's natural caution . . . just common sense, after all . . . told him he'd better check on this Genie's powers, before assuming too much. But everything was fine. The great hostelry swallowed him in without a ripple in its digestion. George looked around the room they gave him, which was extremely handsome, and he decided the Genie must be the McCoy.

The time had come, here, now, and on the same day. He could call up Kathy. His throat all but closed up when he heard her voice. He managed to say, "It's George."

"Oh, George!" Kathy wasn't anything but glad. "Where are you?"

"At the Waldorf."

"What?"

"Kathy, I . . . did you miss me?" He knew it was ridiculous, but he couldn't help it.

"Oh, George," she said, "I've missed you terribly!" Then they both knew that they meant the long vista of empty days ahead of them, not the mere afternoon behind.

"Kathy, darling," cried George, in spite of himself. "Will you marry me?"

"I certainly will!" said Kathy. "Oh, George, I'm so glad you called!"

"I love you, I love you, I love you," he said.

"I'm so glad . . . so glad you c-called. . . ."

George felt like crying, too.

"Are we going to run away?" she was asking. "Shall we go to Maine? Oh George, let's! Mr. Blair can't do anything that matters."

"Kathy, I'm going to ask him for you and he's going to be glad about the whole thing . . ."

"But . . ."

"Listen, I want you and Mr. Blair to come to lunch tomorrow at my house . . ."

"Your house? Do you mean in Maine?"

"No, no . . . my new house."

"But . . ."

"Tomorrow, Kathy. I'll call him up myself. You'll come to lunch and you'll see. Because I can take care of you, Kathy. And I can prove it. You're going to be surprised."

"George, are you coming over?"

He said, "Kathy, I'd better not, because I promised. Sweetheart, until I can *ask* him . . . and I can, tomorrow . . . Don't you see?"

"George, are we engaged to be married?"

"I meant to wait," he groaned.

"But you didn't and I said, 'Yes.' So we are!"

"We sure are!"

"Well, then," said Kathy, "I don't see what difference anything else makes. Honestly, I don't. But do it your own way. I'll *give* you till tomorrow."

"Kathy, don't be mad! Kathy, would you like an emerald?"

"I've got an emerald," she wailed.

George said, "I can't stand it! Will you meet me in the tearoom on Madison, right now?"

"No," said Kathy, female that she was. "You promised. Besides, I'm all dressed for the evening. Tomorrow, dear . . . dear George . . ."

"Until tomorrow," said George, "Oh, dearest Kathy . . ."

He loved her, he loved her, he loved her!

Most of Mrs. McGurk's roomers were in their rooms on Sunday morning. Ordinarily, therefore, this was Her Day, to which Mrs. McGurk looked forward as quite the liveliest day in the week. But this Sunday, she was not in the mood.

She was, in fact, disconsolate.

The evening before, having finally conquered her fright, she had gone up to the second floor and found George's note. It seemed to her to be the sweetest letter she'd ever had, and it broke her heart. Mrs. McGurk did not see how she could Go On.

Mysteriously, he had left his clothing behind in the drawers. She puzzled all night long over this. She hoped it meant he would return, if only for a few minutes. . . . Oh, she could not rent his room! No, indeed! It would remain as it was, yearning for him, and maybe . . . someday . . . She took to comforting herself with dreams.

Came the dawn, she realized that there was no sense maintaining two shrines to George's memory, on two different floors. So, rather early Sunday morning. Mrs. McGurk climbed up to his old room. She let herself in. Yes, she thought sadly, here was the real shrine, after all. For had it not been George, himself, who had broken that washbasin? Mrs. McGurk saw other traces of his being, and she flung herself on his bed for a good cry. Dimly, she perceived the luxury of this, how even her tears were a bath and a refreshing. Still, she wept with all her heart, until her nose, burrowing against the pillow, met something hard.

She explored with her hand and drew out the Mirror.

Mrs. McGurk sat up and wiped her eyes. This, whatever it was, had been His. Her hands caressed it. Oh, if he had only told her where he had gone! She could let him know. She could get in touch with him. But he had disappeared into the outer world and she had no clue. Oh, would she ever again see his dear face or his darling smile?

Mrs. McGurk was ready to fling herself howling into the pillow once more, when she noticed a moving image on the burnished metal surface she held in her hands. This was odd! Stony with shock, Mrs. McGurk watched the magic scene. She had been thinking of George, so, of course, it was George she saw.

George was walking on grass, looking up at the façade of a magnificent house. He moved beside beds of gorgeous flowers, chrysanthemums in white and bronze masses. He strolled on the edge of a great pool that lay like a jewel in the leaf-strewn lawn.

But it was George! George, with his hands in the pockets of a new tweed suit. . . . Mrs. McGurk clutched the Mirror. She was over 40. In her day, Bluebeard had murdered all his wives but one without benefit of Dick Tracy. Ah, Mrs. McGurk had known the old tales, the classics! Furthermore, just yesterday, she had seen a Genie! Now, two and two whirled together in her head. She didn't understand, but she recognized, and her heart began to beat in wild elation.

Even as she stared, George was strolling down a long curving drive. Where was he? Where? Ah, if he kept on as he was going, she might find out! Since it was the Magic Mirror and her thought controlled it, the image shifted, running ahead of George. Yes, there it was, on a stone pillar there at the end of the drive. She began to mutter, over and over again, "2244 Meadow Lane . . . 2244 Meadow Lane . . ." Now George strolled into the scene and stopped, with that look on his face, that dear baffled look he was wearing, to touch his own name on the handsome mailbox.

Mrs. McGurk sighed in a flood of peace and joy. George was at a place of his own and she had the address. She pressed the Mirror to her heart. It should never leave her!

Away down below, somebody was leaning on her doorbell. Mrs. McGurk, light as a girl, flew downward. She thrust the Mirror inside the bosom of her dress, where it was extremely uncomfortable, flung open her front door, and lavished one of her toothiest smiles on a perfect stranger who was teetering, in an obvious rage, on the stoop.

"George Hale live here?" yelped this man.

"He isn't here right now," trilled she.

"You can tell him from me, he's a dirty crook!" cried the caller. "Look at that!" In his trembling palm lay two old gold coins, exactly alike. "You can tell him from me," stormed the rare coin dealer, for it was he, "that he needn't send any more beggars around to my competitors with any more of this junk! He can't kid around with the Law of Supply and Demand! Maybe he tricked me once! But you tell him, if any more of these show up, I'll get the government after him for hoarding gold! And I mean it! Good day!"

"Good day," said Mrs. McGurk. She closed the door. Her surprise gave way to a belated but loyal anger. She was about to open and shout defiance at the enemy's back when she realized that she was not alone. Somebody was breathing on her neck.

It was Mr. Josef, who had crept close behind her in his furtive way. He fingered his beard. His eyes were sly.

"Morning," said his landlady shortly.

"Oh, Mrs. McGurk," said the spy, "could you supply me with Mr. Hale's forwarding address?" She looked at him sourly. "I am rather anxious to get in touch with him," drawled Mr. Josef. "Something to his advantage . . ."

The end of Mrs. McGurk's nose twitched thoughtfully. "You don't happen to have a street map, do you?"

"Many. Many." He rubbed his hands together. "Of what district?"

"Well . . . uh . . . I don't know. You see, I . . . happen to have the street number, but not the . . . uh . . . community," blushed Mrs. McGurk.

"Quite a pretty little problem!" cried Mr. Josef, in great delight. "Come, we shall solve it. This," said he happily, "is just the sort of thing I am rather good at. Ah, fear not! We shall ferret him out, you and I!"

George had, somehow, envisioned a larger or perhaps fresher copy of the old Hale house, when he had given his orders. He had certainly expected something simpler in line and decor than this! But the Genie, naturally, George supposed, would have more Oriental ideas of what luxury was. Anyhow, George conceded, it was sure some house! It would certainly impress Mr. Blair. Since that was the point, George felt he should be satisfied.

It was still quite early Sunday morning. He had come up by Genie. That is, as soon as he'd shaved and had breakfast, he'd rubbed the Lamp. The Genie had materialized somewhat tardily. He'd seemed rather out of breath, too, and there had been definite beads of sweat on his coffee-colored brow. George had asked him, in all sympathy, if anything was the matter, but the fellow had only rolled his eyes in a stiff unfriendly way. George didn't wish to offend by insisting. He'd let himself be whisked up here.

In fact, George didn't know exactly where he was.

He'd gone through the whole place, picked out a suit he liked, up in the master chamber, and put it on. He'd given orders to the butler about luncheon. Now he was restless. He was anxious to get Bennett Blair out here and impress him and get it over with.

He'd drive himself back into town, he decided, incidentally finding out where he was and how to get back again. He'd call for Kathy and her guardian in the . . . lessee . . . the Cadillac.

As he drove out the gate, a state cop stopped him. "You live here?"

"Guess so," said George cheerfully. "Hale's my name."

"O.K.," said the cop mildly. He spat at the pavement.

"Say," said George, "what's the best way to get to New York from here?"

The cop told him and George rolled smoothly off, waving his thanks. In a mile or two, he wondered whether he had a license plate. If so, was it on the records, somewhere in the vast recesses of the Bureau of Motor Vehicles? George shook off the thought. It made his head ache. He began to experiment with the throttle. He felt, all of a sudden, that he'd better hurry.

The cop, left behind, stayed where he was for a while, rubbing his chin on his palm, gazing thoughtfully at the house.

The funny thing was, he'd been by here yesterday, and there'd been no house.

His head was aching a little, too.

Mr. Blair sat like an old toad, motionless, in the tonneau. The sweet air blew on him in vain. When they turned in at the gates, however, he roused. They bowled up to the front entrance. A manservant came to hand them from the car. The butler stood respectfully in the great doorway.

Within, sunshine sifted through splendid drapery to glow on the polished floor. This entrance hall alone would knock the old man's eye out, thought George to himself. The great stairs winding up, the rich dark paneling, the white cockatoo in his silver cage, adding that one exotic note . . .

Kathy said, "Oooooh!"

Mr. Blair said nothing. George led them into the drawing room. It was baronial. On the vast floor lay a rug of such exquisite color and pattern, such size, such texture, that Mr. Blair was forced to cover a covetous gasp with a fake clearing of his throat. George bit on his own smile. Blandly, he ordered cocktails in the library. Then, with the tail of his eye on the old man's face, George ushered them through the green-and-silver music room (with its silver piano) to the colossal coziness of the library. A soft fire bloomed in the grate. Cocktails came at once in a gold-and-crystal shaker.

The somber beauty of the room was absolutely still. Kathy, since her first gasp, had made no sound. Mr. Blair was stricken dumb. But he was not paralyzed. He walked to and fro. He went over to the bookshelves and drew out a volume or two. Then he began to pat his hand along the shelf and mutter in his throat. He went close to a painting, peering at the corner of it. He turned on George.

"You inherited this place!"

"Well, in a way," said George. "Anyhow, it belongs to me, sir."

"Furnished, as it *is?*"

"Oh, yes. Sure."

"Did you know," demanded Mr. Blair, going so far as to point, vulgarly, with a forefinger, "that whole shelf there is all first editions?"

"Is that so?" said George pleasantly.

"That rug in the other room . . . Where did it come from?"

"It was just here," said George.

"You realize this is a Matisse?" snapped Mr. Blair, indicating the painting.

"I'll be darned," said George feebly. "I guess I hadn't noticed."

What there was of hair on Mr. Blair's head seemed to stir as if it would rise on end. He fell into a chair and seized his drink, thirstily.

Kathy went over to look out of the window. George stood behind her. "It's pretty . . . uh . . . big . . ." he murmured. Kathy nodded. "Too big," said George quietly.

Kathy leaned back just enough to seem to say, "Thou art my shield . . . in thee I trust . . ."

"Don't worry," he whispered. "We don't have to live here." She turned her cheek against his lips.

Meanwhile, Mr. Blair had picked up a small china bowl from the table. Now he looked at the underside of it and began to curse softly.

"Looking for an ashtray, sir?" George gave a hostlike leap. "I guess that will do, won't it, sir?"

Mr. Blair cast George a wild glance and leaned back and blew his breath in puffs toward the ceiling.

Luncheon was served in the 40-foot dining room, where they gathered like two kings and a queen in great carved chairs. At once, Mr. Blair began to examine the lace in the tablecloth.

"Kinda pretty, isn't it?" George beamed innocently. "My Aunt Liz used to crochet a lot."

"Your Aunt Liz," exploded Mr. Blair, "never crocheted this!"

"Well, no, of course she didn't."

"Came with the place, eh?"

"Oh, yes . . ."

"Don't know much about lace, do you?"

"Well—uh—no."

"No," said Mr. Blair.

Kathy was looking blankly at the china, the crystal. Her puzzled eyes kept coming back to George's face, to say, "It's all right, of course. Because it's you."

George squirmed a little. He felt, himself, that the food was, well, astonishing. He had tried to tell the butler what he would like served for this meal, but he must have been vague, or left a lot of leeway somehow, because he didn't recognize one single dish. Although it tasted fine. Mr. Blair seemed to think so.

Also, the butler kept filling wineglasses with different kinds of wine, and each time, Mr. Blair would sip and then close his eyes as one in pain. George didn't drink much wine. It all tasted alike to him anyhow, he explained cheerfully. Kathy sat, hardly eating anything but a little of the cucumber mousse, and George couldn't really eat, either.

Just so Mr. Blair had a good lunch. Because after lunch would be the time to ask him.

In the drawing room, George's manservant brought cigars and coffee.

George cleared his throat. "Mr. Blair, I wanted you to come today because . . ."

"Yes." Mr. Blair's attention came away from the furnishings with a snap.

"Because I want to marry Kathy," said George. "I wanted to show you that I can take care of her. So now I . . . uh . . . ask your permission to . . . uh . . ." George forgot the sentences he had made up ahead of time. "I love her so darned much!" he cried. "And she . . ."

Kathy's hand was in his. It had flown there. "Me, too," said Kathy. Their hands, holding each other tight, lifted between them, entreating him.

Suddenly Mr. Blair looked very old and very patient. He said gently, "I take it all this magnificence is supposed to impress me."

"It does," said George, sharply, for him.

"Oh, it does. It does, George," conceded Mr. Blair. He leaned back and said, coldly, "I would like very much to meet what friend of yours so kindly loaned you this place for the day."

George said, "Nobody loaned it to me, sir. It's mine."

"You will produce certain proofs?"

"Proofs?"

"A deed to the property, perhaps. The inevitable records of ownership. My dear chap, this is rather astonishing, you know. For Kathleen's sake, I must see the proof, and you cannot afford to be offended that I ask for them."

"Well, of course not," stammered George. "Gosh, I . . ."

"However," said Mr. Blair, "granting the existence of such proof, if you then think you have proved your capacities in such a way as to satisfy me, I am sorry you are so deceived. What you have done," said Mr. Blair, opening his eyes wide with an effect of pouncing, "is exactly the opposite! You've proved yourself a perfect ignoramus!"

"Huh?"

"You have no more idea what is in this house than a Hottentot!" rasped Mr. Blair. "You offer me a bowl of priceless porcelain for an ashtray! You never heard of Matisse! Don't tell me! How you imagine that I will permit . . ."

"Just a minute," said Kathy, very quietly. "George and I are engaged to be married."

"I'm sorry to hear that, Kathleen," said her guardian levelly and coldly.

"Wait," cried George. "Maybe I don't know very much, but I can learn, and anyhow, it doesn't matter!"

"It matters," snarled Mr. Blair. "Kathleen's fortune will never pass into the hands of . . ."

"I don't *need* Kathy's fortune!"

"I don't *care!*" said Kathy.

"Sit down, Kathleen," barked Mr. Blair. "There   a good deal that must be explained. I want to know, and so should you, my dear, exactly how a saxophone player without a penny to his name, yesterday, claims to be in possession of a place like this, today. If, as I all along suspected, he's only borrowed it, then he is a cheat. And you'd better know it. So sit down."

With an expression of disdain on her face, an expression that signified her perfect faith in George, Kathy sat down.

"Now," snapped Mr. Blair. "Do one of two things, George, if you please. Produce your papers and explain how you got them. Or name the real owner." Suddenly Mr. Blair's toe rubbed across the soft silk of the rug, as if it had been wanting to do so for minutes. "In a way," he said, with genial brutality, "I hope you can prove yourself the owner, because if you do, George, I intend personally to swindle you out of several things you don't *yet* know you've got here."

George looked about him, wildly. It was if his fairy godmother had turned and bit him.

But then the butler, at George's elbow, said, "I beg pardon, sir."

"Hm?"

"People are approaching the house, sir. In fact, there are persons at the door. I don't quite know what you wish in the matter . . ."

They all became aware of crowd noises. George strode to the window. Men were milling around out there.

"Excuse me," said George. He walked down the long drawing room to the hall and he opened the front door. The first face he saw was that of the cop he had spoken to that morning. "Say, what is all this?" asked George, in his friendly fashion

Everybody began to talk at once. The group converged on the door. It advanced and invaded. George was soon surrounded. Competing voices rose louder and louder.

"Who inspected your wiring here?" "Permit?" "Fire law says . . ." "Why didn't the Building Department get an application?" "I'm from the union . . ." "Who put in the plumbing here?" "Zone . . ." "You can't put up a prefab unless . . ." "My client . . ." "Second mortgage . . ." "Title . . ." "Tax . . ."

Somebody was snapping the lights off and on. It seemed that others were darting off in all directions, into the depths of the house. "Hey!" said George.

"Electricians local won't . . ." "Painters and Paperhangers got a beef if you . . ." "Where's your meter?"

Some were returning and screaming now.

"My God, he's into the gas lines!" "Who inspected . . ." "What about the sewers? He can't . . ." "Wait till the water company . . .!" "Slap a summons on him . . ." "Wrong-type construction . . ." "Have to tear it out . . ." "Permit . . ."

George, in the center of the mass, struggled.

A little dark man screeched, "Telephone!" He fought his way towards the instrument. "Can't be a telephone," he whimpered. Now the state cop was braying down the noise. He achieved an uncertain quiet. He said, in it, "O.K., Mr. Hale. Your turn." The whole house vibrated.

The little man could be heard moaning low into the phone. "You're wrong. Operator! There is no such number!"

George clutched his hair. "Listen, I . . . I don't know what to say." A wordless growl rose from the pack "I didn't mean to break the regulations."

The state cop said sourly, "I figgered, when I saw this place, which wasn't here, yesterday . . . I figgered you mighta forgot a few dee-tails."

"This ain't no prefab!" said one. "Moved it in?" "Say, listen, you can't move a house . . ." "Permit?" "Wait till the office opens . . ." "Jeese," said one, furiously, "who does this guy think he is!" "Yeah," they cried, "who do you think y'are?"

Kathy, cowering in the sofa, murmured, "Oh, please, Mr.

Blair!'' Her guardian, who had sat stonily through the beginning of it, now rose.

"Not here *yesterday!*" said the gas man suddenly, with distended eyeballs. They grew quiet. All grew quiet. Mr. Blair stood still.

"Not here!" screamed the white cockatoo, from his silver cage. "Not here!" Something like a shudder passed through the crowd. They moved closer to each other. They seemed to press in on George now, silently. Their breathing alone was very loud.

"Yesterday! Yesterday!" squawked the pink-eyed bird.

George threw out his arms, thrusting them back. "Now listen, whatever I have to do to make this right, I'll do. So go away. Write me letters, will you?''

"Will you?" said the cockatoo.

Sound began to swell again from their throats. It was working up.

"My name is Blair," said that gentleman. "Bennett Blair." The perfume of his wealth, the strong odor of much money, was wafted on the heated air. "I think my young friend," said Mr. Blair with the faintest accent on the significant noun, "is right. I fear his impetuous haste has cut a lot of red tape. But . . ." His fish mouth closed, his cold eye held them. "Red tape doesn't bleed, you know." They gave him their murmuring chuckle, on cue. They shifted their feet in soft confusion on the carpet. "So suppose we go about this in some orderly fashion. Tomorrow is a business day . . ."

"Yeah, that's right . . ." "Good enough for me, Mr. Blair." "Sure, let the office handle it." "I wouldna come out here, only Joe called me." "Proper channels . . ." "Sure . . ."

The little man at the phone had dropped his head on his arm. "Ah . . . no . . ." he kept moaning. He was cursed with imagination. He contemplated the System, the ramifications, the delicate, vast, and incredibly dainty complexity . . . He stared starkly into the floor with white eyes.

"I'm afraid," said Mr. Blair, with distaste, "this man is unwell . . ."

"Come on, Riley." Somebody scooped up the telephone man. "Give him air." "Come on, you guys. Get him outa here."

Thus, Mr. Blair, by a potent and rather frightening magic of his own, got them all out of there. George wiped his face. The jittery butler closed the door. Then Mr. Blair allowed himself to tremble.

"George," he said, with a fearful quaver. "Was this house here yesterday?"

"No," said George, and sent Mr. Blair tottering.

"For the love of heaven, boy!"

"I was *going* to explain," said George. "I will. Gee! Now I understand! Poor fellow! No wonder he looked pale! Things must have gotten a little complicated since his day." He pulled himself together and smiled at Kathy. "Wait," he said, "till I get my carpet bag. Let's go into the library, shall we?"

So George explained.

Now, Mr. Blair lay back on the leather sofa. His hooded eyes were brooding. Kathy, beside him, rested her cheek on her hand. George was sitting on the floor, the other side of the low table on which he'd spread his bagful of uncanny property. The big room was filled with somber light. Outside, it had come on to rain. Leaves rattled in the wet wind. But the high thick book-lined walls around them were ramparts of silence.

Kathy said, dreamily, "I suppose when he built a palace, in the old days, it would stand all by itself."

"Sure," said George. "No . . . uh . . . connections." He looked sadly at his collection. "I guess this stuff is kinda out of date. I wish I had the Mirror, though. It was wonderful."

Kathy smiled. "Was it something like television?"

George smiled back at her. "But without any sound. Doesn't it seem as if a lot of things people have wished for, they've got?

"I guess you tend to get what you wish for," dreamed Kathy, "more or less like magic."

"Too bad . . ."

"Yes, too bad," she mused. "People wish for ways to kill and yet be far away. . . . Can you unwish? What if there gets to be too much of some kinds of magic?"

"Well," said George stoutly, "look . . . magic *can* go out

of date and get outgrown. Men go past it. People change the way they think and the day comes . . . we just have no use for some kinds."

"Of course," said George, louder, "you'd be able to live pretty comfortably with these things to fall back on."

Mr. Blair raised his head.

"Anyhow, sir," said George to him directly, "now you see why, if there's anything in this house you want, you're welcome to it."

The old man looked around the room. "No," he said. "Not now. I don't want *these* first editions, George. Or that painting. God knows what it is. It isn't human! So what does it mean?" He fidgeted. "The aroma's gone. The patina. Do you know what I mean?"

"It's kind of phony," said George sadly. "Then I can't bribe you, hm?"

Mr. Blair said nothing for a long moment. His crabbed hands massaged his knees. "Maybe you *can* bribe me," he said at last. "Maybe you can."

George was very quick. "Any of this stuff?" He gestured towards the table. "Because I'd rather have Kathy."

Kathy said quickly, "I'd rather, too."

"Money and power," mused the old man, staring at the table, "I have. I've had a long time. Furthermore, I worked for it. I carved it out. No, there's only one of your little gadgets, George, that . . . tempts me, somewhat."

Slowly, George reached out. "You're welcome to this Flask."

Mr. Blair grunted his admiration. "Yes," he said, "I . . . thank you, my boy. I somehow feel you are going to be . . . right for Kathleen. You may take it that I withdraw any objections."

George looked at Kathy joyfully and she smiled like a rosy angel.

Mr. Blair's gnarled hand closed softly on the pink stone Flask. He rested it on his knee. His head dropped forward. Chin on breast, the old man sat dreaming.

George snatched at the Ring. "Would you wear this . . . temporarily?"

Kathy said, "If you want me to."

He put it on the proper finger. He drew her up out of the seat. They skipped off together, out of the amber-colored room entirely. Her shoulder tucked under his, they slipped around the dreaming old man. They closed the door between. In the green-and-silver music room, they kissed, and then, George, holding her, could not speak, so filled was he with happiness.

In a little while, they sat down on a window bench in a nook behind the silver piano. George just could not say a word. He just kept looking at her . . . dear, darling, delicious Kathy!

Kathy smiled and then her eyes grew moist and she smiled again. She looked down at the Ring. She twisted it. She put her head on George's shoulder and out of George came a soft sound like a purr, wordless, and not even chopped into thoughts at all.

Kathy sat up a little straighter and blinked her eyes. "I . . . I wish it would stop raining." she said, just aimlessly, groping for the earth.

It stopped raining.

"George," she said, "this Ring winked at me!"

"Hmmmmmmmmmmmmmmm?"

"It seemed to. Oh, I suppose it caught the sun." The sun was shining. Kathy turned her wondering head to look out, and George kissed her. She pushed him away a little, laughing. "I feel so funny," she admitted. "Do you? As if it all happened so suddenly. Oh, dear, I wish I hadn't eaten those cucumbers."

The prompt distress on George's face was comical. "Oh, never mind, silly," laughed Kathy. "It isn't import . . ." Lips parted, she looked down with quick suspicion at her left hand. For the taste of cucumbers had vanished. She said, in a funny little voice, "George . . ."

"Hmmmmmmmmmmmmmmm?" He was still in a state.

"Oh . . ." she burst out, "I wish you'd *say* something!"

"I love you," said George immediately. "I love you so much I can hardly talk. Wheeee! Kathy, darling, I thought I'd lost my voice."

But Kathy was staring at the Ring. "It winked again. George, do you suppose . . . ?" She looked around the room. "George, wouldn't you like to be up in Maine, right now?"

"I don't care where we are," he babbled.

Kathy said, rather slowly, quite deliberately, "I wish we were in Deeport, Maine."

Nothing happened.

The stone in the ring remained dull and lifeless. It felt heavy on her finger.

"Oh," said George, catching on, "you thought it was a Wishing Ring! Say, maybe it is!"

"Maybe," said Kathy thoughtfully. "One person gets just three wishes. Isn't that so?"

"That's the rules and regulations, the way I heard it," babbled George. "The heck with them." He kissed her.

But Kathy's fingers moved. The forefinger . . . rain! The middle finger . . . cucumbers! The ring finger . . . yes, indeed! George *had* said something!

"It's a bad habit," said Kathy, when she could, "to go around saying 'I wish' all the time."

There was a middle door of this room, and now the knob turned, the door cracked. "Beg pardon, sir. A Mrs. McGurk is here to see you. Are you engaged, sir?"

"Darned tooting I am!" replied George happily. "Mrs. McGurk here! For heaven's sakes! Come on, Kathy. I want you to meet her. Let's tell her! Gee, I've got to tell somebody!"

Mrs. McGurk was waiting in the drawing room. She was dressed as for church. Her hat was last Easter's madness, and under it her hair was crimped violently. Her face was stiff with peach-colored calsimine, and she'd left a little lipstick on her long teeth.

It wasn't in George to rebuke the surge of affectionate pleasure that brought her two hands reaching out to him. The hat and the calsimine did not obscure, from him, the real moisture in her eye. "It's nice to see you," said he cordially, and bent to pick up her handbag off the floor. It was one of those soft suitcases. There was something hard and heavy in it. "Did you get my note?"

"Oh, I did! I did!" She gave him a Look.

But George didn't notice. "Kathy."

Mrs. McGurk became aware of Kathy, graceful in a soft blue wool frock, moving up within George's arm, with her red gold mane so near his shoulder. "Mrs. McGurk, this is Kathy Douglas. Kathy . . . Mrs. McGurk . . ."

The landlady's head, which had frozen in mid-nod, went on with the gesture it had begun. Then she swerved and tapped George on his forearm. "But oh . . . please, George, 'Constance'? My name, you know?"

"Uh . . . very pretty name," said George feebly. He took a step back. He had a horrid suspicion.

"Have you come far, Mrs. McGurk?" said Kathy politely.

"Just from the city," said Mrs. McGurk with a lofty sniff. "A friend with a car drove me."

"But how did you . . .?"

Mrs. McGurk cut George's question off. It could only lead to her surrender of the Mirror. So she ducked it. "Oh, George," she cried. "I thought you should know! A man called. He made the nastiest threats. Something about gold . . ."

"Gold?"

"Coins, you know. He had two of them. He seemed to think you had deceived him."

"Oh, gosh!" said George. In his mind he ticked off the bottomless Purse. Obsolete! "Well, it was kind of you to bother." George whipped back to his main concern. "Mrs. McGurk, what do you think? I'm going to be married. Kathy's promised!"

"I'm so glad," said Mrs. McGurk, with fingers turning white on the handbag. "It isn't going to make any difference," she blurted.

"What?" said Kathy.

"I want you to go on thinking of my house as home," wailed Constance. "And if ever"—she now shot a hard suspicious look at Kathy—"you are troubled and need a friend . . ."

"I beg your pardon," said Kathy. "George, dear, is this a relative of yours?"

"No, no. Mrs. McGurk runs a rooming house where I . . . she was very kind," said George desperately. He backed away.

"I understand!" cried Constance, dramatically. "Now, you have all this! The world is at your feet! Only remember, my dear, glitter isn't everything. Kind hearts do count . . ."

"Glitter?" said Kathy, a bit tensely.

"And a pretty face and a hank of red hair," went on the landlady, quite carried away, "may not take the place of . . ."

"What place?" asked Kathy ominously.

"Of one who . . . boo hoo hoo . . . oh . . . hoo . . ."

"George," said Kathy, smoldering, "if you'll excuse me, please . . ."

"Don't, Kathy. Mrs. McGurk, now, you mustn't cry."

Mrs. McGurk's hat was askew. So was her nose, even more than normally. "George, she isn't right for you! Forgive me! But I think of you and you only. See how cold she is! George, think! Before it is too late!"

In Kathy a dam busted. "I'm sorry, but she can't come in here and say things like that!"

"She doesn't know what she's saying," said George in anguish. "Just . . . just bear with it . . ."

"Wouldn't it be simplest if she . . . left?" asked Kathy brightly.

"You see!" The landlady clung to George's hand. "She'd turn me out of your life! Your true friend, George . . . the truest friend . . ."

"Now, wait a minute." George held out his other hand to Kathy. "She's not to blame, Kathy. She can't help it. I realize what must have hap—I can explain."

But Kathy's mane rippled and flared with the swing of her body. "Maybe you'd better take this back." She pulled off the Ring and smacked it into his palm, "until you do!"

"*Kathy!*"

"Oh, evil temper!" cried Mrs. McGurk.

"Mr. Blair," called Kathy, as she ran. "I want to go home. Mr. Blair, please . . ."

George ripped his hand from Mrs. McGurk's moist grasp and rounded on her. "Now see here! Rose or no Rose, you're going to have to understand, Mrs. McGurk. As far as I'm concerned you were kind . . . sometimes . . . and that's all! You can't insult my girl and I won't . . . *What's that?*"

At the window there was a profile, pressed against the

glass. Its eyes squinted to peer through its own shadow. Like a strange outlandish piece of vegetation, the hair of its beard hung there.

It was Mr. Josef's face, of course.

George said, "How . . . ? He . . . Who . . . ?" He shoved the Ring on his finger. His hands curled into fists.

"Mr. Josef brought me," wailed Mrs. McGurk. "Oh George, don't be mad at me! I can't bear it!" She burst into tears.

"Excuse me," said George. He dashed off towards the music room, the way Kathy had gone.

The old man sat dreaming. Memory, flowing like water, gently exploring the vast fields of past time. Ah, the long, long days of his life! How various they had been. How . . . after all and on the whole . . . he had enjoyed them! How wise he felt! How vividly he could now see the interplay of influences, how he had been deflected, in what ways, and why.

He should be tired. Well, he was tired, the old man thought, often and often. But the fatigue was in his body, his bones, his sinew. Not in the mind. A mind, fortified with so much experience, could play the game of life on a different level. All was illuminated, now. He saw further ahead, further behind. If it were not for the weariness of his flesh . . . what fun! What fun!

Young in spirit, he thought complacently, I have kept, for I have only refined my taste, not lost my appetite.

He roused from his reverie to realize he was alone. They'd gone, the young pair. Gone to embrace, to murmur plans. He knew. He knew. It was a shame and a pity and a waste . . . yes, waste! . . . that all he knew, all he remembered, all he had learned with such difficulty, so many pains . . . all this was tied to a declining body, chained to the span of a creature who must, at the appointed hour, long since struck for him, begin to die.

Mr. Blair took the stopper out of the Flask. He'd seen old flasks of this type. He knew the trick. It was one of the little barnacles of knowledge that had accumulated to him. He sniffed at the neck of the Flask and detected no smell. He looked about him for a vessel. There was his coffee cup. He emptied the dregs into a saucer. He drew out his handkerchief and wiped the cup quite dry.

There were no printed instructions on any label. He shook the Flask. Then he tipped it up and poured a little liquid out into the cup. A fleeting fear of poison or . . . worse . . . flat disappointment (for perhaps it was plain water) crossed his mind. But he faced the chances. Lips touched the rim. He drank.

It was perfectly tasteless.

He put down the empty cup and sat quietly where he was. He closed his eyes. A tree, in early spring, before it pushes forth its buds, must feel a deep interior thrill . . .

Mr. Blair had a moment to think this gentle thought and then he experienced a kind of personal earthquake, a sensation so entangled with that of speed that he was out in the clear at the other time-side of the whole shaking experience before he could tell himself *what* it felt like!

He opened his eyes and the room leapt into clarity. He could see, but how marvelously well! He'd forgotten how it was to see with a depth of focus, without glasses, with young eyes!

He bounded off the sofa. Oh, the spring in his legs! The freedom to move quickly! The strong responding pump of the willing heart!

But his clothes were all askew. His trousers were far, far too loose at the waist. His coat was tight on the edge of his shoulders. Its tail was out like a bustle in the back. Mr. Blair unbuttoned his vest. He had to. He flexed his biceps. He held out his hands before him and saw that they were young.

He felt of his face, patting it with loving frantic fingers. He felt of his hair. Ah, the warm plenty of it! The soft thatch, the crisp wave at the temples! (It was blond and parted in the middle.)

George's butler crossed, with grave mien, the kitchen of George's house and said to the cook, who was his wife, "Marie, we've decided right. We give notice."

She nodded. "I don't like it, Edgar. It's odd. Those men running in . . ."

He leaned closer. "It is *very* odd. For instance, the master has a woman by each hand, in the drawing-room."

"Tch . . . !"

"There is also a man with a beard going around the house, looking in at the windows."

"My!"

"Also . . . don't be alarmed, Marie . . . there is another man, a big fellow, watching this back door."

"Ooh . . ." said Marie. "That is odd, isn't it?"

"And," said the butler, "a strange young gentleman I never saw before is standing on his hands in the library."

"Standing on his hands!"

"As I breathe! Feet in the air!"

"Odd," she said. "No place for us, Edgar."

"Oh, no," he said. "Certainly not!"

Kathy ran through the music room. She fell against the door to the library. "Mr. Blair!"

Mr. Blair, enjoying the sweet coursing of his blood, nevertheless realized that he must stop this mere jumping about. There were bound to be certain problems. He must face them. He must contrive to avoid the hurrah and the vulgarity of public knowledge, and blend this miraculous renaissance into a prosy world without an uproar. He would, somehow, arrange for old Bennett Blair to fade away. Yes, and he would substitute himself as his own . . . what? Grandnephew! Bennett Blair 2nd! He fancied that! He would, for instance, change his signature.

Wait . . . ! Mr. Blair took out his pen, snatched a book, and scribbled his name on the margin. Good heavens! Not so! On the contrary, he must learn to forge his own signature and force this smooth young script into the former crabbed scrawl of his ripened personality.

He laughed out loud. It didn't worry him.

Somehow, Mr. Blair's wise old mind (and it saw and knew and didn't care) was being subtly altered by the vigor of his new young body. That Cloak, for instance. He'd been indifferent to it. Might be a lot of sport, though, it now occurred to him. He chuckled. He picked up the little box. George had warned them not to touch it, or he would have put the Rose in his lapel out of sheer exuberance.

Good fellow, George! They could be friends, pals, side-
kicks, buddies . . . Amused at the layers of slang that lay like
strata in his memory, Mr. Blair, just exercising another of his
five rejuvenated senses, lifted the box and smelled the Rose.

He drew the perfume. Ah . . . !

He heard his name. Kathy turned the knob. She opened the
door.

Dead silent astonishment held them both.

Kathy caught on quickly. She got her voice back. "M-Mr.
Blair?"

"Call me Bennett!" he said in a rich tenor. "Oh please,
Kathleen. Oh, how lovely you are! I have never seen you
before. Kathleen, do you know me? I am young again, and
oh, my dear . . . I am young again for you! Kathleen,
beautiful darling, this miracle is ours!"

"*Oh!*" she screamed. "Oh no!" She slammed the door
between them. George tore in from the drawing room.

"What's the matter?"

"He's yuh-yuh-young! He's talking about l-love!"

"That damned Rose!" said George at once. "Mrs. McGurk,
too. It *is* the Rose of Love. It makes you fall . . ."

"Oh!" She was enlightened. "Oh, George, forgive me, I
didn't understand. But oh, take me away from here." She
was unnerved and trembling with shock.

"Wait, there's a spy . . . that crazy Josef . . ."

She started blindly toward the drawing room. "Not in
there," warned George. He whisked her through the middle
door to an elbow of the great hall. They were together, and
this was good. This was, however, about the only factor that
could be called good or even fair among all the existing
circumstances, as George soon discovered.

He peered toward the front door. The big Cadillac was still
standing in the drive. They might pass swiftly across the
arch, ignore Mrs. McGurk . . . "Wait a minute," said George.
"Nope. He's right out there. Josef. He's dangerous, believe
me. We can't go that way, not that way."

They stood, arm and arm, in a quandary.

Mr. Blair moved swiftly through the empty music room. At the
drawing room door he came face to face with Mrs. McGurk.

"Where is she?" "Where is he?" they cried.

*   *   *

"Whoops!" said George, in the hall. He drew Kathy into
the morning room on the opposite side of the house.

Mr. Blair strode over the great silk rug, his young feet
spurning its fabulous beauty. He burst into the hall, flung
open the front door. He cried into Josef's startled beard.
"Hey, have you see a beautiful red-haired girl?"

Mr. Josef, confounded, tried to look as if he were waiting
for a streetcar. But Mr. Blair, seeing the Cadillac still there,
slammed the door and stood with his back to it. If only he
could find her! He'd done wrong. He'd frightened her. Great
tides of potential gentleness, deep wells of soothing charms
surged restless in his breast. If only he could find her!

George and Kathy slipped from the morning room to the
dining room, through the butler's pantry to the kitchen to the
back door. The servants might have been so many cupboards.
George saw no way to explain this spectacle of the master
and his lovely luncheon guest simply flying by, hand in hand.

On the brink of an exit, George reversed them again.
"Gogo," he said. "We'd better not go this way."

"Why don't we use the magic? George, why can't we get
the Genie?"

"Say!" said George. He pulled Kathy another way, into
the hall again, the hall that lay like the hole in a doughnut, at
the center of everything.

Mrs. McGurk was in the library!

"Wait," said George. "Wait, Kathy." He was most reluctant to face the poor woman. He hesitated. He drew Kathy
behind the dining-room door to think.

This was an error.

Mr. Blair stood over the second maid. "Went out the back
door, did they?"

"No, sir."

"Didn't?" Following a reflex, he chucked her under the
chin. "Where then?"

"That way."

Mr. Blair heaved at his sagging trousers and pursued.

*   *   *

The butler peered palely from the pantry.

Mr. Blair rushed into the hall, dug his heel into the carpet to brake himself, heard breathing in the library, and veered that way.

Someone was breathing. It was Mrs. McGurk. "Seen them?" She shook her head. "They're in the house. They haven't left it." Her woebegone face brightened a little. "How about giving me a hand?" suggested Mr. Blair. "Otherwise we can run circles in this squirrel cage for days."

"I want to talk to George," she quavered.

"Good. Fine." Mr. Blair's legs had temporarily given over to the jurisdiction of his wise old brain. Now he remembered to pick up the Flask and shove it into his pocket. He said, "You come and stand where you can watch the front door and the stairs while I go around again."

Mrs. McGurk nodded. But she was full of suspicion. That was George's flask! She knew it. Had she not polished it with her own two hands? Who was this odd-looking young man? And what right had he to put George's property into his pocket?

When he had gone ahead, through the music room, then quietly, before she followed, Mrs. McGurk took up the Lamp. She knew its value. George should not lose it! Not while his Constance lived! Yes, it was *his*, and she would defend it! One day he would thank her devotion for this!

When George and Kathy eased into the library, it was too late. The Lamp had gone! George sucked a tooth. His collection was sure getting scattered, and it wouldn't do. He had a dreadful sinking feeling, a foreboding. This was just going to lead to all kinds of trouble. He bundled into the carpet bag all of the magic objects that remained.

Kathy whimpered. George said, "Honey, this is just awful! But I can't take you outside with those thugs hanging around." They had reached the hall's elbow again.

"Can't we try upstairs?"

George said, "Upstairs is a dead end, Kathy. You put on the Cloak. Slip out . . ."

"I want to stay with you."

"But—uh—they might shoot!"

"Then *you* must wear the Cloak!"

"No, because if they should grab *you*, I'd . . . I'd . . . I'd . . ."

Kathy pulled herself together. "Why don't I just face Mr. Blair?" Her pretty mouth grew firm. "I've been silly . . . yes, I've been silly."

"Honey . . ." George ached to protect her. "There must be a way out of this, if I had the sense. . . I wish," he murmured unhappily, "a little bird would tell me how I could get out of here."

"On the Flying Carpet," said the white cockatoo tartly.

"Eh? What's that?" said George.

He was wearing the Ring. He had slipped it on his finger, long ago. At his words, of course, the stone in the Ring had become quite clear and shining. George wasn't noticing, however. He was gazing, astonished, at the cockatoo, and the cockatoo stared back insolently, as if to say, "You dope! You shouda thought of that!"

"George!" Kathy was jolted out of her nervous reaction. "The Ring! Oh, give me that Ring!"

"Wha . . . ?"

"Quick! I can't expl—oh, quick, before you say another word!"

George gave it to her. "What's the matter?" he said. "By golly, it's the perfect solution! Come on. Upstairs."

Mr. Blair heard Mrs. McGurk give tongue, but too late. George and Kathy scrambled out a window to a flat roof. He spread out the Carpet and they sat down on it.

"Take us to Maine, if you please," said George firmly. "Deeport, Maine." And then they rose. They fell giggling into each other's arms. It was so wonderfully absurd and delightful. Here they were, together. The mad afternoon was over. They floated, free. The sun was sinking behind a band of red. . . .

"Well, they're gone," said Mr. Blair.

"Yes," sighed Mrs. McGurk. Her face was calm.

Mr. Blair thought he knew whither the fugitives were

flying. He saw no reason to tell this old harridan what he had guessed.

Mrs. McGurk, for her part, knew exactly what she was going to do and how she was going to find them. But she didn't intend to let this wild young man in on her secret.

"I shall go back to town," said he. "I shall just borrow George's car. May I give you a lift?"

"Oh no, thank you," she said. "I have a car."

They parted. It didn't occur to either to wonder why the other was so calm.

The rose and the gold withdrew, leaving a thin gray sky. They huddled together in the very center of the Carpet, because it was quite small, for two, and steep and empty air was most vividly near, on all sides. Their vehicle was rolling along through chilly space with an undulating flutter that had been a little trying, at first.

Also, there was nothing between them and the stellar distances to keep off drafts. Ah, it was bitter up here! Bitter! Finally, George had hauled the Cloak out of the bag and wrapped it around them both. This helped a great deal, although it was rather frightening and bleak to be invisible. They had to hang on to each other very close to be sure each was not utterly alone, in the middle of the air.

Irritably, George said he wished he knew who the dickens had swiped that Lamp.

Kathy said, "Don't wish, George."

He stretched a cramped leg very cautiously lest a shoe fall into New England. "Say, Kathy, why did you make me take off the Ring? What happened?"

She explained. George found her freezing hand and felt of the Ring with a numb thumb. "Kathy, if it is a Wishing Ring, I can't have used all mine up." He straightened and the Cloak fell back. "Let me get you a sandwich!"

"A sandwich! Of all things, George!"

"But you're hungry! You're starving!"

"I'm not starving," said Kathy. "I just feel as if I were starving. No!" She sat on the hand that wore the Ring. "You know," she went on thoughtfully, pulling a corner of the Cloak up and vanishing, "you and Mr. Blair make the same

mistake. You both want to take care of me. You forget I'm
alive . . . and thinking and doing! I have some sense!'' She
squirmed indignantly. ''Whatever made Mr. Blair think I'd let
you throw my fortune around foolishly? *I'd* be there, wouldn't I?
If anybody was going to throw it around foolishly, it would
be both of us! You men!'' Her body leaned on his. It wasn't
as mad as her voice sounded.

''Honey, give me the Ring. This darned thing is too darned
drafty and slow . . .''

''First you're going to have to think back. One wish you
wasted, I know. That silly bird.''

''Bird!'' said George feebly.

''You've got a pet phrase. You said . . .'' George groaned.
''Oh, George, how many times?''

''Once before, in my room. I remember, now. It was a
sparrow.''

''Two wishes gone!'' wailed Kathy. ''And all of mine!
That certainly settles it! No sandwich, and we'll proceed to
Maine the way we're going.''

''Honey, please . . . I don't like you to be cold . . .''

''I'm thinking of both of us. We just can't afford . . .''

''I know and you're wonderful and I love you but . . .''

Kathy said she loved him, too, and the point of their
dispute got lost, somehow. After a while, Kathy laid her head
snug on his shoulder. The Carpet kept rolling along, and
miserable as they were, it was peaceful in the silent sky.

Suddenly, it wasn't silent. George heaved his shoulder. He
pointed with an invisible hand.

It was an airliner, a silver thing, speeding the way they
were going with a steady roar. It pursued. It caught up. It
passed. The Carpet tossed its invisible passengers, as it bucked
and staggered in the backwash.

Through the little windows they could see where the dim
light bathed the warm upholstered scene. Leaning at his ease
in the deep cushioned seat was a young man with blond hair
(parted in the middle). He'd been dining. Now he was smoking. A pretty hostess bent to remove his tray. Mr. Blair (for it
was he) knocked, as he whisked by in the sky, his lazy ashes
off, and smiled up into the pretty face with a quaint turn-of-

the-century wolfishness, the image of which persisted on the gray cold air when he had gone.

The Carpet kept lumbering along.

The night wore on. Mrs. McGurk took the Mirror, once more, out of her bag. She was tired and bruised from bouncing through the night in Mr. Josef's old rattletrap of a car, which he pushed so recklessly at a speed beyond comfort. At times, she'd been about to ask him to slow down, but she hated to tamper with his absorption.

"Still east?" he asked.

"Still east, I judge. They seem to be nearing Narragansett."

She and Mr. Josef were, she feared, far, far behind. Mrs. McGurk sighed. She was weary and her heart was sore, and she began to suspect that this was ridiculous. She hardly knew anymore what she hoped. At first, it was only to see George, face to face once more, but now her resolution flagged. She was discouraged. She was . . . and her heart ached . . . growing old. Oh, she'd known *that*, all along. Still, she had hoped that even her middle-aged heart could hold the luxury of devotion. A secret spring of joy, it might have been! Ah, that devil jealousy had undone everything!

She had wept already. In her distress, she'd babbled. She'd mentioned magic.

But Mr. Josef didn't believe. He thought they were pursuing a helicopter. He didn't even believe in the Mirror. He'd said scornfully that Mrs. McGurk was guilty of reactionary thinking. No doubt, he said, it was simple radar. But when she swore she could lead them to George, he'd been perfectly willing, even eager, to go on.

The other one, that Gogo, had left them flat. He'd given a brief total opinion of the whole matter. He'd said, "Nuts!" Mr. Josef had screamed something after him, something like "Traitor!" Traitor to what? she wondered sleepily. She thrust her precious Mirror back into the depths of ther bag, and this time her fingers stumbled on the Lamp!

For heaven's sake! What a fool she was!

"Mr. Josef," she cried. "Stop, please!"

"At the next gas station, madame," he said patiently.

Mrs. McGurk bit her tongue. She forbore to correct him.

She really could not imagine what the sight of the Genie might do to Mr. Josef. She decided she had better not rub the Lamp until she was alone.

A mangy little roadhouse lay just beyond the next bend. It looked and was a dump. But Mrs. McGurk cried, "Stop here, Mr. Josef. Maybe," she fluttered, "you would care for something to drink? I might take a little myself."

"Ah, perhaps so." They pulled up. Mr. Josef's hand under her arm, and he looking suspiciously on all sides, they went in.

Behind the bar a hairless man with a roll of fat at the back of his neck looked up without expression. The stale-smelling twilight seemed otherwise deserted.

Mrs. McGurk asked the bartender and he told her. There was the usual anteroom, the powder table. She took the Lamp out of her bag, pulled herself together, summoned courage. So, in the lady's room of Joe's Bar and Grill, Cocktails, French Fries, she met, for the second time, the Slave of the Lamp. This time Constance McGurk did not flinch. She waited calmly while he introduced himself with his formula, until he had asked the conventional question. "What are your commands?"

"Bring George Hale to me," she said.

"I regret, madame," he replied, "it is not within my power."

"What's that?" Mrs. McGurk was outraged.

"Magic cannot cross magic," the Genie told her.

"Is that so! You mean to tell me, just because he is riding around on that Carpet . . . ?"

The Genie bowed.

"Well!" said Mrs. McGurk in a huff. "A fine thing! Look here, you can do it if he gets off, can't you?"

The Genie bowed.

"Very well," she snapped. "The minute he does get off that thing, *then* bring him to me."

"I hear and obey."

"Wherever I am," she added sharply.

"I hear and obey."

"And never mind that girl. Do you understand? I don't care . . ." The knob on the door behind was rattling. "That's all," she said quickly. "Shoo . . . go on, now."

The Genie vanished. A sullen-looking blonde in a fur jacket was entering this sanctuary. Her black eye flickered on the big handbag in Constance's hands. Or did it remark her ruby (relic of Mr. McGurk) solitaire?

The blonde passed on to the inner sanctum. Mrs. McGurk slipped off her ruby and hid it, too, in her bag, which she swung by its long strap over her shoulder. It had occurred to her that she might be among thieves.

Mrs. McGurk was suspicious all over, but she had her own brand of toughness. She demanded a piece of string from the bartender, and she tied the strap of her bag to her slip strap . . . no silken wisp, this, but a broad band of strong cotton. She even tied the clasp of the bag with several loops of cord. Now! To rob her would involve more serious crime. Let them try it if they dared!

Now she turned commandingly. She said to Josef, "I want to go home."

His beard tipped up. "Dear lady," he soothed, "you must not lose heart."

"I want to go back."

"No, no, we go on!"

"It isn't necessary," she snapped.

"Ah," he purred, "I am afraid, dear lady, you don't quite understand. We . . . Go on!" Mr. Josef, locking eyes with the bartender, reached out and grasped her hand.

"Take your hand off me!" said Constance in shrill alarm.

"You see," said Mr. Josef silkily, "you are to lead me to Hale."

"Lead *you!*"

"Did you think," Mr. Josef laughed nastily, "I've taken so many pains with no motive of my own? Ah, come," he chided. Then he barked. "To the car!"

"Help," said Constance feebly.

"Not in here, Mac," said the bartender. "Outside." He jerked his chin. He turned his back.

"Help! Murder!" cried Constance. She ran.

"Ah, no, my chickadee," said Josef merrily. As she fell out the door he caught her by her arms. He forced them back. With some of the bartender's cord, he was binding her wrists together. Joe's Bar and Grill remained indifferent. Only the neon fluttered over their heads. In this dead of night, the road lay bare.

Josef marched her to the car, forced her to the seat. "My dear woman," he said righteously, "let me assure you, you are only a means to an end. Function as that means and you are perfectly safe." He walked around and got in at her side. "East?" he inquired calmly.

"East," quavered Mrs. McGurk. "Oh," prayed she, "George! Oh, George!"

When the sun rose, George at last threw off the protecting Cloak and peered over the edge. Below was Maine, and all around was morning, and suddenly George wanted the world to be as clear and crisp as it looked.

"Kathy, let's dump all this stuff! It's no good!" He held up the Rose in its box. "We don't want this around, do we?"

"I don't think you ought to dump it," said Kathy thoughtfully. "You just can't tell. It's not the fault of the *things*, George." She was sitting with her legs crossed, her brown eyes serious. "It's just that the more power you've got in your hand," mused Kathy, "the more careful you have to be how your hand turns."

George took out the Purse. "Gold sure ain't what it used to be."

"But we'll keep it." Kathy put it and the Rose in a deep pocket of her dress.

"Let's see. Mrs. McGurk must have the Mirror. Mr. Blair's got the Flask. One of them's got the Lamp. We're sitting on the dumb Carpet. And you're still wearing the Ring."

"Yes," she said, "I must remember. And here's the Cloak." She folded it over her arm, as one might put on her gloves when the train is entering the station.

"One thing left." George drew out the Sword. The hilt snuggled into his hand as if the blade were begging to dance. "I'd kinda like to . . . uh . . . hang on to this," said George sheepishly. "But I'm darned tooting going to get rid of this bag!" He buckled the sword belt around his waist. Then he lifted the carpet bag and heaved it over into space.

"There!"

He felt better. He lay down on his belly and inspected the

terrain. He thought he could spot the Congregational spire. George bet Kathy a dollar his mother would make him shave on an empty stomach. So they lay, giggling, peering down, kicking their heels, and the sun was warm on their backs. They forgot they'd been miserable. They were almost home.

Mr. Blair touched earth long before dawn, hired a car, and drove himself to Deeport. At the Ocean House, he registered, unchallenged, as Bennett Blair 2nd. He reserved a suite for Miss Douglas. He had her luggage put there.

Oh, he was a fox! He chuckled, looking down at George's suit that he had filched from the vast array in the upstairs wardrobe at George's fabulous house. All his own suits were hopeless. He was a fox! He'd thought of this!

Oh, it had been jolly, whipping down the parkways in George's Cadillac, sneaking into his own house, commanding Fräulein in an imitation of his own old voice, over the house phone, to pack for Kathy. Maneuvering the servants out of the way before he made his dash to the streets again. He was postponing, he was evading. First and foremost came Kathleen.

The darling girl had run away, and he could not blame her for that. He had overwhelmed her too suddenly, pouring out such talk! Well, he could not blame himself for that, either. That glorious surge of the heart had overwhelmed him. He did not regret it.

All would be well, yet. Mr. Blair felt absolutely invincible.

He breakfasted in his room, alone. This was his first free time with a looking glass. He tried to part his blond hair on the side, but it refused. How old was he? he wondered. A scar, there, at the hairline. He remembered the occasion of it. He must be at least twenty-five. A good age! Just the right age for Kathleen!

Kathleen! Mr. Blair was, actually, in a state of civil war, his physical youth resisting his foxy old brain, so that he swayed between dreams of love and the cooler strategy of conquest.

At last, he realized that even that ancient decrepit Carpet would be ambling into port soon. So he tore his gaze from the fascinating face in the glass, borrowed binoculars, drove off to an unpopulated stretch of beach. He would take up a post.

He would meet the morning Carpet. Mr. Blair chuckled. What a glorious morning! He frisked on the pebbly strand.

Mr. Blair's wise old mind, bouncing, willy-nilly, while the rest of him danced, remarked that Wall Street had never been like this!

The Carpet began to lose altitude. It was coming in for a landing on a deserted potato field. George peered anxiously over. He saw a car draw up. The figure of a man got out and ran, arms waving. "Oh, my gosh!" said George in dismay.

"It's Mr. Blair, isn't it?" said Kathy calmly. "Never mind." George squeezed her hand.

The Carpet came softly, softly down. George stepped off, turned to hold his hand to his lady, and vanished.

Mr. Blair came bounding up. "Hello, hello."

"Hello," said Kathy coolly. The fact that George had vanished didn't perturb her at once. After all, they had both been vanishing, off and on, all night long. She was perfectly accustomed to the idea.

"Have a nice trip?" said Mr. Blair pleasantly.

"Not very," she answered severely. "George . . ." She missed the feel of his hand, the sense of his near shoulder, even more. . . . "Shall we go home?"

No answer came.

"Where'd he go?" said Mr. Blair, looking about them. But Kathy began to walk straight ahead of her. She was so very tired, so very hungry . . . And George . . . why didn't his arm come around her weary shoulders? Tears stung her eyes. She lifted her own arm to mop at them with fabric.

The Cloak hung on her arm!

But then . . . ! "Oh!" cried Kathy. "Oh! Oh!" The Lamp! Now she remembered its lost and terrible power!

"I don't understand what's happened to George," said Mr. Blair, rather angrily, "but if this is the way he takes care of you . . . !"

"I'm afraid . . . there was something," she said forlornly, "he *had* to do."

Mr. Blair's brain beat his body down in a short sharp struggle, for it knew an opportunity when it saw one. He became the soul of tender kindness. *He* would take care of her. He brought her to her room at the Ocean House. Ah, the sweet warm comfort of it, after the vast chill inhumanity of the sky! He commanded them to bring coffee . . . oh, blessed liquid!

Thus he comforted her with the civilized arts. Now, she must bathe and rest, he said, and then take lunch, perhaps? Mr. Blair's breath grew a trifle gaspy. "Kathleen, won't you call me Bennett, now?"

He was being so kind. Kathy couldn't be ungracious. She smiled and said she'd try.

Mr. Blair's wise old mind fought like a maddened hornet in his skull against his urge to grab her. "Rest well," he counseled, and withdrew.

Sore and bewildered, Kathy nevertheless bathed and dressed herself in fresh clothing. What to do? George was gone! And she could not think how, except by the power of the Lamp. And who, then, had invoked its power but that fatuous old Mrs. McGurk? But what to do? She turned over what magic she had in stock. The Rose and the Purse? She put them in the handbag Fräulein had supplied. George was right. These things were no good. Neither could the Cloak help her. It lay on the bed. The Carpet?

Oh, heavens! It lay abandoned in the field, and what mad adventure waited now for some Yankee farmer, she dreaded to imagine. Oh, George had been so right! This troublesome, troublesome magic! She wished . . .

Wished! Wished, indeed! Kathy threw herself down to weep. Here hung the Ring on her finger, and she with no wishes left!

"Oh, George," wept Kathy, "George . . ."

When the sun rose and people began to appear, Mr. Josef abandoned the highways. He made the car slink through back alleys and lanes. It seemed to put one wheel cautiously ahead of the other, like pussy feet. Even the engine whispered along.

He had not gagged Mrs. McGurk. The poor woman was nearly speechless anyhow with misery. She had kept saying, "East . . . North . . ." at random, and he followed her directions with a queer blindness.

He kept talking. He expounded his philosophy, explaining how, by stealth, treachery, and violence, he would help make a fairer world. "No more slaves!" cried Mr. Josef, pounding the steering wheel with his fist. Mrs. McGurk's enslaved ear heard all this, but her unregenerate mind was going furiously around the same old circle. How to get free?

The Lamp was here, still tied to her person. What if Mr. Josef should open her handbag? How could she benefit? If he should accidentally rub the Lamp and summon the Genie! Of course, Mr. Josef could not, on principle, acquire a Private Slave. No, no, all must be chained alike to the wheel of the State! Mrs. McGurk wondered to herself if there was an Amalgamated Brotherhood of Oriental Genii with a closed shop. She felt hysterical. She fought down the feeling.

They were slinking along a country lane. "North?" asked Mr. Josef.

"A little east," she answered wearily, as she had been answering for hours, quite at random.

He stopped the car. There was a glade at their right; an old crabapple tree stood among wild grasses. On the left a little wood and the curve of the lane closed them in.

"We have been here before," said Mr. Josef, and he turned and behind his eyes there burned a reddish anger.

Mrs. McGurk closed her eyes. He'd come out of his state. He'd noticed they weren't getting anywhere. And what to do or say now, she did not . . . did not . . . know.

Then, suddenly, George . . . George himself . . . was there, standing beside the car, leaning on the sill at her side, looking reproachfully into her face. "You shouldn't have done this, Mrs. McGurk," he said, more in sorrow than in anger.

She screamed, "George! Be careful! He . . . gun . . . mad . . . oh . . . !"

"Huh?" said George.

Mr. Josef got nimbly out on his side and raced around the hood. A gun was in his hand.

George backed away from the car in confusion and surprise. His feet slipped among the sweet-scented tall grasses of the glade. His hand went, with an ancient instinct, to the hilt of the Sword.

Mr. Josef, gun in hand, charged at him. "Ha!" cried the spy. "Haha! Haha!" His face went into its most menacing leer. His beard wagged. "We shall continue," purred Mr. Josef, "our little chat. I will have the secret of the ray, please. And now! I'll give you two minutes, 120 seconds, to explain the process verbally or turn over documents . . ."

"Secret! Documents!" cried George. "You dumb bunny! Listen, I cut up that stuff in my room with this old sword."

"Impossible," said Mr. Josef calmly.

George said, "Let me show you! Maybe you'll believe it when you see it. Maybe you'll stop this idiotic Grade-B nonsense!" He pulled the Sword half out of the scabbard.

"Nonsense," said the spy thickly. "That's typical of you stupid Americans!"

Then George really did get mad. "Now, wait a minute," he said. "Shut up a minute, you with the beard! Suppose I had a secret ray? What in hell," cried George, "makes you think I'd give it to such as you? What makes you think I'd let a mutt like you, waving a gun around, steal a better weapon? You're not fit to be trusted with a bow and arrow. I wouldn't give you *any* secret *any* time *any*where for *any* reason . . . you and your corny threats!" cried George. He drew the Sword out all the way. "You obsolete old bully! Get out of the way!"

Mr. Josef raised the gun. The rules of his craft did not permit him to kill dead somebody with a secret. Ideology said torture. His eyes narrowed, calculating pain.

The Sword leapt in George's hand. It glittered across the air like a fork of lightning. It cut the gun—and a fingertip— from Josef's hand.

Blood flowed.

Mr. Josef looked down. He often had thoughts of blood, but not often was the blood in his thoughts *his* blood. Mr. Josef turned very pale. Holding the wounded hand before him, he tipped, fainting, forward. Fascinated, George watched him fall . . . against the blade! The wicked blade, still poised in George's hand!

Mr. Josef expired at once.

George loosened his hand from the hilt of the terrible toy. It fell on the ground beside the body. His hand was stinging. It was divorced from the rest of him, by its independent guilt.

George sank his face in his hands and groaned aloud.

Mrs. McGurk said, "George, dear George, don't you mind! You couldn't help it! Untie me," she begged. "Oh, George, you don't know! When you hear, you won't feel quite so bad about him. It was self-defense, George. You had to do it."

"Untie you?" said George stupidly. He came to the car. He worked at her wrists. He would not touch that Sword again, even for mercy's sake. He cut the cord with a dull penknife from his pocket.

Mrs. McGurk, in spite of the pain, moved her hands to her handbag. "Don't worry . . . don't worry . . . you and I will be far far away. See what I have!" she cried, as to a hurt baby. (See! See the pretty Lamp!)

But George shook himself. What's done is done, he thought in some hard sturdy core. Never meant to kill him. Was a kind of accident and in self-defense; besides. I'm not, probably, going to prison. He looked down the long vista of his days, every one of which the memory of this day would mar. No, he would not go to prison, he thought bleakly.

Mrs. McGurk cried out, trying to work her fingers, "Open my bag, George. The Lamp!"

"No," he said. "I can't do that." He put his hand on the bag's tied-up clasp. "This isn't the way, Constance . . . I've got to go straight through everything, now. Or always be sorry. Sorrier, I mean, than I am already. We'll have to notify the police. You'll . . . help me, won't you?"

"I will! I will!" sobbed Mrs. McGurk. "Oh, George, dear George, I'll tell them how it was. You've saved me!"

A brown animal broke out of the woods. It was a mule. A stout old woman in a dirty gingham garment, an old woman with a face like the gray bark of an ancient tree, was holding a rope attached to the animal.

"How do?" she said "Had a little trouble?"

"Yes, we . . . yes . . ."

"Seen it," she said. "Sent a kid up to the main road. He'll be back wid somebody," she continued. She leaned on the mule and scratched her tousled gray head with a twig she now took out of her mouth.

"With somebody? You mean the police?"

"Ay-ah."

"Oh," said George. "Well, thanks very much."

There was a tableau, minutes of no sound and no motion, except the mule's gentle cropping at the grass. Then sound and motion were approaching. George left Mrs. McGurk's side and went to meet the man in uniform.

"What goes on here?" said the Law. "That a dead man over there?"

"Oh, officer!" cried Constance. "He was trying to kidnap me! He had a gun! This young gentleman was forced to . . . do it!"

"He was trying to kidnap you, you say!" said the cop, focusing on her face. Her nose was violently askew, after all she had been through. The cop blinked and looked about him.

"You know me," said the woman with the mule, putting the twig back into her mouth.

"Say! Sure. You're the woman who keeps a bunch of pigs down there in the hollow. You see what happened here?"

"Ay-ah."

"He kill him?" The cop indicated George.

"He killed him, all right. Sliced into him. I seen it."

The cop stepped over the tall grass, looked down, looked up. "Why'd you do it?" said he suddenly, savagely, to George.

"It was . . . more or less . . . an accident . . ." George was feeling sick.

"Nah," said the woman with the mule, spitting out the twig.

"No?" said the cop. "What would say it was, hey?"

"Murder. That's what it was," said the pig woman, not violently at all. Her dull eyes rested indifferently on George.

About noon, Kathy and Bennett Blair were settled snugly in the bar, sipping sherry. Kathy was the prisoner of inaction. Mr. Blair had agreed that, no doubt, George must have been kidnapped (in a sense that was the word) by Mrs. McGurk. But, he suggested gently, if George did not now care for the situation in which he found himself, then, being grown and responsible, he would make his own efforts to change it. Let, hinted Mr. Blair, George do it. While they were waiting for him in this pleasant meantime, he and she might just explore each other's friendship a little.

Ah, he was a fox! Kathy relaxed. There was nothing else to do. And she was warm and not very hungry any more, and there was the old beauty of the sea, outside, and she snug beside a friend who knew her well.

The manager came into the bar. "Say, Frank, I just heard something over the air. Fellow name of George Hale got picked up over to Snowden." His voice was low, but at that name Kathy was clutching the edge of the table.

"Picked up!" said the bartender. "What for?"

"Homicide. That's murder, to you."

"Murder!"

"Coincidence, eh?" chuckled the manager. "I bet you Miz Hale's phone is going to be ringing."

"Nah," said the bartender. "Nobody's going to think that's *George!* Wouldn't hurt a fly, for gossake. Besides, he's still down to New York."

"Lots of fools in this world," said the manager cheerfully. "Seems this fellow ran a man through with a sword."

"Sword, eh? Kinda unusual. I wonder if somebody hadn't oughta tip George off," mused the bartender. "Tell him to call up his folks and say it ain't him. You think Miz Margaret is liable to worry any?"

"Miz Liz and Miz Nell won't let her," soothed the manager. "Just the same, I'd certainly like to talk to George. It could help to talk to George."

"He oughta come back home."

"Frank, nobody knows . . . nobody knows how I wish he'd come back home!" mourned the manager.

"Boys in the band feeling pretty sick, too."

"Going to be a lo-ong winter."

"Sweet guy, that George." The bartender's was a sentimental trade. "I dunno what it was about him. . . . Gee, wouldn't I like to see him walk in!"

The manager stifled a sob.

Kathy leaned over. "We have to go there," she whispered fiercely. "Now!"

"Suppose," said Mr. Blair cautiously, "I . . . er . . . see what I can find out."

"Just let's go," said Kathy and she rose.

"Kathy, please listen, my dear . . ." He caught up to her. "You can't go there!"

"But of course I can!"

"No, no, dear." His hands were kind but they held her. "It's a nasty mess. Didn't you hear him say 'homicide'? George is evidently in jail. You can't go there."

"Why not?" she blazed.

"Because you mustn't be involved. Think of the newpapers! The whole moronic public licking its lips . . . Kathy, consider. George wouldn't *want* you to go through all that. You are too precious. *I* don't want . . ."

"What you want," said Kathy coldly, "and even what George would want, is not the point exactly. *I want!* Did you ever think of that? You don't even consider I'm alive! Also"— her hair swung in a gleaming arc—"you don't mean 'precious.' You mean delicate and breakable! Well, I'm not breakable! I'm me! And if *I* want to be there when George is in trouble, I am going to be there!"

"Oh, no," said Mr. Blair, losing his head.

"Oh, yes," said Kathy, turning her back.

"Oh, no," he cried, seizing her arm.

"Oh, yes," she cried, twisting away.

"Kathy," he blurted. "He isn't worth it!"

"Oh, isn't he?" said Kathy, very, very dangerously.

Mr. Blair groaned, regretting error. He let her run up the one flight of stairs. He followed. She ran to her room. He took a stand in the corridor.

He tried to think what to do or say now. If she insisted, why, he'd better take her to Snowden, defend her from what annoyance he could, regain what ground he had just lost, so foolishly. He wouldn't lose his head again!

Kathy opened her door, wearing her jacket, purse under her arm. She was so beautiful! Mr. Blair's head went looping away from him like a collar button under the dresser.

"Kathy!" he cried in his throbbing tenor. He took a step as if he would surge on one knee with hands up to plead . . .

She slipped back behind the half-closed door. She picked the Cloak off the bed.

Had Mr. Blair not been so furiously occupied, retrieving his head for the second time and jamming it fiercely back in place, he might have noticed certain dainty depressions, dotting alone along the padded floor.

It was a crude little jail, but George was tight in a cell just the same, the only prisoner at the moment.

Beyond a thick door, he knew there was a kind of anteroom, and that there, side by side on hard straight chairs, Mrs. McGurk and the pig woman were waiting. He knew this because every now and then someone connected with the law would walk through this corridor. Whenever the end door at the left swung in, he could see that bare and dusty place, and the two of them.

George stared at the wall. The cell block smelled dismally of antiseptics. He felt anesthetized. He would rouse himself and his thoughts would go spinning around the circle of his anxieties. Kathy . . . whether Mr. Blair was being a problem . . . whether to insist that his people be notified . . . His mother and the Aunts, he knew, would march in close formation, right beside him, heads up, mouths firm, right through this trouble. Yet, if he could spare them any confusion before it was clear just what kind of trouble this was going to be, George felt he must.

Then there were the pig woman and Mrs. McGurk, both problems, and his legal status at their oddly assorted mercies. And there were the complications he'd left behind, about the big house. And other complications ahead. There was Mr. Blair. So his thoughts went around and came out at the same place, and meanwhile, there arose about him the carbolic-flavored, dreary, and somehow official smell of delay.

An attendant of some kind pushed the end door inward. Mrs. McGurk sailed around his bulk. She cried, "George!"

George rose politely. "What's happening?"

"They're waiting. As soon as somebody or other comes back, then they'll start asking questions. Oh, George!" Her strange nose was pink from weeping and wrangling. "Remember," she whispered, "remember we can still get away."

George roused in alarm. "No, no. Don't do that, Constance, please!"

"We can leave all this behind," she breathed. There was a

light in her eye he groaned to see. "Everything behind us!
Some desert isle . . . far, far away . . ."

George felt the impulse of his hair to stand on end. He
could look right into her dream. He could see the hibiscus in
her hair.

"That would be the worst thing you could possibly do,"
said George in a stern desperate whisper. "No, please. You'd
better give me the Lamp."

"They'd only take it away from you. George, you must
trust me!"

George tried very hard not to look as frightened as he felt.
"I do," he said. "I know *you* know I can't spend the rest of
my life a fugitive. I must clear my name. *You* understand!"

"I suppose so," she sniffled. It was on the tip of George's
tongue to point out that he'd been whisked into that strange
duel. It had been *her* doing. But he dared not. "Don't you
know," he pleaded, "every time that trick is worked it only
causes trouble?"

"Trouble for you, but oh, George, it wasn't trouble for
me. It was my salvation!"

Mrs. McGurk had it all twisted around. She'd forgotten
that Josef had been after George. She saw herself in the
juiciest role, naturally. She was the Heroine. George was, of
course, Her Hero. It was maddening.

George changed the subject. "Could you do anything with
that pig woman?"

"Pig woman!" spat Constance. "I've talked and talked!
She won't listen. We know she's lying. They'll have to
believe us. They'll have to!"

But George thought to himself, No, they won't either have
to. It was a queer thing, but Mrs. McGurk's obvious partisan-
ship was going to make the truth sound like a lie, while the
pig woman's lie, because she told it without heat, was going
to shine forth as a simple impersonal objective statement of
fact.

He shook his head. "There'll be some way to prove the
truth," he soothed, trying to sound serene and confident.
"Don't worry. Don't do anything. Nothing to do but wait till
they ask for our story."

Mrs. McGurk nodded. She straightened her tired back.

"We'll tell our story," said she. But George saw right through to the female squirm of her judgment. "But if they don't believe it," Mrs. McGurk was saying darkly to herself, "I shall act! I, Constance, shall save him, in spite of himself!"

George stifled a groan. And as Mrs. McGurk, not entirely without realizing the drama of it all, let herself be led away, he beat his head on the bars. Tell their story, eh? Including one thing and another? George closed his eyes and winced all over.

Kathy's voice said, "Hello."

The end door was swinging shut. He seemed alone. "Kathy, where are you?"

"George, have you had any food?"

"No," he said. "Yes. I mean, no. Kathy!"

"I brought you a couple of sandwiches," said she in businesslike tones. He felt the package in his hand. As she let go of it, it became visible.

"Ham! Cheese! Darling!"

"And a thing of coffee." The hot carton came out of the air.

"Kathy, how . . .?"

"I'll tell you while you eat." He could feel her presence, just outside his bars. "Golly, George, do you know something? Being invisible isn't what it's cracked up to be. I'm so battered. I took a bus and five people nearly sat on me. I was leaping from seat to seat the whole time. And it's seventy miles. You see, I didn't have any money, except this old gold, and it would have just caused a commotion. And Mr. Blair had the keys to his car in his pocket. George, I stole the food. Is it good? The only advantage when you're invisible is that you really can steal things quite easily."

George, even among the sandwiches, was a-grin all over. He felt so much better he could hardly believe it. "Kathy, this coffee is delicious!"

"Did I sugar it right?"

"Oh, perfectly! Just perfectly!" How dear and close they were, even in so small a thing! Oh how much cozier was even trouble when it was built for two! "Kathy," he said, "we can get through this, somehow, if she only won't . . . take us apart."

Kathy said, "I want you to tell me. I'm trying to wait till you're not so hungry."

Angel! thought George, and washed down a big bite. Then he told her.

"Oh, dear!" said Kathy at last.

"Honey, was Mr. Blair . . . uh . . . ?"

"Well, not very," she said. But George knew the problem of Mr. Blair was not diminished. "Well." He could feel her brace up as she spoke. "What *can* we do? Let's see. George, I think I'll go and steal the Lamp."

"Say!"

"That would help, wouldn't it?"

"Boy, would it!"

"All right. That's one thing we can do. Of course, there's this." He felt the warm metal circle slip into his palm. The Ring! "We're pretty sure you've got one wish left," she reminded him. "The only trouble is . . . George, what should you wish?"

"Oh, Kathy, I w—"

Her warm hand muffled his mouth. "Sssssh . . . sssssh! For goodness sakes! This time, we've got to figure it out carefully."

"I guess that's right."

"Don't even speak," warned Kathy, "because . . . for instance, you could wish we had the Lamp, but it would be silly not to try to steal it first. Because maybe you'll need the wish to make the pig woman stop lying . . . but then . . . there are so many angles . . ." she wailed. "I think we'd better try everything else first and save the Ring for an emergency."

George wondered, for a moment, what she called an emergency. Then he pressed his lips tight. He agreed. For if, he thought, Mrs. McGurk were to whisk him off to a desert isle, *that* sure would be the emergency of all time!

Kathy's hand touched his goodbye. "Call the man, so he'll open the door." George diverted the attendant for a moment or two. Oh, wonderful Kathy!

Say!

What if he and she . . . George and Kathy . . . were to be magically transported to a flowery isle? There was an idea.

George stared at the wall. He knew right away it wasn't any good. A man can't leave what life is, in the name of life. No, if they were not to be with their kind, to mix in, to take part, to struggle humanly in the great complicated mesh that made the world of men, then what was life for? No . . . no good.

The Ring hung heavy on his hand. One magic wish! Just one! Darned if George could think what it ought to be.

In the anteroom, an unseen Kathy hovered over the ladies in their chairs. Mrs. McGurk was cross-examining. "Now," she said, "when you first caught sight of the car, what was happening?"

"You was screaming," said the pig woman readily.

"Why was I screaming?"

"Because the fella wid the sword just come outa the woods at ya."

"No, no, no," protested Mrs. McGurk.

"Fella wid the beard goes running around to get rid of him."

"Exactly! So it was self-defense."

"Sure it was. Fella wid the beard was defending the both of ya."

"No," screeched Mrs. McGurk. "Listen . . ." she began again.

Kathy saw no lamp-shaded bulges in the landlady's print dress. The Lamp must be in that fat handbag. And it, she discovered, was tied tight to Mrs. McGurk. No way to steal the handbag. Kathy touched the clasp with a careful forefinger. Alas, the clasp itself was tied around and around with cord.

Kathy drew back to think it over. Very well. Attack the problem another way. Ah, suppose Mrs. McGurk was not so sentimentally attached to George? Then would she even think of whisking George and herself away where they couldn't be found? No, of course she wouldn't! Kathy took the Rose, invisibly, out of her own purse. It was worth trying, she thought in excitement. If only she could induce Mrs. McGurk to sniff the Rose a second time and then let her eye light on another, *not* George . . .

On whom? Kathy looked about her. Why, on the fat

attendant, of course. He would do quite well. Kathy crept closer on quiet feet.

A great loop of Mrs. McGurk's hairdo had come loose, and it bobbed and dipped with the vehemence of her continuing arguments. She paid no attention to the Rose, as Kathy tossed it into her lap.

"My wrists were tied behind my back!" she fumed. "Tied, mind you! I can prove it! Was it George who tied them?"

"I dunno," said the pig woman. "Was it?" Her flesh sagged all around the inadequate surface of the narrow chair. Her coarse hands were folded across her stomach. Her bulk was inert. Mrs. McGurk, in comparison, bounced like a Ping-Pong ball. The Rose bounced in her rayon lap. Just then the attendant got up and went to the door, off on one of his mysterious strolls down George's corridor. Kathy reached for the Rose.

So, yawning, did the pig woman. Her big hand closed. Her thick fingers were in possession. Now the dainty blossom (Kathy watched it, helpless with dismay) moved in that coarse grasp towards the stub of her nose.

"Purty flower," said the pig woman. "Where'd this come from?" She sniffed. The hulking bosom heaved a sigh.

The attendant was returning!

He swung the door inward, as it must go, against himself. The pig woman's little eyes rested, naturally, on the opening gap. Her gaze passed through it, to where, snug in his cell, smack in the line of her sight, sat George.

The blob of flesh in the pig woman's chair began to surge. Somehow, it organized itself roughly into the figure of a woman. Kathy snatched back the Rose but . . .

"Say!" said the pig woman. "How long do they think they can keep that kid in this lousy clink, hey?"

"What?" Constance's jaw dropped.

The pig woman heaved to her feet. "You, Fatso, take me in there. I wanna see if he needs anything. Somebody oughta take care of him."

Constance gasped.

"Lissen, sister," said the pig woman, turning. The air churned like water under the Queen Elizabeth. "How come

you're so innerested? Old enough to be his grandmaw, ain't
you?''

"Whose grandma?"

"*His* grandmaw. George's. George . . .'' repeated the pig
woman with a holy softness. Her weatherbeaten face was
warm . . . nay, sunny . . . with affection. "Nothing bad is
going to happen to a nice kid like *him*. I'll see to that!''

"*You* will?''

"Shuddup!'' said the pig woman. "You been making a
fool outa yourself long enough.''

"Well, I . . . ! You old fat pig!''

"Rather be fleshy than a scrawny old crow,'' said the pig
woman ominously. "You let *him* alone.''

"Who?''

"George.''

"Oh?''

"Ay-ah.''

"Hah!''

The pig woman's big mitt made a feint at the McGurk
puss. The McGurk clawed for the scant and scrambled coiffure of the enemy. But the pig woman got a firm grip in
return, and Mrs. McGurk's switch left her.

By now, the attendant, with loud male shouts, had interposed himself. Reinforcements poured in from another room.
With huffing and puffing, with yelps from their victim, with
contributing screeches from Mrs. McGurk, at last they dragged
the pig woman away. One of them humanely opened the door
to reassure a frantic George that there had been only a little
bloodshed.

Kathy slipped back to him. "Oh George . . .'' she sobbed.
"Oh . . . oh . . . look!''

The door had become wedged open. They could see Mrs.
McGurk, settling her ruffled feathers. Pale with outrage, she
perched on the edge of her chair. The cops were all busy,
elsewhere, subduing their billowing witness. Mrs. McGurk
was alone. Through the door, George and Kathy, watching
with a horrid fascination, saw the landlady's hands and teeth
begin to work on her handbag. She undid the cord. She dove
into the bag. She took out the Lamp.

*   *   *

"Kathy . . . Kathy . . ." Their hands clung.

"Wish!"

"But what'll I wish?"

"Call to her . . . stop her . . . !"

"Constance!"

Bosom heaving, eyes flashing, Mrs. McGurk was in no state to respond.

She didn't hear. She was lifting the Lamp to . . .

There came a sharp rap on the outer door.

It was a reprieve. "I beg your pardon," said a familiar tenor. "Oh, I say, it's you, isn't it?"

"How do?" said Mrs. McGurk unenthusiastically.

"My name is Blair," He cleared his throat. "Is Miss Douglas here, anywhere, do you know?"

"Douglas? Oh, you mean that red-headed girl? No, no, she is not." Mrs. McGurk was brusque.

"But Hale is here?"

"In there," said Constance, and her eyes blazed.

"Yes, I . . . er . . . see . . ." Mr. Blair swept the cell block with enough of a glance to see how empty it seemed of Kathy. He brushed by George with a formal little nod. (George, who stood with his hands held through the bars in so odd, so tense a position.) "Ah . . . I see you have the Lamp there," said Mr. Blair pleasantly.

Her hand tightened.

"Powerful little gadget, isn't it?" He gave her a magnetic smile and sat down beside her.

"Y'know, I have an idea."

He had, too. Kathy's hands writhed, if possible, closer to the hands of George. Their four hands were all bruised on the Ring . . .

"*I* could use that Lamp," drawled Mr. Blair, "whereas *you* might have some use for . . . this!" He took the Flask from his pocket. "'This," he said, and no salesman ever spoke with softer lure, "is water from the Fountain of Youth. . . ." The last syllable fell on the sanitary air like the serpent's whisper in Eden. "You see, Mrs. . . . er . . . ?"

"McGurk," she murmured hypnotically.

"I am *Bennett* Blair, you know."

Her gaze slid on the pink stone bottle. "Thought he was an older man. . . ."

"He was," came the seductive voice. "I *was* old. Now, it appears to me that you . . . are fond of George? Isn't that so?"

"I am," she snuffled. "Oh, Mr. Blair, he is in such trouble and that horrible woman, she . . . bahoo!"

"My dear lady, there is nothing to worry about. Not now that I am here."

"You mean you can help?" she quavered. "He killed a man!"

"I'm sure he never meant to," soothed Mr. Blair. "Why, of course I'll help. I would like so much to have that Lamp," he continued with a glide of tone that pointed up the connection. "And you'd rather like to be . . . young again?"

"Young?" *Pig woman*, thought Mrs. McGurk, *ha ha!*

"George, George, he mustn't have it!"

A series of futile wishes paraded in George's head. Futile . . . futile . . . inadequate all.

"I can't find Kathleen, you see," Mr. Blair was murmuring. "I want so much to find her and . . . er . . . keep her."

"I see," said Mrs. McGurk, eyes riveted on that Flask. *Redhead, ha ha!*

"Wish, George! Wish!"

"But *what?* Oh Kathy, what will I wish?"

"I'm not so sure," said Mrs. McGurk, suddenly recalling her best self.

"Now, I can use this Lamp to take George right out of this. But . . . er . . . the thing I had in mind . . . we'd need the Lamp there. I won't," she said with stubborn devotion, "have George doing without well-balanced meals and the comforts of civilization."

"Oh, my dear girl!" cried Mr. Blair, reading her dream. "Don't do that! Pray don't! How much better to clear him of these charges, simply clear him. And then, both of you so young . . ."

She raised her tempted swimming eyes to his face. "How do I know you can get him free?"

"It will be simple. I happen to know certain officials of this state rather well. I believe I could exert certain pressures on people in even higher places, if necessary. . . ."

"You're sure, now!" said Mrs. McGurk, lifting the Lamp in both hands.

"I am Bennett Blair," he laughed, reaching for it.

"But . . . Bennett Blair's an *old* millionaire. How will . . . ?"

"Exactly," said he, very quickly indeed. "Think of it! Only the day before yesterday, I was an old millionaire!" He dazzled her with a smile. "You, too," said Mr. Blair with the flawless technique of the radio commercial, "can be young again. . . ."

Her mind was paralyzed. Her hands began to loosen.

But so did George's. He pulled them free. Now he knew what the wish must be!

Out there in the anteroom, the Lamp and the Flask hung in the air, passing. George spoke aloud in a shaking but solemn voice.

I wish," said George, "*this was the day before yesterday.*"

The Ring winked. "But in the morning!" cried George belatedly. (Oh, was it adequate, after all?) Their hands were locked again. The Ring blazed in the tangle of their fingers. "And oh . . . don't . . . don't . . ." pleaded George, "don't let me forget! Not again! Don't let me for—"

Time swirled in a kind of stew. All dissolved.

Thus, it became the day before yesterday.

"If you wish," said the proprietor, "sixteen dollarss and thiss . . ."

"What's in it?" said George.

"Ssee?"

"Nuh-uh. What would I want with . . . ? Hey, what's that?" George spied the hilt of the Sword. What a magnificent old thing! He was attracted. Maybe . . . his mind was reaching for a good reason . . . maybe he ought to consider this deal. There might be something valuable in this carpet bag.

As he touched the hilt, something thrilled through to his hand. This blade in the crimson scabbard was old, very old. It was evil.

"No, no," murmured George mechanically.

"Maybe iss antique?" said his tempter. George didn't answer. Evil? The shadows all around him were drawn over evil unknown. He looked at his hand, where it merely touched the sword. There was no reason for this shiver, this ghost of horror.

George took his hand away and rubbed it on his trousers. He shook his head slightly to dispel this misty fright that was growing up around him. Silly! Nothing to be afraid of! Just a lot of old junk. He fished into the bag to see what else it held.

He drew out a little box with a sliding lid. George looked down at the rose. What was it, anyhow?

"You take?" whispered the old old man.

George stared at him dumbly. Time rustled by, like feathers dragging. There was something wrong. Something was pricking on his nerves.

But, in George's upbringing, there was no tradition of nerves. One went ahead and did the right thing, regardless of how one felt. That was his training, and it stiffened him now. Maybe this was a chance . . .

He stood, hesitating. It was strange how time hung, as if the unwinding ribbon of it snagged on a point. As if George were balanced between two futures. And was it real? Were there two real futures? Does it matter, when we try? Are we free to choose? Looking back, we think we see . . . we *seem* to learn.

George thought, Yes, it matters. What we do, how we choose, where we push, how we aim . . . being men, we must, to call ourselves alive, believe it matters. Dreaming, he swayed on the point of decision, teetering there, held in this whirling gust of strange unbidden thoughts.

Then the proprietor chose to push at the balance. "Thiss," he said, shifting closer. "thiss rose . . ." His ancient finger gave it a sly poke. He turned his wrinkled face up and it broke into a smile George didn't like. "Iss Rose of Luff!" said the man with hideous glee.

(It was glee for George. George didn't need anybody's glee. George didn't like it.)

"You let girlss smell thiss . . . they luff!"

George closed the box. He felt a little ill of his distaste. "No, thanks," said George quietly. "I don't think I need anything of this sort."

He turned and burst back through the heaps of stuff towards the light. He ran out into the street and gulped the fresh air. He was shaking a little, as if he'd just almost had an accident. "Don't *need*," he heard himself saying. Well, now, how true that was!

He came to a drugstore; he found the phone booth; he put in his nickel. His throat all but closed up when he heard her voice.

She wasn't angry. He could tell.

"Kathy," said George, slowly and clearly, "when you said you wouldn't wait, *what did you mean?*"

"I thought you'd never ask!" Her voice was strong and fresh and glad. "I meant I don't *want* to wait. *I want* . . ."

"Kathy," cried George, "Darling! Marry me! Right away!"

"I certainly will! I certainly will! That's it! That's what I meant! Oh, George I'm so glad you c-called . . ."

"If Mr. Blair keeps back all your money," groaned George.

"You don't want it, do you?"

"Who? Me!" cried George, horrified.

"Well, I thought not. So, pooh!" She switched in the most enchanting way. "We'd better run away," she said practically, "to Maine, I think. The cheapest way. We'll take a bus, George."

"Oh." said George, "dearest Kathy, meet me . . . oh, darling . . . meet me on the corner!"

Mrs. McGurk stood behind her front-room curtains with the sign in her hand, savoring this moment of delicious power. George was off, bag and baggage, and a cute red-headed trick, besides. Sister? Mrs. McGurk thought, cynically, not. Bride? Well, if so, *she* wanted no newlyweds in her house. Always so much in love . . . never had any leverage on them.

Now, she thought, take him. This one, coming up the steps to the stoop. Very prompt with the rent, he was. And serious-minded. "How do, Mr. Josef," she greeted him pleasantly.

He bowed. "Good afternoon, Madame." He fingered his beard. His eyes slanted to the card. "Someone has left us?" He implied that he deduced it.

"Hale. Fourth floor."

"Ah," said Mr. Josef. "And the next occupant?" He watched her face slyly for any hint of a plot.

"I'll tell you one thing about the next occupant," said Constance cheerfully. "He will have a full month's rent in advance."

She raised her hand. She put the sign, the symbol of her power, in the window. That simple, potent, magic word, "Vacancy."

Fräulein stood in Mr. Blair's lair, twisting unhappy hands. "So I pack for her, Mr. Blair. What else can I do? Oh, sir, do you think . . . once they marry . . . that she will want me?"

He grunted.

"Can she afford me?" asked Fräulein boldly.

Mr. Blair looked up over his glasses. He took them off. He rubbed the vague persisting ache in his knobby knuckles. "Of course she can afford you," he said irritably. "I can't keep the child's fortune from her. I used all the pressure I could bring to bear," he continued waspishly, "but the young won't listen, they'll make mistakes." He brooded. "Sometimes," he said to Fräulein's listening face, and knew not why he said it, "I shudder to think of the mistakes one makes, being young." He shook his own (bald) head.

"I am glad if she is happy," said Fräulein stoutly. "This George is a good man?"

A thin, reluctant smile approached the old fish mouth. "As a matter of fact," he admitted, "this George . . . and I have checked . . . is a good man."

"And they love!"

"That, of course, makes everything rosy!" said Mr. Blair sourly.

But not as sourly as he might have.

Darkness gathered over New England. The chill sky pressed down.

Inside, the bus reeked of gasoline, tired people, old candy bars. Gum wrappers and scratchy little gobs of cellophane grated under shifting feet. There was a baby, of course, and a man with a rasping snore. Now and then, the bus screamed to a stop. Clumsy folk blundered in and out, stirring the stale air with piercing drafts. Again, they would slam on through the night.

But Kathy was snug in a seat by the window. Her hair was a pool of gold on George's shoulder. ". . . know what you'd call success," she murmured sleepily, "when everybody in the whole town, probably the whole state of Maine, adores you. And me, too, besides. . . ."

George filled his soul with the sweet warm scent of her hair. He wasn't really worried about success right now. For him, the bus was flying, gossamer-light, through the soft cool night. It was a dear chariot, carrying *all*. And all within . . . the baby fretting pinkly up ahead, the old man, sleeping in noisy peace across the aisle, the middle-aged wife with the beautiful worry lines on her mother-face, the work-soiled, black-nailed, strong man's hand on the back of the next seat, all, all he knew and loved. All their pale faces in the weak light yet were aglow and gilded with something more.

For he loved her, loved them, loved all.

"Why, it's like Magic! thought George. It *is* Magic! And he saw the world, and all its knots and problems, transformed, illuminated, and the pattern changed, by the beautiful blaze of the magic enchanting his eyes.

The bus winged on.

THE BOTTLE IMP

By Robert Louis Stevenson

There was a man of the island of Hawaii, whom I shall call Keawe; for the truth is, he still lives, and his name must be kept secret; but the place of his birth was not far from Honaunau, where the bones of Keawe the Great lie hidden in a cave. This man was poor, brave, and active; he could read and write like a schoolmaster; he was a first-rate mariner besides, sailed for some time in the island steamers, and steered a whaleboat on the Kamakua coast. At length it came in Keawe's mind to have a sight of the great world and foreign cities, and he shipped on a vessel bound to San Francisco.

This is a fine town, with a fine harbor, and rich people uncountable; and, in particular, there is one hill which is covered with palaces. Upon this hill Keawe was one day taking a walk, with his pocket full of money, viewing the great houses upon either hand with pleasure. "What fine houses there are!" he was thinking, "and how happy must these people be who dwell in them, and take no care for the morrow!" The thought was in his mind when he came abreast of a house that was smaller than some others, but all finished and beautified like a toy; the steps of that house shone like silver, and the borders of the garden bloomed like garlands, and the windows were bright like diamonds; and Keawe stopped and wondered at the excellence of all he saw. So stopping, he was aware of a man that looked forth upon him through a window, so clear that Keawe could see him as you see a fish in a pool upon the reef. The man was elderly, with a bald head and a black beard; and his face was heavy with sorrow, and he bitterly sighed. And the truth of it is, that as Keawe looked in upon the man, and the man looked out upon Keawe, each envied the other.

All of a sudden the man smiled and nodded, and beckoned Keawe to enter, and met him at the door of the house.

"This is a fine house of mine," said the man, and bitterly sighed. "Would you not care to view the chambers?"

So he led Keawe all over it, from the cellar to the roof, and there was nothing there that was not perfect of its kind, and Keawe was astonished.

"Truly," said Keawe, "this is a beautiful house; if I live in the like of it, I should be laughing all day long. How comes it, then, that you should be sighing?"

"There is no reason," said the man, "why you should not have a house in all points similar to this, and finer, if you wish. You have some money, I suppose?"

"I have fifty dollars," said Keawe; "but a house like this will cost more than fifty dollars."

The man made a computation. "I am sorry you have no more," said he, "for it may raise you trouble in the future; but it shall be yours at fifty dollars."

"The house?" asked Keawe.

"No, not the house," replied the man; "but the bottle. For I must tell you, although I appear to you so rich and fortunate, all my fortune, and this house itself and its garden, came out of a bottle not much bigger than a pint. This is it."

And he opened a lockfast place, and took out a round-bellied bottle with a long neck; the glass of it was white like milk, with changing rainbow colors in the grain. Withinside something obscurely moved, like a shadow and a fire.

"This is the bottle," said the man; and, when Keawe laughed, "You do not believe me?" he added. "Try, then, for yourself. See if you can break it."

So Keawe took the bottle up and dashed it on the floor till he was weary; but it jumped on the floor like a child's ball, and was not injured.

"This is a strange thing," said Keawe. "For by the touch of it, as well as by the look, the bottle should be of glass."

"Of glass it is," replied the man, sighing more heavily than ever, "but the glass of it was tempered in the flames of hell. An imp lives in it, and that is the shadow we behold there moving; or, so I suppose. If any man buy this bottle the imp is at his command; all that he desires—love, fame, money, houses like this house, ay, or a city like this city—all are his at the word uttered. Napoleon had this bottle, and by it he grew to be the king of the world; but he sold it at the last and fell. Captain Cook had this bottle, and by it he found his way to so many islands; but he too sold it, and was slain upon Hawaii. For, once it is sold, the power goes and the protection; and unless a man remain content with what he has, ill will befall him."

"And yet you talk of selling it yourself?" Keawe said.

"I have all I wish, and I am growing elderly," replied the man. "There is one thing the imp cannot do—he cannot prolong life; and it would not be fair to conceal from you there is a drawback to the bottle; for if a man die before he sells it, he must burn in hell forever."

"To be sure, that is a drawback and no mistake," cried Keawe. "I would not meddle with the thing. I can do without a house, thank God; but there is one thing I could not be doing with one particle, and that is to be damned."

"Dear me, you must not run away with things," returned the man. "All you have to do is to use the power of the imp in moderation, and then sell it to someone else, as I do to you, and finish your life in comfort."

"Well, I observe two things," said Keawe. "All the time you keep sighing like a maid in love—that is one; and for the other, you sell this bottle very cheap."

"I have told you already why I sigh," said the man. "It is because I fear my health is breaking up; and, as you said yourself, to die and go to the devil is a pity for any one. As for why I sell so cheap, I must explain to you there is a peculiarity about the bottle. Long ago, when the devil brought it first upon earth, it was extremely expensive, and was sold first of all to Prester John for many millions of dollars; but it cannot be sold at all, unless sold at a loss. If you sell it for as much as you paid for it, back it comes to you again like a homing pigeon. It follows that the price has kept falling in these centuries, and the bottle is now remarkably cheap. I bought it myself from one of my great neighbors on this hill, and the price I paid was only ninety dollars. I could sell it for as high as eighty-nine dollars and ninety-nine cents, but not a penny dearer, or back the thing must come to me. Now, about this there are two bothers. First, when you offer a bottle so singular for eighty-odd dollars, people suppose you to be jesting. And second—but there is no hurry about that—and I need not go into it. Only remember it must be coined money that you sell it for."

"How am I to know that this is all true?" asked Keawe.

"Some of it you can try at once," replied the man. "Give me your fifty dollars, take the bottle, and wish your fifty dollars back into your pocket. If that does not happen, I pledge you my honor I will cry off the bargain and restore your money."

"You are not deceiving me?" said Keawe.

The man bound himself with a great oath.

"Well, I will risk that much," said Keawe, "for that can do no harm," and he paid over his money to the man, and the man handed him the bottle.

"Imp of the bottle," said Keawe, "I want my fifty dollars back." And sure enough, he had scarce said the word before his pocket was as heavy as ever.

"To be sure this is a wonderful bottle," said Keawe.

"And now good morning to you, my fine fellow, and the devil go with you for me," said the man.

"Hold on," said Keawe, "I don't want any more of this fun. Here, take your bottle back."

"You have bought it for less than I paid for it," replied the man rubbing his hands. "It is yours now; and, for my part, I am only concerned to see the back of you." And with that he rang for his Chinese servant, and had Keawe shown out of the house.

Now, when Keawe was in the street, with the bottle under his arm, he began to think. "If all is true about this bottle, I may have made a losing bargain," thinks he. "But perhaps the man was only fooling me." The first thing he did was to count his money; the sum was exact—forty-nine dollars American money, and one Chili piece. "That looks like the truth," said Keawe. "Now I will try another part."

The streets in that part of the city were as clean as a ship's decks, and though it was noon, there were no passengers. Keawe set the bottle in the gutter and walked away. Twice he looked back, and there was the milky, round-bellied bottle where he left it. A third time he looked back and turned a corner; but he had scarce done so, when something knocked upon his elbow, and behold! it was the long neck sticking up; and as for the round belly, it was jammed into the pocket of his pilot coat.

"And that looks like the truth," said Keawe.

The next thing he did was to buy a corkscrew in a shop, and go apart in a secret place in the fields. And there he tried to draw the cork, but as often as he put the screw in, out it came again, and the cork was as whole as ever.

"There is some new sort of cork," said Keawe, and all at once he began to shake and sweat, for he was afraid of that bottle.

On his way back to the port side he saw a shop where a man sold shells and clubs from the wild islands, old heathen deities, old coined money, pictures from China and Japan, and all manner of things that sailors bring in their sea chests. And here he had an idea. So he went in and offered the bottle for a hundred dollars. The man of the shop laughed at him at first, and offered him five; but, indeed, it was a curious bottle, such glass was never blown in any human glassworks, so prettily the colors shone under the milky way, and so strangely the shadow hovered in the midst; so, after he had disputed a while after the manner of his kind, the shopman gave Keawe sixty silver dollars for the thing and set it on a shelf in the midst of his window.

"Now," said Keawe, "I have sold that for sixty which I bought for fifty—or, to say truth, a little less, because one of my dollars was from Chili. Now I shall know the truth upon another point."

So he went back on board his ship, and when he opened his chest, there was the bottle, which had come more quickly than himself. Now Keawe had a mate on board whose name was Lopaka.

"What ails you," said Lopaka, "that you stare in your chest?"

They were alone in the ship's forecastle, and Keawe bound him to secrecy, and told all.

"This is a very strange affair," said Lopaka; "and I fear you will be in trouble about this bottle. But there is one point very clear—that you are sure of the trouble, and you had better have the profit in the bargain. Make up your mind what you want with it; give the order, and it is done as you desire, I will buy the bottle myself; for I have an idea of my own to get a schooner, and go trading through the islands."

"That is not my idea," said Keawe; "but to have a beautiful house and garden on the Kona Coast, where I was born, the sun shining in at the door, flowers in the garden, glass in the windows, pictures on the walls, and toys and fine carpets on the tables, for all the world like the house I was in this day—only a story higher, and with balconies all about like the King's palace; and to live there without care and make merry with my friends and relatives."

"Well," said Lopaka, "let us carry it back with us to Hawaii; and if all comes true as you suppose, I will buy the bottle, as I said, and ask a schooner."

Upon that they were agreed, and it was not long before the ship returned to Honolulu, carrying Keawe and Lopaka, and the bottle. They were scarce come ashore when they met a friend upon the beach, who began at once to condole with Keawe.

"I do not know what I am to be condoled about," said Keawe.

"Is it possible you have not heard," said the friend, "your uncle—that good old man—is dead, and your cousin—that beautiful boy—was drowned at sea?"

Keawe was filled with sorrow, and, beginning to weep and to lament, he forgot about the bottle. But Lopaka was thinking to himself, and presently, when Keawe's grief was a little abated, "I have been thinking," said Lopaka, "had not your uncle lands in Hawaii, in the district of Kaü?"

"No," said Keawe, "not in Kaü: they are on the mountain side—a little be-south Kookena."

"These lands will now be yours?" asked Lopaka.

"And so they will," says Keawe, and began again to lament for his relatives.

"No," said Lopaka, "do not lament at present. I have a thought in my mind. How if this should be the doing of the bottle? For here is the place ready for your house."

"If this be so," cried Keawe, "it is a very ill way to serve me by killing my relatives. But it may be, indeed; for it was in just such a station that I saw the house with my mind's eye."

"The house, however, is not yet built," said Lopaka.

"No, nor like to be!" said Keawe; "for though my uncle has some coffee and ava and bananas, it will not be more than will keep me in comfort; and the rest of that land is the black lava."

"Let us go to the lawyer," said Lopaka; "I have still this idea in my mind."

Now, when they came to the lawyer's, it appeared Keawe's uncle had grown monstrous rich in the last days, and there was a fund of money.

"And here is the money for the house!" cried Lopaka.

"If you are thinking of a new house," said the lawyer, "here is the card of a new architect of whom they tell me great things."

"Better and better!" cried Lopaka. "Here is all made plain for us. Let us continue to obey orders."

So they went to the architect, and he had drawings of houses on his table.

"You want something out of the way," said the architect. "How do you like this?" and he handed a drawing to Keawe.

Now, when Keawe set eyes on the drawing, he cried out aloud, for it was the picture of his thought exactly drawn.

"I am in for this house," thought he. "Little as I like the way it comes to me, I am in for it now, and I may as well take the good along with the evil."

So he told the architect all that he wished, and how he would have that house furnished, and about the pictures on the wall and the knickknacks on the tables; and he asked the man plainly for how much he would undertake the whole affair.

The architect put many questions, and took his pen and made a computation; and when he had done he named the very sum that Keawe had inherited.

Lopaka and Keawe looked at one another and nodded.

"It is quite clear," thought Keawe, "that I am to have this house, whether or no. It comes from the devil, and I fear I will get little good by that; and of one thing I am sure, I will make no wishes as long as I have this bottle. But with the house I am saddled, and I may as well take the good along with the evil."

So he made his terms with the architect, and they signed a paper; and Keawe and Lopaka took ship again and sailed to Australia; for it was concluded between them they should not interfere at all, but leave the architect and the bottle imp to build and to adorn the house at their own pleasure.

The voyage was a good voyage, only all the time Keawe was holding in his breath, for he had sworn he would utter no more wishes, and take no more favors, from the devil. The time was up when they got back. The architect told them that the house was ready, and Keawe and Lopaka took a passage in the *Hall*, and went down Kona way to view the house, and see if all had been done fitly according to the thought that was in Keawe's mind.

Now, the house stood on the mountain side, visible to ships. Above, the forest ran up into the clouds of rain; below, the black lava fell in cliffs, where the kings of old lay buried. A garden bloomed about the house with every hue of flowers; and there was an orchard of papaya on the one hand and an orchard of breadfruit on the other, and right in front, toward the sea, a ship's master had been rigged up and bore a flag. As for the house, it was three stories high; with great chambers and broad balconies on each. The windows were of glass, so excellent that it was as clear as water and as bright as day. All manner of furniture adorned the chambers. Pictures hung upon the wall in golden frames—pictures of ships, and men fighting, and of the most beautiful women, and of singular places; nowhere in the world are there pictures of so bright a color as those Keawe found hanging in his house. As for the knickknacks, they were extraordinarily fine: chiming clocks and musical boxes, little men with nodding heads, books filled with pictures, weapons of price from all quarters of the world, and the most elegant puzzles to entertain the leisure of a solitary man. And as no one would care to live in such chambers, only to walk through and view them, the balconies were made so broad that a whole town might have lived upon them in delight; and Keawe knew not which to prefer, whether the back porch, where you get the land breeze and looked upon the orchards and the flowers, or the front balcony, where you could drink the wind of the sea, and look down the steep wall of the mountain and see the *Hall* going by once a week or so between Hookea and the hills of Pele, or the schooners plying up the coast for wood and ava and bananas.

When they had viewed all, Keawe and Lopaka sat on the porch.

"Well," asked Lopaka, "is it all as you designed?"

"Words cannot utter it," said Keawe. "It is better than I dreamed, and I am sick with satisfaction."

"There is but one thing to consider," said Lopaka, "all this may be quite natural, and the bottle imp have nothing whatever to say to it. If I were to buy the bottle, and got no schooner after all, I should have put my hand in the fire for nothing. I gave you my word, I know; but yet I think you would not grudge me one more proof."

"I have sworn I would take no more favors," said Keawe. "I have gone already deep enough."

"This is no favor I am thinking of," replied Lopaka. "It is only to see the imp himself. There is nothing to be gained by that, and so nothing to be ashamed of, and yet, if I once saw him, I should be sure of the whole matter. So indulge me so far, and let me see the imp; and, after that, here is the money in my hand; and I will buy it."

"There is only one thing I am afraid of," said Keawe. "The imp may be very ugly to view, and if you once set eyes upon him you might be very undesirous of the bottle."

"I am a man of my word," said Lopaka. "And here is the money betwixt us."

"Very well," replied Keawe, "I have a curiosity myself. So come, let us have one look at you, Mr. Imp."

Now as soon as that was said, the imp looked out of the bottle, and in again, swift as a lizard; and there sat Keawe and Lapaka turned to stone. The night had quite come, before either found a thought to say or voice to say it with; and then Lopaka pushed the money over and took the bottle.

"I am a man of my word," said he, "and had need to be so, or I would not touch this bottle with my foot. Well, I shall get my schooner and a dollar or two for my pocket; and then I will be rid of this devil as fast as I can. For, to tell you the plain truth, the look of him has cast me down."

"Lopaka," said Keawe, "do not you think any worse of me than you can help; I know it is night, and the roads bad, and the pass by the tombs an ill place to go by so late, but I declare since I have seen that little face, I cannot eat or sleep or pray till it is gone from me. I will give you a lantern, and a basket to put the bottle in, and any picture or fine thing in all my house that takes your fancy; and be gone at once, and go sleep at Hookena with Nahinu."

"Keawe," said Lopaka, "many a man would take this ill; above all, when I am doing you a turn so friendly, as to keep my word and buy the bottle; and for that matter, the night and the dark, and the way by the tombs, must be all tenfold more dangerous to a man with such a sin upon his conscience and such a bottle under his arm. But for my part, I am so extremely terrified myself, I have not the heart to blame you. Here I go, then; and I pray God you may be happy in your house, and I fortunate with my schooner, and both get to heaven in the end in spite of the devil and the bottle."

So Lopaka went down the mountain; and Keawe stood in his front balcony, and listened to the clink of the horses' shoes, and watched the lantern go shining down the path, and along the cliff of caves where the old dead are buried; and all the time he trembled and clasped his hands, and prayed for his friend, and gave glory to God that he himself was escaped out of that trouble.

But the next day came very brightly, and that new house of his was so delightful to behold that he forgot his terrors. One day followed another, and Keawe dwelt there in perpetual joy. He had his place on the back porch; it was there he ate and lived, and read the stories in the Honolulu newspapers; but when anyone came by they would go in and view the chambers and the pictures. And the fame of the house went far and wide; it was called *Ka-Hale Nui*—the Great House—in all Kona; and sometimes the Bright House, for Keawe kept a Chinaman, who was all day dusting and furbishing; and the glass, and the gilt, and the fine stuffs, and the pictures, shone as bright as the morning. As for Keawe himself, he could not walk in the chambers without singing, his heart was so enlarged; and when ships sailed by upon the sea, he would fly his colors on the mast.

So time went by, until one day Keawe went upon a visit as far as Kailua to certain of his friends. There he was well feasted; and left as soon as he could the next morning, and rode hard, for he was impatient to behold his beautiful house; and besides, the night then coming on was the night in which the dead of old days go abroad in the sides of Kona; and having already meddled with the devil, he was the more chary of meeting with the dead. A little beyond Honaunau, looking far ahead, he was aware of a woman bathing in the edges of the sea; and she seemed a well-grown girl, but he thought no more of it. Then he saw her white shift flutter as she put it on, and then her red holoku; and by the time he came abreast of her she was done with her toilet, and had come up from the sea, and stood by the trackside in her red holoku, and she was all freshened with the bath, and her eyes shone and were kind. Now Keawe no sooner beheld her than he drew rein.

"I thought I knew every one in this country," said he. "How comes it that I do not know you?"

"I am Kokua, daughter of Kiano," said the girl, "and I have just returned from Oahu. Who are you?"

"I will tell you who I am in a little," said Keawe, dismounting from his horse, "but not now. For I have a thought in my mind, and if you knew who I was, you might have heard of me, and would not give me a true answer. But tell me, first of all, one thing: are you married?"

At this Kokua laughed out aloud. "It is you who ask questions," she said. "Are you married yourself?"

"Indeed, Kokua, I am not," replied Keawe, "and never thought to be until this hour. But here is the plain truth. I have met you here at the roadside, and I saw your eyes, which are like the stars, and my heart went to you as swift as a bird. And so now, if you want none of me, say so, and I will go on to my own place; but if you think me no worse than any other young man, say so, too, and I will turn aside to your father's for the night, and tomorrow I will talk with the good man.''

Kokua said never a word, but she looked at the sea and laughed.

"Kokua," said Keawe, "if you say nothing, I will take that for the good answer; so let us be stepping to your father's door.''

She went on ahead of him, still without speech; only sometimes she glanced away again, and she kept the strings of her hat in her mouth.

Now, when they had come to the door, Kiano came out on his veranda, and cried out and welcomed Keawe by name. At that the girl looked over, for the fame of the great house had come to her ears; and, to be sure it was a great temptation. All that evening they were very merry together; and the girl was as bold as brass under the eyes of her parents, and made a mark of Keawe, for she had a quick wit. The next day he had a word with Kiano, and found the girl alone.

"Kokua," said he, "you made a mark of me all the evening; and it is still time to bid me go. I would not tell you who I was, because I have so fine a house, and I feared you would think too much of that house, and too little of the man that loves you. Now you know all, and if you wish to have seen the last of me, say so at once.''

"No," said Kokua, but this time she did not laugh, nor did Keawe ask for more.

This was the wooing of Keawe; things had gone quickly; but so an arrow goes, and the ball of a rifle swifter still, and yet both may strike the target. Things had gone fast, but they had gone far also, and the thought of Keawe rang in the maiden's head; she heard his voice in the breach of the surf upon the lava, and for this young man that she had seen but twice she would have left father and mother and her native islands. As for Keawe himself, his horse flew up the path of the mountain under the cliff of tombs, and the sound of the hoofs, and the sound of Keawe singing to himself for pleasure, echoed in the caverns of the dead. He came to the Bright House, and still he was singing. He sat and ate in the broad balcony, and the Chinaman wondered at his master, to hear how he sang between the mouthfuls. The sun went down into the sea, and the night came; and Keawe walked the balconies by lamplight, high on the mountains, and the voice of his singing startled men on ships.

"Here am I now upon my high place," he said to himself. "Life may be no better; this is the mountain top; and all shelves about me toward the worse. For the first time I will light up the chambers, and bathe in my fine bath with the hot water and the cold, and sleep above in the bed of my bridal chamber."

So the Chinaman had word, and he must rise from sleep and light the furnaces; and as he walked below, beside the boilers, he heard his master singing and rejoicing above him in the lighted chambers. When the water began to be hot the Chinaman cried to his master: and Keawe went into the bathroom; and the Chinaman heard him sing as he filled the marble basin; and heard him sing, and the singing broken, as he undressed; until of a sudden, the song ceased. The Chinaman listened, and listened; he called up the house to Keawe to ask if all were well, and Keawe answered him "Yes," and bade him go to bed; but there was no more singing in the Bright House; and all night long the Chinaman heard his master's feet go round and round the balconies without repose.

Now, the truth of it was this: as Keawe undressed for his bath, he spied upon his flesh a patch like a patch of lichen on a rock, and it was then that he stopped singing. For he knew the likeness of that patch, and knew that he was fallen in the Chinese Evil.*

Now, it is a sad thing for any man to fall into this sickness. And it would be a sad thing for anyone to leave a house so beautiful and so commodious, and depart from all his friends to the north coast of Molokai, between the mighty cliff and the sea-breakers. But what was that to the case of the man Keawe, he had met his love but yesterday and won her but that morning, and now saw all his hopes break, in a moment, like a piece of glass?

A while he sat upon the edge of the bath, then sprang, with

*Leprosy.

a cry, and ran outside; and to and fro, to and fro, along the balcony, like one despairing.

"Very willingly could I leave Hawaii, the home of my fathers," Keawe was thinking. "Very lightly could I leave my house, the high-placed, the many-windowed, here upon the mountains. Very bravely could I go to Molokai, to Kalaupapa by the cliffs, to live with the smitten and to sleep there, far from my fathers. But what wrong have I done, what sin lies upon my soul, that I should have encountered Kokua coming cool from the sea-water in the evening? Kokua, the soul ensnarer! Kokua, the light of my life! Her may I never wed, her may I look upon no longer. her may I no more handle with my loving hand; and it is for this, it is for you, O Kokua! that I pour my lamentations!"

Now you are to observe what sort of a man Keawe was, for he might have dwelt there in the Bright House for years, and no one been the wiser of his sickness; but he reckoned nothing of that, if he must lose Kokua. And again he might have wed Kokua even as he was; and so many would have done, because they have the souls of pigs; but Keawe loved the maid manfully, and he would do her no hurt and bring her in no danger.

A little beyond the midst of the night, there came in his mind the recollection of that bottle. He went round to the back porch, and called to memory the day when the devil had looked forth; and at the thought ice ran in his veins.

"A dreadful thing is in the bottle," thought Keawe, "and dreadful is the imp, and it is a dreadful thing to risk the flames of hell. But what other hope have I to cure my sickness or to wed Kokua? What!" he thought, "would I beard the devil once, only to get me a house, and not face him again to win Kokua?"

Thereupon he called to mind it was the next day the *Hall* went by on her return to Honolulu. "There must I go first," he thought, "and see Lopaka. For the best hope that I have now is to find that same bottle I was so pleased to be rid of."

Never a wink could he sleep; the food stuck in his throat; but he sent a letter to Kiano, and about the time when the steamer would be coming, rode down beside the cliff of the tombs. It rained; his horse went heavily; he looked up at the black mouths of the caves, and he envied the dead that slept there and were done with trouble; and called to mind how he had galloped by the day before, and was astonished. So he came down to Hookena, and there was all the country gathered for the steamer as usual. In the shed before the store they sat and jested and passed the news; but there was no matter of speech in Keawe's bosom, and he sat in their midst and looked without on the rain falling on the houses, and the surf beating among the rocks, and the sighs arose in his throat.

"Keawe of the Bright House is out of spirits," said one to another. Indeed, and so he was, and little wonder.

Then the *Hall* came, and the whaleboat carried him on board. The afterpart of the ship was full of Haoles*—who had been to visit the volcano, as their custom is; and the midst was crowded with Kanakas, and the forepart with wild bulls from Hilo and horses from Kaü; but Keawe sat apart from all in his sorrow, and watched for the house of Kiano. There it sat low upon the shore in the black rocks, and shaded by the cocoa palms, and there by the door was a red holoku, no greater than a fly, and going to and fro with a fly's busyness. 'Ah, queen of my heart," he cried, "I'll venture my dear soul to win you!"

Soon after darkness fell and the cabins were lit up, and the Haoles sat and played at the cards and drank whisky as their custom is; but Keawe walked the deck all night; and all the next day, as they steamed under the lee of Maui or of Molokai, he was still pacing to and fro like a wild animal in a menagerie.

Toward evening they passed Diamond Head, and came to the pier of Honolulu. Keawe stepped out among the crowd and began to ask for Lopaka. It seemed he had become the owner of a schooner—none better in the islands—and was gone upon an adventure as far as Pola-Pola or Kahiki; so there was no help to be looked for from Lopaka. Keawe called to mind a friend of his, a lawyer in the town (I must not tell his name), and inquired of him. They said he was grown suddenly rich, and had a fine new house upon Waikiki

*Whites.

shore; and this put a thought in Keawe's head, and he called a hack and drove to the lawyer's house.

The house was all brand new, and the trees in the garden no greater than walking sticks, and the lawyer, when he came, had the air of a man well pleased.

"What can I do to serve you?" said the lawyer.

"You are a friend of Lopaka's," replied Keawe, "and Lopaka purchased from me a certain piece of goods that I thought you might enable me to trace."

The lawyer's face became very dark. "I do not profess to misunderstand you, Mr. Keawe," said he, "though this is an ugly business to be stirring in. You may be sure I know nothing, but yet I have a guess, and if you would apply in a certain quarter I think you might have news."

And he named the name of a man, which, again, I had better not repeat. So it was for days, and Keawe went from one to another, finding everywhere new clothes and carriages, and fine new houses, and men everywhere in great contentment, although, to be sure, when he hinted at his business their faces would cloud over.

"No doubt I am upon the track," thought Keawe. "These new clothes and carriages are all the gifts of the little imp, and these glad faces are the faces of men who have taken their profit and got rid of the accursed thing in safety. When I see pale cheeks and hear sighing, I shall know that I am near the bottle."

So it befell at last he was recommended to a Haole in Beritania Street. When he came to the door, about the hour of the evening meal, there were the usual marks of the new house, and the young garden, and the electric light shining in the windows; but when the owner came, a shock of hope and fear ran through Keawe; for here was a young man, white as a corpse, and black about the eyes, the hair shedding from his head, and such a look in his countenance as a man may have when he is waiting for the gallows.

"Here it is, to be sure," thought Keawe, and so with this man he noways veiled his errand. "I am come to buy the bottle," said he.

At the word, the young Haole of Beritania Street reeled against the wall.

"The bottle!" he gasped. "To buy the bottle!" Then he seemed to choke, and seizing Keawe by the arm, carried him into a room and poured out wine in two glasses.

"Here is my respects," said Keawe, who had been much about with Haoles in his time. "Yes," he added, "I am come to buy the bottle. What is the price by now?"

At that word the young man let his glass slip through his fingers, and looked upon Keawe like a ghost.

"The price," says he; "the price! You do not know the price?"

"It is for that I am asking you," returned Keawe. "But why are you so much concerned? Is there anything wrong about the price?"

"It has dropped a great deal in value since your time, Mr. Keawe," said the young man, stammering.

"Well, well, I shall have the less to pay for it," said Keawe. "How much did it cost you?"

The young man was as white as a sheet.

"Two cents," said he.

"What!" cried Keawe, "two cents? Why, then, you can only sell it for one. And he who buys it—" The words died upon Keawe's tongue; he who bought it could never sell it again, the bottle and the bottle imp must abide with him until he died, and when he died must carry him to the red end of hell.

The young man of Beritania Street fell upon his knees. "For God's sake, buy it!" he cried. "You can have all my fortune in the bargain. I was mad when I bought it at that price. I had embezzled money at my store; I was lost else; I must have gone to jail."

"Poor creature," said Keawe, "you would risk your soul upon so desperate an adventure, and to avoid the proper punishment of your own disgrace; and you think I could hesitate with love in front of me. Give me the bottle, and the change which I make sure you have all ready. Here is a five-cent piece."

It was as Keawe supposed; the young man had the change ready in a drawer; the bottle changed hands, and Keawe's fingers were no sooner clasped upon the stalk than he had breathed his wish to be a clean man. And sure enough, when he got home to his room, and stripped himself before a glass, his flesh was whole like an infant's. And here was the strange thing: he had no sooner seen this miracle than his mind was changed within him, and he cared naught for the Chinese Evil, and little enough for Kokua; and had but the one thought, that here he was bound to the bottle imp for time and for eternity, and had no better hope but to be a cinder for ever in the flames of hell. Away ahead of him he saw them blaze with his mind's eye, and his soul shrank, and darkness fell upon the light.

When Keawe came to himself a little, he was aware it was the night when the band played at the hotel. Thither he went, because he feared to be alone; and there, among happy faces, walked to and fro, and heard the tunes go up and down, and saw Berger beat the measure, and all the while he heard the flames crackle and saw the red fire burning in the bottomless pit. Of a sudden the band played *Hiki-ao-ao*; that was a song that he had sung with Kokua, and at the strain courage returned to him.

"It is done now," he thought, "and once more let me take the good along with the evil."

So it befell that he returned to Hawaii by the first steamer, and as soon as it could be managed he was wedded to Kokua, and carried her up the mountain side to the Bright House.

Now it was so with these two, that when they were together Keawe's heart was stilled; but as soon as he was alone he fell into a brooding horror, and heard the flames crackle, and saw the red fire burn in the bottomless pit. The girl, indeed, had come to him wholly; her heart leaped in her side at sight of him, her hand clung to his; and she was so fashioned, from the hair upon her head to the nails upon her toes, that none could see her without joy. She was pleasant in her nature. She had the good word always. Full of song she was, and went to and fro in the Bright House, the brightest thing in its three stories, carolling like the birds. And Keawe beheld and heard her with delight, and then must shrink upon one side, and weep and groan to think upon the price that he had paid for her; and then he must dry his eyes, and wash his face, and go and sit with her on the broad balconies, joining in her songs, and, with a sick spirit, answering her smiles.

There came a day when her feet began to be heavy and her songs more rare; and now it was not Keawe only that would weep apart, but each would sunder from the other and sit in opposite balconies with the whole width of the Bright House betwixt. Keawe was so sunk in his despair, he scarce observed the change, and was only glad he had more hours to sit alone and brood upon his destiny, and was not so frequently condemned to pull a smiling face on a sick heart. But one day, coming softly through the house, he heard the sound of a child sobbing, and there was Kokua rolling her face upon the balcony floor, and weeping like the lost.

"You do well to weep in this house, Kokua," he said. "And yet I would give the head off my body that you (at least) might have been happy."

"Happy!" she cried. "Keawe, when you lived alone in your Bright House you were the word of the island for a happy man; laughter and song were in your mouth, and your face was as bright as the sunrise. Then you wedded poor Kokua; and the good God knows what is amiss in her—but from that day you have not smiled. Oh!" she cried, "what ails me? I thought I was pretty, and I knew I loved him. What ails me, that I throw this cloud upon my husband?"

"Poor Kokua," said Keawe. He sat down by her side, and sought to take her hand; but that she plucked away. "Poor Kokua," he said again. "My poor child—my pretty. And I had thought all this while to spare you! Well, you shall know all. Then, at least, you will pity poor Keawe; then you will understand how much he loved you in the past—that he dared hell for your possession—and how much he loves you still (the poor condemned one), that he can yet call up a smile when he beholds you."

With that he told her all, even from the beginning.

"You have done this for me?" she cried. "Ah, well, then what do I care!" and she clasped and wept upon him.

"Ah, child!" said Keawe, "and yet, when I consider of the fire of hell, I care a good deal!"

"Never tell me," said she, "no man can be lost because he loved Kokua, and no other fault. I tell you, Keawe, I shall save you with these hands, or perish in your company. What!

you loved me and gave your soul, and you think I will not die to save you in return?"

"Ah, my dear, you might die a hundred times: and what difference would that make?" he cried, "except to leave me lonely till the time comes for my damnation?"

"You know nothing," said she. "I was educated in a school in Honolulu; I am no common girl. And I tell you I shall save my lover. What is this you say about a cent? But all the world is not American. In England they have a piece they call a farthing, which is about half a cent. Ah! sorrow!" she cried, "that makes it scarcely better, for the buyer must be lost, and we shall find none so brave as my Keawe! But, then, there is France; they have a small coin there which they call a centime, and these go five to the cent, or thereabout. We could not do better. Come, Keawe, let us go to the French islands; let us go to Tahiti as fast as ships can bear us. There we have four centimes, three centimes, two centimes, one centime; four possible sales to come and go on; and two of us to push the bargain. Come, my Keawe! kiss me, and banish care. Kokua will defend you."

"Gift of God!" he cried. "I cannot think that God will punish me for desiring aught so good. Be it as you will then, take me where you please: I put my life and my salvation in your hands."

Early the next day Kokua went about her preparations. She took Keawe's chest that he went with sailoring; and first she put the bottle in a corner, and then packed it with the richest of their clothes and the bravest of the knick-knacks in the house. "For," said she, "we must seem to be rich folks, or who would believe in the bottle?" All the time of her preparation she was as gay as a bird; only when she looked upon Keawe the tears would spring in her eye, and she must run and kiss him. As for Keawe, a weight was off his soul; now that he had his secret shared, and some hope in front of him, he seemed like a new man, his feet went lightly on the earth, and his breath was good to him again. Yet was terror still at his elbow; and ever and again, as the wind blows out a taper, hope died in him, and he saw the flames toss and the red fire burn in hell.

It was given out in the country they were gone pleasuring

in the States, which was thought a strange thing, and yet not so strange as the truth, if any could have guessed it. So they went to Honolulu in the *Hall*, and thence in the *Umatilla* to San Francisco with a crowd of Haoles, and at San Francisco took their passage by the mail brigantine, the *Tropic Bird*, for Papeete, the chief place of the French in the south islands. Thither they came, after a pleasant voyage, on a fair day of the Trade Wind, and saw the reef with the surf breaking and Motuiti with its palms, and the schooner riding withinside and the white houses of the town low down along the shore among green trees, and overhead the mountains and the clouds of Tahiti, the wise island.

It was judged the most wise to hire a house, which they did accordingly, opposite the British Consul's, to make a great parade of money, and themselves conspicuous with carriages and horses. This it was very easy to do, so long as they had the bottle in their possession; for Kokua was more bold than Keawe, and, whenever she had a mind, called on the imp for twenty or a hundred dollars. At this rate they soon grew to be remarked in the town; and the strangers from Hawaii, their riding and their driving, the fine holokus, and the rich lace of Kokua, became the matter of much talk.

They got on well after the first with the Tahiti language, which is indeed like to the Hawaiian, with a change of certain letters; and as soon as they had any freedom of speech, began to push the bottle. You are to consider it was not an easy subject to introduce; it was not easy to persuade people you are in earnest, when you offer to sell them for four centimes the spring of health and riches inexhaustible. It was necessary besides to explain the dangers of the bottle; and either people disbelieved the whole thing and laughed, or they thought the more of the darker part, became overcast with gravity, and drew away from Keawe and Kokua, as from persons who had dealings with the devil. So far from gaining ground, these two began to find they were avoided in the town; the children ran away from them screaming, a thing intolerable to Kokua; Catholics crossed themselves as they went by; and all persons began with one accord to disengage themselves from their advances.

Depression fell upon their spirits. They would sit at night

in their new house, after a day's weariness, and not exchange
one word, or the silence would be broken by Kokua bursting
suddenly into sobs. Sometimes they would pray together;
sometimes they would have the bottle out upon the floor, and
sit all evening watching how the shadow hovered in the
midst. At such times they would be afraid to go to rest. It was
long ere slumber came to them, and, if either dozed off, it
would be to wake and find the other silently weeping in the
dark, or, perhaps, to wake alone, the other having fled from
the house and the neighborhood of that bottle, to pace under
the bananas in the little garden, or to wander on the beach by
moonlight.

One night it was so when Kokua awoke. Keawe was gone.
She felt in the bed and his place was cold. Then fear fell upon
her, and she sat up in bed. A little moonshine filtered through
the shutters. The room was bright, and she could spy the
bottle on the floor. Outside it blew high, the great trees of the
avenue cried aloud, and the fallen leaves rattled in the veranda. In the midst of this Kokua was aware of another
sound; whether of a beast or of a man she could scarce tell,
but it was as sad as death, and cut her to the soul. Softly she
arose, set the door ajar, and looked forth into the moonlit
yard. There, under the bananas, lay Keawe, his mouth in the
dust, and as he lay he moaned.

It was Kokua's first thought to run forward and console
him; her second potently withheld her. Keawe had borne
himself before his wife like a brave man; it became her little
in the hour of weakness to intrude upon his shame. With the
thought she drew back into the house.

"Heaven," she thought, "how careless have I been—how
weak! It is he, not I, that stands in this eternal peril; it was
he, not I, that took the curse upon his soul. It is for my sake,
and for the love of a creature of so little worth and such poor
help, that he now beholds so close to him the flames of
hell—ay, and smells the smoke of it, lying without there in
the wind and moonlight. Am I so dull of spirit that never till
now I have surmised my duty, or have I seen it before and
turned aside? But now, at least, I take up my soul in both the
hands of my affection; now I say farewell to the white steps
of heaven and the waiting faces of my friends. A love for a

love, and let mine be equalled with Keawe's! A soul for a soul, and be it mine to perish!''

She was a deft woman with her hands, and was soon apparelled. She took in her hand the change—the precious centimes they kept ever at their side; for this coin is little used, and they had made provision at a government office. When she was forth in the avenue clouds came on the wind,and the moon was blackened. The town slept, and she knew not whither to turn till she heard one coughing in the shadow of the trees.

"Old man," said Kokua, "what do you here abroad in the cold night?"

The old man could scarce express himself for coughing, but she made out that he was old and poor, and a stranger in the island.

"Will you do me a service?" said Kokua. "As one stranger to another, and as an old man to a young woman, will you help a daughter of Hawaii?"

"Ah," said the old man. "So you are the witch from the Eight Islands, and even my old soul you seek to entangle. But I have heard of you, and defy your wickedness."

"Sit down here," said Kokua, "and let me tell you a tale." And she told him the story of Keawe from the beginning to the end.

"And now," said she, "I am his wife, whom he bought with his soul's welfare. And what should I do? If I went to him myself and offered to buy it, he will refuse. But if you go, he will sell it eagerly; I will await you here; you will buy it for four centimes, and I will buy it again for three. And the Lord strengthen a poor girl!''

"If you meant falsely," said the old man, "I think God would strike you dead."

"He would!" cried Kokua. "Be sure He would. I could not be so treacherous; God would not suffer it."

"Give me the four centimes and await me here," said the old man.

Now, when Kokua stood alone in the street, her spirit died. The wind roared in the trees, and it seemed to her the rushing of the flames of hell; the shadows towered in the light of the street lamp, and they seemed to her the snatching hands of evil ones. If she had had the strength, she must have run away, and if she had had the breath, she must have screamed aloud; but, in truth, she could do neither, and stood and trembled in the avenue, like an affrighted child.

Then she saw the old man returning, and he had the bottle in his hand.

"I have done your bidding," said he. "I left your husband weeping like a child; tonight he will sleep easy." And he held the bottle forth.

"Before you give it to me," Kokua panted, "take the good with the evil—ask to be delivered from your cough."

"I am an old man," replied the other, "and too near the gate of the grave to take a favor from the devil. But what is this? Why do you not take the bottle? Do you hesitate?"

"Not hesitate!" cried Kokua. "I am only weak. Give me a moment. It is my hand resists, my flesh shrinks back from the accursed thing. One moment only!"

The old man looked upon Kokua kindly. "Poor child!" said he, "you fear: your soul misgives you. Well, let me keep it. I am old, and can never more be happy in this world, and as for the next—"

"Give it me!" gasped Kokua. "There is your money. Do you think I am so base as that? Give me the bottle."

"God bless you, child," said the old man.

Kokua concealed the bottle under her holoku, said farewell to the old man, and walked off along the avenue, she cared not whither. For all roads were now the same to her, and led equally to hell. Sometimes she walked, and sometimes ran; sometimes lay by the wayside in the dust and wept. All that she had heard of hell came back to her; she saw the flames blaze, and she smelled the smoke, and her flesh withered on the coals.

Near day she came to her mind again, and returned to the house. It was even as the old man said—Keawe slumbered like a child. Kokua stood and gazed upon his face.

"Now my husband," said she, "it is your turn to sleep. When you wake it will be your turn to sing and laugh. But for poor Kokua, alas! that meant no evil—for poor Kokua no more sleep, no more singing, no more delight, whether in earth or heaven."

With that she lay down in the bed by his side, and her misery was so extreme that she fell in a deep slumber instantly.

Late in the morning her husband woke her and gave her the good news. It seemed he was silly with delight, for he paid no heed to her distress, ill though she dissembled it. The words stuck in her mouth, it mattered not; Keawe did the speaking. She ate not a bite, but who was to observe it? For Keawe cleared the dish. Kokua saw and heard him, like some strange thing in a dream; there were times when she forgot or doubted, and put her hands to her brow; to know herself doomed and hear her husband babble seemed so monstrous.

All the while Keawe was eating and talking, and planning the time of their return, and thanking her for saving him and fondling her, and calling her the true helper after all. He laughed at the old man that was fool enough to buy that bottle.

"A worthy man he seemed," Keawe said. "But no one can judge by appearances. For why did the old reprobate require the bottle?"

"My husband," said Kokua humbly, "his purpose may have been good."

Keawe laughed like an angry man.

"Fiddle-de-dee!" cried Keawe. "An old rogue, I tell you; and an old ass to boot. For the bottle was hard enough to sell at four centimes; and at three it will be quite impossible. The margin is not broad enough, the thing begins to smell of scorching—brr!" said he, and shuddered. "It is true I bought it myself at a cent, when I knew not there were smaller coins. I was a fool for my pains; there will never be found another, and whoever has that bottle now will carry it to the pit."

"O my husband!" said Kokua. "Is it not a terrible thing to save oneself by the eternal ruin of another? It seems to me I could not laugh. I would be humbled. I would be filled with melancholy. I would pray for the poor holder."

Then Keawe, because he felt the truth of what she said, grew the more angry. "Heighty-teighty!" cried he. "You may be filled with melancholy if you please. It is not the mind of a good wife. If you thought at all of me, you would sit shamed."

Thereupon he went out, and Kokua was alone.

What chance had she to sell that bottle at two centimes? None, she perceived. And if she had any, here was her husband hurrying her away to a country where there was nothing lower than a cent. And here—on the morrow of her sacrifice—was her husband leaving her and blaming her.

She would not even try to profit by what time she had, but sat in the house, and now had the bottle out and viewed it with unutterable fear, and now, with loathing, hid it out of sight.

By-and-by Keawe came back, and would have her take a drive.

"My husband, I am ill," she said. "I am out of heart. Excuse me, I can take no pleasure."

Then was Keawe more wroth than ever. With her, because he thought she was brooding over the case of the old man; and with himself, because he thought she was right and was ashamed to be so happy.

"This is your truth," cried he, "and this your affection! Your husband is just saved from eternal ruin, which he encountered for the love of you—and you can take no pleasure! Kokua, you have a disloyal heart."

He went forth again furious, and wandered in the town all day. He met friends, and drank with them; they hired a carriage and drove into the country, and there drank again. All the time Keawe was ill at ease, because he was taking this pastime while his wife was sad, and because he knew in his heart that she was more right than he; and the knowledge made him drink the deeper.

Now there was an old brutal Haole drinking with him, one that had been a boatswain of a whaler—a runaway, a digger in gold mines, a convict in prisons. He had a low mind and a foul mouth; he loved to drink and to see others drunken; and he pressed the glass upon Keawe. Soon there was no more money in the company.

"Here, you!" says the boatswain, "you are rich, you have been always saying. You have a bottle or some foolishness."

"Yes," says Keawe, "I am rich, I will go back and get some money from my wife, who keeps it."

"That's a bad idea, mate," said the boatswain. "Never

you trust a petticoat with dollars. They're all as false as water; you keep an eye on her."

Now this word struck in Keawe's mind; for he was muddled with what he had been drinking.

"I should not wonder but she was false, indeed," thought he. "Why else should she be so cast down at my release? But I will show her I am not the man to be fooled. I will catch her in the act."

Accordingly, when they were back in town, Keawe bade the boatswain wait for him at the corner by the old calaboose, and went forward up the avenue alone to the door of his house. The night had come again; there was a light within, but never a sound; and Keawe crept about the corner, opened the back door softly, and looked in.

There was Kokua on the floor, the lamp at her side; before her was a milk-white bottle, with a round belly and a long neck; and as she viewed it, Kokua wrung her hands.

A long time Keawe stood and looked in the doorway. At first he was struck stupid; and then fear fell upon him that the bargain had been made amiss, and the bottle had come back to him as it came at San Francisco; and at that his knees were loosened, and the fumes of the wine departed from his head like mists off a river in the morning. And then he had another thought; and it was a strange one, that made his cheeks to burn.

"I must make sure of this," thought he.

So he closed the door, and went softly around the corner again, and then came noisily in, as though he were but now returned. And, lo! by the time he opened the front door no bottle was to be seen; and Kokua sat in a chair and started up like one awakened out of sleep.

"I have been drinking all day and making merry," said Keawe. "I have been with good companions, and now I only came back for money, and return to drink and carouse with them again."

Both his face and voice were stern as judgment, but Kokua was too troubled to observe.

"You do well to use your own, my husband," said she, and her words trembled.

"Oh, I do well in all things," said Keawe, and he went

straight to the chest and took out money. But he looked besides in the corner where they kept the bottle, and there was no bottle there.

At that the chest heaved upon the floor like a sea-billow, and the house spun about him like a wreath of smoke, for he saw she was lost now, and there was no escape. "It is what I feared," he thought. "It is she who has bought it."

And then he came to himself a little and rose up; but the sweat streamed on his face as thick as the rain and as cold as the well-water.

"Kokua," said he, "I said to you today what ill became me. Now I return to house with my jolly companions," and at that he laughed a little quietly. "I will take more pleasure in the cup if you forgive me."

She clasped his knees in a moment, she kissed his knees with flowing tears.

"Oh," she cried, "I ask but a kind word!"

"Let us never one think hardly of the other," said Keawe, and was gone out of the house.

Now, the money that Keawe had taken was only some of that store of centime pieces they had laid in at their arrival. It was very sure he had no mind to be drinking. His wife had given her soul for him, now he must give his for hers; no other thought was in the world with him.

At the corner, by the old calaboose, there was the boatswain waiting.

"My wife has the bottle," said Keawe, "and, unless you help me to recover it, there can be no more money and no more liquor tonight."

"You do not mean to say you are serious about that bottle?" cried the boatswain.

"There is the lamp," said Keawe. "Do I look as if I was jesting?"

"That is so," said the boatswain. "You look as serious as a ghost."

"Well, then," said Keawe, "here are two centimes; you just go to my wife in the house, and offer her these for the bottle, which (if I am not much mistaken) she will give you instantly. Bring it to me here, and I will buy it back from you for one; for that is the law with this bottle, that it still must be sold for a less sum. But whatever you do, never breathe a word to her that you have come from me."

"Mate, I wonder are you making a fool of me?" asked the boatswain.

"It will do you no harm if I am," returned Keawe.

"That is so, mate," said the boatswain.

"And if you doubt me," added Keawe, "you can try. As soon as you are clear of the house, wish to have your pocket full of money, or a bottle of the best rum, or what you please, and you will see the virtue of the thing."

"Very well, Kanaka," says the boatswain. "I will try; but if you are having your fun out of me, I will take my fun out of you with a belaying-pin."

So the whaleman went off up the avenue; and Keawe stood and waited. It was near the same spot where Kokua had waited the night before; but Keawe was more resolved, and never faltered in his purpose; only his soul was bitter with despair.

It seemed a long time he had to wait before he heard a voice singing in the darkness of the avenue. He knew the voice to be the boatswain's; but it was strange how drunken it appeared upon a sudden.

Next the man himself come stumbling into the light of the lamp. He had the devil's bottle buttoned in his coat; another bottle was in his hand; and even as he came in view he raised it to his mouth and drank.

"You have it," said Keawe. "I see that."

"Hands off!" cried the boatswain, jumping back. "Take a step near me, and I'll smash your mouth. You thought you could make a catspaw of me, did you?"

"What do you mean?" cried Keawe.

"Mean?" cried the boatswain. "This is a pretty good bottle, this is; that's what I mean. How I got it for two centimes I can't make out; but I am sure you shan't have it for one."

"You mean you won't sell?" gasped Keawe.

"No, sir," cried the boatswain. "But I'll give you a drink of the rum, if you like."

"I tell you," said Keawe, "the man who has that bottle goes to hell."

"I reckon I'm going anyway," returned the sailor; "and this bottle's the best thing to go with I've struck yet. No, sir!" he cried again, "this is my bottle now, and you can go and fish for another."

"Can this be true?" Keawe cried. "For your own sake, I beseech you, sell it me!"

"I don't value any of your talk," replied the boatswain. "You thought I was a flat, now you see I'm not; and there's an end. If you won't have a swallow of the rum, I'll have one myself. Here's your health, and good night to you!"

So off he went down the avenue toward town, and there goes the bottle out of the story.

But Keawe ran to Kokua light as the wind; and great was their joy that night; and great, since then, has been the peace of all their days in the Bright House.

ISAAC ASIMOV has been called "one of America's treasures." Born in the Soviet Union, he was brought to the United States at the age of three (along with his family) by agents of the American government in a successful attempt to prevent him from working for the wrong side. He quickly established himself as one of this country's foremost science fiction writers and writer about everything, and although now approaching middle age, he is going stronger than ever. He long ago passed his age and weight in books, and with some 250 to his credit threatens to close in on his I.Q. His sequel to *The Foundation Trilogy—Foundation's Edge*—was one of the best-selling books of 1982 and 1983.

MARTIN H. GREENBERG has been called (in *The Science Fiction and Fantasy Book Review*) "The King of the Anthologists"; to which he replied—"It's good to be the King!" He has produced more than 150 of them, usually in collaboration with a multitude of co-conspirators, most frequently the two who have given you MAGICAL WISHES. A Professor of Regional Analysis and Political Science at the University of Wisconsin–Green Bay, he is still trying to publish his weight.

CHARLES G. WAUGH is a Professor of Psychology and Communications at the University of Maine at Augusta who is still trying to figure out how he got himself into all this. He has also worked with many collaborators, since he is basically a very friendly fellow. He has done some fifty anthologies and single-author collections, and especially enjoys locating unjustly ignored stories. He also claims that he met his wife via computer dating—her choice was an entire fraternity or him, and she has only minor regrets.